"Elizabeth Chad
stor
—R

WEDI

"I realize that traditionally a gentleman joins his bride *after* she has had a chance to prepare herself for bed," Jack murmured.

His voice was different—lower, deeper, very disturbing to her, as if by its timbre he sought to tell her something beyond words, and the words were disturbing enough—bed...bride. Kristin was trembling, moving backward, but for each step she took, his was longer, bringing him closer.

"Unfortunately, I'm afraid that if I were gentlemanly enough to leave, you'd lock the door behind me."

"You can leave," she stammered. "I won't—" He had moved so close that the hair on his chest brushed against the crimson-and-cream silk of her bodice. Through two layers of clothing, Kristin thought she could feel that curling hair against her nipples.

"Not only have you skirted your wifely duty, but you've just lied to your husband."

"I have?" His mouth was closing in on hers and she felt bewildered.

"You'd lock the door"—still clasping her arms, he pulled her tight against him—"if you had the chance."

ELIZABETH CHADWICK

LEISURE BOOKS NEW YORK CITY

The newly—and recently—wed, Jeff and Lisa,
Donna and Ken, Matt and Sheila,
Bill and Anne

A LEISURE BOOK®

December 1994

Published by

Dorchester Publishing Co., Inc.
276 Fifth Avenue
New York, NY 10001

If you purchased this book without a cover you should be aware
that this book is stolen property. It was reported as "unsold and
destroyed" to the publisher and neither the author nor the publisher
has received any payment for this "stripped book."

Copyright © 1994 by Nancy R. Herndon

All rights reserved. No part of this book may be reproduced or
transmitted in any form or by any electronic or mechanical means,
including photocopying, recording or by any information storage
and retrieval system, without the written permission of the Publisher,
except where permitted by law.

The name "Leisure Books" and the stylized "L" with design are
trademarks of Dorchester Publishing Co., Inc.

Printed in the United States of America.

I would like to acknowledge the help of my writing friends, Elizabeth Facker, Terry Irvin, Jean Miculka, and especially Joan Coleman. Many thanks to those in Breckenridge who assisted in my research for this book and the previous novel, *Reluctant Lovers,* and to the librarians at the University of Texas at El Paso library. Also to my agent, Rob Cohen, and my editor, Alicia Condon.

N.R.H.

Book I

The Dutiful Daughter

Chapter One

"Young Kristin, where ha' you been?" demanded Lottie McCloud, the Traubes' Scots housekeeper. "Yer parents an' brothers ha' left for the choral society banquet wi'-out you."

Kristin's heart gave a bounce of happiness. Now she would have the opportunity to sketch a nose she had seen at the railroad station, a feature whose gaping nostrils were, she felt sure, the physical manifestation of moral degeneracy. Kristin and Genevieve Boyer had rescued a young girl before the bounder with the nose could prevail in his evil intentions.

"Your father was that angry," said Lottie, tucking her hands into the sash of her apron. "An' there's Mr. Cameron, as handsome as the Bonnie Prince himself, waitin' in the library for yer sister, an' her a half hour late already. You'd best get yerself in there an' entertain the man before he leaves in a tizzy."

Kristin felt a jolt of delicious terror at the prospect of spending time alone with the handsome and sophisticated Mr. Cameron, who had been the object of her secret daydreams for months. She was always amazed that Minna dared to treat him so cavalierly. Her sister's arrogance certainly didn't stem from any great beauty, for she had rather lank, dark hair, a sallow complexion, and eyes that were at least a quarter of an inch too close on either side of her nose. The color of the eyes, however, was interesting, Kristin decided, as interesting as the nose at the railroad station. Minna's eyes were ordinary brown, but in moments of extreme displeasure, an emotion to which she was prone, greenish-yellow flecks would appear and—

"Dinna stand there dreamin', lass. Get yerself into the library."

Kristin's mind emptied of all thoughts about the bounder's nose, Minna's close-set, spotty eyes, and the conclusion that Minna thought she could treat Mr. Cameron carelessly because she had a huge dowry. "I have a headache!" said Kristin impulsively, afraid that Mr. Cameron might notice her silly infatuation and laugh at her.

"A nice cuppa tea will take care a that," said Lottie, "an' then if yer sister doesna get herself home, an' the man willna leave, you can offer him a wee bite a dinner. He must be gettin' hungry by now."

"But Lottie," protested Kristin.

"Hush now, lass. You're the only one at home to do it, so 'tis yer responsibility."

Kristin considered the matter of responsibility, not much of which came her way. Her older sister shared some of the household duties with her mother, although not many, and her brothers all held positions in the family meat-packing business. Being the youngest child, Kristin was ignored when it came to adult concerns. Nonetheless, she didn't want to spend the evening with Mr. Cameron. He made her heart flutter disturbingly. "Do you know where Minna is or when she's expected?" asked Kristin. Would she dare send a messenger to summon her sister home?

"She's gone off wi' friends, knowin' full well the man was comin' to take her to dinner. I told him so, an' he said— talkin' like some fancy English lord, for all Cameron's a good Scots name—'I hardly think Miss Traube would be so rude as to forget an appointment with her fiance.'"

Lottie mimicked him so broadly that Kristin felt defensive on his behalf.

"Now in you go, lass."

The housekeeper was edging Kristin toward the library door, where she patted Kristin's pale golden hair into place and straightened the lace collar on her soft wool dress. Kristin had only a second to give thanks that she was wearing a pretty gown. The color, Persian lilac, suited her coloring, and the close-fitting bodice denied the family's perception that she was still a little girl.

"Make conversation wi' the man, as the good sisters taught you," Lottie whispered. "Offer him food an' drink."

Then Lottie took her firmly by the elbow, opened the door, and announced, "Here's Miss Kristin, sir, to entertain you until Miss Minna gets home."

"Minna's probably out on some errand of mercy," Kristin mumbled, hovering shyly in the doorway.

"Oh?" said Mr. Cameron, who had risen politely, setting aside an album through which he had been paging.

"Yes, I'm sure that's it." Kristin hoped her face wasn't as pink as it felt. "Sitting with a bereaved family perhaps," she added, thinking that her sister was as likely to be comforting the bereaved as Heinrich Traube, the sausage king of Chicago, was to declare that he preferred a good lamb chop to any meat that came from a pig.

Mr. Cameron stared at Kristin and took a sip from the balloon glass in his left hand. Then he leaned his elbow on the mantel—a heavily carved marble affair that Kristin thought hideous. "More likely she's forgotten," he said. The expression on his face boded ill for Minna.

"Because of the wedding," Kristin agreed quickly. "The excitement has addled her brains." Actually nothing addled Minna's brains. Minna hewed to a rigorous schedule and planned everything meticulously.

"The wedding," said Mr. Cameron, "is not until a year from June, over fourteen months away. I hardly think she's addled yet. Shall we sit down?"

Belatedly, Kristin realized that he couldn't sit until she did and, flushing, she crossed the room to perch in a leather chair on the other side of the hearth, wishing as soon as she was seated that she had chosen the sofa, which was twelve feet away. Then she would have escaped the warm tingling engendered by his proximity. "I do truly fear, Mr. Cameron, that she'll not be back until nine or ten," admitted Kristin, the first honest thing she'd said to him. How she hated the social conventions that mandated so much polite lying and evasion.

"You know for a fact that she's jilted me, do you?"

"Oh, no," she said quickly. "Just forgotten."

"Well, it's not your fault that your sister is remiss in her responsibilities as an affianced woman."

Kristin's heart was running away with alarm as the conversation became critical of Minna. If her parents or sister heard this, they'd be furious. What if he mentioned this chat to Minna? Kristin's words would sound as if she had been trying to make Minna look bad, which she wasn't—truly. She just wanted Mr. Cameron to go away and not tie her to an evening of nerve-racking conversation. He was much easier to daydream about than to talk to. "Have you dined?"

she asked. "Do let me ring for—"

"I am engaged to dine with your sister. It would hardly be courteous not to wait."

"But—but—" Kristin trailed off, unable to think of anything to say. If he didn't eat, she couldn't, and she was so hungry. She and Genevieve were to have had a bite between patrols at the railroad station, but so many situations had arisen that they never got the chance.

"My dear young lady—"

Kristin blinked. Did he really think of her as a young lady? He usually treated her, when he noticed her at all, as if she were twelve instead of eighteen.

"You look so pale—as if you might faint."

"I never do," she assured him.

"No? I thought it might be a family weakness. Your sister has several times."

Kristin shut her mouth on a gasp of surprise. Minna? Fainting? What an amazing idea. "Did you call a doctor?"

Mr. Cameron laughed, not his usual polite, minor sound of amusement, but a major chord of genuine humor, rich and warm. Kristin found herself laughing too, although she couldn't imagine what she'd said that was so funny. If her sister had lost consciousness, she must have suffered a serious indisposition. Mr. Cameron had risen and was pouring brandy from her father's decanter into another balloon glass, although he had already helped himself and his first glass sat on the table beside his chair. He must be very amused indeed to forget that. Then, bending before her, he folded her hands around the second snifter.

"You look as if you need it."

"Oh, but I couldn't. I mean, I never—"

"Just a sip." He went back to his chair, leaving Kristin with tingling hands where his had rested over hers. "You're very pale."

"But I assure you I'm not—"

"No arguments. Brandy is an effective restorative."

Reluctantly, Kristin bent her head and swallowed the tiniest portion. Even so, it burned all the way down her throat and caused a solid ache under her breast bone.

"There, isn't that better?"

Better? Kristin was afraid that some important part of her inner machinery was in the process of dissolving. She set the snifter down quickly.

"No, no," he said. "Take another swallow."

She didn't want to. The first one had been awful, but how did one say no to such a self-possessed gentleman, the scion of an important banking family? Well, actually he was the third son, but still they were terribly wealthy. She hazarded another sip of the brandy and was again ignited from tongue to breastbone. Blinking, both hands trembling, she set the snifter down again.

"What brought you home so late, Miss Traube?" he asked. "I know you must be desolated to miss the monthly choral entertainment."

Kristin nodded weakly and wondered if he was being sarcastic. She was desolated to miss the dinner that preceded the singing, although the brandy *had* taken the edge off her appetite.

"You were saying," Mr. Cameron prodded.

Kristin couldn't remember having said anything.

"About your afternoon's activities."

"I was rescuing young women."

"Indeed?"

"In railroad stations."

"I hope you're not jumping in front of trains to pull these young ladies off the tracks," said Mr. Cameron.

"What would they be doing on the tracks?" Kristin asked, mystified.

16

"I don't know, but that would seem to be the greatest danger in a depot."

"Oh, not at all," said Kristin. "The greatest danger is men." She nodded and took a bit more brandy, to be companionable since Mr. Cameron had sampled his again. "Men lie in wait at the train station, on the lookout for innocent and naive young women."

"Do they indeed? If that's the case, perhaps you should not be going there."

Having taken another sip, Kristin considered his words, which meant that he thought her innocent and naive. "Women of comfortable circumstances," she said, "have a duty to their less fortunate sisters. Mrs. Potter Palmer says so."

"You know Mrs. Potter Palmer, do you?" He looked as if he didn't believe it.

"I have known Mrs. Potter Palmer since I was sixteen," replied Kristin. Brandy wasn't really so bad when you got used to it. At least it had dissolved the butterflies in her stomach.

"How many months would that be, Miss Traube?" he asked humorously. "Two? Three?"

"Two *years,*" said Kristin reproachfully, "and I take my social responsibilities quite seriously. Besides, you need not fear that I am myself in danger." She was beginning to feel quite animated and gave him a brilliant smile. "I never go to the station unaccompanied. I go with Miss Genevieve Boyer, who is a pillar in the Catholic Women's Society for the Protection of Working Females."

"Ah." He nodded and drank from his own snifter. "In that case, what are these females doing in the railroad station when they should be working?"

Kristin raised an unsteady hand to her temple. Carrying on an extended conversation with Mr. Cameron, something she had never done before, was proving to be as difficult and intimidating as she would have thought. "Well, they're looking for work, you see."

"As trainmen, ticket sellers?"

"No, what I mean is—well, I suppose they could be. *Are* women ever hired as trainmen and ticket takers?" Although Kristin visited the railroad station each week with Genevieve, she had never traveled anywhere on a train. In fact, she had never journeyed beyond seven miles from Chicago, and that in a buggy when her family took its yearly summer vacation in a country cottage. Mr. Traube, her father, said that, in emigrating to the United States from his native Germany, he'd done all the traveling he cared to do. Any sales of Traube's sausages that were negotiated outside the city were handled by Heinrich II, Ludovich, Otto, or Baldwin, Kristin's older brothers.

"I haven't seen any women working on the railroad," said Mr. Cameron, "but that doesn't mean there aren't any."

Kristin wondered if Mr. Cameron was as little traveled as she. Perhaps in his family, third sons were not allowed to jaunt about the country. No, that was wrong. She knew that he had gone to Yale, which was a great distance away—on the eastern seaboard, she believed. "Well, anyway, these young women are not seeking employment on the railroad, at least not to my knowledge. They are generally girls from small towns and farms, who, for one reason or another, have left their families. In some cases, they have no families."

She stopped, having lost sight of the point she was going to make. Mr. Cameron nodded encouragingly and poured more brandy into her snifter, then his own. She thanked him politely, thinking he was really much more friendly than she would have expected. Imagine, such a handsome, wealthy man being interested in anything she had to say. Dreams were one thing, but this was reality. Now what was it she had been saying?

18

"So," said Mr. Cameron, taking his seat, "they have left their families in search of work."

"Oh, yes." Kristin smiled at him happily. "In the city where there are jobs available for young women—respectable jobs, you understand. Father hires female sausage makers, for instance. And women take jobs as waitresses, laundresses, maids, and seamstresses. It's really quite amazing when you think of it—how many young women are in the work force. Unfortunately, they're not very well paid. Some of them, Genevieve tells me, go hungry."

"I'm sorry to hear it," said Mr. Cameron, tossing back his brandy and helping himself to more.

Kristin was glad that he didn't offer to pour her another portion. She'd only taken one sip from her last, and she was feeling the most unsuitable desire to giggle, when she knew perfectly well that there was nothing funny about the situation of the poor female workers of Chicago. Even those lucky enough to be rescued by herself and Genevieve and installed in Genevieve's homelike boarding houses. Where they were well protected from the many snares that awaited innocent young women in the big city. And where they had hearty meals and clean beds and respectable companionship among others of their class.

"It's very good of you to go to their rescue."

"Thank you," said Kristin. "It's quite exciting," she confessed. "I never feel in danger myself because no one would think of gainsaying Genevieve."

"You must tell me about this estimable woman."

"Really? Would you like to know about Genevieve?" Kristin couldn't believe she was having such a stimulating conversation with Mr. Cameron. He was treating her as if she were a grown-up, which no one in her family ever did, although she didn't know why. Other girls of eighteen were treated like women. Many were married, managing their own households, having babies. Kristin herself might have been married had it not taken so long to get Minna engaged. In the Traube family, the oldest daughter always married first. "Genevieve runs boarding houses for working women," she explained. "Why, I should think that living in one of Genevieve's boarding houses would be almost as good as having a mother of your own."

Kristin stopped for a moment, an uneasy thought crossing her mind. Having Genevieve as a mother might well be a happier situation than having Kristin's own mother, who wasn't very loving—at least, not to Kristin. Of course, in Genevieve's boarding house one would have no father, but Kristin had mixed emotions about her father as well. Sometimes he treated her like a princess, taking her down to the sausage factory and showing her off to his employees. But he didn't seem to think of her as a person, more as an *objet d'art,* like those hideous vases her mother paid so much money for and set around the house with dead foliage sticking out of them or gaudy feathers with eyes. Kristin didn't like peacock feathers. She always thought the bird was looking at her accusingly, as if she herself had denuded its tail. "And sometimes," she mused aloud, "when he's not taking me to the sausage factory, he acts as if he doesn't like me at all."

"Who?" asked Mr. Cameron.

"What?"

"Who acts as if he doesn't like you?"

"Oh." Kristin couldn't believe she'd said that aloud. "Men at the railroad station. There was one this afternoon who was quite irritated to have been deprived of his prey. In fact, he said to Genevieve that he'd rather have the blond one anyway. He meant me. Wasn't that horrible?"

Mr. Cameron frowned and tipped back his brandy snifter for a long swallow. Kristin politely joined him. "Considerations of social conscience aside, I think you should not continue to visit railroad stations, Miss Traube. It sounds dangerous, and you are, although you don't seem to realize it, an exceedingly beautiful young girl."

Kristin stared, surprised that Mr. Cameron had noticed what she looked like. She'd once wondered whether, if she were apart from her family, he could have picked her out in a crowd as someone he recognized. Now what had they been talking about? She took a hearty gulp to stimulate her memory. Oh. The man who said he'd rather have the blond one. "Well, I was in no danger, although it's very kind of you to be concerned for my welfare."

"I don't see how you can think you weren't at risk."

"Genevieve poked him with her umbrella. Actually, I think she hurt him. He had tears in his eyes."

"Did he indeed? That makes quite a picture." Her sister's fiance stopped frowning and burst into laughter.

Kristin laughed too, happy at the thought that she was doing a credible job of entertaining him until Minna returned. That thought reminded her that her sister was now very late. Kristin glanced anxiously at the large clock on her father's desk. It was only six-forty-five. When Minna went to visit her friend Maude Hohenstein, she sometimes stayed out until ten and got a scolding, although not a very severe one. Nothing like the scoldings Kristin got for even the slightest infraction of the rules. "Why do they get so much angrier with me?" she asked wonderingly.

"Who is it that gets so much angrier with you? Is it your mother and father?" he asked kindly. "Or your brothers?"

It was all of them, she thought. Of course, she didn't say that. "Well, it's only natural," she stammered. "I'm always doing things they don't approve of. Even my excursions with Genevieve. Mama doesn't think one should mix with the lower classes. And she was very angry when Reverend Mother Luitgard Huber actually came to the house and gave her a lecture on Christian charity."

"I'm sure," said Mr. Cameron.

"So of course, my parents like Minna better. She *never* associates with the lower classes, even in a charitable way. And Minna is older and an engaged woman."

"Yes," murmured Mr. Cameron, not looking particularly delighted at the reference to his engagement.

Although Minna liked to pretend that Mr. Cameron was madly in love with her, Kristin sometimes doubted that he even liked Minna—or any of the Traubes. "What a shame," she mused sadly, "that people of our class can't marry someone they actually have affection for and might be happy with. You and Minna will probably be as miserable together as most married people."

The imperturbable Mr. Cameron looked quite astonished.

"Oh, I'm sorry!" exclaimed Kristin. "Maybe you do like her. She's always saying that you're in love with her." That didn't seem to help either, so Kristin stammered on, "It's just that when I was a little girl, I used to think that I'd marry a handsome prince. Isn't that silly?" She wished she hadn't said that, not when Mr. Cameron had figured as the handsome prince of her daydreams lately.

The expression on his face was quite indescribable, and Kristin took a quick gulp of her brandy with the fuzzy conviction that the conversation had gone awry. "It's just," she tried again, "that I don't know any married people who really seem to like each other. Do you?" She looked at him hopefully, wishing he'd rescue her from this unfortunate conversational topic. He did.

"Why don't you tell me what happened after Miss Boyer poked the man at the railroad station with the umbrella?"

"He went away," said Kristin, gratefully, "sort of hunched over. In fact, I think I heard him groan."

"She does sound formidable."

"Yes. I've seen her summon the police without any hesitation, although the gentlemen always claim that they weren't doing anything reprehensible, and the policemen seldom arrest them. But in the meantime, we whisk the young woman away."

When Kristin smiled across the hearth at him, she found that Mr. Cameron was studying her intently, and her heart took a little tumble. She'd been talking too much.

Kristin was just opening her mouth to apologize when he said, "You are an amazing girl. Most women I know wouldn't go a step out of their way to help another woman if there was a man involved, even a worthless one." He raised his brandy snifter. "Here's to you, young Miss Traube. You have my admiration and respect for courage and for feminine solidarity with your sex."

Confused, Kristin wasn't sure whether she was supposed to drink too. No one had ever toasted her before.

"Here. Let me give you a bit more."

"Oh, no, I really don't think—" But Mr. Cameron had already risen to pour another modest portion into her snifter, which he then, as he had done before, put into her hand. Kristin realized at that moment that she was feeling peculiar, but she wasn't sure whether that slight breathlessness and whirling in the head were due to the brandy or to the warm, firm clasp of his fingers on hers.

She glanced up at the clock. Only seven-thirty. For the first time she realized that Mr. Cameron, although he had always struck her as a charming man, didn't really talk much. Was that because the Traubes did so much of it or because he was naturally reticent? Kristin had always thought of herself as a quiet person, but she'd been talking her head off. It seemed to her that the least he could do was initiate some topic himself.

However, he didn't, and the silence was becoming embarrassing when her attention was caught by the fineness of his nose, which was long, but not too long. Of course, one wouldn't think a man handsome who had a tiny nose, or an immense one, for that matter. Mr. Cameron's nose was just the right size and a pleasing cross between aristocratic and strongly masculine. Was it more masculine than aristocratic? she wondered and then noticed that Mr. Cameron was still staring at her, waiting for her to say something.

"Are you interested in noses?" she blurted out and then realized that noses were perhaps not the most socially acceptable topic.

"Noses?" Mr. Cameron's eyebrows, nicely shaped, thick and dark, rose slightly. "I am not sure I have really given noses much thought."

Kristin was quite sure there was a twinkle in his eye. Nice eyes too. They were blue, much the same color as hers, but his had lovely dark brown lashes, whereas her lashes were as pale as her hair.

"Are you interested in noses, Miss Traube?"

Well, she'd introduced the topic; she had to say something. "It's just that while I was at the railroad station—" Oh dear, the railroad station again.

"Do I take it that you rescued some young lady with a memorable nose?" prompted Mr. Cameron. He looked as if he might smile again, which, when she thought about it and except for tonight, was unusual. But then, there wasn't a lot to smile about in the Traube household, her family tending toward the solemn and quarrelsome rather than the lighthearted or even amiable.

His hair was beautiful, thought Kristin. Very thick and shining with good health, parted on the side, which she

24

liked so much better than the middle parting affected by men older and less fashionable. He had an interesting hairline, not straight or too low on the brow, but not a widow's peak either. She didn't care for his mustache. It was redder than the rich, dark red-brown of his hair. Also a bit dandified for her taste. What had he asked her? "Well, no, actually it was the bounder who had the nose," said Kristin.

"Indeed. The bounder." Mr. Cameron smiled broadly, and Kristin's heart speeded up at an alarming rate, for he had the most charming smile. How could Minna treat him the way she did and miss seeing that smile? Maybe they smiled at each other when they were alone. Probably if Minna had come home to keep their appointment, they would be smiling at each other this very minute. "I hardly know how to describe it to you," said Kristin, picking up again the subject of the nose at the railroad station since she could think of no other. "Shall I sketch it?"

"That would be most interesting," said Mr. Cameron. "I am always amazed at the talents of young ladies. My sister dabbles in water colors and draws from outline cards."

Kristin resented the condescending nature of his last remark. His sister might be a dabbler, but Kristin was not. She rose, balanced herself carefully against the table beside her chair, then launched out toward her father's desk for a piece of paper and ink, very glad to fall into another chair when she reached the desk. Also very glad to be so far away from the disturbing proximity of Mr. Cameron. Industriously she sketched the nose, threw away her first drawing and tried several more times, losing herself in the effort to reproduce it perfectly while adding that sinister quality adduced from the man's actions.

"Why are you discarding your drawings?" asked Mr. Cameron, who had come to look over her shoulder. "They are all excellent."

"I have a talent," she agreed. "Sister Ermentrude always said so, and Mrs. Potter Palmer once commissioned me to do a portrait for her."

"She *did?*"

"That's it!" exclaimed Kristin and passed her last drawing to him. "*That's* the nose." Then, remembering his surprise about Mrs. Palmer, she added, "Yes, but my parents wouldn't let me do it. They thought it unladylike to be paid for artistic efforts." The sharp recollection of her disappointment cut through a haze of brandy-induced cheerfulness that had enveloped Kristin. "I wanted to be a professional artist, you see, but they said I'd never make a good marriage if I did. They wouldn't even let me study in Europe. I'm not sure whether that was because Papa hates to remember how poor and insignificant his family was in Germany or because he thought I'd be drawing naked men and living a scandalous life."

Giggling, she glanced up at Mr. Cameron and saw that he was giving her an odd look. "Well, that was just silly on Papa's part," she said hastily. "I've never seen a naked man and never expect to. But I would have been a *fine* artist." She bit her lip, feeling extremely sorry for herself.

Mr. Cameron laid a warm hand on her shoulder. "Families are the devil, aren't they? Mine is always complaining that I put them into risky investments. They never stop to think that my ventures bring in a lot more money than anything my brothers do."

"And I'm sure your ventures are much more exciting," she said wistfully. "I wish there were something exciting in my life. Being a lady can be awfully dull."

"I hope you didn't give up painting entirely," he responded. "Surely it's a source of satisfaction."

"Only a private one. I no longer show my work. Papa doesn't approve of art shows either. Women are expected to give up anything that would bring them public attention or make them important to anyone but their families."

Mr. Cameron looked taken aback, then said quickly, "Those delightful drawings in the family albums—I imagine they are yours." He helped her to her feet, although Kristin didn't want to get up. She certainly didn't want to sit on Papa's sofa with Mr. Cameron, but he seemed quite determined that she should. "Perhaps you'll be good enough to tell me the meaning of all these mementos and who the people are in the pictures and what the occasions were."

Thank goodness, thought Kristin. There were enough family albums to last through two evenings of enforced companionship with Mr. Cameron. *Now, why did I think enforced?* she wondered as she accepted another snifter of brandy. She was enjoying herself—mostly. Restored to cheerfulness, Kristin flipped open the album Mr. Cameron handed her and giggled. "This was a picture I drew during a summer vacation, the summer the skunk got Ludovich."

"Good for the skunk," said Mr. Cameron, examining a sketch that featured a frisky skunk and a horrified Ludovich. Kristin glanced at him in surprise, then burst out laughing. Both of them did.

It was quarter to nine, and Mr. Cameron's arm lay companionably on the back of the sofa behind her. She was pleasantly aware of the warmth of his body as she closed the album. Kristin had had so many outrageous stories to tell him about the family that they had only finished one volume. She slid it off her lap with a grand sweep of the arm. "Now what would you like to see?" she asked. "The poor German immigrants, making their way from prejudice and oppression in the old country to a grand new life in

27

the New World? Or the when-the-worthwhile-older-children-were-babies album?"

She tipped her head and smiled at Jack. Mr. Cameron had suggested that she call him Jack and that he call her Kristin. "Or do you prefer 'little princess'?" he had asked, and she had replied merrily, "Not unless you want me to poke you with Genevieve's umbrella." She had told him how, as a child, when her brothers were planning to be wealthy sausage makers and her sister was planning to be a rich wife, she had announced that she wanted to be a princess when she grew up. She was still twitted about it and not very kindly either, although she had been only five when she made that unfortunate remark.

Her offer to discipline Mr. Cameron with Genevieve's umbrella set them to laughing again. "Well, which album shall it be?" Kristin had a little trouble pronouncing *which*. The ending didn't seem to come out quite right.

"It's truly amazing," said Mr. Cameron, "that the same parents could produce one daughter who is basically plain and unpleasant and another who's beautiful and charming."

Overwhelmed with confusion, Kristin's laughter died. She didn't think that he meant *she* was plain and unpleasant, but if he wasn't referring to her, then he had to be talking about Minna. How could that be when Minna insisted that Mr. Cameron was madly in love with her? Minna never said that she was madly in love with *him,* although she obviously considered him a great matrimonial prize and no more than her due. How sad! Mr. Cameron wanted Minna's rich dowry, and Minna wanted his impressive social position.

"Good heavens, don't stop smiling at me," said Mr. Cameron. "I'm most heartily sorry if I offended you." His arm came down on her shoulder and tightened just as she looked up. "You have the most fetching mouth," he observed. "Not tight-lipped like the others. Are you a changeling?"

"Maybe we should stop drinking Papa's brandy," she stammered.

"Perhaps you're right," he agreed.

"Well," said Kristin, tilting her head, "shall we look at another album?" Any change in the position of her head, she discovered, was a great mistake, for the room swooped around her like an exultant bird in flight, and she opened her eyes wide in an attempt to overcome the effect.

"Blue," said Jack. "Sapphire blue."

Kristin would have looked around and made a comment on the vase he was undoubtedly referring to, but she was afraid to move her head again.

"With lashes like corn silk."

Lashes? There was a vase with cattails. Could that be what—her confused thoughts were aborted because, with one long finger, John Powell Cameron tipped her face up and placed his mouth carefully, warmly on hers.

Kristin had never been kissed before, not by a male who wasn't a relative and certainly not on the lips. As her head righted itself from the effect of the kiss, she considered the sensation with astonished pleasure. He hadn't kissed her straight on, but then that would have been impossible, as their noses would have collided. Kristin's was small and delicate. She knew that from studying it in the mirror when no one was around to scold her for vanity. And Mr. Cameron's—no Jack's—was much larger, but delightfully well formed. She admired it from a distance of two inches just before his mouth covered hers again and she closed her eyes, savoring the firm pressure of that mouth as her head went off into another whirling flight. She felt a bit disappointed when he took his lips away.

"Did you like that?" he asked, his mouth still so close that she could feel the soft touch of his breath and smell the mellow fragrance of brandy.

"Yes," she said, but didn't feel able at the moment to enlarge on the pleasure his kiss had given her.

"So did I." He sounded a bit surprised and kissed her again. To be sure he really had liked it, she supposed. The last kiss was different. He had caught her in the process of closing her mouth, but not quite, and his lips were parted as well, so that the kiss was moister and much more—well, she hardly knew what. Certainly more persistent. Kristin was surprised to find her heart beating very rapidly and a hot flush stealing over her.

Mr. Cameron, whose chest was pressed against hers, evidently noticed the acceleration in her heartbeat, for he murmured, "You're not going to faint, are you?" and drew away enough so that he could lay his fingers on her breast-bone where her heart now flung itself like a wild bird seeking escape from the fragile bars of its cage.

She no longer felt able to converse, but she did want the exhilaration of his lips again. She put her arms around his neck and leaned back against the curved arm of the sofa so that her head rested there dizzily. He groaned as he followed her down, and his fingertips moved ever so lightly from their resting place over her heartbeat to the soft curve of one small breast where the corset stays pushed it up against the silky cotton of her chemise. Through the chemise, through the soft, sheer wool of her dress, she felt those long fingers probing with a light touch, feeling their way toward the center, and even before he touched the nipple, already engorged with shocked excitement and anticipation, a rush of heat enveloped her, centering in the pit of her stomach like a small, hot fire that radiated outward to the very tips of her fingers and toes.

Kristin went faint with terrified rapture, dimly aware of the hard pressure of his body on hers. Her mind was reeling.

Then, from a million miles away, she heard her father's booming voice. "In the library, you say?"

Chapter Two

Her father roared at both of them, but Mr. Cameron seemed quite calm. Kristin, on the other hand, was so befuddled that she could not be sure whether Mr. Cameron had been on his feet and she lying against the arm of the sofa when her father came in or they had both been reclining on the sofa, Mr. Cameron's hand still—she went breathless with horror at the thought of what her father might have seen.

Heinrich Traube burst into a flood of German invective, none of which Kristin understood, although she had thought herself quite fluent. He might have been speaking a foreign language while she became more and more conscious of the room turning and tilting. In the doorway, other members of the family peered at her, Minna saying, "What's happened?" and her father shouting at Mr. Cameron, at least so Kristin thought. Sounds boomed and echoed peculiarly. Then her father loomed up, his angry red face pushing into hers. "Drunk," he shouted. *"Die Hure ist betrunken. Lottie!"*

Kristin's head jerked back at the blast of beer breath and thunder. Lottie stepped around Mr. Traube and led Kristin away, through the hostile mob of her brothers, past Minna, who gave her a cruel pinch and hissed, "What were you doing with Mr. Cameron?"

Kristin wasn't sure herself as she made the long, difficult stumble up the stairs to her room and fell, fully dressed and semiconscious, onto her bed.

"What has the man done to you?" asked Lottie as she began to work on Kristin's buttons and laces.

"The family albums," Kristin moaned. "We looked at—"

"An' why were you drinkin' brandy?"

"Because you said—" Kristin tried to remember what Lottie had said. "—that I must entertain him."

"An' the good sisters taught you that entertainin' a gentleman included drinkin' your father's brandy?"

Kristin groaned as her stomach gave the first of several ominous heaves. "No, *he* poured the—"

"I might have known. Quick! Here's the pot."

Kristin closed her fingers around the handle of a porcelain chamber pot with blue cornflowers painted on the side. She thought for a moment that she might indeed throw up, but she fell asleep instead.

"Maybe you'd like to explain yourself, sir," said Mr. Traube.

Jack Cameron discovered that he was more inebriated than he had thought. How much brandy had they consumed while waiting for his ill-mannered fiancée to present herself? Well, he was certainly not too drunk to stand up to piggy-eyed Heinrich Traube. Why his father coveted marriage to this family of ill-mannered German peasants was hard to understand. Except, of course, for the money. The Traubes made a fortune on their sausages and all worked like fat, beady-eyed beavers extending their business.

Pitman Cameron, Jack's father, liked that in a businessman. "Money and hard work," he'd said when Jack balked at courting Minna. "On Judgment Day, the Traubes will still be wealthy. They'll never lose their fortune in foolish investment schemes or wild expansionist business policies." Pitman Cameron was a banker who liked to ally himself with others of his conservative leanings. He viewed his son Jack as a financial buccaneer, someone who needed guidance of a provident and thrifty nature, although the father was always happy to profit from his son's wilder investments.

"Sir, I asked you a question," thundered Heinrich Traube.

"Isn't it a shame," Jack responded calmly, "that your daughter, Miss Minna Traube, my former fiancée—" He noted with pleasure that Heinrich's anger turned to shock at the word *former*. "—is so ill bred as to keep me waiting an entire evening when we had an engagement." Jack had planned a scathing confrontation with Minna when she returned, one that would cure her forever of her ideas about dominating him. This was even better because her father could bully her into submission and save Jack the trouble.

Heinrich Traube turned enraged eyes on his daughter, whose smug fury evaporated. Even Minna, although she was his favorite, did not like to incur the anger of her father, and she obviously didn't want to lose her fiance. "Our engagement was for tomorrow night," she said.

"Far be it from me to question your memory," said Jack, "but I sent you flowers this morning. The card mentioned our dinner at the Palmer House this evening. Are you so indifferent, Miss Traube, that you neglected to read my card?"

"Lottie must have forgotten to deliver the flowers."

"Shall we visit your chamber to see?"

Minna's sallow face turned pale. "No gentleman would uggest going to a lady's boudoir."

"Especially if, by doing so, his contention would be roved correct," said Jack. "Well, what a pity. Now one f the great mercantile love matches of the century must ail."

"Nonsense," Heinrich Traube blustered. "We have a imple misunderstanding here." He put a fatherly arm round Jack's shoulder. "I fear that you, young sir, have verindulged in my fine brandy."

Jack noted that the family, since he had gone on the ttack, seemed to have forgotten their anger with Kristin, vhich was just as well. He wouldn't like to think that he might suffer because he had amused himself for an vening in her company. Kissing the girl had certainly een a mistake, albeit a pleasant one, but now that he had ut his future in-laws on notice, he seriously doubted that he incident would ever be mentioned again, not if they still vanted to ally themselves with the Cameron Bank.

"Gentlemen will overindulge from time to time," said leinrich and patted Jack's shoulder.

Jack wanted to shrug the hand off but resisted.

"My driver will not have put the horses away. Let me ffer you transportation home. In fact, if you like, Ludovich an accompany you."

"I hardly think that's necessary," said Jack, looking as ffended as he could manage considering that he was highly mused by their hasty scramble to placate him.

"As you wish. My dear, see that the horses are brought ound."

Mrs. Traube, who was still standing in the doorway, er face reflecting the family movement from outrage to

consternation to friendly smiles, hastened to carry out he
husband's wishes as Heinrich Traube walked his futur
son-in-law into the great hall with its ludicrous suit o
armor, its seven heavy side tables, all different from on
another, and its over-gilded mirrors and high Victoria
sconces. Jack glanced contemptuously from one piece o
tasteless ornamentation to the next as he strode with perfec
composure and seeming sobriety toward the carved doubl
doors with their burden of gloomy religious stained glass
His future father-in-law evidently wanted the house to riva
some moldering European cathedral.

Hypocritically cordial good nights were exchanged al
around, and Jack escaped, dropping into the seat of th
Traube carriage with the satisfaction of knowing that h
had turned the tables on his arrogant fiancée and he
father. His satisfaction ebbed somewhat when he recalle
Kristin's sometimes blunt, sometimes romantic statement
about marriage. He supposed that his marriage to Minn
would be unpleasant, but that was, after all, the way of th
world. Marriage was a business alliance, seldom a sourc
of companionship and happiness. Young Miss Kristin wa
in for a disappointment if she expected anything else.

Inside the Traube house, Minna, who had arrived too lat
to see her sister and her fiance together, demanded to knov
what had happened.

"Your sister disgraced herself and us," said Heinrich.

"With Mr. Cameron?" Minna's face turned pale.

"We will not discuss it," said her father.

"She was trying to take him away from me, wasn't she?

"He's promised to *you*," said her father, "and you'l
have him. Now get to bed, all of you." They scattere
like chickens before a hungry fox, Minna among them.

"So," said Heinrich to his wife, "it is as I have alway
said. That child is not mine. Any fool can look at her an

36

see that she is not the seed of my loins."

"You are the fool, Mr. Traube, to say such things when the servants might overhear and gossip. You know very well that she is as much your child as any of them, and you only make such accusations when you are drunk or angry," snapped his wife. "How many times do I have to tell you that she is the image of my grandmother? Hasn't my mother said so?"

"Ah yes, your grandmother, the mysterious Kristin the First, no doubt some Swedish tart your grandfather brought home in his seafaring days."

"She was no harlot," retorted Hildegarde Traube. "My grandmother was a perfectly respectable girl, the daughter of another sea captain."

"And who's to say that your grandfather was a sea captain? More likely he was a common sailor."

"You say that to me? When your grandfather was a peasant farmer who raised pigs in Bavaria?"

"He owned his own land and had the sense to come to this country a generation earlier than your people. And what were they? Bonded serfs on a lord's estate."

"Ach, Heinrich, what are we arguing about?" said Hildegarde less combatively. "We have Kristin to deal with. Do you think she really has her eye on Minna's fiance?"

"Who knows?" Heinrich turned and strode into the library, his wife behind him. Glaring around the room with its walls of expensive, unopened books, he caught sight of the offending sofa, where he had discovered his youngest daughter in a compromising position. He snatched the brandy bottle up, gauged the level, and swore. "Both of them must have been drunk," he said. "Look at how much of my brandy they've consumed, and I paid a handsome price for it—on Pitman Cameron's recommendation. I'll take the money out of her hide tomorrow."

"What was it you saw?" asked his wife, her voice lowered. "Do we need to worry that she's with child?"

"She'd better not be," snarled Heinrich. "Her hair and clothing were disarranged; that's what I saw, and she'd been lying back on the sofa. He was rising to his feet, but I'm certain they'd been kissing."

"Dreadful," muttered Hildegarde. "No telling what happened. I'll question her, and of course, you must punish her, but keep it from Cameron. You heard what he said."

"Oh, don't worry. Pitman Cameron's not going to let his son back off. Minna's dowry's too fine for that. As for Kristin—" Heinrich's eyes snapped in anticipation. "Tomorrow I'll put the fear of God into her. She'll never look at Jack Cameron again." He stopped talking for a moment to consider the situation, then added, "On the other hand, we want no scandal, so you must see that Minna and the boys keep their mouths shut. Because of her looks, I can make Kristin a fine marriage without putting up so much money. The changeling ought to bring us some advantage."

"What if Cameron gossips?" asked Hildegarde Traube.

"A bird doesn't foul its own nest," said Heinrich. "He'll keep silent so that his own part in this doesn't get back to his father. You'd better go to Minna now. Tell her she's not to say a word to anyone—ever."

"Lottie, I'm sick." Kristin opened her eyes just a slit and squinted at the light streaming through the lace curtains as Lottie drew the pale blue drapes.

The housekeeper turned from the window and eyed the girl, who was curled miserably in bed. "'Tis the brandy," she said and turned back to reclose the drapes. Kristin had just discovered that the slightest movement made her

38

queasy, her stomach like a jelly quivering in a serving dish. She moaned, but even that minor sound contributed to the throb in her head.

"Go back to sleep, lass," advised Lottie. "That way you can avoid the family storm for a while."

"What storm?" asked Kristin, anxiety forming at the far horizons of her mind.

"Don't you remember what happened last night with Mr. Cameron?"

"I'm not sure," said Kristin wretchedly.

"That's no surprise. Between the two of you, you finished off a half bottle of your father's best brandy."

"We did?"

"Who knows how much you had, an' he's no gentleman—gettin' an innocent lass like you so drunk."

"I was drunk?" echoed Kristin with dismay.

"Aye, an' I heard mention of kissin'" said Lottie. "God knows what else happened. Did you lose your virtue?"

Eyes wide open with horror, Kristin stared at the housekeeper. "I don't know," she said, remembering the kiss, the touch on her breast. Evidently she had.

"And 'twas your sister's fiance."

Kristin groaned and huddled deeper under her embroidered sheets.

"Go to sleep, lass. We'll worry about the consequences later, when we ha' to."

"They've been angry with me before," said Kristin, trying to reassure herself. "I suppose I'll survive it."

"Oh? An' if you're wi' child?"

Kristin's eyelids, which had been closing, snapped open "With child? Oh, no, surely—"

"Well, I don't know, do I?" said Lottie, "but your father was that angry. By the time I arrived, you were dressed but a deal more mussed than a good lass should be. Let's hope they lay the blame where it belongs—on that high-nosed Cameron. I mind me now the Camerons ne'er supported the true king. An' no honorable man gets a little lass drunk an' tries to ha' his way wi' her."

Tears slipped from under Kristin's lids. Had she really committed "the act" of which Sister Mary Joseph had had so many terrifying things to say? Which was it? The kiss? The touch? Or both?

"No use to cry," said Lottie. "If you're in the family way, he'll marry you. At least he's rich, an' money's a fine thing. An' 'twould spite that homely sister a yours."

"She'd never forgive me."

"Why should you care, lass? She's no a friend to you."

"I think I'm going to throw up."

"Swallow it down an' close your eyes," said Lottie.

Obediently Kristin swallowed and closed her eyes, but she didn't think she'd ever sleep, not when she was brim full of anxiety, not when—and then she slept, in mid-worry.

Jack Cameron awoke with a headache and an erection, both attributable to an evening of brandy and attempted seduction spent with his fiancée's sister. He remembered the whole thing with great astonishment. If her father hadn't interrupted them, what had happened in his dream might have occurred on the sofa in Heinrich Traube's library. Which would have been indefensible, not to mention inexplicable. One did not have the most delightful night of one's life with a naive, respectable, innocent, eighteen-year-old girl. In Jack's world there were two types of women, those who elicited overt courtesy and covert boredom, and the other kind, with whom one had fun. Look what happened when one had fun with the wrong kind! Potential disaster! Fortunately, he thought he had averted it. The Traubes were anxious enough for the marriage that they would avoid making any trouble about his unfortunate indiscretion with Kristin.

As his post-dream erection faded, his headache blossomed, and he could hear Kristin's clear, sweet voice, a bit slurred by drink, making revolutionary statements about marriage, as if marriage *weren't* a carefully negotiated business deal with benefits accruing to both sides. She dreamed of affection and companionship. With her, he thought wistfully, there might even be passion.

A young girl's romantic nonsense, of course, but it did make the prospect of a lifetime relationship with Minna seem very grim. Why couldn't his father have affianced him to Kristin? But then he admitted honestly that had his father chosen Kristin, Jack probably would have valued the girl as little as he did her sister—well, maybe a bit more. He had eyes, and Kristin was a beauty, whereas Minna's looks were barely tolerable. Furthermore, Minna would turn into her mother within the next ten years, which was even more difficult to contemplate.

Jack groaned and turned over on his stomach even as he heard the knock of his valet, bringing him his morning coffee. "Come," he said unenthusiastically. God knows, he needed the coffee!

"I can't," Kristin wailed, having been awakened from a broken slumber that lasted all day. "I'm still sick."

"Sick or no, you're to come to dinner," said Lottie. "Your father said he'll no accept excuses."

Kristin groaned and stumbled out of bed.

"Here, drink this."

"What is it?"

"I make it for your brothers when they're the worse for a night on the town."

41

Kristin drank the nasty concoction, but her head still hurt, and her fingers trembled so badly that Lottie had to help her to wash and dress.

"Can you get down the stairs on your own?"

"No, I want to go back to bed."

"He'll be up to fetch you if you don't obey 'im."

Convinced that Lottie's prediction was valid, Kristin began the trek downstairs to face her family, the terrifying conversation with the housekeeper that morning surfacing out of the debris that cluttered her aching head. Lottie had said she might be with child. Then Mr. Cameron would have to marry her, awesome Mr. Cameron, who had sunk as low yesterday evening as she herself.

Clutching the bannister tightly, she inched down, wondering if anything had happened beyond the kiss and the touch. Sister Mary Joseph, who had conducted secret classes on "the marriage bed" and "the act" for four years of girls at St. Scholastica before she suddenly and inexplicably disappeared, had had a lot to say about "preserving one's virginity" and "remaining chaste even in the face of a husband's lust," about submitting to "the act" for no reason other than procreation and many other confusing and frightening instructions.

However, Sister had never told her students what "the act" entailed, nor had anyone else. The rites of the marriage bed were to remain a mystery until the husband revealed them; that much Kristin knew. But she had no husband, and if Mr. Cameron had revealed anything else to her last night, she couldn't remember it, which was perhaps just as well. She couldn't believe that he'd actually touched her breast. Worse, she had found it very exciting. She supposed that was part of the allure of sin—it took you by surprise and made you experience exciting feelings you'd never had before.

At the bottom of the stairs, she panicked. Suddenly the family dining room was a more threatening place to Kristin than the lion's den in the story of Daniel. Daniel had at least believed that God would rescue him; Kristin, having evidently lost her virtue to brandy and Mr. Cameron, had no hope of divine intervention. She could hear their voices behind the double sliding doors, which were usually left open until everyone had assembled. Now they were closed.

She fretted a moment, fingers clenched at her sides; then, tentatively, she slid the doors open a mere three inches and peeked through to find them staring at her, silent and condemning. When she reached her place at the bottom of the table, everyone sat down. Her presence acted on conversation like a blanket smothering a fire, and her fingers shook as she unfolded her napkin and placed it in her lap. Grace was said, soup served. Twice her spoon clinked against the edge of the soup bowl, but Kristin dared not look up to see if this breach of etiquette had been noticed by the rest.

When the roast was brought in, her father spoke at last. "Well, have you nothing to say for yourself?"

By this time Kristin was beginning to feel resentful. No matter what had happened last night, Minna and Mr. Cameron bore some responsibility. She looked toward her father, who held the carving knife clutched in a red fist.

"You have disgraced us all. Now I want to know what you thought you were doing," he said.

Kristin clenched one hand over the other in her lap.

"Well, speak up."

"I don't know, Papa," she quavered.

"You don't know? What does that mean?"

"I don't remember very clearly." Nor was she sure what he had seen.

"She doesn't remember." Various members of the family echoed him in sepulchral tones.

"Well, let me tell you what you've done."

Kristin waited to hear.

"You have disgraced your family. You have attempted to lure your sister's fiance away from her."

"I have not!" said Kristin, surprised out of her anxiety and humiliation.

"Perhaps hoping that the bigger dowry would be yours."

A silence ensued as Kristin wondered why, aside from her most recent transgression, her dowry had to be smaller than Minna's. Her father seemed to be waiting for her to speak. Finally he said, "It would seem that you cannot find an excuse for your conduct."

No one seemed to be blaming Mr. Cameron for what had happened. A seed of bitterness that had lain fallow in the meadow of Kristin's family feelings began to grow. Mr. Cameron was wealthy and could contribute to their prosperity, while she, being a girl, had nothing to offer and no defense unless she spoke up for herself.

"It seems to me, Papa," she said, trying to sound brave and reasonable, "that any man who urges strong spirits on his fiancée's sister and then makes an attempt on her virtue, which you seem to think he did—well, he's no gentleman. Hardly someone you'd want to marry your daughter."

"Don't you dare suggest," shrieked Minna, "that I give up Mr. Cameron!"

"And how can any woman call herself a lady," said Kristin, "when she deliberately leaves her fiance cooling his heels while she sits gossiping with female friends?"

Minna turned scarlet and began to stammer with fury.

"Be silent, both of you," roared Mr. Traube. "And you, Kristin, since you think yourself old enough to lecture me—and your sister—and to sit in my library drinking brandy as if you were a man, as if you were one of your brothers instead of a mere girl, perhaps you also think you're old enough to go into the world and fend for yourself."

Did he mean to put her to work at the sausage factory like Heinrich II, Ludovich, Otto, and Baldwin? Kristin wondered apprehensively. It was a terrible place. She couldn't imagine working there in all the heat and noise, where everything was permeated with grease, and pig innards lay slippery and noisome under foot.

"Very well," said her father, as if she had agreed. "Go. Pack your things."

He stood and took his money clip from the inner pocket of his frock coat. "Nor do I intend to be stingy with you, even though you have been a thankless, disgraceful daughter. I have started your brothers off in life, and I will do the same for you. With the fine education I've given you, you will doubtless find a job somewhere."

Kristin stared at her father. He meant for her to leave the house? To leave the protection of her family? To look for work and live in some shabby room, eating what little she could afford, never enough, like the poor creatures she had heretofore rescued in railroad stations?

He counted out a pile of greenbacks on the table. "Pass that to your sister," he said grandly, handing the lot to Heinrich II. As the money traveled from Heinrich to Otto to Kristin, Mr. Traube said, "Go out into the world. Make your own way, since you cannot keep the rules of my house or of society. Then perhaps, if you prove to me that you can live a respectable life and if you see the error of your ways, we will readmit you to this family. I expect you to leave after breakfast tomorrow."

Kristin sat staring at the stack of bills that rested beside her plate. Part of her wanted to spurn the money. However, good sense prevailed. She raised a hand from her lap and closed slender fingers around the greenbacks.

"Now leave the table."

Kristin rose. In a second she was gone from the room.

Mr. Traube carved the roast with a grand ferocity. Minna was the first to break the silence. "You have done just right, Papa," she said triumphantly.

"I do not need you to pass judgment on my conduct of family affairs," said Mr. Traube, using the knife to cut slices of roast and place them on each plate.

"No, of course not, Papa," said Minna, "but she had no right to throw herself at my fiance. I shall have to teach Mr. Cameron a lesson about—"

"You will treat Mr. Cameron with the respect and duty you owe him," said Mr. Traube. "If you had kept your dinner engagement, this would not have happened."

Minna flushed. "I think he got the night wrong."

"She's lying," said Otto. "I saw the card in his flowers. She means to make him a hen-pecked husband."

Heinrich Traube, in whose mind all respect and obedience were owed to the man of the family, said to his daughter, "I have provided you with the handsomest of dowries. If, after my generosity, you destroy this opportunity, I may reconsider what you are worth on the marriage market. You may find yourself married to some butcher down in South Chicago or not married at all. Do I make myself clear?"

Minna went pale. "Yes, Papa," she hastened to assure him. "I will not let Mr. Cameron get away. I understand that he is of financial importance to the family."

"Good. See that you do not put your pride above our interest."

"Kristin's banishment," said Heinrich II, "may prove an embarrassment to the family. And we should remember that Minna hates Kristin."

"Why do you say that?" demanded Hildegarde Traube.

"Minna used to pinch her," said Ludovich, "even when she was a baby. That's why Kristin cried so much."

"I did not," said Minna.

"You did too," said Otto. "Because she was pretty and you were jealous."

"She's jealous of me!" screeched Minna and pinched Otto.

"Did you see that?" Ludovich crowed. "She's still pinching."

"Silence!" roared Mr. Traube. His offspring all cowered against the backs of their chairs. Then Mr. Traube smiled. "Who knows," he said, having exacted his due in terror, "I may relent by breakfast time and let her stay."

"A fine joke, Papa," said Ludovich admiringly, and the family members began to pile their plates with creamed potatoes, bread, and vegetables richly drenched in lard, the product of Mr. Traube's own sausage-making empire.

"What are you doing, lass?" asked the housekeeper.

"I'm packing," said Kristin, brushing away another fall of tears. "I've been told that I must leave the house."

"Pish-posh. He'll ha' changed his mind by mornin'."

"Papa never changes his mind, Lottie. He's always telling us that. He said that I must make my own way in the world." The very thought terrified her, but she was too proud to show it. "I see this as a great opportunity," she said, trying to sound brave and optimistic. "Now I can pursue the career as an artist that I gave up two years ago because Papa insisted." She bent to fasten a strap, hiding her tears. "Of course, I can never marry, having been dishonored, but I shall become a famous artist. Papa will wish he hadn't driven me away."

"And who will buy enough paintings to support you?"

"Mrs. Potter Palmer." Just thinking of Mrs. Palmer gave Kristin courage. "And Papa has given me money to make a start on my new career."

"Has he? How much?" asked Lottie. Kristin pointed to the pile of greenbacks on the table by her bed. Lottie counted it. "Stingy as always," she muttered.

"Really?" Kristin's heart sank. She knew very little about finances, having been given only trifling sums each week. Her major expenses—clothing and gifts—came out of her father's pocket, so the amount he provided had seemed generous, a small source of reassurance—that and her talent— as she faced the frightening prospect of being separated from a lifetime of security.

"This won't last long," said Lottie. "You're a babe in the woods where money's concerned. And where will you go?"

"To my friend Genevieve's." Kristin had considered taking refuge with Aunt Frieda, the only member of the family who was consistently kind to her, but she had decided that such a course would be unfair to Aunt Frieda. Her aunt might take her in, but it would cause a rift between the sisters and would endanger Aunt Frieda's position in society now that Kristin was an outcast. Also Kristin's father hated Aunt Frieda for her anarchist opinions on women's suffrage and property rights. Therefore, it had to be Genevieve's. Instead of feeling terrified and bereft, she should be thanking God that she had a talent on which to build a new life and a friend to take her in.

Kristin finished tying another bundle. "Now, I have packed enough canvas to start my professional life, but I must choose what clothes to take. Several dresses suitable for tea with Mrs. Palmer, of course, smocks for when I am painting, a ball gown for exhibitions—why are you groaning, Lottie? That seems a practical list to me."

"Even if he lets you go, he'll soon decide that it's a shame to ha' a daughter in exile. After all, no one knows of your disgrace except the family. Is this Genevieve a good woman? Yes? Then I suppose she can watch over you an' see you come to no harm. 'Twill only be a day or so." Lottie patted Kristin's shoulder. "You'll see, lassie."

Once Lottie had gone, Kristin thought about facing the family at breakfast. No one had defended her at the dinner table. No one had come to commiserate with her since. And they wouldn't. Her mother and brothers, even if they felt sorry for her, wouldn't risk Papa's wrath. Breakfast would be more hurtful than dinner had been.

Hearing on the street below the rattle of a carriage and the clip-clop of horses' hooves, she fantasized that Mr. Cameron was coming to rescue her from her cruel family. But what nonsense that was, she chided herself. Mr. Cameron was no handsome prince! He was a scoundrel, and no one would be coming to rescue her. So why wait? She might as well go tonight. Obviously, she could not call upon Mrs. Palmer at such an hour, but Genevieve took in young women at all hours, and Kristin had money to pay for a cab.

Not sure whether this decision represented bravery or cowardice, Kristin rang for the upstairs maid and sent her to the attics to fetch down the cases Kristin used on summer trips to the country. Having packed her art supplies—paints, brushes, pencils, drawing paper—she strapped an easel to the side of the suitcase. Then she selected the clothing she had mentioned to Lottie and packed those items, followed by everything else she had room for. Maybe she would never return. Instead she would become a famous artist, the toast of Chicago society, from which position she could snub Mr. Cameron and her parents. By the time she had finished packing, the house was silent, all the occupants

49

having gone to bed. Kristin herself was sleepy.

She lugged the cases, one by one, down the stairs and placed them at the front door in the great hall, which was now silent and dark, lit by only one lamp, trimmed low, its flame safe in the glass casing.

She went to the back of the house and knocked timidly at the door of her father's driver. When Carl answered, he was clad only in his trousers and undershirt, a pipe clenched in his teeth.

"Carl," she said, embarrassed to have him staring at her puffy, tear-reddened eyes, "I must impose upon you to get me a hackney cab."

The man shook his head. "*Gross Gott!*" he exclaimed. "What are things coming to in this family when the little princess is put out in the street?"

Kristin flushed. Obviously the story had been whispered through the servants' quarters already. Perhaps Carl would refuse to help her because she was a fallen woman. She sniffed back tears. "I don't want to have to go afoot, Carl. Surely it's not good for a young woman to be on the streets at night."

The driver turned, tapped out the bowl of his pipe into a dish he kept for that purpose, and got his shirt. "I'll find you a cab, miss." And so he did, first packing it with her mountain of luggage, then helping her in. "Go with God," he muttered as he closed the door and Kristin waved to him through the window, taking a last look at "the house that sausage built," as she often thought of it. Her father's mansion, of which both parents were so proud, was massive, ornate, and tasteless. When she was famous and could afford her own house, she would build something much nicer, she told herself.

Still, it was terrible to leave home with no member of the family to see her off. Would they have done so had she stayed for breakfast? Well, no matter. She must face the change bravely. Her grandmother had come to this country all on her own when her family died in a typhoid epidemic. If Grossmutter could do that, Kristin could surely embark on a new life in the country where she had always lived. Tomorrow she would call upon Mrs. Potter Palmer and make a start.

During the cab ride between her father's mansion and Genevieve's boarding house, Kristin's fears were forgotten in the wonder of nighttime Chicago. Because she was alone, she could look at everything, breathe in, with the cold March air, the mystery of her own city. Shades of black. Halos of gaslight blossoming tenuously in the dark, shining on cobblestones like oil swells. Flashes of color as people appeared and disappeared, moving indistinctly through pools of soft radiance and her field of vision.

Oh, if she could paint this, catch the black glow, the golden aureoles crowning the lamp posts, under which stood men in evening clothes and top hats, impressions without details or color, only line and shadow. What techniques would she use? Perhaps those of the new school rising in Paris—Independents they called themselves, or Impressionists. Kristin had seen a few pieces of their work at Mrs. Palmer's house and at exhibitions. There was an American woman among them—Mary Cassatt. Perhaps someday Kristin could go to Paris herself.

Her heart raced with excitement as in her head the painting of midnight streets took shape. "Nightscape in Chicago," she'd call it. Her fingers trembled for the feel of a brush, the smell of oils. How could she have frittered away these two years in desultory activity, seeing and painting nothing new, expending her time and energy on good works and social calls when she should have been reaching for new goals that beckoned the eyes and fingers of an artist? And she *was* an artist!

Perhaps Mr. Cameron had done her a favor in forcing her out of her safe, dull niche. Lottie had said the family would come for her. But did Kristin want that? Maybe God didn't mean for her to live an ordinary life circumscribed by the expectations of her father and thereafter whatever man her father chose for her, a husband who would have to be deceived into thinking that she was pure. How much better to stay single, live a Bohemian life, and put onto canvas insights into places and people that came from her heart, her eye, her brush.

"We're here, miss," called the driver. "You sure this is the address you want?"

Kristin peered out and saw a three-story frame house, many-windowed but of no architectural distinction, on a street crowded with similar structures. She noticed for the first time the stench of the slaughter houses. She had arrived in South Chicago, the least desirable of districts. Even so, she was filled with glowing optimism as she hastened up Genevieve's steps, hugged the surprised woman, and tipped the driver generously to carry in her fourteen trunks, suitcases, and bundles.

Book II

The Bohemian Spinster Artist

Chapter Three

Nothing had worked out as she'd hoped, as she'd dreamed, Kristin thought. She huddled into the Medici collar of her blue mantle and boarded a narrow-gauge train in Como, Colorado, a nasty little coal-mining and railroad town in the middle of a treeless plain surrounded by mountains. She was on her own and terrified, thousands—maybe millions—of miles from home. The difficulties of getting here had certainly made it seem that far.

Once aboard, she folded the mantle carefully on the seat beside her. She was wearing a cream-colored suit with elaborate blue cording rising in points from the bottom of her flared skirt and the wrists of her jacket and decorating the lapels. The bright blue of her hat and gloves and the blue leather of her high-buttoned boots matched the passementerie on her suit. Kristin's traveling costume would have been seasonable in many sections of the country. Here in April, winter still had a grip on Colorado. The previous train had traveled through snow from which spring flowers had just begun to peek. Birds exploded ahead of the engine from evergreens still frosted with white. Small ground creatures scuttled about, their tracks pocking snow fields. As the second train wound higher into the next mountain range, a rotary snowplow cleared the tracks ahead of them and sent whirlwinds of snow crystals to either side of the engine.

Still, whether or not her costume was seasonally appropriate, Kristin was the most fashionably dressed person on the train. She had more baggage, undoubtedly, than anyone else—fourteen pieces, which had caused endless commentary at Genevieve's house, at the Chicago railroad station where the conductor had made her pay extra, by Maeve Macleod, to whose house Kristin went in Denver, and now by various railroad employees between Denver, Como, and Breckenridge. She had a more extensive wardrobe than a bride on a wedding trip, than a famous artist setting across the ocean to paint on the continent, but she had no money. Kristin was probably the best dressed woman in all of Colorado. And the poorest. The most disillusioned. The most disheartened and melancholy.

Dreams, she had discovered, were not the forerunners to reality. She had dreamed of being a famous, Bohemian, spinster artist. But Mrs. Potter Palmer had been out of the country, unavailable to launch Kristin's career. Then Kristin had turned to Mrs. Sara Hallowell of the Chicago Interstate Industrial Exposition, an art expert who advised the Palmers on their collection, a woman so forceful that she had almost succeeded, just the year before, in forcing Heinrich Traube to let one of Kristin's paintings be shown at the exposition. But Mrs. Hallowell was no help! She had advised Kristin to go home to her family and make a good marriage.

Mrs. Drusilla Weems, a member of the Palette Club at whose exhibitions Kristen's paintings had been shown when she was still the schoolgirl protege of Sister Ermentrude, had told Kristin that it took years, even decades, to establish oneself as a self-supporting artist. She showed Kristin a picture of an elk with immense, overbalancing antlers, painted in Colorado and already sold. Then she offered Kristin a glass of wine, had three herself, and advised Kristin to try for mural commissions at businesses or in the nurseries of women with child since Kristin couldn't afford to travel to Colorado to paint elk. Unfortunately, the Palmer House, even given Kristin's connection to Mrs. Potter Palmer, had not been interested in a mural, and an expectant mother in Genevieve's district, when Kristin offered to paint a nursery mural, had called her a lunatic and summoned a policeman. So much for her dreams of being an artist!

She had dreamed that her family might relent and bring her home. Instead, she found herself on the streets in the Slaughterhouse District looking for work, any kind of work. She had dreamed that Mr. Cameron would arrive on Genevieve's doorstep, begging Kristin's pardon for his shocking conduct in the library, heartsick at the disaster he had brought into her life, declaring that he had always secretly loved her and wanted nothing more than to marry her and make an honest woman of her. No Mr. Cameron had appeared!

Instead, Genevieve, wondering why the Traubes did not come to retrieve their daughter, had wormed the story out of Kristin and then declared that, had the evil seducer planted his seed in Kristin's womb and got her with child, he would have to marry her whether he wanted to or not. Many a terrified night Kristin had spent puzzling over seeds. How were they planted? Would the seed have jumped from Mr. Cameron's mouth to hers while he was kissing her?

Horrified that she might be with child, Kristin had imagined her own death in childbirth, her funeral, the pitifully emaciated body in its coffin with the dead infant alongside, all the Traubes weeping around the grave, blaming themselves and Mr. Cameron for her untimely death. "Even though she lost her virtue, we should have stood by her," they'd say. Mr. Cameron a distant, tragic figure in the graveyard, heartsick at the betrayal that had brought about her untimely death, would vow never to marry but to remain faithful forever to her memory.

Instead of dying a tragic death, Kristin secured a job as a waitress in a working man's cafe, washing dishes and carrying heavy plates of greasy sausage and odoriferous cabbage. The wages were pitiful, and her only tip was a penny given by a sewing machine salesman whose patent leather hair was so interesting that she made a sketch of him. That one penny, however, spawned fantasies in which she was the toast of glamorous Chicago restaurants in which she did witty cartoons of the patrons, received huge commissions, and invested her money, becoming rich, independent, and famous—astonishing Mr. Cameron, who was said to be such an investment genius. She'd say to him some day, "Although you were a cad, sir, I forgive you."

What actually happened was that the proprietor, while she was wiping off dirty tables, said, "Give us a kiss, sweetheart." Kristin, terrified of further dishonor, had flung the dirty cloth in his face and fled his establishment with the owner in noisy pursuit, crying, "Stop, thief. Bring that apron back." The next day Genevieve had to go to the cafe to return the apron and collect Kristin's winter coat and day's pay.

As a last resort, with no job, no prospects, and the money her father had given her dribbling away in fees to get her badly packed clothes pressed and cab fares to take her on fruitless job searches, Kristin had begged Genevieve to send her to Colorado as she did other Chicago girls in need of jobs and husbands. Kristin was then dreaming of painting majestic Colorado landscapes, maybe even saleable if bizarre elk, becoming the talented Miss Traube, a second Bierstadt. Instead, after a disastrous train ride from Chicago to Colorado, she became the maid of a woman who resented the fact that Kristin couldn't iron or bake, who inexplicably demanded to know if Kristin had a sister named Ingrid, and who, for no known reason, hated blond hair and became upset when Kristin went off to make contact with Chicago artists residing in Denver.

None of *them,* thought Kristin, could make a living as an artist either, but she had managed to leave a portrait of Aunt Frieda for showing in a new gallery owned by Mrs. Helen Henderson Shane, painter of a famous picture of the Royal Gorge. Emma Richardson Cherry, an important landscapist who had studied in Chicago, New York, and Paris, accepted a Chicago scene bustling with street urchins, pushcart pedlars, and poor, shabby tenement dwellers. Mrs. Cherry promised to enter it in the next Denver art contest. Surrounded by her fourteen pieces of luggage, Kristin had painted the cityscape in Maeve Macleod's shabby guestroom and delivered it wet.

However, before Kristin could benefit from any of these new contacts, Mrs. Macleod decided to ship Kristin off to her daughter Kathleen Macleod on the frontier. In parting, Kristin gave Mrs. Macleod a pastel of her younger daughter, horrid little Bridget, and Mrs. Macleod gave Kristin a basket lunch and a book of saints' lives to see her through the trip to the wild frontier. So much for dreams, thought Kristin sadly. The handsome prince had asked her to call him Jack and ruined her life. The famous Bohemian spinster artist was going to become a housemaid, probably in a log cabin, cooking at an open hearth, dusting firearms, tending children with runny noses while mountain blizzards whistled between the logs.

If she hadn't been dishonored, she might have married. A number of men, most of them virtual strangers, had proposed to her, but of course she could not accept. She couldn't even talk to them. Genevieve's last admonition as the train was pulling out of the great railroad station in Chicago had been, "Don't talk to strange men."

"May I take this seat, miss?"

Kristin looked up to see a strange man. Trembling, she lifted her mantle from the aisle seat, wondering if he was a vile seducer or some other evil type. Sister Mary Joseph had indicated that the varieties of evil particular to the male gender were legion. As the train began its descending spiral, the drummer introduced himself to a determinedly silent Kristin and spent the rest of the trip extolling the merits of Dr. Witt's Little Early Risers, a miracle-working patent medicine of which he was the sole Western Slope purveyor. At Argentine, halfway down the mountain, Kristin was shrinking back in her seat, hideously embarrassed to hear mention of diarrhea and constipation.

"And biliousness," said the salesman enthusiastically, shouting above the shriek of the brakes that kept them from hurtling off the hairpin curves and running away on the steep grades. "It's a fine specific for biliousness. Perhaps you'd like to buy some."

Kristin bent over her sketch book to hide her blush.

"Female problems," he cried. "My lady customers tell me it's a marvel for female problems."

At the Washington Spur, a crowd of men wearing shapeless canvas pants, flannel shirts with their long underwear showing at the neck, gaudy suspenders, and hobnailed boots clumped aboard and divested themselves of heavy jackets.

Because there were not seats enough for them, they crowded the aisles, laughing and talking.

"Those are miners," said the salesman, "going into Breckenridge for a Sunday drunk."

She made hasty line drawings of their faces, remembering with a shiver that spirituous drink had got her into her present situation.

"Do you have a place to stay in Breckenridge?" asked the salesman.

Kristin refused to answer, fearing that he meant to offer her one.

"I hope it's with a big family and you'll tell them about Dr. Witt's Little Early Risers. Families are my best customers. The more members, especially children, the wider the variety of ailments for my Early Risers to cure."

Kristin had no idea how many were in the family to which she was going and whether there would be children—children she would perhaps be expected to tend. Bridget, badly spoiled by her father, had been a real trial to Kristin.

"This is the Gold Pan Trestle," said the salesman.

Kristin glanced up from a sketch of a bearded miner with a droopy nose that hung off his face like a sack of Red Devil Chewing Tobacco. The train was pulling onto a fragile wooden structure that bridged two sides of a canyon.

"We're crossing Illinois Gulch," said the salesman.

Cold sweat broke out on the palms of her hands, and she could hardly hold her pencil as she anticipated immediate death when the trestle buckled and plunged into the gulch. In fact, gulch seemed much too modest a word for the abyss they were crossing. How ironic if she should meet her end at a place named for her own home state, where she had once felt so secure. Swallowing hard, hands trembling, she started a wobbly sketch of the trestle.

"Here now," said the salesman. "Nothing to be afraid of," and he put his arm around her shoulders.

"Unhand me, sir!" she cried, remembering Jack Cameron's arm as he urged another snifter of brandy on her. "Look what you've done to my drawing." She pointed to the place where her pencil line had skidded off the page, forgetting in her dismay that she wasn't supposed to talk to strange men.

The salesman drew back, flushing, and heads turned all down the car. Kristin glared at the gawking passengers. She didn't care what they thought; no man was having his way with her, even if she wasn't sure what "having his way" entailed. She turned the wiggly skid line into a flight of birds. Nasty man! Genevieve was right. One should never talk to strangers. Sister Mary Joseph was right. Men were evil creatures.

"Breckenridge! Breckenridge!" called the conductor not long afterward. Kristin, ignoring the offered help of the Dr. Witt's Little Early Riser salesman, climbed down on the platform, glad to escape that car full of terrifying men.

The station master came hurrying toward her, saying, "Get back on the train, miss. Ladies don't step down here."

"Isn't this Breckenridge?" asked Kristin.

"Yep, but you're supposed to get off at the edge of town."

"Why?"

"Because—because this ain't a fit section of town for a lady. Now hurry, miss."

Bewildered, Kristin looked from the scowling station manager to the porter who had just dumped the last of her belongings on the platform to the conductor who was calling, "All aboard." Miners streamed by on either side.

"Well, hell," muttered the station manager.

Kristin began to cry. "I can't reboard when all my luggage is here on the platform."

"That's fourteen, miss," said the porter, "just like in Como. Ain't you never heard of tippin'?" Grumbling, he climbed back aboard and the train left.

"I'm sorry to have flouted your rules," stammered Kristin, "but how was I to know?" She hoped this wasn't an omen, that she hadn't already made herself an outcast in her new home. "I'll need a hack to carry me and my luggage to French Street," she said.

"Breckenridge don't have hacks."

"Then what am I to do?"

"Burro maybe," he responded grudgingly. "Probably take two of 'em. If you'd got off where you was supposed to, I wouldn't be havin' this problem."

"There are hacks at the edge of town?"

"Nope. But I wouldn't be there neither." He turned and left her alone on the platform in front of the little depot. Kristin wondered what was wrong with this section of town and how she would get to French Street when she had no knowledge of the town and no conveyance, not to mention no money and no sense of direction.

"Can I offer myself as your rescuer?" asked the Early Riser salesman.

Kristin stumbled over her art supply case in an attempt to back away from him.

"Here now, just because she got off at the wrong stop, don't mean you can treat her like a west side female," barked the station master, who had returned with a dreadful-looking man whom Kristin could smell at twenty yards.

As she wondered what a west side female was, the station master said, "Henry, here, has two burros—old, retired

63

from haulin' ore sacks near Montezuma, but likely they can get your cases up the hill."

Kristin tried to smile at Henry while holding her breath to block out his odor. Henry said nothing, simply hauled off her cases, trunks, valises, and parcels to load on two scruffy, ancient, unwashed, bug-ridden beasts of burden. They looked remarkably like their master and were so small that she expected them to sink under the weight.

Kristin, Henry, and his overloaded burros plodded across the bridge behind the throng of men from the Washington Mine and continued to Main Street. Its many business establishments looked reassuringly substantial until she noticed that most of the second and third stories were just elaborately constructed facades with windows, gables, and fancy eaves, but not a thing behind them except air. She shook her head in amazement. Was this the frontier? An elaborate false front with no substance?

The miners had stopped in front of the Miner's Home Saloon and were roaring with anger and frustration. Kristin's eyes opened wide, since it appeared that they intended to riot.

"Here, miss," said a portly gentleman with a curly gray beard, "let me escort you to the other side of the street."

She glanced with dismay at the muddy expanse she had to traverse if she were to accept his arm, and she did want to because the milling crowd in front of the saloon was becoming noisier, their language shocking. Weren't there *any* paved streets in Colorado? Denver called itself the Queen City, yet she hadn't seen one paved street during her stay there, and this town was even muddier.

"Hurry, miss. They're in no mood for gentlemanly behavior." The man clamped a firm hand on her elbow and urged her into the mud. Holding her skirts up to the very tops of her boots, Kristin waved Henry on, then glanced worriedly at her boots as she slogged across. "What is wrong with them?" she asked the gentleman, looking back every few minutes to see that her belongings were not falling off the burros into the mud.

"Colorado legislature passed a Sunday closing law, and the saloon keepers decided to honor it this one Sunday in hopes of getting folks mad enough to force a repeal."

"But surely, if it's just one day a week—" Kristin protested.

"'Tis their only day to drink, young lady. They work the other six. Poor fellows have come all the way from their mines to enjoy themselves, and now they find there's nothing to do but stand around on the street with their hands in their pockets."

The miners didn't look to Kristin as if they planned to stand about with their hands in their pockets. They looked as if they might tear open the doors to the saloon and help themselves to the spirituous liquors. "I'm trying to find the house of the Macleod family," she stammered, anxious to be away from the center of town. She drew out Maeve's instructions and stared at them helplessly.

"Would that be Connor Macleod?" asked the man.

"Oh, yes," she said. "Do you know them?"

"Everyone in Breckenridge knows everyone else."

Kristin wasn't sure she liked the sound of that, not with her dubious reasons for being here.

"Walk up Lincoln and turn left at French," he ordered. "Look for the house with the five-sided tower. Now, there's a story. Mrs. Macleod's carpenter didn't know what octagonal meant, so he built her tower room with five sides instead of eight. Then he kidnapped her."

Kristin's eyes grew wide.

"Oh well, *you* needn't worry. He's in prison, and even if he weren't, he was taken with that curly black hair of hers.

65

She had maids as blond as you, and he never gave them a second glance."

"Oh." Why was it that nobody out here liked blondes? She thanked the man for his help and turned toward Lincoln, again calling to the silent Henry, who had halted with his burros ten feet away from her.

Trudging wearily up the incline, she came upon the house at last, having turned the corner at French Street. "Oh, thank goodness!" she exclaimed. It was not a log cabin. The place even had charm of a bizarre sort, and her artist's eye was immediately engaged. The house had been painted a deep blue-green and rambled about, disparate sections tied together by a long front porch, a turret thrusting up on one side with a balcony around it, and gingerbread everywhere. Smiling with delight and relief, she mounted the steps and knocked on the door. She had never seen any edifice so quaint.

A stocky, handsome man with ginger-colored hair answered, and she exclaimed, "Your house is a whimsical work of art, sir."

He looked surprised to hear it. "You aren't by any chance the new Chicago girl, are you?" he asked.

Kristin nodded, happy to know that she was expected. Maybe life wouldn't be quite as grim as she had thought. After all, she had traveled through beautiful mountain ranges. All around her would be vistas which she could paint. Although no one in this frontier outpost would buy her paintings, she could send them by train to Denver, even to Chicago or Paris! Miss Kristin Traube, the female Bierstadt, they would say.

"Kat!" shouted the man, breaking in on Kristin's newest fantasy.

A beautiful woman with black hair and large green eyes appeared, a miniature version of herself in pinafore and white stockings clinging to her hand. The woman and her child were obviously dressed for calling. "Are you the new maid?" she demanded eagerly.

"Yes, I am," said Kristin. "I was just telling this gentleman what a delight your house is."

The woman's face lit with a radiant smile. "How nice to find someone who agrees with me. I designed it myself— more or less. At least, I had it put together. It was originally two houses, one a log cabin."

Kristin shivered. A log cabin after all?

"Don't you love the scrollwork? And the stained glass?"

"Oh yes," Kristin agreed. "The scrollwork shows a wonderful sense of humor. So antic."

"Humor?"

"And the stained glass is ever so much prettier than my father's. You wouldn't think stained glass could be gloomy and depressing, would you? But my father managed to find some, while yours—well, it makes the spirit sing." She couldn't *see* evidence of a log cabin.

"I've always felt that way about it myself. I'm Kat Macleod," said the lady, "and this is my husband, Connor."

"And I'm Kristin Traube."

"You've arrived not a moment too soon. I'm on my way to Robinson on business—Fitzgerald Sweet Cream Butter and Eggs. Molly, this is Kristin. She'll look after you."

"What a pretty child," said Kristin, her short, difficult acquaintance with Bridget coming to mind. "I'll look forward to painting her."

"Painting her!" Mr. Macleod exclaimed.

"Her portrait."

Both parents looked astounded.

"I'm an artist."

"How nice," murmured Mrs. Macleod. "Well, you'd best get into your working clothes and make a start on the house. I'm afraid things are a mess. First, you need to bake some bread. Molly will be as good as gold watching you. Then you can get on with the cleaning."

"I don't know how to bake bread," said Kristin.

"You don't?" Kat Macleod frowned. "You do know how to clean houses, don't you?"

"Well, I was learning as fast as I could when I left your mother's. Would you prefer your daughter's portrait in oils or pastels? I did a lovely pastel of—well, I guess little Bridget would be your sister. Mrs. Maeve Macleod was delighted with it."

"Was she?" The enthusiasm on Kat Macleod's face was leaching away, and Kristin felt a twinge of anxiety. She hoped they wouldn't fire her before she'd even got started.

"Do you know any stories?" asked Molly.

"Yes, I do," said Kristin. "If you'll show me where I am to sleep, I'll start telling you one right away."

"Oh, goody," cried the child and transferred her hand from her mother's to Kristin's.

"Connor, why is that man standing out in the yard with two overloaded burros?" asked Kat Macleod. "I think it's shocking the way animals are treated by the mining population, and I should certainly launch a crusade to do something about it if I weren't so busy with Sunday closing and women's suffrage, not to mention my business affairs. At least you could reprimand your employees for—"

"He's no employee of mine," said Connor Macleod, "and while we're on the subject of your crusades, you are not to recruit this young woman. She's here to do the housework."

"Oh, you needn't worry, Mr. Macleod," said Kristin. "My particular area of social concern is the rescue of women in railroad stations, and I do not think your station large enough to provide much opportunity for that."

"Now, don't fret, Connor." Kat Macleod went on tiptoe and kissed her husband so heartily that Kristin was embarrassed and experienced little shocks of memory and excitement. Mr. Cameron had kissed her that way.

"Actually, that's my baggage on the burros," Kristin explained when the Macleods finally let go of one another.

"Your *baggage*!" cried Kat. "I've never had a maid who came with more than two valises. How many are there?"

"Fourteen," admitted Kristin.

"Good lord," said Connor, "what will we do with them?"

"Heaven knows," muttered Kat, "but I really must be on my way. Stow what she doesn't need in one of—"

"I need it all," said Kristin.

"Well, if you can get it into your room, that's your business." Mrs. Macleod bustled down toward the street, one valise in her hand.

She certainly travels light, thought Kristin, *for a woman who is evidently going to another town.* Mr. Macleod was eyeing the mountain accumulating on his porch as Henry unloaded the burros.

"I wonder if you could pay him and take it out of my wages," said Kristin. "I have literally no money left."

"In that case," said Connor Macleod, "you might consider selling some of the things in your fourteen pieces of luggage."

Kristin looked shocked. "I couldn't do that."

"Then good luck getting them into your room."

"You expect me to haul all this stuff in?" asked Henry. "If your wife's gonna start one a them campaigns a hers agin my animals, Connor, I'm gonna—"

"She's not, and I'm not going to play porter to my own maid," said Connor Macleod. "I've business of my own. Talk to Augustina." He pointed to the left side of the house. "Augustina!" he shouted. Then he turned back and instructed Kristin to wash and iron all his shirts by nightfall because he'd been wearing the same shirt for three days. Kristin didn't get a chance to tell Mr. Macleod that she had yet to master the art of ironing, even though Mrs. Maeve Macleod had stood at her shoulder for several hours giving ill-natured directions and making Kristin very nervous.

A tall, red-headed woman appeared in the doorway on the left. "Wasn't that Connor? Where is he?"

"He has business elsewhere," said Kristin and introduced herself.

Augustina was staring at her in astonishment. "Good heavens," she said. "You look—" She paused, her expression puzzled. "—familiar."

"Do I? Maybe you know someone with blond hair. I don't know why, but people seem to take blond hair amiss. Mrs. Macleod in Denver certainly did. I need to know where my room is so that this man can put my luggage there."

Augustina stared at the pile. "There may not be room for you and all those things in that bedroom," said Augustina. "In fact, you'll never be able to make your way to the bed."

"But I hardly know of anything I can dispense with." Kristin bit her lip.

"It's not," said Augustina, "as if you're going to be needing a huge wardrobe. Just a few wash dresses and one Sunday outfit for when your suitors come to call."

"I don't plan to have any suitors," said Kristin, "and I guess I'd better tell you right off, I don't know how to make bread, and I'm a terrible ironer. Do you live here?"

"I'm Augustina Fitzpatrick, the wife of Mrs. Macleod's brother Sean, and we live on the left side of the house, although my husband actually owns the right side, except

70

for the tower room, which his sister had built when she thought he was going to die and wouldn't be back from Denver."

Kristin tried to digest this information while Mrs. Augustina Fitzpatrick began to look put out. "You say you can't bake? Where did Maeve find you?"

"Well, Genevieve found me. Maybe you don't know Genevieve, but——"

"Of course, I do. She sent me out here, but everyone she sends has practical skills."

Kristin felt terrible to hear that she was the least acceptable of Genevieve's protegées.

"You'll have to learn baking this afternoon," said Augustina Fitzpatrick and led Kristin and the burro man across the house to Kristin's very small room.

"Your room's next to mine," said Molly, "and now I'll have my story."

"Mrs. Fitzpatrick is going to teach me to bake," said Kristin, "so I'm afraid——"

"You promised," wailed the little girl.

"Then I guess I'll have to tell the story as I'm learning," she said and began to take her parcels and bags from the burro man. They did indeed fill up every inch of space, mounting up around the bed, the chiffonier, and the one chair. Kristin sighed, thinking of her chamber at home with the blue brocade drapes. Even the guest room at Genevieve's had been better than this, although her room at Mrs. Maeve Macleod's had been small and pedestrian.

And where will I put my easel? Kristin wondered. She also noted that the light was bad. She'd have to paint in the back yard or on the front porch. Would they give her time during the daylight hours to do so? Already she'd been asked to bake bread and to wash and iron shirts, although the afternoon was half gone.

"Story, story," wheedled Molly, clambering over the trunk that held Kristin's ball gown.

"Once upon a time," began Kristin sadly, "there was a little princess who thought that she'd grow up and marry a handsome prince and live happily ever after." Oh dear, she thought, this was an unfortunate beginning—too like her own story. One didn't say, "Then the princess drank too much brandy in her father's library, and the handsome prince was really a scoundrel in disguise." She'd have to improvise rather wildly as she went along.

"The bread," Augustina reminded her.

"She was an elk princess," said Kristin, remembering Mrs. Drusilla Weems's elk picture. Kristin lifted Molly over the luggage, then climbed over herself. "And the prince had huge horns that weighed his poor head down so the princess could hardly see his handsome elk face."

"Whee-e-e!" cried Molly.

"Elk princess?" muttered Augustina.

Chapter Four

Jack Cameron didn't know what else he could do. After the Traube dinner party, from which Kristin was missing, he'd bullied Minna into admitting that Mr. Traube had told his younger daughter she had to leave. Not that Papa really meant it, Minna hastened to add. He had been prepared to relent in the morning, only stupid Kristin had run away that night. Jack had been furious, appalled. He told Minna that, as nothing of importance had happened in the library, they were impugning his honor and that if they didn't retrieve Kristin and treat her decently, the engagement was off. Much good it had done. They claimed they couldn't find her.

He couldn't find her himself. Assuming that she had gone to the house of her fellow reformer, he had canvassed every parish priest in Chicago looking for the address of Genevieve Boyer, berating himself for having touched the girl, for having found her so attractive, for having all those blasted erotic dreams about her ever since. A gentleman sought his sexual pleasures among women most likely to see sex for what it was, an enjoyable and profitable diversion. He kept his procreative efforts for the marriage bed, and he eschewed everything in between except polite flirtation. Jack had forgotten the code and was paying for it.

Now everything was at sixes and sevens, the Traubes running all over town trying to find their daughter and their curmudgeonly Aunt Frieda treating Jack like the villain in a melodrama, insisting that he should be horsewhipped for besmirching the reputation of her innocent niece. Frieda believed that women should have control of their own property and the right to vote. She'd even told Heinrich Traube that he was a bully and a tyrant, and that men of his sort should be gelded before they could beget children. That had been amusing, Jack recalled with a chuckle, but on the whole the situation was no laughing matter, especially since Heinrich Traube had demanded an audience with Pitman Cameron and Jack now had to tell his father the whole unfortunate story. God knows how his father would take it.

And the confession would take place before Jack could get Kristin back into the bosom of her family. He finally had a lead. At the corner of Forty-Fifth and Lowe in Canaryville, a poor section of Chicago, Jack, trying not to breathe the fetid stockyard air too deeply, had questioned Father Maurice Dorney of St. Gabriel's. The priest said, yes, of course, he knew Genevieve Boyer, a bit of a saint, that woman. He gave Jack the address. If only Jack could have followed up and retrieved Kristin before he had to tell his father what had happened.

But his father surprised him. Traube arrived and, instead of complaining about Jack's treatment of Kristin, the sausage maker insisted that Jack meet his obligations to Minna by escorting her to a cotillion.

"Well, sir," said Pitman Cameron, "it appears to me that, since you have not brought your younger daughter home, you intend her absence as a rebuke to my son. He feels that his honor is at stake here, and so do I."

Mr. Traube looked astounded. Obviously he had not believed that Jack would tell his father the story.

"'Twas your son who was caught kissing my daughter," stammered Traube. "No one has said why he'd do such a thing. What was I to think?"

"I kissed her on the cheek," said Jack, stretching the truth a bit. He *had* kissed Kristin on the cheek, and that cheek had been as soft as down, although not as soft as her lips. He had a sudden sharp memory of how her mouth had tasted beneath his, so sweet, so tempting that he felt himself stir with excitement and had to tamp down those emotions lest he embarrass himself. "I hardly think a kiss on the cheek of one's future sister-in-law constitutes just cause for throwing the poor girl out on the street. Yet if you know where she is, why isn't she home?" demanded Jack.

"True," agreed Mr. Cameron, "which leads us to believe that we are being manipulated in this matter. If you think to renege on the dowry agreement—"

"I've said nothing about the dowry," blustered Traube.

"Then if this is not a financial ploy, you must have had some previous quarrel with your younger daughter and are seeking to blame your actions on my son. An innocent kiss—"

"There was much more to it than that," said Mr. Traube.

"Are you saying that Jack debauched your daughter?"

Mr. Traube turned the color of wet putty.

"If so, sir," said Pitman Cameron, "I must ask myself why you are not demanding that Jack make an honest woman of her, rather than asking that he take the elder girl to a cotillion. It seems to me that you are not only

75

defaming my son and my family but that your values are strangely awry. If I thought someone had dishonored *my* daughter—"

"I didn't say he had," muttered Heinrich.

"Then why have you not brought your daughter back into the bosom of her family? Why did you send her away?"

"She ran away," Mr. Traube muttered. "And perhaps I did act hastily with her, but—"

"I wouldn't have taken you for a hasty man where money is involved, Mr. Traube, not to mention reputations. Surely you are aware that we would not think of allying ourselves to a family touched by scandal. You must tell me honestly, sir, what scandal is attached to your younger daughter."

"None," sputtered Heinrich. "We were angry when she ran away and shocked to think she might be trying to spite her sister by pursuing your son."

"Well, that's hardly Jack's fault, is it? I shall have to think on this, sir, but in the meantime I do not see that it would be at all proper for my son to escort Miss Minna Traube to the cotillion. We must consider the engagement in abeyance until you show your good faith by bringing your younger daughter back into your home." Mr. Cameron stood up, signifying that the interview was at an end.

Once Mr. Traube had left the office, Pitman Cameron turned to Jack. "I think that until this contretemps has been resolved, it would be better if you were out of town."

Jack started to protest but was overridden. Pitman Cameron said, "I've been thinking about that gold mine in Colorado, which has shown little profit for our money. Someone should go out there and investigate."

Jack's heart leapt. He would have loved to go to Colorado, but if he left before Kristin was found and reunited with her family, he'd be shirking his duty as a gentleman. He'd got her into this fix; he had to get her out.

"You'll leave tomorrow," said Pitman Cameron.

"But—"

"This is not something that I intend to discuss, Jack. We have the Cameron reputation to protect—not to mention the money. Why I ever let you talk me into a gold mine . . ."

Jack Cameron was thinking of his trip to Colorado as the hack took him to Mrs. Boyer's house in the Stockyard District. He'd had good advice on that gold mine and was determined to turn it into a moneymaker. Then he felt a stab of regret. Once he rescued Kristin, he wouldn't see her again for weeks, maybe months. By the time he returned from Colorado, she might be married. He found that he didn't like the idea at all, nor that by the time he got back, he'd be expected to marry Minna.

If he had to marry, why not Kristin? Maybe he should suggest that, since the Traubes were trying to make out that he'd dishonored her. Of course, they probably hoped to make a fine marriage for Kristin without providing a dowry as big as Minna's. Pitman Cameron would never agree to any diminution of the dowry. He'd say, "It's the money that counts. Pretty faces don't last." Jack's own mother hadn't been a beauty; she had been rich and well connected.

With the ways of the world firmly in mind, he alighted from the hack and mounted the steps to knock on Genevieve Boyer's door, hoping this last stop would be the one that discovered Kristin and freed him of his moral obligation. It had to. Tomorrow he left for Colorado.

"Mrs. Genevieve Boyer?" he asked when a dark-haired, graying woman opened the door.

"That's right."

"I'm Jack Cameron."

To his astonishment, she tried to slam the door in his face. "If you'll just give me a minute, ma'am," he cried, stepping forward quickly.

"I ought to give you a horsewhipping."

Jack blinked. Surely Kristin had told her that there had been nothing but a kiss between them. Well, actually he had touched the girl's breast, but Kristin probably didn't remember that, not after all the brandy. What was wrong with these people? Making such a fuss over a kiss. "I wonder if I might speak to Kristin?" he asked. Genevieve didn't budge. "Then maybe you'd give me a minute of *your* time." Nothing from her but a scowl. "Truly, Mrs. Boyer, I mean no harm to you or Kristin. In fact, I hope to reunite Kristin with her family,"

"Her father won't have her back."

"Ah, but he will. I've refused to marry Minna unless he does." Happily, he thought, the wedding was a year away, and he'd be in Colorado for as long as he could manage. Minna wouldn't like having a fiance who wasn't available to escort her around town. Maybe she'd jilt him.

"I knew I shouldn't have let her go off so fast," muttered Genevieve and relented, waving him into the parlor.

"What do you mean?"

"I mean she's gone."

"Gone where?" He hoped it wasn't too far. Today was his last chance to—

"Gone to Colorado, where they take in Chicago girls and find them husbands. She couldn't get work here, so I gave in and sent her."

Jack felt dazed. Was this good news? Or bad? "Where in Colorado?"

"Denver first, then the frontier I should imagine. Colorado is a wild place, but full of men who want wives."

Jack wondered if Breckenridge, his destination, was a wild place. And how big was the frontier? He might not have the time or know-how to find Kristin.

"Your gentleman's games have turned her life completely out of its path. She may even be married by now."

Appalled, Jack tried to imagine fragile Kristin married to some hulking miner or tobacco-chewing cowboy. He'd never get her off his conscience if he didn't save her from that fate. "Do you know where exactly she might be going?"

"Why do you ask?" Genevieve looked suspicious again.

"Because it's my duty as a gentleman to find her."

"I sent her to Mrs. Maeve Macleod in Denver," Genevieve answered reluctantly.

"And after that?"

"It's up to Mrs. Macleod."

Jack frowned. No matter what the priest had said, this woman was acting too cagey about Kristin's whereabouts to be an honest protector of young girls. Father Dorney had said nothing about Colorado. "If I find that she's not with this Mrs. Macleod or that she's come to harm—"

"'Twas you she came to harm with," said Genevieve. "We're trying to help her after you wrecked her life."

Jack flushed. "Just remember what I've said. I'll have the police on you if you've sold her."

"*Sold* her?" Genevieve had caught the implication. "Out of my house, young man!" She leapt from her seat and rushed to the umbrella stand in the hall.

"Not until I've got the address of Mrs. Macleod," said Jack, who followed Mrs. Boyer only to face an umbrella coming at him point first.

"Out!" ordered Genevieve.

Remembering Kristin's story of the bounder in the railroad station, doubled over with pain in a skirmish with

79

Genevieve Boyer's umbrella, Jack reconsidered his demand for information. Since he couldn't knock the woman down, he backed out, wondering if her indignation meant that she was, in fact, a fine, charitable person or that she was a seller of young innocents into sin and putting up an indignant front in order to bamboozle him.

"That miserable hypocrite," muttered Genevieve as she strode down the hall to check on the preparations for dinner. How dared Jack Cameron, who was the cause of all Kristin's troubles, suggest that Genevieve might be a procurer? The man had an evil mind. And no doubt his intentions toward Kristin were evil. Men were creatures of great lust and no conscience. Fortunately, she doubted that he'd bother to chase the girl all the way to Colorado when he had only a name in Denver to guide him. No, he'd give it up, turn his desires elsewhere, and Kristin would be safe.

At the end of her first day in Breckenridge, Kristin was in the kitchen. Having finished washing the dinner dishes, she had gone back to ironing Mr. Macleod's shirts. As she worked, she tried to sort out the children, of whom there were so many. The two blond ones, Phoebe and Sean Michael, evidently belonged to Mr. Fitzpatrick and some former wife. There was a red-headed toddler, Liama, daughter of red-headed Augustina and black-haired Sean Fitzpatrick, the half-brother of the now absent black-haired Kat Macleod, daughter of Maeve. Kat was married to Connor Macleod, son of James Macleod, a Denver photographer who was married to Maeve. James had been as nice to Kristin as Maeve had been hard-hearted. Kristin sighed. What a confusing family! She thought she had the names and relationships right. Molly, three years old and daughter of Connor and Kat, was black-haired like her mother and uncle, and then there was a sandy-haired teenager named—what was his name?—he was evidently a son by some previous marriage of Connor Macleod's. Connor also had a grown daughter who was married and lived somewhere else.

Kristin had just scorched another of Mr. Macleod's shirts with the flat iron when she heard Mr. Fitzpatrick in the dining room say, "I thought I'd seen a ghost when she sat down to dinner."

"Nonsense," said Connor. "She's eight or nine inches shorter."

"Still, the resemblance is uncanny. I can't stop looking at her."

"You'd better," said Connor, "if you don't want to find yourself in hot water with your wife."

Are they talking about me? Kristin wondered. Then she was distracted from that question when Connor Macleod said, "Did you see that mob of angry men down by the saloon? They'll probably show up at our door any minute."

Sean laughed. "And Kat out of town. I always said my sister was a troublemaker. I used to catch it for her antics when she was just a tyke."

"Maybe they'll call on Reverend Passmore instead of us," said Connor. "How Kat could team up with him to campaign for Sunday closing is beyond me."

"She'd team up with the devil if it meant closing a saloon," said Sean.

Kristin shivered to think that frightening mob of thirsty miners might come up French Street. Surely they'd have gone back to their mines by now? Bone-tired, she hung one shirt and picked up another. They seemed awfully limp, not at all like her father's and brothers'. Was there something else she was supposed to have done beside wash and iron them? Mr. Macleod hadn't said. Then she whipped her hand away from the iron, having burned herself for about the fortieth time. The iron made another yellow-brown patch on the shirt. She hoped Mr. Macleod wouldn't notice. Maybe he'd be so glad to have a clean shirt that he wouldn't care.

"He's left Chicago," shrieked Minna. "I've been jilted!"

"Now, now. Maybe he has business out of town," said Heinrich Traube, but he too looked anxious. He couldn't find his youngest daughter, and now his eldest daughter's fiance had disappeared as well. Mr. Traube hadn't had the heart to tell Minna that Pitman Cameron had declared the engagement "in abeyance" until Kristin was returned.

Jack Cameron spent three days in Denver trying to trace Kristin Traube and Maeve Macleod, which was two days longer than he had planned. He found a Macleod photographic studio, but it was closed each time he visited it. He found a Timmie Macleod, who was a burly teamster and the foulest-mouthed man he had ever met. He found a Red Betty Macleod, who was a lady of the night in a Market Street crib, but no one knew Maeve Macleod or Kristin. Even in the railroad station where someone should have noticed a beautiful young girl climbing off the train by herself, no one admitted to having seen Kristin. The depot baggage manager became downright belligerent when closely questioned by Jack.

"And what would you be wanting with such a young lady if there was one?" he asked, eyeing with suspicion Jack's velvet-collared Chesterfield overcoat.

"I am a friend of the family," said Jack.

"Are you now? Well, I've not seen her," said Mr. Seamus McFinn and slammed down his rolling shutter.

Jack shook his head and went on to canvas the business district. He also slept uneasily in luxurious accommodations at the Windsor Hotel, dined expensively but with a nervous stomach at Charpiot's, which called itself "the Delmonico's of the West," and saw a rousing prize fight at the Palace Theater. Denver was a fine town—muddy but exhilarating. He'd have enjoyed it a lot more if he could have found Kristin, but after three days he'd still located neither Kristin nor the mysterious Maeve Macleod. Genevieve Boyer must had been lying to him, and by God, he would see that she paid for it. He was relieved to locate a Pinkerton's branch in Denver and engaged their services.

Then, knowing that he had done all he could for the moment, Jack climbed onto the train to Breckenridge and read over the reports he'd received on the Chicago Girl gold mine, in which the Cameron Bank had a fourth share. He knew his engineering study had been good, so why weren't they producing more gold? Perhaps they were stinting on the development of the mine, even though they had received a healthy infusion of capital from the bank on his recommendation. The interesting thing was that the partners were named Macleod—Connor and Kathleen Macleod. He hadn't noticed that before. Maybe they'd know Maeve.

"I see you're lookin' at gold-mine papers there," said a fellow sitting beside him, wearing a crushed hat and a embroidered waistcoat with red and purple *fleurs-de-lis* on a gold background.

Jack frowned at him. "Do you always read strangers' papers over their shoulders?" he asked.

The man grinned, revealing a missing tooth on the left front side. "When I ain't got nuthin' else to do, why not? *Rocky Mountain News* hadn't come out when I left Denver."

Jack had noticed that too. No doubt, out here on the frontier, reading material was scarce and anything would do, even someone else's reading material.

"You lookin' for a good gold mine, I got one," said the man. "Assayed out at twenty ounces of silver and forty ounces of gold per ton."

Jack's eyebrows lifted, and he knew the skepticism showed on his face.

"It's a winner," said the fellow, "or would be if I had me the money to develop it."

"Where is it located?" asked Jack.

"Well, I ain't tellin' that," the man replied. "Cain't have Yankee strangers jumpin' my claim, now can I?"

"I'm from Chicago," said Jack, "not the Northeast."

"Chicago's north to me. Makes you one a them big city slickers, don't it?"

Twenty ounces of silver didn't stir Jack's gambling instincts, but forty ounces of gold was another matter. "How much money are we talking about?"

"Why would you be askin'?"

"Because I'm a banker, and I've already, as you've just ascertained, invested in one gold mine."

"You got money in the Chicago Girl? Well, I swan. Got yerself a good one there. I'm surprised them Macleods sold you shares. Miss Kathleen, she loves that mine. Found it her ownself. Best business woman on the Western Slope. I know 'cause I married one of her Chicago girls."

"One of her Chicago girls?" Jack's attention sharpened. "Connected by any chance with Genevieve Boyer or Maeve Macleod?" he asked eagerly.

"Cain't say as I know either a them ladies," said the miner. "My girl's Hettie Mann that was. Now she's Hettie Wapshot, and I'm Aloysius Wapshot." The man thrust out a callused paw and shook Jack's hand. "So you're a Chicago banker an' you put money in gold mines?"

"Only after I've had them inspected by an engineer of my own choosing," said Jack. "Now about your wife—"

"Ain't sellin' my wife," said Aloysius Wapshot.

"I'm not asking you to. I want to know about the Macleods and the Chicago girls."

"Nuthin' to tell. They brings 'em out and finds husbands fer 'em—substantial fellas like me, fellas who might consider partin' with half the shares in a good mine, given enough capital money to develop it."

Jack studied the man carefully. He had found in the past that he had a good eye for swindlers, and he didn't think Mr. Wapshot was one.

"By God, you're interested. I kin see it. I knew this was my lucky day when I found that horseshoe on the street. Sunk in mud it was, but I seen it. Where you plannin' to get off? Breckenridge I reckon, if you was goin' to see the Macleods. Well, the Macleod mine ain't goin' nowhere. Why don't you just stay on the train with me and come to Aspen. I'll find you a good engineer."

"Thanks, but I'll find my own," said Jack. With the scent of profit in his nose and the conviction that Kristin was safe and could be found next week, he added, "I think I *will* accompany you to Aspen, Mr. Wapshot."

Kristin stared woefully at Molly's ruffled frock. The iron was cold again, the ruffles scorched. As patient as she'd been, Miss Kat would not be pleased. Kristin sniffed and brushed away a welling tear. This housewifery was a depressing business, and she hadn't painted a single picture since she'd got here, although the mountains rose majestically at the edges of the valley that held Breckenridge. Not that the valley was any beautiful sight with its muddy river, misnamed the Blue, and its inexplicable piles of gravel.

The town was small, undoubtedly too small to harbor any art collectors, if Kristin ever managed to produce any art in between the ironing, the dusting, the washing, and all those other activities at which she was so inept. She was trying to act as servant to *nine* people. In Chicago there would have been a swarm of knowledgeable servants to take care of so many masters. Here there was just Kristin, the hopeless housemaid.

Still, it was a wonder Miss Kat seemed so anxious to marry her off. Surely even an inept housemaid was better than none. And it was so embarrassing. Kristin didn't want to tell Kat Macleod why it was that she refused to entertain suitors, although they had collected on the front porch after church. Evidently word of an unmarried female ran through the bachelor community of the Western Slope like wildfire. Men from miles away had come to meet her.

Curse Jack Cameron! If she ever saw him again, she'd—she'd—well, she didn't know what she'd do, but she'd better not find herself with child. Kristin's hand had been pressed against the small of her back, which was aching. Now she moved it around to pat her waistline. No sign that she was turning into a pickle barrel, thank God. That was the only sign of pregnancy she knew.

Chapter Five

"Excuse me, sir."

Jack looked up from his newspaper. He was traveling to Breckenridge from Aspen, where he had been offered shares in numerous silver mines and refused them all. He did wire his father for money to invest in the Wapshot gold mine. Pitman Cameron had replied that he did not appreciate buying into a second gold mine when he had sent his son west to investigate the first, which was not yet showing much profit. However, he had sent the money. The Cameron Bank, not to mention Jack himself, were now part owners in Aloysius Wapshot's venture.

"Sir," prompted the unknown gentleman, seating himself beside Jack, "I believe you are Mr. John Powell Cameron, who bought into an Aspen gold mine."

"I am," said Jack, deducing from the accent that the fellow was a New Yorker.

"I am Melrose Farr."

"The fellow who tried to buy Wapshot out for a practically nothing?"

"All in the way of business," Mr. Farr responded. "And I am still interested in that mine."

"Well, now it will cost you a good deal more than you would have paid had you offered him a fair price in the first place," said Jack, turning the page of his newspaper. There was nothing he relished more than a good financial haggle, and he knew how to conduct one—by exhibiting disinterest to the party who wanted something Jack controlled.

"Are you disinclined to sell?"

"It would depend on the price." Jack named an outrageous one.

Mr. Farr blanched.

"I see that you are not a serious buyer," said Jack and returned to his newspaper. He was reading of Aspen's attempts to clean up its red light district, which he had visited for the local interest, not to search for Kristin. He had convinced himself that she was safe in Breckenridge under the protection of the Macleods. Jack looked forward to seeing her, poor girl. What an adventure she had had. And women were not appreciative of adventure.

"Fifty thousand," said Mr. Farr, his voice tense.

"That might be enough for my shares, certainly not enough for the bank's as well." Jack gave his newspaper a shake and began to read about a lady of the night named Merciful Minnie, who had injured an Aspen policeman by cudgeling him with a wooden leg, which she had snatched from a one-legged customer on the second floor of the brothel.

"Seventy-five thousand," said Mr. Farr.

"Make it a hundred, and I might consider your offer," said Jack.

"Sir, that is outrageous."

"Then you don't really want the mine." Jack returned to Merciful Minnie who, on the way to jail, had screamed obscenities at several respectable ladies on the street. A charge of public indecency and lewd language had been lodged against Minnie for her remarks.

"Very well, a hundred thousand," said Mr. Farr. "Dammit, what did you pay Wapshot?"

"That's my business," said Jack, but he had just tripled his money and felt very happy about it. Although the mine was a good one, Aloysius Wapshot had not struck Jack as a reliable partner. Jack would have had to hire a manager and oversee the venture himself. "If you are able to produce the hundred thousand by close of business tomorrow in Breckenridge, the Cameron shares will be yours."

They shook on it, and Mr. Farr fell into a brooding silence, no doubt wondering whether he had made a wise investment. Jack picked up his newspaper, which also contained information about Merciful Minnie's colleagues, who had caused such a ruckus in the local jail that the police chief was quoted as saying, "From here on, if the citizens of Aspen want to interfere in the operations of the red light district, they'll have to do it themselves."

Jack chuckled. Although the towns were smaller, the West was much more amusing than Chicago. Maybe he'd stay. A profit of sixty-six thousand dollars might convince his father that the Cameron Bank needed a branch in Colorado. As long as they didn't put any money into silver, the price of which was falling and would, in Jack's opinion, continue to fall, Cameron's of Colorado should be very profitable.

"Mummy," said three-year-old Molly Macleod, "the ruffles on my petticoat have turned brown."

"Mine too," said Phoebe Fitzpatrick.

"I suppose the water's bad again," said Kat.

Kristin, as soon as she heard the words *brown ruffles,* departed hastily for the kitchen, knowing that she had scorched them all.

"Kristin," called Kat, "do let the mud settle in the river water before you wash the clothes."

"Yes, ma'am," called Kristin from the kitchen and breathed a sigh of relief just before she discovered that her stew had burned again. She quickly poured what was not blackened and stuck into another kettle and hid the burned pot on the back porch. Someone would comment on the peculiar flavor, but the Macleods and Fitzpatricks had been remarkably tolerant of her novice efforts.

In fact, Sean, Miss Kat's brother, seemed to like everything she did and followed her constantly with his eyes. She could tell that he was making his wife, Augustina, nervous. In fact, everyone who looked into Kristin's face, except the children, seemed alarmed or bemused, as if they were looking at a ghost instead of a pretty girl. At least, friends in Chicago had said Kristin was pretty, but perhaps only in contrast to the rest of her family.

Not that it mattered. Because of Jack Cameron, she was unmarriageable, even if she *had* wanted a husband to take care of her. She told herself every night before she went to sleep that she no longer wanted to marry, that she truly looked forward to becoming a famous and wealthy spinster artist. But it was getting harder to believe she would succeed when all she'd done in Breckenridge was housework.

Thinking of Mr. Cameron reminded her of the Breckenridge priest, Father Boniface Wirtner, whom she found very intimidating. Kristin had yet to go to confession because she did not want to confess her loss of virtue. But if she never confessed, she could never be forgiven. It was a frightening thought.

She had got the stew boiling in the second pot and decided there ought to be some sort of award for bravery, an award intended just for housewives and maids. What a terribly difficult activity it was! She hadn't yet managed to light the stove on her own. Mr. Sean did that for her, and he had trouble because he kept staring at her. Then, with the stove lighted, she never knew how much wood to feed it or how hot it should be to bake bread, as opposed to meat or cake. Nothing came out right when Kristin cooked.

To forget her troubles, she slipped over to the heavy oak table where she kept a sketch pad hidden under a pile of dish towels. Looking out the window, she did a quick drawing of the mountain range. If only she could get back into those mountains and do some painting. Were maids in Colorado ever given a day off? She'd forgotten to ask how much money she'd be making after she paid off her Denver-to-Breckenridge ticket and the burro man's fee. Life was so difficult. And all because of Jack Cameron. She hoped he was marrying horrid Minna this very minute and would be wretched for the rest of his life.

Then Kristin fell to daydreaming over her sketch, imagining that she was a princess in a mountain kingdom and a prince came riding up on a white horse while she was doing a beautiful oil painting. He dismounted and fell in love immediately with both Kristin and her painting and offered a thousand dollars for the picture and a lifetime of happiness if she would accept his hand in marriage. Oddly enough, he looked like Jack Cameron. Kristin sighed. Even in her daydreams, she wasn't convincing as an independent woman.

"What's that peculiar smell?" Kat sniffed and turned toward the stew pot, shaking her head. "Burned again. Oh well, just so I don't have to do the cooking myself."

91

Kristin shoved her sketchbook under the dish towels and turned to smile at Kat, who was a wonderful mistress if you had to be a maid. "You are the nicest person."

"Why, thank you, dear," said Kat. "Perhaps you'd like to join me at the women's suffrage torchlight parade."

"I don't know," said Kristin. "I've never been a suffragette, although my Aunt Frieda is." Kristin had finally written to her aunt to assure the lady that she was safe and eating regularly.

"Well, there's nothing more exciting than a torchlight parade. You'd better come."

Kristin sighed. Another evening when she would not be able to paint after her chores were done. Not that she had so far. She was always so tired that she fell into bed as soon as she could. One night she hadn't even managed to get her clothes off and had left her candle burning, only to be awakened and scolded by Phoebe, who had a great deal to say on the dangers of fire in frontier communities.

Kristin had been terribly embarrassed to be lectured by an eight-year-old child, who knew more about frontier life than she did.

Jack Cameron didn't get the reception he expected from the Macleods. Connor was friendly, but his wife acted as if the Camerons had stolen their fourth interest in the Chicago Girl mine. She wouldn't even invite Jack to their house, so he had to ascertain from other sources that Kristin was living there. Jack sent word to Pinkerton's that they could discontinue their search. Then he leased space on Main Street near the corner of Washington Avenue.

The store front had been a barber shop that lost half of its clientele because the barber, somewhat the worse for alcohol, shaved the lobe off a patron's ear. The other half of the clientele, who had been accustomed to taking their baths in the back room, scowled at Jack on the street because he wouldn't rent out the tub after he took over the lease. He hired a sign painter, and within several days a sign was raised over the door that said:

Cameron Investment Co.
A Branch of the Cameron Bank of Chicago
John Powell Cameron, President

Much to his astonishment, merchants and other citizens began to bring money in. "I am not a depository bank," he tried to explain. They said, "Fine. Invest it." Everyone had heard of his sixty-six-thousand-dollar profit on the Wapshot mine transaction and how Wapshot had been drunk ever since, much to the distress of the partners from New York. A canny Scot, was the word around town about Jack Cameron, and people wanted to profit from his good luck and good sense. Accordingly, Jack sent to Denver for a safe and hired a teller, who slept in the back room on a pallet beside the bathtub, armed with a double-barreled shotgun to protect the money.

In the meantime Jack was keeping a sharp eye out, hoping that Kat Macleod would leave town so he could rescue Kristin. He realized that he would have to curtail his Colorado operations long enough to take her home, but then he planned to return. He himself was living at the Denver Hotel and had gone hunting with the proprietor, Robert Foote, after which Jack ate the birds he had shot. This was life as it should be lived, he had decided exuberantly, his mouth full of some unidentified feathered creature that tasted wonderful, except for the buckshot.

Kristin tried to brush the flour off her apron, her dress, her face, and out of her hair as she hurried toward the front door where someone was pounding impatiently. She swung it open, about to give the visitor a piece of her mind; then she gasped in shock.

"Don't faint," said Jack and caught her before she could do so. "I always seem to make an upsetting first impression upon you."

The sight of him, the protective touch of his hands on her arms flooded her with the happiness she had felt that night in the library. She had liked Jack Cameron better than any person, man or woman, she had ever met. And the man had used her happiness to seduce her. "Go away, or I'll call the sheriff."

"Now Kristin, I realize that this must have been a difficult and frightening time for you," said Jack, edging in and closing the door behind him, "but you have to look at it as an adventure. How many girls from your circle in Chicago have had the new experiences, met the new people, seen the sights that you've seen, and come out of it unscathed?"

"Unscathed!" exclaimed Kristin. "I haven't been unscathed. Since you plied me with brandy and ruined me on my father's sofa—"

"I didn't ruin you," Jack interrupted, laughing.

"I don't know how you can say that. And as for adventures, the whole experience has been one long disaster. Mrs. Palmer wasn't even in the country to launch my art career so that I could become a famous spinster artist."

"My dear girl, you'll never remain a spinster," he protested, chuckling.

"I have to," said Kristin. "What else can I do now? All my daydreams are squashed, and to think that I once considered you the handsome prince—"

"You did?" Jack looked pleased.

"—when you're really a follower of the devil."

He grinned. "That's just your innocence speaking."

"What innocence?" she muttered. "You think I've been having an adventure? The restaurant owner where I worked as a waitress tried to kiss me."

"A waitress?" Jack was horrified. "What's his name?"

"What difference does it make? I lost the job and had to leave Chicago. I didn't even have enough money to eat on the train to Denver. Some stranger offered to pay for my dinner, but of course it wouldn't have been proper to accept, so I didn't get any."

Jack felt conscience-stricken, remembering his own sumptuous meals on the train.

"Then I got off the train at some little town to buy food from a hawker, and it left without me, taking all my baggage on to Denver."

"So you *were* the blond girl in the dining car who got off in Southern Illinois?"

"How would you know that?" she asked suspiciously.

"I've been trying to find you ever since I discovered that you'd left."

"You followed *me* out here?" said Kristin, surprised and thrilled.

"Well, actually my father sent me about the Macleod gold mine, so I combined the errands—"

"Errands!"

"But I'd have come for you even if my father hadn't—"

Disappointed all over again because she hadn't been his main object, Kristin said, "You're no friend of mine. Only Mr. McFinn's my friend. He's the baggage man who saved my cases and gave me directions when I arrived in Denver, penniless."

"McFinn at the Union Depot? He said he never heard of you."

"Good! He knew a bounder when he saw one. And then I had to be a housemaid in Maeve Macleod's house, and she didn't like my cooking, or my ironing, neither of which, I'll have to admit, I knew how to do."

"Well, there you are," said Jack. "This experience has taught you all the things you'll need to know to make someone a fine wife."

She glared at him. "No man who knew anything about me would marry me," she said bitterly. "About twenty of them have proposed, all strangers."

"I'm glad you refused them," said Jack. "You shouldn't marry anyone you don't know and who doesn't have the approval of your family."

"You had the approval of my family, and look how you treated me," she snapped. "Because of you I ended up working as a housemaid for a woman who shipped me off to Breckenridge without even considering that I didn't want to go. And when I finally arrived, I had to hire a man to take my baggage here, and I didn't have any money to pay him, so I'll never get out of the Macleods' debt. I'll be a household slave for the rest of my life."

"I'll pay them off and take you home," Jack promised.

"No one wants me at home."

"Believe me, they'll take you back."

"No, they won't. And even if they did, they'd treat me worse than they ever did."

"Nonsense. You won't be there that long. With your looks and all your experience, as I said, you'll make someone a wonderful wife."

Kristin burst into tears, and Jack had a terrible, sinking sensation. Something much worse than anything she'd mentioned must have happened to her somewhere between Chicago and Breckenridge, something that really did make her unmarriageable. "What is it?" he asked, afraid to hear. "What's happened that you haven't told me?"

"It's the bread," said Kristin, weeping harder.

"What bread?"

"I told you, I'm the housemaid. They expect me to make bread, and I just can't learn how. It won't rise, and it sticks all over the table when I try to roll it out for biscuits, and it tastes terrible when I cook it, so nobody will eat it, and—"

"I'm so sorry," said Jack, "but you mustn't cry. I've come to—" He stopped talking as he looked into those tear-drenched blue eyes. "Good lord, I'd forgotten how beautiful you are." And he kissed her.

Because of the shocking pleasure of that kiss, Kristin forgot about her dreadful experiences. Her breast tightened in anticipation of his touch. Horrified, she gave him a powerful shove as a little voice said, "Come quick, Liama. Some strange man is kissing our housemaid."

"Kissing isn't allowed," said Sean Michael importantly. "You can argue with her. We heard all that from the back yard. And you can court her in the parlor on Sundays, but you can't kiss her, or Aunt Kat and Augustina, who is our stepmother, will be very angry."

"And nobody crosses Aunt Kat," said Phoebe. "She can be ever so fearful if she gets put out."

"Then I'll try not to irritate her," said Jack, who had been unnerved both by the kiss and then by the shove that Kristin gave him. Four children, three girls and a boy, were staring at him. Where had they come from?

"I'm Sean Michael," said the boy. "And this is my sister Phoebe, and my half-sister Liama, and my cousin, Molly."

"I'm older than Liama. I should get introduced third, not fourth," said Molly.

"I the baby," said Liama.

"You vile seducer," Kristin hissed. "Don't you ever touch me again."

Jack's mouth dropped open. Why was she calling him a vile seducer? One—no, two kisses—well, perhaps a few more than that, but they hardly merited such an accusation. She was acting as if they were characters in a melodrama, with Jack cast as the villain. Did Kristin really look at it that way? She did, of course, have cause to be angry with him since she'd ended up a Colorado housemaid instead of a Chicago heiress, but he'd come to rescue her. He was the *hero* in this story. "Kristin, I'm here to—"

"Go away," said Kristin. She opened the door, gave him another push, and closed the door behind him. He could hear the children giggling inside.

"Don't you say a word about this," came Kristin's voice through the wood, "or I'll never tell you another story."

"We won't," cried Sean Michael.

"Don't you tell, Liama," said Phoebe and Molly, "or we'll all pull your pigtails."

"And you'll never find out what happened to the handsome elk prince," added Sean Michael.

Liama burst into tears, and Kristin said, "Oh, hush. Come into the kitchen. "Once upon a time there was a big, bad wolf—"

"No, no," cried four young voices. "The elk prince and princess."

"Oh. All right. The fairy godmother looked at those huge, ungainly horns on his head, and she said . . ."

Jack shook his own head in confusion and walked down the front steps. Here he had thought he was the hero, come to rescue her, and it seemed that she didn't look at it that way at all. And the children were right; their Aunt Kat was a formidable woman. Good lord, if Kristin had told her the whole story, it was going to make the partnership in the gold mine even more difficult.

Chapter Six

Kristin was upset over her conduct with Mr. Cameron. Admittedly she had pushed him away, but not nearly soon enough, and she certainly should not have enjoyed his kiss, which she had.

"So then what happened?" asked Molly. All the children sat in a circle listening to the bedtime story in the corridor parlor that linked the two houses. Across the room, Kat rocked in her rocking chair and Connor read a newspaper.

"Well, then the elk prince, who now had no horns at all because the fairy godmother had taken them away, was confronted in the forest by an evil elk knight who challenged him to a duel."

"Are there really elk knights and princes?" asked Sean Michael.

"Of course, there aren't," said Kat. "Why don't you tell them a good, rousing saint's tale, Kristin?"

"Oh, Aunt Kat," complained Phoebe, "you've already told us every saint's tale there ever was."

"Are there any St. Elks?" asked Molly, who had some of her mother's religious fervor.

"I don't know," Kristin replied. "The sisters at St. Scholastica never mentioned any."

"You went to St. Scholastica?" asked Kat, amazed.

"Yes," said Kristin.

"So did I."

"Did you know Sister Mary Joseph, the one who told us about marriage?" Relations between men and women had been on Kristin's mind since Jack's appearance.

"She must have been after my time," said Kat. "Nobody told us about marriage when I was there."

Kristin mused on that interesting information. "Maybe that's why Sister Mary Joseph disappeared so suddenly. Maybe she wasn't supposed to tell us about marriage."

"What about the elk prince?" demanded Sean Michael. "I'll bet the evil elk knight, who still had his horns, killed the elk prince, and then the elk princess—"

"Hush, Sean Michael," said Kat. "I don't know where you get that taste for violence, unless it's that you're male."

"I resent that," said Connor. "You're the one who attacked Medford Fleming with his own gold nugget."

"Are you saying I wasn't within my rights to hit him?" asked Kat indignantly.

Kristin was always amazed at Macleod family stories. They made Ludovich's encounter with the skunk seem mundane.

Kristin couldn't stop thinking of Jack Cameron, his reappearance, his kiss, his claim that he had come to rescue and return her to her family in Chicago. Much good that would do; they didn't want her back. She dreamed of him a night and daydreamed about him as she did her chores, one result being that she left the meat for the evening meal out on the table and Connor's dog ate it. Everyone was angry except Kat, who said during the meatless dinner, "You seem rather blue, Kristin. What you need is a good cause to take your mind off whatever's bothering you. You should come along with me to the march for women's suffrage tonight."

"What does one wear to a suffrage march?" asked Kristin.

"Well, the night air will be nippy. Bring a cloak."

"Yes, but what sort of dress?"

Augustina had lent her wash dresses after she appeared for her first full day of work in an afternoon calling gown. "Good heavens," Augustina had said, "didn't you bring anything but church clothes and art supplies?"

Without explaining the whole humiliating situation, Kristin could hardly say that she had never expected to be a maid. So she was wearing made-over, out-of-style dresses, and a seamstress had had to be called in to do the alterations on those that had belonged to Augustina since Kristin didn't know how. The fees, which Kat had paid, were to come out of Kristin's salary. What with the railroad ticket, the burro rental, and the sewing charges, she'd never get her debts paid and actually collect her pay.

And the very worst was that Jack Cameron had seen her wearing one of those shabby dresses—and covered with flour. The gown was a faded purple-and-white print, flowers on stripes, very tasteless and old. She imagined Jack comparing the wash dress to the lilac gown she'd been wearing in the library the night he—well, anyway, he was probably wondering why he'd ever been attracted enough to bother seducing her.

Still, she thought, trying to cheer herself up, she could wear something decent to the torchlight parade and pretend she was still a lady of means. Feeling better, she went to her room and donned a smart dress and a beautiful gray felt hat with black wired ribbons rising in back and blue velvet flowers under the brim against her hair. "My goodness," said Kat when Kristin reappeared. "Don't you look elegant? But you didn't really have to wear your best clothes, dear. You should save them for church and Sunday courting."

Kristin didn't correct Miss Kat because she didn't want to argue about Sunday courting. Instead she put on her gray cloak with its dark blue passementerie braid trim and walked with Kat to the Episcopal Church, where the converts to women's suffrage were assembling. There they lit the torches. "Here's yours, dear," said Kat. Kristin juggled it awkwardly and set fire to the feathers on the hat of a Methodist lady, causing great consternation among the assembled suffragettes and a dreadful odor. Kat decided that Kristin should carry a sign rather than a torch. Then other problems plagued the ladies. As they marched down Lincoln Avenue, chanting "Women Should Vote" and other such slogans, miners began to drift out of the saloons, muttering and then shouting angry remarks. By the time they reached Main Street, one very rude fellow yelled, "Close down the saloons, will you?" and he scooped up a handful of mud from the street and flung it at the torch of the lady whose feathers had burned.

"Get off the sidewalk," shouted another man. "You want to set the town aflame?" Then a handful of mud actually connected with a lady. By that time the women were running toward the Denver Hotel, Kristin in the forefront.

Women's reform movements in Chicago, where the streets were paved, never had problems like these, she thought, hoping that no mud would connect with her outfit since she was the one who would have to deal with the damage. It had taken her three days and lots of advice to get the mud spots off the hem of the cream-and-blue suit in which she had arrived at the Macleod house. While she was trying to remember that recipe for mud removal, someone caught Kristin's arm and jerked her under the overhang of a store. She shrieked loudly for help and tried to poke the attacker with her sign.

"Hush," said Jack Cameron. "What are you doing with those women? You could be injured." He removed the sign from her hand and tossed it into the alley behind him.

"Let go of me." She recognized his voice, although it was dark under the overhang, with only dim light from the passing torches. "Why haven't you left for Chicago?"

"Because I have business in Breckenridge," he replied, tightening his grip on her arm. "For heaven's sake, Kristin, I came out here to rescue you, not to see you attacked by drunken miners while you are supporting women's suffrage, to which you'd probably never given a thought."

"I have too," said Kristin. "Aunt Frieda told me about it." The pressure of his chest and body against hers made her panicky and short of breath. "If women had the vote, maybe we could do something about men like you," she gasped, trying to pull away and failing. "*You* probably don't approve of women's suffrage."

"I love it," said Jack, "especially watching your Aunt Frieda attack your father on the subject."

Forgetting her anger for the minute, Kristin started to giggle as she remembered those delightful interludes at dinner. It never took Aunt Frieda more than two or three minutes to turn Papa absolutely apoplectic on the subject of women's suffrage. However, Kristin had never realized that Jack enjoyed it too. How mismatched he and Minna were. Minna had no sense of humor. "Are you still engaged to my sister?" she asked and tried to squirm away. She had to stop because the proximity and friction caused that

103

peculiar, melting sensation in her body.

"Not unless you return home," said Jack. "I told them I wouldn't marry her until they took you back. That being the case, maybe we should both stay here," he added wryly.

Kristin was touched that he'd forgo a huge dowry for her sake—touched until she thought of all the trials she'd been through because of Jack Cameron, until she realized that he'd stay here rich and she'd stay poor. Unless he meant they'd—but he didn't mean anything, certainly not marriage to the girl he'd wronged. He just wanted to get her off his conscience. If only he didn't have such a nice, warm laugh, and a sense of humor that triggered hers. *No* one in her family had a sense of humor. Just then Jack brushed an escaping curl back toward her hat, touching her ear, making her shiver. "Let go," she ordered, a bit hysterically.

"As soon as the rowdies have passed. Then I'll walk you home."

"Absolutely not," said Kristin.

"Absolutely yes," said Jack. "Any young woman who looks as fetching as you do—that's a wonderful hat—"

"Oh, do you think so?" She touched the blue velvet flowers self-consciously, knowing that they looked good with her blond hair. It was nice to look fashionable again after weeks of wearing dumpy wash dresses while she scrubbed floors and ironed.

"Actually, you'd look charming in just about anything," said Jack, "even that dreadful rag you were wearing under your apron the day I first visited the Macleods."

"Well, I wouldn't be wearing rags if it weren't for you," snapped Kristin. "What do you expect me to wear for bread baking? A ball gown?"

"Now, now," said Jack. "I didn't mean to insult you. In fact, I was paying you a compliment. Most women wearing ugly clothes look ugly. You look wonderful in anything."

Again Kristin felt her heart give a little squeeze of pleasure. Then she remembered that Jack would remain engaged to Minna if she agreed to go home and spend the rest of her life being picked on by her family. At best, she'd be condescended to by some second-rate husband they managed to find for her, someone old and mean who thought he was doing her a favor by marrying her. "Well, I'm afraid you'll have to give up your plans to get richer on my father's money because I'm not going home," she announced.

"Now, Kristin," said Jack, "the princess is never unkind to the prince when he comes to rescue her."

"I'm a housemaid, not a princess. And you are certainly no prince. More like the snake in Eden."

"And here I always thought you were such a quiet, retiring girl," said Jack. "I'll swear you've got a tongue as sharp as your Aunt Frieda's."

"I'd be proud if I really were like Aunt Frieda," said Kristin. When was he going to let go of her? The crowd of miners was thinning out. If he really insisted on walking her home, it might be another occasion for sin. Even if he was a snake, he was a charming one, and remarkably good humored. She'd never have got away with saying anything so outrageous to her brothers as she had to Jack Cameron.

Her thoughts were interrupted by a stream of profanity from a passing miner. Jack pulled her closer and murmured, "There's no need to be afraid."

"Who's going to protect me? You? Those men out there are always drunk and fighting."

"Actually, I'm fairly handy with my fists," said Jack, "and besides that, I'm armed."

"You mean with a—a gun?"

"That's right, armed and ready to defend your honor," he murmured. Kristin looked up into his face with surprise.

Elizabeth Chadwick

Her blond hair gleamed from beneath the brim of her hat
in the dim rays of a newly risen moon. Jack inhaled sharply
and, giving in to impulse, bent his head.

Because her mouth was open in surprise when he kissed
her, Kristin experienced a mixed flood of passion and panic, but in this instance, panic prevailed. She now knew
about baby seeds and twisted so violently that she managed
to break free and run out among the last of the passing
miners.

"May I take your arm, sir?" she said to the first miner
she got hold of. "A bounder just accosted me."

Confused, the miner dropped the handful of mud he was
carrying. "Are you from West Breckenridge?" he asked.

"Of course not. I understand that West Breckenridge is
a den of—of—disreputable females."

"Yeah. Well, I guess you don't sound like one a them—
uh, disreputable females. Where'd you wanna to go?"

"To the Denver Hotel."

"That's where them suffragettes are headin'."

"Really?" Kristin tried to look as if she hadn't realized
that suffragettes were on the march.

"Well, obviously you ain't one a them. But it's a dangerous place. You sure you wanna go there?"

"Well, I can't ask you to escort me home when I don't
know you," said Kristin. "That would be improper."

"Improper?" He scratched his stubbled chin. "Guess I got
a real, sure-enough lady on my hands," he mumbled and
dutifully escorted Kristin through the crowd of his angry
confederates and on to the Denver Hotel, getting pelted
with mud in his attempts to shield Kristin and then pum-
meled with an unlit torch in the hands of a lady who wanted
to vote. "I hope you appreciate this, miss," he shouted to
Kristin before he bolted away from the hotel. "This here's
about the most gentlemanly thing I ever done in my life."

"Kristin, what happened to you?" cried Kat.

"I was accosted on the streets by a cad," said Kristin, about to name Jack Cameron. Kat didn't give her a chance.

"How lucky that you found a protector. I *am* sorry the poor fellow was attacked by one of my ladies. It looks bad when our male supporters are set upon, but now I must make my speech." Kat took a place in front of the assembled women and said, "Ladies of Breckenridge, the vote is ours if we but—" A large clod of mud skimmed the edge of her hat.

Kristin did not really feel that the torchlight parade was a success, although she managed to keep her own outfit intact, and Kat didn't seem to care what happened to her clothing. No doubt that was because she had money and could afford to buy new clothes and hire maids, even inept ones.

Kristin went to bed that night and dreamed of Jack Cameron's arms pressing her against his chest in the darkness on Main Street and of his kiss, even of how funny he was. She woke up several times during the night wishing he weren't a bounder and semi-engaged to her sister Minna. What if he had been *her* fiance? Would the kiss have dishonored her then?

"I knew it," said Maeve. "The girl is some relation to Ingrid and is little better than a harlot."

"Why do you say that?" asked James absently. He was studying a set of photographs.

"Because she's a fallen woman. Genevieve has just written me to say that the girl lost her virginity to her own sister's fiance, who is now chasing after her and has accused us of being procurers. Can you imagine? We must leave immediately for Breckenridge."

"What for?" asked James.

"Because Kat shouldn't have another fallen woman in her household. It's bad enough that Phoebe and Sean Michael were born of one. They certainly don't need the influence of another serving as a maid in the household. And what if her seducer finds her and tries to start up an affair while she's living at Kathleen's? There'll be a scandal."

"Do stop wiggling, Molly." Kristin had finally discovered a way to get some painting done. When Kat and Augustina were out of the house with Kristin left in charge of the children, she painted the portrait of one while the others played house. Although it was hard to get a child to hold still, they did make delightful and charming portrait subjects. She was sketching Molly this afternoon, seated on the floor with a doll in her lap, one leg extended, shoe sole foremost, one leg tucked under. The sketch was going well until Phoebe screamed, "Liama, you nasty thing."

"I the baby," said Liama. "Babies do that."

"She's wet the carpet," Sean Michael announced.

To Kristin that was the last straw. She rose, forgetting Molly, and went to peer despairingly at the spot.

Liama was grinning at her with devilish pride. "Sean Michael's fault," she said. "He tickle me."

Kristin turned sad eyes on Sean Michael, who shrugged and said, "I thought that's what you did with babies."

"You know she always wets when you tickle her," said Phoebe. "Now, don't cry, Kristin." Phoebe looked conscience-stricken when she saw Kristin's expression. "I know how to clean it up, but oughten you to start dinner?"

Before Kristin could respond to that suggestion, there was a crash, and they all whirled to find that Molly had toddled over to the lamp table, grasped its embroidered skirt and, in falling over on her bottom, pulled the lamp with her. The crash signified the demise of Miss Augustina's fake Tiffany lamp.

"You're in for it, Molly," said Sean Michael.

Molly burst into noisy tears, and Kristin, feeling the accident was partly her fault, didn't know what to say.

"It's Liama's fault," said Phoebe. "If she hadn't wet the carpet—"

"I the baby." Liama wasn't going to be blamed.

"Go on and fix dinner, Kristin," said Sean Michael. "If we pick up all the pieces, they'll never even notice that the ugly old lamp's missing."

When evening came and they wanted to light the lamp, they'd notice. With that daunting thought, Kristin went off to the kitchen to start dinner, a process for which she had minute instructions from Miss Augustina, who was the cooking person in the family. Miss Kat evidently never cooked except in cases of dire need, and from all the jokes made about her efforts, no one wanted her to. But then Miss Kat was far too busy for domestic activities.

Kristin took out potatoes and began to peel them—very carefully because she already had cuts on her fingers, one of which had required bandaging. Kristin had thought her finger might fall off, ending her faltering career as a professional artist. However, nobody in the household had paid her injury any mind. They acted as if they came close to slicing off their fingers everyday.

Fingers or no, she'd best hurry up, or there'd be no dinner on the table when the adults returned. But wait. She was supposed to have warmed the stove up before she began preparations. She rose, ticking off in her mind the steps in the stove-lighting process. Miss Augustina had impressed them upon her. Kristin actually got the stove going. Pleased, she sat down again with the potatoes. Happy chatter drifted in from the children and they began to sing a song, Liama joining in boisterously with inarticulate hums and joyous shrieks since she didn't know and probably couldn't have pronounced the words.

Sean Micheal interrupted Kristin's musings by pointing out that the stove had begun to smoke. She turned and found that smoke was indeed trickling from every aperture. The volume increased in the few seconds she spent looking at it.

"Fire, fire," shouted Sean Michael. "The house is on fire again."

"Aren't you going to put it out?" screamed Phoebe.

"I don't know how," Kristin replied.

"With water," said Sean Michael.

"We'll have to get the fire department," said Phoebe and dashed out the door. Terrified, Kristin followed, scooping up Molly as Sean Michael grabbed Liama.

"There's Father Boniface," shouted Phoebe. The priest was standing across the street in front of St. Mary's talking to a parishioner.

"Our house is on fire," screamed Phoebe. By this time they had all reached the gate and pelted through. Kristin, trying to be a responsible adult, closed it behind them.

Father Boniface said to the parishioner, "I told the congregation we needed a belfry. If we had a bell, we could summon the fire department."

"I'll spread the word," said the parishioner and dashed down the street.

"Come over here, children," called Father Boniface. "We don't want you getting burned to crisps."

Kristin wondered if the invitation extended to her, or was she, as the adult who had started the fire, responsible for staying near the house, even going in and throwing a bucket of water on it? She didn't want to be burned to a crisp. Turning Molly over to Phoebe, Kristin settled for hovering anxiously by the gate. How she hated Jack Cameron! She should have been safely home in Chicago instead of out here on the frontier letting people's lamps get broken and setting fire to their houses.

As yet there were no flames showing in front, so Kristin supposed the back was afire, the kitchen and the bedrooms of Sean Michael, Phoebe, Liama, and their parents. *Holy Blessed Virgin,* she prayed, *don't let the whole house burn down.* Where were the firemen? If they didn't hurry, Miss Augustina would get back from fixing up the Rheinhardts' cottage. She might try to save her house and be burnt to death. Then Mr. Fitzpatrick would be heartbroken. Kristin, conscience-stricken, would be thrown out in the street to fend for herself, and no one would ever hire her, knowing that she'd set fire to a house. She'd freeze to death under some bush. Even if she put on every piece of clothing she had, the temperatures became terribly cold after dark, and she'd never survive even one night.

Then she saw Miss Kat, turning the corner and running down French Street, interrupted, Kristin supposed, in the meeting she'd been having with Reverend Passmore. Did she already know that her house was on fire?

Well, it was Mr. Cameron's fault. For putting a stain on the virtue of his fiancée's sister, which no true gentleman would do. That stain was a good deal on Kristin's mind now that she had seen Mr. Cameron again and also because Miss Kat kept bringing home young men and trying to leave them alone with Kristin in the parlor, which paralyzed Kristin with alarm. She never wanted to be alone with another man. And she knew Miss Kat didn't like it when Kristin ran away from them. She'd like it even less that Kristin had set fire to the house, even if it wasn't Miss Kat's side. Well, technically it was, that side and the tower, where Miss Kat and Mr. Connor slept. Not that the

Macleods seemed to sleep that much. Kristin often heard them laughing in the middle of the night, not to mention the squeaks, thumps, sighs, and groans.

Miss Kat and Mr. Connor seemed to be very fond of each other. She was always making him laugh, and he was always kissing her. Wasn't that amazing? Kristin's parents never kissed each other, not even on the cheek, whereas Miss Kat and Mr. Connor kissed each other on the mouth as Mr. Cameron had Kristin. She put a palm to her waist and found it still reassuringly flat. As much as the Macleods kissed, it was surprising that they had only the one little girl, although they had been married four years.

Well, it was all a puzzle to Kristin. With Miss Kat only one house away, she glanced apprehensively over the gate. Still no smoke or flame showing. Maybe the fire had gone out on its own. Why hadn't she thought of that? It wouldn't be the first fire that had gone out on Kristin. The other three she had tried to set had done so.

"Out of the way."

With her eye on Kat, Kristin hadn't seen the men approaching from Lincoln Avenue.

"Damn," shouted one. "Who's locked the gate?" He leapt over it, a whole crowd of men following him. Now she could see the fire equipment being trundled down the street.

"Good lord, have you set fire to the house?" asked Miss Kat. Kristin whirled the other way to see her mistress jerking the gate open and holding it for the firemen. "I swear you're worse than Diederick."

Who was Diederick? Kristin wondered.

"He's the carpenter who set fire to the house the first time," said Sean Michael, who had crossed the street to get a better look at the action. "And then he kidnapped Aunt Kat. That was after our first mother ran off with a gambler and was never seen a—"

"Get back across the street, son," said his father, who was evidently a fireman too. "And keep all the girls over there. You too, Kristin," he added gently.

Kristin felt terrible. Mr. Sean had been so kind to her, for all he looked at her in the strangest way. She noticed with astonishment that Miss Kat was following the firemen into the house. What a brave woman! Augustina had arrived also, but she stayed across the street with Father Boniface Wirtner and the children.

"How did it happen?" she asked Kristin.

"I don't know. I lit the stove, the first time I ever managed it, and suddenly there was smoke."

"Well, don't look so stricken," said Augustina. "Fires are common enough in Breckenridge. This house has already burned once."

"Yes, but that one was set. I didn't mean to—"

"Of course you didn't."

"My stars, Augustina, who's this girl? She looks just like Phoebe and Sean Michael." A hefty lady had come puffing up, having run all the way from her own house to participate in the excitement.

Augustina turned pale, and Kristin felt a new wave of anxiety. Several strangers had pointed out that she resembled Sean Fitzpatrick's blond children, and she now remembered what Sean Michael had said about his mother running away. *I'm not their mother,* thought Kristin, *so why does everyone in the family stare at me? And since he married Augustina, he can't be still mourning a woman who ran away from him, a woman whose name is never mentioned.*

Oh, life was such a puzzle. Always more confusing and less satisfying than one's daydreams. In her daydreams, Jack Cameron was still the handsome prince. She couldn't seem to overcome her infatuation completely.

113

Chapter Seven

"I don't know what I'm going to do with Kristin," said Kat as she and Connor lay curled together in the tower room. "She simply will *not* entertain suitors, and the girl's a dreadful housekeeper."

"Worse than you?"

"Not that bad," admitted Kat, laughing, "but she did almost burn the house down."

"Nonsense. She forgot to open the flue."

"And in case you haven't noticed, my brother's mooning after her as if she were really Ingrid, and Augustina's miserable even though I don't think she knows why Sean seems so taken with the maid. And then I caught Kristin painting a picture of Phoebe instead of doing the ironing, and she allowed Liama to wet on the carpet and Molly to smash Augustina's favorite lamp. I've never had a worse housemaid, except perhaps for Colleen."

"The one who eloped to the Sisters at St. Gertrude?

Maybe Kristin would like to become a nun. She seems to be a devout Catholic."

"Well, the nuns are no longer here," said Kat in such a woebegone tone that her husband gave her a consoling kiss. "I do miss Sister Freddie since they moved to Mason City," said Kat, sniffing. "Maybe I can set Kristin up in business," she mused.

"You'll send us to the poor house trying to make entrepreneurs out of these girls. Are you hoping, if you make enough women into proprietors, you'll convince the state of Colorado that women should have the vote?"

"Women *should* have the vote," said Kat.

"Well, at the moment men have the vote, and this man casts a vote for making love."

"I'm tired," said Kat, trying to sound reluctant.

"If you're so tired, why are you snuggling up to me?"

Downstairs Kristin had heard Connor's first outburst of laughter, then Kat's, then the sighs and groans. What was going on up there? she wondered. For some reason, they made her think of Mr. Cameron.

"Have you ever thought of going into business for yourself, Kristin?" asked Kat, who had stayed home to help with dinner and have this conversation.

"My ambition is to be a professional artist." The two were sitting on the back porch shelling peas grown by a man in Braddock who had to cover his vegetables at night lest they freeze. *Maybe Miss Kat will find me a studio and art patrons,* Kristin thought with dawning excitement.

"You'd starve to death painting pictures," said Kat. "We need to find something practical and lucrative for you."

Kristin stared out at the mountains, sadly disappointed. No one thought she could be an artist.

"How did your father make his living? Was he a farmer? Vegetable growing has been profitable for Dave Braddock."

Kristin was so surprised at the idea that Kat might try to make a farmer of her that she dropped a handful of pea pods. "Sausage-making," she muttered.

Kat's face lit up. "Do you know how?"

Kristin mumbled that yes, she did know how to make sausages. Anyone with an ounce of wits would know how, more or less, if they'd gone to the sausage factory as many times as she.

"Well, I think that's a wonderful idea," said Kat, as if Kristin had suggested it. "Sausages should sell very well in the mountains. Miners love sausages."

"Excuse me," said Kristin, "I have to use the necessary house," and she dashed away toward the amazing little structure with its window and scrollwork. Probably the design of the kidnapper carpenter.

Sitting on the back porch with an apron full of peas, Kat stared after Kristin. What was wrong with the child? Lack of confidence, in all likelihood. She probably thought women couldn't make their own way in the world.

Kat decided to investigate the sausage-making business. Now what would they need? Well, pigs, obviously. The Landis family, who leased her ranch outside Dillon, would have to raise the pigs. Kristin could make and sell the sausages to Kat's Fitzgerald Sweet Cream Butter customers. But what could they use for a place of business? Kat didn't want the sausages made in her own house. She ran over various unoccupied properties in her mind and settled, with malicious glee, on the Fleming mansion on Nickel Hill. It had been vacant for four years. Considering its state of disrepair, she ought to be able to get it in lieu of the slander judgment she'd won against Medford. The Fleming Mansion would get Kristin off French Street and away from Sean. He certainly didn't need to be reminded of Ingrid now that he was married to Augustina.

On the other hand, Kristin was such a spineless little thing; she might be afraid to live by herself. *Who can I get to live with her who might be interested in sausage making?* Kat wondered. *I'll write Genevieve.*

"Care for another?" asked Robert Foote, the owner of the Denver Hotel in which Jack was staying. Foote was a friendly man, but not given to dispensing free drinks. However, it was after legal hours, and his bar was closed, so Jack accepted the offer.

Why the devil couldn't Mrs. Macleod see that he hadn't stolen a portion of their mine from them? Jack wondered. He'd rescued them. They hadn't, as he'd originally thought, been diverting Cameron money to their losing silver mines. They'd lost the vein at the Chicago Girl for a time while expanding to try to increase their profits. Jack was convinced that the bank's money would be returned manyfold, but in the meantime his father had just sent a telegram saying, in essence, that the Wapshot profits were all very well, but why was nothing being done about the Chicago Girl?

Some investments took longer to pay off than others. Jack had yet to inform Pitman Cameron that there was a new branch of the Cameron Bank in Breckenridge, which would pay for itself many times over, although his father would complain at every turn, might even refuse to participate. If so, Jack had inheritance money, the investment profits on that, and his own share of the Wapshot deal.

The fly in his ointment was Kristin. He'd managed to corner her twice since their first meeting, and their last confrontation had been as angry as the first. "I only want to help you," he'd said.

"You came here on business, not because of me," she'd retorted.

"That's not true. Well, not entirely."

"Leave me alone," she'd said. "If you don't, I'll tell Miss Kat and everybody at St. Mary's what you did to me, and they're very devout and upright people. Kat will have you run out of town."

Jack could believe that. Kat Macleod, who was loved by one and all, still disliked him intensely. He had on his hands two women he couldn't win over, when in all his life heretofore he hadn't found one he couldn't charm, except for Kristin's Aunt Frieda. Well, he'd not let them ruin his plans to settle in Breckenridge. He wanted to stay, and there were townsfolk aplenty who wanted him to.

Which would win out? he wondered. Moral indignation or greed? Greed, he thought. But lord, he didn't want to hurt Kristin. If she told Kat what she thought had happened to her—did she think a kiss amounted to seduction? It was possible. She was such an innocent girl.

The worst of it was that every time he saw her, he dreamed of her, the most incredibly erotic dreams, and in the dreams he did seduce her. In dreams she was a better bed partner than any of the experienced women he'd been involved with. *I'm turning into a fool,* he thought, *and over a woman. No, not even a woman. A slip of a girl.* She'd never welcome his advances as she did in his dreams. He'd probably have to get her drunk again to win so much as another kiss. Jack shook his head.

"Aye," said Robert Foote, "if Passmore and Kat Macleod have their way, every bar and saloon in town will have to close on Sunday."

Jack smiled at his host. He did have friends in this town, even if Kat Macleod and Kristin weren't among them.

"Have another shot, my boy. We'll drink to—what? Perdition to the Brother Passmores of the world."

"Perdition," said Jack companionably and raised his glass. He didn't mind drinking with Foote, but a whole barful of friendly natives would have cheered him more. Foote was abysmally distressed at the Sunday closing ordinance, afraid that eventually the temperance contingent would get a court order for its enforcement in Breckenridge.

"Perdition to Kat Macleod," said Foote.

Jack grinned. "I dare not drink to that. If it got back to her, she'd treat me worse than she does already."

"Oh, Connor will bring her around. She may be hardheaded, but she's also the prettiest woman in town."

Jack thought Kristin prettier, but he couldn't say so. He wasn't supposed to know Kristin.

"So if you won't drink perdition to Kat, how about the Methodist Ladies Aid Society? Teetotalers, the whole lot."

As a Catholic, although not a very devout one, Jack didn't mind that toast. "All right. Perdition to the Ladies Aid Society." As he raised his glass, his mind wandered back to Kristin and how pretty she had looked the last time he saw her, how sweet her mouth had tasted when he kissed her at the Macleods' house and in the dark on Main Street. "Perdition to women," he muttered in frustration.

"Oh now, I wouldn't go that far," said Robert Foote.

"Kristin, I wonder if I might have a word with you?" asked Connor Macleod.

"Certainly, sir," she replied and tucked her hands into the pockets of her apron.

"Why don't we go into the corridor room where we'll have some privacy."

Why did he want privacy? she wondered, remembering that one of the maids at home had accused her brother

Ludovich of making advances. The girl had been fired.
Was Mr. Connor going to make advances when they were
alone in the corridor room? Very reluctantly, she followed
him out of the kitchen. Where was Miss Kat? she wondered
desperately. Miss Augustina and Mr. Sean were at choir
practice and the children all abed.

"Kristin, I've been wondering whether you've thought
about your future."

"My future?" she echoed in a wobbly voice.

"Yes. You don't seem to be interested in any of the
suitors Kat's turned up for you."

*Oh lord, they're going to ask me to leave because I won't
get married.*

"I was thinking you might want to become a bride of
Christ?"

"What?"

"The Benedictine Sisters. Maybe you'd like to join."

"Become a nun?" Although her girlhood had been spent
at school with the sisters, Kristin had never considered
becoming one. Jack Cameron's handsome face flashed in
her mind. If she became a sister, she'd never—never what?
she asked herself sternly. She wasn't going to see Jack
Cameron again. "Do I have to?" she asked Connor.

He looked quite taken aback. "No, of course not. I just
thought you'd like it."

"I don't think so," said Kristin.

"Well, that settles it. I'll bid you good night." Connor
Macleod rose and left.

Was he angry? she wondered. Was that why he had
ended the conversation so abruptly? He'd said she must
think about her future. What was it? Housemaid? Sausage maker? Nun? She supposed that if she became a
nun, she could teach art like Sister Ermentrude, but surely
God wouldn't like it if someone joined a convent because

they couldn't find anything better to do. A pox on Jack Cameron, she thought. No matter how handsome he had looked the last time she saw him, he was a bad person. She must stop thinking about him.

"Mother!" cried Kat. "I'm so glad to see you. And who's this young woman?" She glanced at the stocky girl who stood behind Maeve on the porch. The girl had a broad face that might have been pretty except that the eyes were narrow and set too close together over a thin blade of a nose.

"Patsy Monroe. Genevieve sent her, and I brought her straight along, knowing you needed better help."

"Kristin is improving." Kat waved them in and picked up Bridget. "Have you a kiss for your big sister?"

"You're too old to be my sister," said Bridget. "I don't see why I can't call you Aunt Kat like Sean's children do." She gave Kat a kiss on the cheek and then drew back to pat her curls into place.

Kat set Bridget down and turned to the new maid. "Patsy, your room is just behind the parlor to your right. You'll be sharing with Kristin. Why don't you unpack while Mother and I sit down to chat?" Patsy, lugging her own bag, went off, although in no great hurry.

"Has a Mr. Jack Cameron come to visit here?" asked Maeve, getting right to the point.

"Of course he has," said Kat. "He owns part of the Chicago Girl and wants the controlling interest. I'm sure I wrote about that."

"I thought Mr. Cameron was coming here about Kristin."

"I don't think he even knows her." Kat passed her mother a cookie from a plate on the lamp table. "She's such a shy thing, Mother. She hides every time we bring a man into the house. I despair of ever finding her a husband."

121

"Well, you've found her one," said Maeve. "Bridge
why aren't you playing with the other children?"

"I want to stay and listen, Mama."

"Kristin and your cousins are in the back yard, Bridge
Take off your hat, dear, and run out." Kat relieved the chil
of her boater with its blue bow and streamers. "Are yo
saying that Kristin and Mr. Cameron know each other?
Kat asked her mother.

"That they do, and in the biblical sense."

"Oh Mother, I can't believe that. There never was a mor
virginal girl than Kristin. She's—" Kat stopped becaus
Kristin herself came in from the yard with a basket o
flowers. Kat wondered how much of the conversation th
girl had heard. Most of it from the look of her.

"Sit you down, girl," said Maeve, "while I tell Kathlee
how you've bamboozled us all. She was disowned by he
family, weren't you?" demanded Maeve. Kristin looke
stricken, but Maeve continued, "Because she'd been pur
suing her own sister's fiance."

"I wasn't," cried Kristin.

"And because her father caught them together. Right i
his own house they were. Genevieve told me about it."

"Genevieve would never have betrayed me."

"Ah, but she did. Wrote me a letter because that Jac
Cameron came to her and she didn't know what to think
He claimed he wanted to make it right."

"How can he make it right?" Tears began to roll dow
Kristin's face.

Kat moved to the sofa and put her arm around Kristi
"Has he offered, child?"

"He wants to take me back to my family, but they won'
have me."

"Well, you certainly can't stay here," said Maeve.

"Now, Mother."

"Do you want your children growing up in the house with a fallen woman?"

"Mother, I'm not throwing any young person out in the street," said Kat, "especially one as unprepared to take care of herself as this one."

"Kathleen, I intend to stay with you until James arrives, and I don't want to set my eyes on this girl. I haven't any doubt that she led that Mr. Cameron on."

Did I? Kristin wondered. Maybe if she hadn't been fantasizing about him, she'd never have got in trouble, never have sipped the brandy, never told him about her activities with Genevieve. He must have thought that if she would associate with lower-class women, he could treat her just as he liked.

"He'll have to marry her," said Kat.

"I doubt that's what he wants," warned Maeve.

Kristin agreed silently. Jack Cameron had never mentioned marriage. Not to her. What would she have said if he had?

"What have you got against Cameron?" Connor Macleod asked his wife. "Jack's a fine fellow."

"The devil he is," said Kat and told him the story she'd heard from her mother.

Connor shrugged. "You and I jumped the gun."

"You're no gentleman to remind me of that."

"Several times," said Connor, grinning, "and we loved every minute of it, both of us. I swear I thought that you meant to keep sleeping with me but never marry."

Kat felt the color staining her cheeks. "What are we going to do about Kristin and Mr. Cameron? He's left town, undoubtedly to escape his duty to her."

"He's just gone to Denver on business. Jack couldn't have had any idea we'd hear the story. Wait until he gets back and talk to him then if you must."

"I don't think Kristin wants to marry him. She wants
be a famous spinster artist."

"Well, surely you can find something more sensible f
her."

"But she's been dishonored."

"No one will know if you don't tell them."

Kristin and Patsy were sharing dishwashing duty aft
an unnerving dinner. Maeve, having insisted that Kristi
be sent away, had stared at her throughout as if she we
a leper plopped down in their midst. And now that K
and Connor had an efficient maid in Patsy, they wouldn
need Kristin. But where could she go? Kristin wondered.
she'd taken up Mr. Cameron's offer, she'd be on her wa
to Chicago—and what? Mama and Papa wouldn't welcom
her. Oh, it was all his fault! If he hadn't gone lookin;
Genevieve would never have written to Maeve, and Kristi
would have been safe here. Kat Macleod was too charitabl
a woman to throw her out under ordinary circumstances.

Patsy interrupted Kristin's thoughts by saying, with a sl
look, "I heard something from Mrs. Macleod that you oug!
to know—Mrs. Macleod that brought me from Denver."

Had Maeve told Patsy the story of Kristin's disgrace?

"I heard her saying to her daughter, 'The girl's got t
go.' Her exact words. 'The girl's got to go.' She said ?
how Mr. Fitzpatrick couldn't take his eyes off you."

"What?"

"She says you're ruining the marriage, and Mi
Augustina's glum all the time."

Miss Augustina did seem to be getting glummer. Kristi
had thought perhaps it was her nature or female troubles.

"She says as how the marriage won't last another yea
with you in the house, even if Miss Kat's willing to kee

you after the other thing. I don't know what she meant by that. Have you done something else to displease them?"

"I haven't done anything," said Kristin despondently.

"Well, that's what I heard."

And pleased to hear it too, Kristin thought. Patsy was like Minna, who had always been happy when their parents turned on Kristin. And Maeve reminded her of her parents. Not one of them had stopped to ask where the fault of Kristin's dishonor lay. It was his fault! And now he'd brought more trouble upon her and then gone off to Denver, leaving her to bear the consequences again.

She'd heard Kat complaining about Jack's departure. Maeve said it was because Jack didn't want to marry Kristin. How would it be if he hadn't left and Maeve had insisted that they marry? What if she and Jack went away somewhere? A place where no one knew them, where Jack could kiss her without bringing everyone's wrath down on her head.

She thought about that first kiss, and the second one here in the Macleod house and the third on Main Street. He'd had no right to any of them. Still, she felt warm and unsettled when she thought about kisses, especially married kisses. After kisses, there would be babies. Pretty, funny babies like Molly and Liama. Babies who laughed and patted your cheeks. Babies who blew funny bubbles and had curly hair. Babies who dirtied their linen.

Kristin sighed. She couldn't even work up a good daydream these days. She was thinking of returning to the kiss dream when Miss Kat came into the kitchen and said, "Kristin, I'd like to speak to you. Patsy, you can finish the dishes."

Kristin saw the flash of anger in Patsy's eyes. Miss Kathleen didn't. They went into the Fitzpatrick parlor beside the dining room and sat down in rockers.

What did Miss Kat want? Surely, they weren't going to make her leave tonight. It would be dark in another hour or so.

Her gloomy thoughts must have shown on her face because Miss Kat said, "Now, Kristin, don't look like that. One way or another, I'll take care of you."

Kristin swallowed hard. This was a good woman! "Your mother—" she began.

"Mother means well, but she can be narrow-minded. She and James are thinking of moving to Breckenridge. Did you know that?"

Kat's face brightened; Kristin's fell. Just what she needed, the elder Mrs. Macleod in Breckenridge telling tales.

"Well, enough of that. Kristin, I think you'd better tell me the whole story of what happened to you in Chicago."

Kristin bit her lip. There was no need to hide anything now. Genevieve had not kept her confidence. "I used to go with Genevieve to the railroad station to rescue young women," Kristin began.

"Did you? What a fine thing to do! Was your family, as Genevieve said, a wealthy one?"

"Yes, ma'am," said Kristin. "At any rate, I'd been out with Genevieve and got home late. My sister was supposed to go out to dinner with her fiance, Jack Cameron."

"Oh dear. Then it is as Genevieve said?"

Kristin nodded. "But Minna hadn't bothered to come home. She did that sometimes just to remind him that he should be thankful for her dowry."

"I was under the impression that he had lots of money."

"That's true," said Kristin. "The Camerons are rich bankers. If he hadn't been rich, what would my parents have wanted with him? All they ever think about is money."

126

"Money's not to be sneezed at. If we hadn't been short of it, part of our best mine wouldn't be in Jack Cameron's hands. Well, go on with your story."

"The housekeeper said I had to entertain Mr. Cameron until Minna got home."

"I see." Kat frowned and tapped her chin thoughtfully. "Still, Kristin, entertaining him doesn't mean that—"

"She just meant that I should sit with him," Kristin hastened to add. "And I didn't even want to do that. He's so sophisticated, and he always treated me like a little girl. That being the case, I don't know why he'd want to—" Kristin stopped, flushing.

Kat, obviously thinking she was too embarrassed to say what had happened, didn't press her. Instead, she exclaimed, "You're quite right. The nasty lecher. If he thought of you as a child, goodness, I must keep him away from my children." Kristin looked at her in astonishment. "Well, there are men like that, you know," said Kat.

"Like what?" asked Kristin.

Kat shrugged, her expression one of distaste. "Go on with your story."

"So I went into the library because Lottie insisted. Then *he* insisted that I have some brandy."

"And did you?"

Kristin could see the disapproval in Kat's face and realized that she shouldn't have mentioned the brandy since she knew how much Miss Kat hated drinking. "I didn't like it," said Kristin. "It burned my throat, but he kept pouring more into my glass while he asked me questions about my work with Genevieve. He seemed so interested." She remembered sadly how flattered she had been. "And the brandy made me feel—well, not myself at all."

"I should think," said Kat.

"I just talked and talked, whereas before I never said more than 'good evening' to him."

"Liquor does make fools of folk," said Kat. "You must remember that, Kristin."

Kristin nodded. "And once I'd told him all about the rescue missions, we got out the family albums, and I told him stories of our childhood. And then he kissed me."

"Yes, yes," said Kat. "You don't have to tell me any more. Poor child. It's all the fault of drink and, as my mother would say, evil seducers. But you mustn't worry. You have a fine new life ahead of you. We'll go to Dillon tomorrow."

"Dillon?" asked Kristin anxiously. Was she to be forced out of town?

"Yes, my ranch is up near Dillon. We have to find a place to raise the pigs."

"What pigs?" asked Kristin with a sinking heart.

"The pigs for the sausage factory, of course. You're about to become the sausage queen of the Western Slope, and I'll only ask one thing in return, except for the repayment of my money, of course."

"What's that?" asked Kristin.

"That you never drink again."

Of course, she wouldn't! Look what had happened to her the last time. But she also didn't want to become a sausage maker. Still, what choice had she? And to think that she'd once wanted to be a princess!

"What are you going to call your new company?" asked Kat, full of enthusiasm. They were on the train, returning from Dillon.

"I don't know," said Kristin gloomily. "You decide." Kristin couldn't imagine that the company would be a success after such an unseemly beginning. Mr. Landis, who ran Kat's Dillon ranch on shares, had said right off that he didn't want to raise pigs.

"There's a good profit to be made in pigs," said Kat.

"How good a profit?" asked Mrs. Landis.

Kat had then quoted figures quite knowledgeably, as if she'd been in the pig business all her life. Kristin was amazed. Was Kat making them up? Or had she really assembled all that information in the one day between Maeve Macleod's insistence that Kristin leave the house and the train trip to Dillon?

A terrible argument had followed between Mr. and Mrs. Landis. "And how are we supposed to git all them pigs into Breckenridge?" shouted Mr. Landis. "You expectin' me to herd 'em like cattle?"

Kristin couldn't help herself; she started to giggle at the idea of Mr. Landis on horseback shouting, "Giddyup, pigs," and herding a group of oinking, grunting "dogies" to Breckenridge. Did one call traveling pigs "dogies" as one did trail-herded cattle? And how many days would the pig drive take? she had wondered, knowing some of the terminology from an exciting book she'd found hidden under the mattress in Baldwin's room.

"I'm not sure pigs can be herded," Kat said quite seriously. "I think we'd best send them by train. In the winter I suppose you could slaughter them here."

"Well, I draw the line at butchering," said Mrs. Landis.

"I'm not doin' it," said Mr. Landis. "A cow's a creature you can have some feelin's for, but a pig—a pig's just plainly disgustin'."

Kristin felt the same way but didn't dare say so.

"Well, if you're so fond of cows," said Mrs. Landis, red-faced, "then the cow business is yours. *You* can do the milking from here on. When do the pigs arrive?" she asked Kat, arms folded militantly over a flat bosom.

"Day after tomorrow," said Kat, and they'd left with Mr. Landis shouting at Mrs. Landis, and Mrs. Landis maintaining a dignified, stubborn silence.

"She'll bring him around," Kat had assured Kristin during the buggy ride back to Dillon. "He didn't want the butter machine either, but it's been a great money-maker."

And now here they were on the train, having already arranged to buy and ship the pigs, some to be delivered to the Landises for breeding and raising, some to be delivered to Kristin for butchering and sausage making.

"You must see Chris Kaiser and arrange for outright sale of some of the meat."

Kristin didn't want to do that and couldn't imagine asking a virtual stranger to take pig parts off her hands. "Miss Kat, are you sure this won't cost too much money? After all, you didn't have enough to keep the mine to yourselves, so how are you—"

"Now, now," Kat had said. "Don't you give it a thought. I have friends in banking."

Not Jack Cameron; he was gone. Kristin looked out the window and noticed that they were getting close to Breckenridge. She felt that stepping off the train would commit her for the rest of her life to being a spinster sausage maker. What a fate for a girl who had once dreamed of being a princess and then a famous artist.

"Traube's Colorado Sausage!"

"What?" Kristin turned to look at her benefactor.

"The company. We'll call it Traube's Colorado Sausage. Because when you really get going, you can sell in Denver. If I hadn't thought of that possibility, we'd call it Traube's Western Slope Sausage."

Chapter Eight

From the porch steps, they could hear the raised voices inside. Instead of opening the door, Kat stopped dead, her face pale.

"What is it?" asked Kristin.

"Ingrid's back." Kat took a deep breath and pushed the door open.

An ominous tableau greeted their eyes—Augustina on the verge of tears; Sean, pale and stunned; Connor frowning; and Maeve shouting angrily, "You've no place in this house any longer. You gave up your right to come here years ago." The person to whom these remarks were addressed was a woman, very tall, very blond and, if Kristin was any judge, very ill. She was flushed and unsteady on her feet, but no one offered her a chair. The whole company stood in the corridor room that joined the two houses.

"My goodness, Ingrid, is it you?" Kat's voice faltered on the question.

The woman turned and tried to focus on Kat Macleod. "This is my house," she said, words all slurred as if she were talking around a mouthful of oatmeal. "I only left because of you."

Kat went pale at that accusation.

"I always loved him." Ingrid swayed and righted herself. "I didn't want to leave, but you said I was a bad mother. Had to go while I had the chance . . . 'cause I knew he'd die . . . an' then you'd have all the money . . . an' my children . . . an' I'd be out in the street."

"Ingrid, I never said—"

"Hardly ever spoke to me." Ingrid swayed again and caught her balance on a small table. The cloth slipped, and the lamp teetered.

Kristin rushed over and grabbed it.

"Who are *you?*" asked Ingrid, then shook her head like a puppy shaking off water. "Oh, don' tell me. Some Chicago girl. An' now they say, she"—Ingrid pointed a trembling hand at Augustina—"they say she's his wife."

In rescuing the lamp, Kristin had come close to the woman, who reeked of brandy, bringing back the evening with Jack as clearly as if Kristin were there, as clearly as if he were kissing her again as she lay against the sofa arm.

"I'm his wife," said the stranger, Ingrid. "We were married . . . legal . . . front of a judge. So this is my house, an' you're jus' his whore."

Augustina burst into tears. Sean wavered helplessly between the two women who claimed him. "I divorced you, Ingrid," he confessed.

"Divorced me?" She looked confused. "How could you divorce me if I din know about it?"

"I divorced you for desertion."

"I din desert you. I jus' . . . jus'—"

To Kristin it looked as if Ingrid couldn't remember what she had meant to say.

"—jus' in Aspen," she finished, stumbling over the "s." "Been in Aspen all along . . . thinkin' you were dead . . . tryin' to live decent, so I could tell her"—she turned accusing eyes on Kat—"tell her . . . I had a right to my children."

"Oh, lord," said Kat, looking appalled.

Maeve said, "Don't tell us about living a virtuous life. You left town with a gambler—"

"Hadda get away, an' you woun let me have any money—" She looked again at Kat. "All these years . . . I been supportin' myself . . . thinkin' when I got money—"

"Supporting yourself how?" demanded Maeve.

"Not what *you* think," muttered Ingrid defensively.

Kristin put an arm around her waist and helped her to a chair because she looked as if she were about to fall.

"No one said she was welcome to sit," snapped Maeve. "I told you you should get the German out of the house, Kathleen. Get both of them out. They've no place among decent folk."

"I'm decen'," said Ingrid. "I nearly starved bein' decen'. Soon as I got 'nough money, I came."

"Well, you're four years too late," declared Maeve. "Be off with you. Augustina is Sean's wife now."

"'S not right," mumbled Ingrid. "We married, an' marriage is forever. This is my house. I should . . . I should . . ."

"Can I come in yet, Mama?" asked Bridget. "Oh, my goodness, are you Kristin's sister?" The child was staring from Ingrid to Kristin.

Then Kristin understood why the adult Macleods and Fitzpatricks treated her so strangely. Why Sean stared at her. Because she looked like the wife he'd put aside. At least in coloring. Ingrid had the same blue eyes and hair so blond it was almost white.

"Bridget, leave the room," said Connor, who until then had been silent.

"I don't want to, and you're not my mama or papa, so I don't have to."

"If you're not out of this room before I count to three, you'll get the spanking of your life, young lady," said Connor. "One, two—"

Bridget's eyes rounded as if no one had ever threatened her before, and she scampered off.

Then Connor turned to Ingrid. "Ingrid, you can't stay here."

"'S my house," Ingrid insisted. "'S my piano. If you make me leave, I'll take my piano with me." There were tears in her eyes. "An' where's my red velvet furniture? I want my furniture. An' my husband. An' my babies. At leas' you can let me see my babies."

"Never in this world," said Maeve.

Connor gave her a hard look, but she persisted. "You should go straight back where you came from." Maeve's statement was punctuated by Augustina's quiet sobs. Sean was no longer staring at Kristin as he used to; now he was staring at Ingrid.

"How could you?" Ingrid asked him. "You tole me you'd come back to me."

"Obviously you didn't believe it," said Sean.

"I'll take her to a hotel," said Connor. "Come along, Ingrid," and he all but lifted her out of the chair. Ingrid was weeping. "Hitch up the buggy, Sean," Connor ordered. "She's in no condition to walk. I'm surprised she managed to get here from the railroad station."

"I'll take care of her," said Sean.

"No, you won't," said Maeve.

Sean turned on her. "Maeve, I want you to stay out of this." But Sean did go for the horses, and Connor led a stumbling Ingrid away, still mumbling about her house, her piano, her red velvet furniture, and her babies.

Kristin thought it the saddest thing she'd ever witnessed, even sadder than the night her own father had ordered her out. How could people treat one another so badly?

"Kristin, I need to talk to you," said Kat.

Having ejected one blond woman from the house, were they about to banish another? Kristin wondered.

"You heard everything that was said?"

Kristin nodded.

"'Tis a terrible situation. We never thought to see her again after she ran away, and now Connor tells me that she's ill and needs looking after."

"It's the brandy, don't you think?" asked Kristin. "I recognized the smell. It nearly made me retch."

"It did make her retch," said Kat. "She must have been drinking all the way from Aspen."

"And for years before that."

Kat nodded. "Poor woman. I suppose she was terribly afraid to come here. We didn't treat her very kindly in the old days." Kat looked troubled. "I shall wonder for the rest of my life how much I am to blame in this. She spoke so rarely when we were sharing a house that I never knew what to make of her." Kat sighed. "Still, something must be done on her behalf. There are folks who have given up drinking. Maybe we can help her to do it."

"You're going to take her in?"

"Here, you mean? We can't do that. Poor Augustina's distraught, and who can blame her? She now thinks she's not legally married, although the priest married her in the church. She thinks Liama's illegitimate."

135

Kristin nodded. Augustina's situation was as bad as her own. Worse. Augustina had a child. Kristin, still looking for signs of impending motherhood, hadn't noticed any in herself.

"I wonder, Kristin, if you could help us out?"

"What could I do?" asked Kristin.

"Well, there's a house for sale, more or less on the outskirts of town and too big for your purposes, but I think I can claim it in lieu of a court settlement that was never paid me. I'll even turn the deed over to you if you'll take Ingrid with you and look after her until she's well enough to function on her own. Maybe you can talk her out of the belief that she's married to Sean."

Kristin stared at Kat with astonishment. "I don't know how to deal with people who have taken to the bottle."

"You just keep her from drinking, and I'll call by to see how you're doing."

"Does that mean I won't be running the sausage factory?" asked Kristin. She'd take care of five drunken women and get them all off demon rum if she didn't have to make sausages.

"Well, of course, you'll have the factory. That's to be your means of support once Ingrid's left, and you'll also have a house of your own. Doesn't that sound fine?"

Nothing about sausages sounded fine to Kristin, but she dared not object lest all the offers be withdrawn.

"In fact, maybe you can get Ingrid to help you with the sausages. Hard work and the prospect of making money ought to keep a person away from the bottle."

Kristin had never heard that. Still, turning Ingrid into a sausage maker wasn't a bad idea. Better than Kristin having to do it herself. With the help of the Blessed Virgin, she'd keep Ingrid from falling into bed senseless and waking up sick. Kristin wanted an efficient sausage maker, not a drunken one. "I'll do it."

"Oh bless you, child. This is a heavy burden to put on one so young, but I'm at my wit's end, what with Sean staring at Ingrid as if he still loved her, Augustina sobbing in her room with the door locked, and all the children trying to find out what's happening. It's almost worse than having drunken men staggering in and out of saloons, shooting at innocent passersby."

"My goodness," exclaimed Kristin, "does that happen?"

"Yes, indeed. I had a guest break a tooth once at a dinner party because he bit into a bullet in a potato I served him. 'Twas a drunk who shot the potato."

Kristin's eyes grew wide. She hadn't heard any gunfire since she came to Breckenridge and was glad of it. No matter what her brother's books about the exciting western frontier said, gunfire didn't sound exciting to her, just dangerous, although the idea of someone shooting a potato tickled her fancy. She imagined herself painting a picture of an outlaw riddling a potato with bullets. *I'm becoming giddy,* she thought. *No one would want to hang such a picture above their sofa.*

"And you'll have a good start on furniture. I'll send that red velvet stuff straight over."

"And the piano?" asked Kristin.

"Well, Phoebe's taking piano lessons."

"Of course," said Kristin quickly. "It probably wasn't really Ingrid's piano."

Kat sighed. "It is Ingrid's piano, so it'll have to go too. Sean's not going to be pleased to know he has to buy another. Oh, this is going to cause no end of trouble, and just when I hoped to devote more time to women's suffrage."

"It seems to me that I'm the one who'll have more demands on my time," said Kristin, wanting to remind

Kat that she, their inept housemaid, was the solution to the problem and therefore deserving of help and consideration. She'd never get either from Maeve, who hated Germans, blondes, and people who looked like Ingrid. "We don't really look alike, you know." said Kristin defensively. "It's just the hair color."

Kristin stood high on Nickel Hill, savoring the irony of the fact that Kat had just given her a mansion in which to establish a sausage factory. The ramshackle house before her had once been grand until deserted by a man named Medford Fleming, who had been attacked with a gold nugget by Kat in retaliation for something shocking he said to her. The mansion was neoclassic, rectangular, with columns across the front supporting a porch roof, above which was a balcony and classic ornamentation rather than elaborate scrollwork. Backed by beautiful mountains and forest, it could be quite handsome if fixed up.

"You're my little sister, aren't you?" said Ingrid, badly hungover and obviously confused by the day's events.

"No, I am not your little sister. You and I are about to become sausage associates. Do you know how to make sausages, Ingrid?" Kristin spoke very loudly on the theory that the more noise she made, the more likely she was to get through the alcoholic haze that fogged Ingrid's brain.

"You look like my little sister. I had one."

"I am not your little sister. Put that in the large room to the right," she instructed a driver, who was lifting a chair down from the wagon on which it had come up hill.

"My beautiful furniture," said Ingrid and burst into tears.

"Yes," said Kristin, thinking the red velvet stuff tasteless enough to have been picked out by her own mother. It was going to look even worse with the green rugs that had been left in the drawing room—like a pauper's tawdry Christmas. "About sausage, Ingrid—"

"I made sausage when I was a girl on the farm."

"Good," said Kristin. "We'll establish our recipe with meat we buy from Mr. Chris Kaiser. Later we'll have our own pigs. I don't suppose you know how to slaughter a pig?"

"No, but my father came after me with a butcher knife once. That's why I left home."

Kristin's head swiveled. Ingrid didn't *look* as if she'd just said anything shocking. Kristin swallowed hard. "If Genevieve will agree to send the Chicago girls to us," she resumed, "they can make the sausage, and you will be the sausage superintendent."

"Is that like a mine superintendent?" Ingrid hung back while Kristin tried to tug her across the yard to their new home.

"This place needs painting," said Kristin. "I must think on what colors would go well with the mountain scenery. One wouldn't want one's personal foreground to clash with the natural background."

A teamster who was walking by, carrying a red velvet settee on his shoulder, stopped to cast her a puzzled glance. "When it comes to paint, you takes what you can git, ma'am."

"I don't," said Kristin. "I'm an artist. Now, Ingrid"— They were entering the reception hall—"as I said—"

"I had a friend who was a mine superintendent. He bought me a bottle of champagne."

"I don't doubt it," said Kristin, "but your champagne days are over. We'll have no drinking in this house."

Ingrid began to cry again.

"There's no use in that," said Kristin. "We are turning our fortunes around. As I said, you will be the sausage

...will be the president in charge of
...nd the countryside finding customers
...painting pictures."

...g me to make all the sausages?"

...dent does not *make* the sausages. I have
a... ...o a friend, asking that she send the Chicago
girls ... ...ead of Maeve. They will make the sausages
until suc... ...e as they are married. We can allow suitors
in the drawing room on Sundays, but at no other time since
we do not want our business affairs interrupted by men in
search of wives."

"I was married," said Ingrid. "I still am."

"I'm afraid you're not," said Kristin sympathetically.

"I need a drink."

"No, you need to decide on equipment for the kitchen.
'Twill serve Maeve Macleod right to lose her supply of
maids. I do hope Genevieve agrees to my proposal."

"I was proposed to once," said Ingrid. "Actually I was
proposed to a lot, but only once in a marriage way."

"I know about Sean. Now will you look at the kitchen
and try to remember your family sausage recipes? Write
them down, please."

"I can't write."

"Oh. Well, you can dictate yours to me. The kitchen's
that way." Ingrid drifted off toward the kitchen, and Kristin
went into the drawing room to supervise the placing of
Ingrid's dreadful furniture. On looking at it again, Kristin
decided that she simply could not spend the rest of her life
with tasteless furnishings. As soon as she became the sausage queen and famous spinster artist of the Western Slope,
she would buy new furniture. Poor Ingrid had terrible taste,
but then Kat expected Ingrid to sober up and leave town;
maybe she'd take her furniture along. On the other hand,
if she should want to stay, Kristin would never force her to
leave, although she would insist on redecorating when she

had money enough. At least sausage making was profitable. Her father had proved that.

Kat had supplied them with beds, which had already been placed upstairs, and had promised sausage-making and other kitchen equipment, which would have to be purchased. Kristin sighed. Two women alone in this huge, decaying house, one of them a drunkard. Well, Ingrid couldn't continue as a drunkard if she couldn't get any alcohol, and Kristin would simply throw it away if it appeared.

That plan turned out to be more difficult to implement than she anticipated. When she finished in the parlor and went to the kitchen, Ingrid was gone and didn't return until well after dark, drunk and garrulous. Kristin had to force six cups of coffee down her throat before she even made sense, and then Ingrid insisted on telling Kristin her pitiable life story—the flight from home in Illinois, drifting west from town to town as a prostitute until she married Sean Fitzpatrick, how happy she had been, the sweet children, the loving husband. Although the ladies of Breckenridge had never accepted her. But what did she need *them* for, Ingrid said, as long as she had Sean? Then he had fallen ill and written his sister for help. "He didn't trust me to see to things," said Ingrid, tears streaming down her cheeks. "He thought I was careless with money."

"Were you?" Kristin asked.

"We had lots," said Ingrid. "I didn't see why we should worry about such things. But then he went to Denver to the sanatorium. I thought he would get well and come back to me, and I *planned* to wait for him. I really meant to. But I was so unhappy. Because I knew that his sister thought I was a terrible person and a bad mother. I'd sleep in the daytime to get away from her. Then I couldn't sleep at night, so I wandered the town."

"What must they have thought?" murmured Kristin.

"Oh, I wasn't doing anything wrong. Just walking around. Feeling sorry for myself. Having a drink now and then with an old friend. I never, well, I didn't—take customers or anything, even though I hadn't a penny of my own because he left the money in Kat's hands." Ingrid mopped her wet eyes with her sleeve.

"It was terrible," she continued. "I couldn't have a new dress without asking her. And I was expected to make ladylike conversation. Which I'd never learned to do. So I never had anything to say. And then Sean came home, and I thought, 'He's well, and she'll go away,' but it wasn't two days before he got sicker than ever. After that I knew he'd die, and there was no hope for me."

"What did you do then?" Kristin asked.

"Sean went back to Denver, and I met a gambler at one of the town balls. I made him think that I liked him so that he would take me to Aspen. But I—I just couldn't stand being with him—you know?"

Kristin didn't.

"He got mean after a couple of days and kicked me out. So I took a job as a laundress. It was the worst four years of my life. I meant to save my money and come back. I knew I'd made a mistake. That I should be home with my children. But I was so sad that I always drank the money up. It took me four years to save enough, and look what's happened."

"Things aren't so very bad," Kristin assured her. "We shall become respectable spinster sausage makers and live here together in this fine house."

Ingrid looked around, puzzled. "What fine house?"

"Well, it will be," said Kristin defensively. How many people knew about Ingrid's background? she wondered. And if they did, would they buy sausages from a woman with such a history?

*   *   *

Jack Cameron poked his head in the kitchen door. "Don't you ever answer a knock?"

"What are you doing in town?" Kristin demanded. She'd never expected to see him again, yet there he was, looking sinfully handsome, while she was wearing one of Augustina's old wash dresses, a stupid pink thing with a loose neckline and waist. "Ingrid! Come here!" she shouted, panic-stricken, knowing full well that the chances of getting Ingrid out of bed after a long, drunken sleep were minimal. "You're supposed to have left town," she said to Jack.

"I went to Denver on business."

"Well, go away." Kristin was very upset to think that he might be staying longer in Breckenridge. Why would he? Surely he knew that Connor Macleod could take care of that mine they owned in common.

"I've come to give you a commission."

"I thought you hated pork." Kristin was standing over a bowl of sausage meat, carefully measuring and dumping in spices. Ingrid had proved to be no help whatever. Kristin was having to make and test the recipes herself, although the very thought of sausage made her bilious. "I hate you," she said to Jack. "Go away."

Jack Cameron looked taken aback. "I want you to paint my portrait," he explained.

"You do?" *The devil is tempting me,* she thought.

"Yes, a large portrait, and I'm willing to pay very well for it."

"A hundred dollars," said Kristin, thinking that if she set the price high enough, he would refuse and leave, thus removing from her path any occasion for sin. Unfortunately, every time she saw him, her heart gave a skip of excitement, and she felt warm and fluttery all over her body.

"Done," said Jack. "Shall we shake on it?"

"No."

"But you *are* going to paint my portrait?"

She thought about the hundred dollars. Her first commission. She just couldn't turn it down. "All right."

"When shall I come for my first sitting?"

"Tomorrow afternoon, and you have to pay then." He nodded agreeably. Kristin anticipated that he would leave town before she finished the painting, but she could insist on keeping the money. In the meantime, she'd just have to be strong. Treat him with ladylike dignity and disdain. "And dress up," she ordered. She'd paint him looking like the unprincipled rake he was. For a hundred dollars she'd give him a picture of his own soul.

"Good," said Jack. "One o'clock?"

"One o'clock," she agreed uneasily and turned back to her sausages.

Chapter Nine

"That foolish Patsy Monroe has spread the tale of Kristin Traube's dishonor all over town," said Maeve. "If Cameron doesn't marry the girl, the scandal will fall on us as well."

Kat sighed. "I thought he'd left town for good, but he's back. Worse, Mrs. Pringle said he's sitting for his portrait at Kristin's house. Surely the girl doesn't consider Ingrid an adequate chaperone."

"We must get him over here," Maeve decided. "Patsy!" The new maid appeared with suspicious rapidity. "Don't let me catch you rattling your tongue about our affairs again."

Her thin blade of a nose twitching in her broad face, Patsy sniveled, "I didn't mean no harm."

"Well, you've done it. Now you go into town and fetch Mr. John Powell Cameron and Mr. Connor Macleod. They both have offices on Main."

"Yes, ma'am."

"And you're not to open your mouth except to pass on the messages."

"Yes, ma'am."

"Or you'll find yourself sleeping with the horses tonight."

"Yes, ma'am," said the girl and fled.

"Stupid busybody," muttered Maeve. "Some people just can't keep their mouths shut, and that one's an eavesdropper as well. You'd best get *her* married off quickly."

"I've already had an offer," said Kat. "A fellow who wanted Kristin but is willing to take fifth best."

"Why do you say fifth best?" sputtered Maeve. "At least Patsy's virtue is intact."

"I'm sure," Kat agreed. "As homely as she is, I was surprised to get any offer at all."

"Marry her?" echoed Jack.

"It's the least you can do," said Maeve. "You've ruined her reputation, and now the scandal has spread."

"I never said a word," Jack protested. Evidently, they'd been looking for him all day, while he'd been in Montezuma saying no to silver-mine owners. Jack realized that he'd never convince these Macleod women that he'd done little more than kiss their former maid, but their chances of forcing this marriage were minimal. Given the way Kristin treated him during the portrait sittings, she'd never agree.

"Of course, I wish to do the gentlemanly thing," he said with every appearance of sincerity. Let Kristin refuse and incur their wrath. She was being extremely unpleasant over a little kiss. Instead of accepting his help and going home to her parents, she insisted on staying in Breckenridge to pursue her career as an artist.

Well, he'd done the best he could for her by offering to pay an outrageous one hundred dollars for a portrait. And what the devil would he do with it? She had him posing in a

gray frock coat with satin-faced lapels, a crimson silk handkerchief in the pocket, creased trousers, and a silly-looking
homburg hat, his hand on the head of a walking stick like
some minstrel singer. He hated homburgs, and nobody
wore one for a portrait. The picture was bound to be dreadful. He gathered that she was accustomed to painting children's portraits, and she seemed to have some sort of hat
fetish. Propped all over her studio were pictures of Macleod
and Fitzpatrick children wearing strange headgear.

While Jack was stewing over Kristin's unforgiving attitude, Maeve was ordering Patsy to the rectory to tell Father
Boniface Wirtner that he'd be performing a marriage ceremony the next day at ten. "You, Mr. Cameron," Maeve said,
"will meet us here at nine tomorrow morning. From here
we'll walk to Miss Traube's new establishment, which my
free-spending daughter insisted on giving to your fiancée. If
you've a decent bone in your body, you'll repay Kathleen."

"Do you plan to give the bride any forewarning of her
impending nuptials?" asked Jack dryly.

"We'll tell her tomorrow," said Maeve.

"Mother, I think there may be some difficulty with
Kristin," said Kat Macleod.

"Right," Connor agreed. "The girl didn't want either
secular or sacred marriage the last time we brought up
the subject. I suggested a nunnery, but she wouldn't—"

"Look," said Jack. "You're all under a great misappre-
hension about what happened between Kristin and me."

"We are men and women of the world, Mr. Cameron,"
said Maeve. "Be here at nine. I don't want to hear that
you've left town again."

Jack decided that someone should warn Kristin of what
the Macleods were planning. The girl deserved the opportunity to prepare a dignified refusal. He was glad that *he*
wouldn't be the one refusing to cooperate with two such

single-minded women. How had they managed to marry men as pleasant as Connor and James Macleod? Jack had met James, quite by accident, in a saloon in Denver and found him a very jolly fellow.

"Tomorrow at nine then, Mrs. Macleod," he said, rising to leave. Jack walked up the hill from French Street to the decaying mansion, surprised that the artist in Kristin had not moved her to have the place painted. And sausage making? Surely the daughter of Heinrich Traube did not want to follow him into sausages. And what about the neighbors? Connor had told him that when Fleming built the mansion, others, thinking Nickel Hill would become the showplace of Breckenridge, had built up here as well, only to see the house they had followed fall into ruin. How would they take to having pigs and sausage making in their midst? Not well, he thought.

He knocked loudly at the door and got no answer. Surely, Kristin was not asleep so early. Jack circled the mansion looking for a light. Ah, there—Kristin was working in her studio. He tapped on the window, causing her to jump and drop her paint brush. Looking alarmed, she came over and peered out at him.

"It is not time for your sitting," she called.

"I have news that you will want to hear," he shouted back.

Kristin glared at him. "Well, come in the back way."

She's becoming as bad-tempered as Kat Macleod, Jack decided as he tramped around the house to a door that led into the kitchen. And she had once been such a sweet, well-mannered girl. Still, the transformation was partly his fault. No doubt hard times affected one's disposition and manners, as well as one's financial status.

She had not come to admit him, so he let himself in, thinking that two women alone in such a large house should be more careful about locking doors, even if no one else in town did. He quickly located the studio where Kristin was working on his portrait, then stared at the work with dismay. She had never let him see it before. "Good lord," he exclaimed, "do I look that decadent?"

"Are you saying you do not find it a good likeness?" There was a little smile lighting her eyes and tilting her lips, one of the few he had seen there since the night they had laughed together in her father's library.

"I suppose it's a good enough likeness," he mumbled, and it was, except for something there that he did not see in himself. She was painting what she thought to be his flawed character. That's why she had insisted on the fancy clothes, the cane and the homberg, which covered up one of his best features, his hair. She thought him a bounder, had said so, and was now painting him thus. Jack shifted uncomfortably. He hoped that he didn't really look so shallow and self-centered. Did others see him that way? Perhaps he should shave off his mustache.

"Well, what news is this you've brought?"

"The Macleods will be coming here tomorrow between nine and ten to insist that we marry."

Startled, Kristin put down her brush and turned to him, searching his face for a clue to his feelings. She was hurt to find that he looked amused. "What woman would marry a person of no morals or decency?" she snapped.

Although her response was exactly what he expected, Jack felt aggrieved at her tone and retorted, "I simply wanted to warn you so that you'll be prepared and can answer accordingly." He then noticed what she seemed to have forgotten. She was wearing a demure nightdress, all tucks and embroidery, under a loose silk robe. She looked unbelievably fetching. "I see I caught you in your preparations for bed."

Kristin blushed. "Well, no one asked you to come here at this time of night and peer in my window. I ought to send for the sheriff."

"It seems to me," said Jack, "that you have threatened to do that before. Are you going to dispatch your drunken housemaid to fetch him?"

"She is not drunken—or my housemaid!" said Kristin indignantly, reminding him that he had just spoken rudely to a lady, a very pretty one. Her pale blond hair was hanging in a long braid with curls escaping around her face and wisps curling from the braid itself. Her face was flushed with anger, and her demure nightdress seemed astoundingly alluring, since he assumed that there was nothing but Kristin underneath.

"Just go," she said with great dignity.

"Certainly," Jack responded, bowed sardonically, and headed for the door, where he was confronted by Ingrid, an amazing replica of Kristin, at least in coloring, although much larger and very drunk. Now that Jack thought of it, Kristin had behaved herself with commendable aplomb while under the influence of alcohol—a few giggles, the telling of family stories that were perhaps not discreet, but still she had been charmingly tipsy, whereas this woman— good lord!

Jack tried to back away, but Ingrid reached out for his arm. "Hallelujah!" she cried. "A handsome visitor!" Giving him a provocative smile, she lurched in his direction, stumbled, and threw up on his waistcoat.

Horrified, Jack tried to free himself from his attacker, who was clutching him for balance. "Ingrid, how could you?" cried Kristin. "You know you're not supposed to drink."

"Nothin' else to do," said Ingrid morosely, a hand at her forehead, an eye on Jack's ruined waistcoat. "No husband, no children. Only got my pretty furniture an' my piano—"

"And the sausage business," Kristin reminded her.

"No pigs yet," Ingrid replied. She released Jack and stumbled backwards.

"Yes, but you were supposed to help with the recipes, and you didn't. Now you've taken to drink again, when you promised me just this afternoon—"

"Well, I forgot," said Ingrid. "An' I don't feel too good."

"Don't you dare throw up again," said Kristin. "You must go to bed immediately."

"Can't get upstairs," said Ingrid. "Could sleep on my velvet settee, but I—"

"I'll help you take her upstairs," said Jack, who had been wiping off his soiled waistcoat with an initialed linen handkerchief.

The two of them assisted a tottering Ingrid up the curved staircase. Kristin put her quickly to bed, giving the same admonitions that Lottie had given to Kristin in her time of alcoholic distress. She was disconcerted when she came down to find Jack still there.

"I stayed in case you needed additional assistance," said Jack stiffly.

"You're the one who needs assistance," replied Kristin, tempted to giggle. He looked as if he couldn't believe what had happened. "Come into the kitchen, and I'll try to clean up your waistcoat."

He followed her and let her scrub industriously at the garment. It was pleasant to stand so close, thought Jack, distracted from his embarrassing condition. To inhale the fragrance of her hair, feel the brush of the silky wrapper against his hand . . .

"Maybe you should take it off," said Kristin. "It smells, and I don't seem to have done much good." She helped him to remove his coat and then the offensive waistcoat.

Jack so savored the touch of her hands that he thought better of exposing himself to temptation any longer. He bade her a hasty good night and retrieved his clothing before she could do any more damage.

As he walked down the hill toward the Denver Hotel and a drink before bedtime, he thought it wouldn't have been so bad to marry Kristin, although he knew that tomorrow she would refuse the Macleods' plans. Had he told her of all the gossip that maid had spread? Perhaps he should have. What if, when he had established himself here, the family insisted that he marry Minna? What if the Traubes sent her out here? Good lord, life with Minna, which he had once viewed with complacency because of her dowry, now seemed impossible, whereas life with Kristin, if he could keep her from turning into a shrew like the two Macleod women, would be very pleasant. She had been a biddable girl when he first met her, and she was pretty—beautiful, in fact—and would make him a lovely hostess and give him handsome children.

But none of that was going to happen. Kristin would make an embarrassing scene tomorrow morning when he and the Macleods arrived at her doorstep, and that would be the end of it.

If he'd asked me, if he'd given me the least hint that he really wanted to marry me, she thought despondently, *I'd have said yes.* Instead he'd treated it lightly. A joke. Just because Kristin Traube's reputation was in ruins, the foolish Macleods thought he should marry her. What nonsense! That was Jack Cameron's attitude. He wasn't even honest enough to refuse on his own behalf. He was leaving that to her, endangering her one hope of supporting herself. Kat might very well pull out of the sausage venture if Kristin refused.

152

And the hope of becoming an artist? What had that come to? One commission. From Jack Cameron. A sop to make up for the grave injuries he'd done her, the complete dislocation of her life. He wouldn't even acknowledge that she couldn't go home, that her parents, if forced to take her back, would make her life miserable. How could he be so indifferent to her plight? So amused. So heartless. She was *glad* that Ingrid had thrown up on him.

If one had to live with a drunkard, her drunkard had certainly committed that terrible *faux pas* in the most appropriate place. Right on his fine brocade waistcoat. Who did he think he was? Some traveling gambler? Well, maybe he did. He was gaining a reputation for creative investment in Breckenridge and he had had it in Chicago, although there his father had restrained Jack's penchant for risk. No doubt, he would be in terrible trouble with Pitman Cameron when he got home. She nodded with gloomy satisfaction and stored her cleaned brushes in a jar.

And she was *glad* that he hated his portrait. It had accomplished exactly what she planned. He had looked into his own black soul, aghast at what he saw. Maybe he would reform, she thought, although she doubted it. She placed her palette neatly on the table where she kept her supplies, climbed the broad staircase, and looked in on Ingrid, who was sleeping heavily. Tomorrow Kristin would pay closer attention to her, so that she could not get away from the house and obtain alcohol. Ingrid seemed to have found Mr. Cameron attractive. Perhaps she would be embarrassed to remember what she had done and change her ways.

These thoughts carried Kristin into bed, where she closed her eyes, eaten up with worry as she thought of the argument she faced the next morning with the Macleods. Pride told her to refuse their intervention, even if her refusal meant that they washed their hands of her. She couldn't agree to a marriage that Jack considered a joke.

Or could she? Why not? she asked herself bitterly. Let *him* say no and incur their wrath. They couldn't blame her if he did the refusing. Wouldn't he be surprised if she agreed! The arrogant bounder! Oh, why couldn't he have liked her? Why couldn't he have been a good person instead of a charming one?

From the corner of her eye, Kristin could see the wedding guests walking up the hill. She wanted to run; instead she ignored them just as she did Ingrid, who was sitting on the front steps of the Fleming mansion, neatly dressed, haggard, and verbosely apologetic. Kristin was trying to discuss colors with the house painter, but Ingrid kept interrupting to say how sorry she was that she had thrown up on the waistcoat of Kristin's guest, that had she not been drunk, she would never have dreamed of doing such a thing to the gentleman caller of her only friend in the world.

To each apology Kristin nodded and found a new way to say that Ingrid must give up alcohol. The side conversations seemed to upset the painter almost as much as Kristin's insistence that not only would she choose her own paint, she would mix it so as to get exactly the right colors.

Mr. Arbol-Smith, who had the widest selection of paint in town and not too many customers, what with the falling price of silver, said, "If I'd a known what you wanted all this here paint for, I wouldn't a brought it. I never heard of mixing paint. It'll git us a streaky house."

"Now that would be interesting," said Kristin. "However, I think I would like two solid colors of my own choosing."

"Two!" exclaimed Mr. Arbol-Smith. "Well, I guess if we run outa one—"

"No, not if we run out of one," said Kristin, and she poured half of one can and half of another into her own bucket, much to Mr. Arbol-Smith's dismay. "One color will be used for the trim, the doors, and the shutters. The other—"

"Don't know why you'd want to paint this old wreck anyway," said Mr. Arbol-Smith, considerably upset by Kristin's revolutionary ideas on house painting.

"What are you doing, Kristin?" demanded Kat, who had arrived at the steps ahead of the others. "I didn't authorize any house painting. Good morning, Mr. Arbol-Smith."

"Our agreement mentioned reasonable repairs," said Kristin. "I'd certainly consider this the first of them." She was vigorously stirring the two paints together. "Just as I thought. Clotted cream." She had mixed yellow and white to get a bold cream color.

"I ain't doin' no paintin' less I git paid," said Mr. Arbol-Smith. "Didn't you say Miz Macleod here was payin'?"

"The question is, do we want this for the house or the trim?" Kristin mused, pointedly ignoring Jack's approach.

"You go paintin' trim, it gits sloppy," said Mr. Arbol-Smith.

"Not if you want to be paid, it doesn't," said Kristin and began to rummage among the other paint cans, looking for colors that would provide her with a nice slate blue.

"Well, Miz Macleod ain't said yit that she's payin'."

"I suppose I must," said Kat.

"I don't see what paint has to do with sausage making," grumbled Connor, arriving with the rest.

"Actually, Mr. Cameron should pay for the painting," said Kat.

"That would depend upon the outcome of your mission, Mrs. Macleod," said Jack.

"I want something that will look good with snow," said Kristin hurriedly, "but not clash with the greenery of the mountain side. A color to match an oncoming storm."

Everyone in the group turned and stared except Jack. He looked as if he might laugh, which infuriated her.

"Here. Let's try these." She slopped two more shades together and began to stir.

"Enough of this foolishness," said Maeve. "We are here on important moral business."

"Mrs. Macleod," said Kristin, still ignoring Jack's presence, "I think that you have said everything to me on the subject of morals that can be said. Now, just a touch of that black, Mr. Arbol-Smith."

"Black? You're gonna put black in there?"

"For lack of gray," said Kristin, "Black and a bit of white."

"Mr. Cameron has agreed that the two of you should be married," said Maeve, "lest scandal ruin your lives."

The hypocrite! thought Kristin. "I find it hard to believe that Mr. Cameron worries about scandal." Kristin poured a bit of black into her mixture and whirled it around until the streaks disappeared. "Now white," she said to Mr. Arbol-Smith.

"Well, we will not discuss fault here, since there is fault on both sides," said Maeve.

"I deny that," protested Kristin. "A convent-bred eighteen-year-old girl has no idea what effect brandy will have on her when she has never drunk it before. Therefore, I am not to blame. Mr. Cameron is."

Absolutely fascinated with the conversation, the painter passed her the white paint, muttering, "I won't never be able to duplicate these here strange colors."

"Of course not," said Kristin, "but I have a true eye and shall mix subsequent lots myself. So Mr. Cameron has agreed to marry me?" She eyed Jack balefully. "Very well, we must do it." Let him explain his refusal!

156

Jack looked surprised, but not as surprised as Kristin had anticipated.

"Good. Father Boniface Wirtner is expecting us at the church," said Maeve.

Ingrid rose and glared at Jack. "You dishonored my friend?" she asked. "I'm glad I threw up on you." Then she turned to Kristin. "I'll be your witness," she offered, "to be sure that it's done right. We'll have to ask the priest about divorce."

"We weren't married by a priest, Ingrid," said Sean.

"Yes, but you didn't warn me we should be," Ingrid retorted, rubbing her forehead, which undoubtedly ached.

Kristin was cleaning paint from her hands as if she expected Jack to go through with the wedding. "I believe you have enough to get started with, Mr. Arbol-Smith," she murmured. "I shall need a hat for the ceremony." She marched up the steps to the Fleming mansion, Ingrid standing guard at the door as if the Fitzpatrick-Macleod crowd might storm the house and do her friend some injury. Kristin returned wearing a wide-brimmed leghorn hat decorated with pink roses and green ribbons. "I'm ready," she said and looked at Jack challengingly. She had *not* changed her dress.

He smiled at her and offered his arm. Disconcerted, Kristin took Ingrid's instead. Did he really mean to go through with it? If so, he'd hate her for the rest of their lives. He'd insist that they go back to Chicago, where she'd be treated with disdain by her husband, her family, and everyone in society. But what if she refused to leave Breckenridge? Could a wife refuse? Of course, she could! What was he going to do about it? Drag her home? That would be humiliating for him, surely. He'd have to leave her here, perhaps conceal the marriage. Maybe he'd help support her to keep her quiet. What a fine revenge! Minna with no rich husband! Mr. Cameron without the fine dowry, and with no wife to look after him! She felt like crying. It took Maeve's sharp tones to stiffen her backbone.

"*She's* not coming to the ceremony," said Maeve, pointing at Ingrid.

"Of course she is," said Kristin. "You and Kat placed her in my care, and I try to keep her always under my eye."

Ingrid said, "I've learned my lesson about drinking."

Kat nodded with satisfaction as if to say there was nothing she would like to see better than a reformed Ingrid. Then the whole party started down the hill toward St. Mary's, leaving Mr. Arbol-Smith behind them, a dripping paintbrush laden with winter-storm blue in his hand. "Who's gonna pay me?" he yelled.

"Looks like that's going to be me," said Jack.

"I expect to see at least half the front side of the house done when I return, Mr. Arbol-Smith," Kristin called over her shoulder.

"Then you'd best go on your honeymoon before comin' back here," he replied.

Kristin knew there'd be no honeymoon. If the groom didn't run now, he'd run later.

Kat, who was walking beside her, across from Ingrid, glanced at Kristin with a frown. "You *are* willing to do this, aren't you?"

"Of course," Kristin replied. "Who would not want to marry a rich and handsome man who will support her in the style to which she was accustomed before he ripped her old life away from her." She said it loudly enough so that Jack Cameron would hear and realize that, just like Minna, she coveted his money.

"My sister was certainly anxious for such a marriage. What a misfortune for the female race that there are not wo Mr. Camerons, or ten, or fifty." Kristin heard Jack, who was walking with Connor, mutter something under his breath. She hoped it was a reconsideration of the marriage. She did hope that, didn't she? Kristin was distracted in her moment of doubt by the voice of Augustina, who was bringing up the rear with her husband.

"Stop staring at them," said Augustina.

"I wasn't staring at both of them," said Sean.

"No, of course not. You were staring at your ex-wife."

"I don't believe I am an ex-wife," said Ingrid.

Augustina burst into tears.

"I notice that you have not brought the children," said Kristin. "Is this too shocking an event for them?"

"It seems to be getting that way," said Kat dryly.

"Have you looked into the Oro?" asked Connor from behind them. "Barney Ford owns a big piece of that one, and it promises to be a winner."

"Really? Do they need financing?" asked Jack.

"Be careful how you spend our money," warned Kristin. "You'll have a wife to support in about a half hour."

"Don't you dare buy into anything with him, Connor," said Kat. "I don't know how you can bear to be friends with such a scoundrel."

"Enough of this quarreling," said Maeve. "It's unseemly in a wedding procession."

"St. Mary's used to be there," said Kat, pointing to the old site of the church. "Do you remember, Ingrid?"

"How could I forget?" said Ingrid, surprised to be addressed by her former sister-in-law. "It's the coldest church I ever sat in."

"Probably the only one you ever sat in," said Maeve.

"My family went to church," retorted Ingrid.

"Are you planning a wedding reception for us, Mrs. Macleod?" Kristin asked.

"Certainly not," said Maeve. "This is hardly an occasion for celebration—more in the nature of a necessity."

"What a shame to have one's nuptials slighted," said Kristin. "With the attitude you're taking, Mrs. Macleod, I'll hardly want to remember them. But then, no one can consider me fortunate in my bridegroom."

"I resent that," said Jack. "Everyone's making me out to be the villain, although I've agreed to this marriage and with little cause to do so."

"Little cause!" exclaimed Maeve. "You are indeed sunk deep in debauchery, sir."

By that time they had arrived at St. Mary's. Father Boniface Wirtner, standing in front of the church, heard the last remark. "Which one of you is the bridegroom?" he asked.

"I am," said Jack, "the one they all consider a debaucher."

"And I," said Kristin, "am the debauchee. Shall we get on with this before the whole group comes to blows?"

Father Boniface Wirtner looked quite shocked. "Have you lost your virtue to this man, Miss Traube?"

"I have," said Kristin.

"She hasn't," said Jack.

"How can you tell lies on your own wedding day?" asked Maeve. "The Holy Mother will never forgive you."

"I imagine the Holy Mother will be casting a hard eye on you, Mrs. Macleod, for slandering my good name."

"Perhaps we'd better leave the Holy Mother out of this," said Father Boniface Wirtner. "I am not sure that I should perform this ceremony. No banns have been posted. The two potential celebrants of the sacred rites do not seem to be—"

"When a sin has been committed, Father, it must be made right," said Maeve, fixing him with a hard eye.

160

"Are you willing to go through with this, young lady?" asked Father Boniface Wirtner.

"If he is," said Kristin. She slanted Jack a glance.

Jack said, "I'm willing if she is," as if daring her to actually marry him.

Maeve went on tiptoe and whispered fiercely into the priest's ear.

"Very well," he muttered, "let us go inside the church." Then he spotted Sean. "I'll want to talk to you after the ceremony, Mr. Fitzpatrick. I've been hearing the most appalling rumors about bigamy."

"He's guilty," said Ingrid.

"Who are you? The bride's sister?" asked the priest.

"No, I am the bridesmaid, and Mr. Fitzpatrick is my husband."

"That is a serious charge, madam," said the priest.

"It's not true," said Sean. "I divorced her legally."

"The church does not recognize divorce."

"We weren't married in the church."

"Then the church does not recognize the marriage."

Ingrid burst into tears. "I was tricked," she said.

"I'm the one who was tricked," said Augustina.

"I'm the one upon whom the most trickery was practised," said Kristin. "No gentleman pours brandy into an inexperienced, eighteen-year-old girl."

Father Wirtner's eyebrows rose into his hairline. "Are you with child, young woman?"

"How would I know?" Kristin responded. "I don't look like a pickle barrel, so I would think not."

"You could have asked me," said Kat. "I would have been happy to instruct—"

"Well, I was embarrassed. Who wants to talk about such things? I hardly think it's seemly for the good Father to mention it at this time or any other."

"Who else would one speak with about sin if not one's priest?" said Father Boniface Wirtner.

"Oh, for heaven's sake," said Jack. They were now at the altar. "Let's get this over with, shall we?"

"What a charming groom you make," said Kristin, and the wedding ceremony was performed, Maeve keeping the priest under a threatening eye.

"Do I get to kiss the bride?" Jack asked Father Boniface Wirtner when the ceremony was over.

"No," said Kristin, turned around, and marched out of the church on Ingrid's arm.

"He's a handsome fellow," said Ingrid, "and rich if what they say is true. You haven't done badly for yourself. Of course, this may be the same kind of trickery Sean practiced on me. Maybe you're not married at all."

"I don't care if I never see him again," muttered Kristin.

"My goodness, you're a peculiar woman," said Ingrid. "Men are real pleasant, especially in bed."

"Not in mine," said Kristin, who was walking up hill as fast as she could, trying to stave off tears, thinking that this was *not* the wedding of which she'd dreamed, although it need not have been so awful, not if Jack had an ounce of consideration.

The Macleods and the Fitzpatricks murmured uneasily among themselves. The bridegroom tried to look amused. The priest, who had never seen the bride leave on the arm of the bridesmaid without saying another word to anyone, turned to Maeve Macleod and said, "For your sins—"

"What sins?"

"Threatening a priest."

"Mother, what did you say to him?" cried Kat.

Chapter Ten

Kristin looked at herself in the long, clouded mirror that had been left behind by the mansion's previous owners. At the sight of her hat, she burst into tears. If she'd believed she was actually to be married, she'd have chosen a better hat; she'd have changed her dress. Pink was not her color! And she was wearing a wash dress—green with slate-blue paint spots she hadn't noticed until now.

At least there were no photographs of the wedding party with her looking like a housemaid and Jack in his fine morning coat. Then it occurred to her that Jack would now leave, and she'd have no photograph of him, only that awful portrait. And he *had* looked handsome this morning. He'd even shaved off his mustache. Crying harder, she threw herself on the bed. In no time her eyes would match the pink flowers on her wretched hat.

"You going after her?" asked Connor.

Jack shrugged. "Later is soon enough. Let's go see Barney Ford about the Oro." Jack was very irritated with his bride. He'd married her, hadn't he? Given up a lot of money to do it. They should have been drinking champagne in a honeymoon suite or at least taking a train that would deliver them to a honeymoon suite. Instead he was heading for the Saddle Rock Cafe. He'd have dinner with Connor and Barney Ford, a Negro. Jack had never done business with a Negro. And a man shouldn't be doing business on his wedding day or spending his wedding night at home. Kristin probably didn't even have a double bed for the occasion.

Kristin mopped her eyes and got up when she heard the knock on her door. What if it was Jack? Her heart gave a little flutter. Then she considered how embarrassing it would be if he realized that she'd been crying.

"You all right?"

Ingrid, not Jack. "Fine," Kristin replied in a quavering voice.

"Maybe we should make some dinner. He'll probably be back pretty quick."

"I imagine he's already on the train to Chicago," said Kristin.

Ingrid muttered something; Kristin couldn't tell what. "You want some dinner?"

"I'm not hungry." Kristin straightened her dress, hastily wet a cloth in the basin, and held it against her swollen eyes. "I have a headache," she called to Ingrid.

"That must set the record for wives with headaches," said Ingrid.

What did that mean?

"Guess I'll go make some sausages."

Kristin could hear Ingrid's footsteps on the stairs. Would

he come to say good-bye before he left town? she wondered. She *had* been rude. But then, he hadn't even bothered to be charming.

"Mr. Cameron!"

Jack tried to look as if he'd heard what the lawyer said.

"The man's newly married, Charlie," said Connor jovially. "I didn't touch ground for six months after I married Kat."

"There are those who think you still haven't, Connor," said Sean.

"Sounds like a good provision to me," said Jack. He'd lose his shirt on this deal if he didn't stop thinking about Kristin and pay attention.

She couldn't even look at the portrait of Jack, so she spent the afternoon, all dressed up in an emerald silk dress in case he came back, painting from memory the stream near the cottage where the Traubes had gone in the summer. Those had been happy days, at least when Mama let her sit at stream-side watching the fish.

She'd never painted fish as seen through running water. It was an engrossing project. Not a success, but interesting. Reflections of sunlight and trees. Distortions of form caused by the water. She almost managed to convince herself that she wasn't wondering where Jack was, what he was doing and thinking. The priest had married them. Her name was cleared. What now? She knuckled a tear away and dabbed yellow flecks of sunlight around her fish.

"Feel like eating something?" Ingrid asked from the doorway.

"Why not?" said Kristin and put her brushes away.

They sat at the table in the kitchen, picking at bread and the sausage Ingrid had made that afternoon.

"It's good," said Kristin, "for sausage." She could see that Ingrid felt sorry for her.

"I say we see the bridegroom home," said Connor. "Have a shivaree."

"The bridegroom has to go to the hotel and pack up," said Jack. "How about letting me stand you to a drink, in return for which you'll let me go home by myself?"

The men headed for the Miner's Home Saloon. "Nobody better tell my sister that Connor had a drink," said Sean. He turned to Jack, grinning. "Marriage is hell."

"I hope not," said Jack, who rather thought he'd like it. He estimated that he'd now stayed away from the Fleming house long enough to worry his rebellious bride. Time to go home and reap the rewards accruing to a man who'd done his gentlemanly duty and won a beautiful girl in doing it.

"You plan to live in my house?" gasped Kristin. Several hours ago, she'd given up thinking he'd come to say good-bye.

"Certainly," said Jack. He directed the deposit of his possessions in the entrance hall by an unemployed miner glad to get the work. "Or would you rather I bought us another house. You can use this for—"

"This is my house and my place of business. I intend to live here," said Kristin.

"Very well, we'll both live here." He paid the fellow off and urged him out the door before the conversation deteriorated into a squabble.

"No one invited you," said Kristin.

"I'm your husband. We'll be sharing a house, not to mention a bed."

"We certainly will not." He'd stayed away to pay her back for walking off without him at the church. "You will never share my bed," she cried resentfully. "I have been dishonored by you once, and I don't intend to let you anywhere near me ever again."

"Kristin," said Jack, "I don't know what you think happened in that library, but I did not dishonor you. I kissed you; that doesn't constitute dishonor, at least not among sensible people."

"It doesn't?"

"Of course not."

"Then why did my father throw me out of the house?"

"I'm not sure he did. It seems he meant to frighten you and then let you stay."

"But Lottie and Genevieve thought I might be with child."

"From a kiss? That's impossible."

"Am I still a virgin?"

"Well, you must answer that yourself." He lit one of the hanging lamps in the hall since they were talking in semi-darkness. "If you're not a virgin, it has nothing to do with me."

"I didn't *have* to marry you?"

"I've tried to tell everyone that, but no one would believe me, including you."

"Well, you might have stated it more forcefully," said Kristin, her face pale. Now she didn't know *why* he'd married her. "Why did you agree?"

"Because some maid gossiped about us all over town and everyone believed the lies."

Not because he cared for her, she thought despondently. Of course, he didn't. "I didn't know they *were* lies," said Kristin. "I thought kisses—oh, do go away!"

"Nonsense," said Jack. "The deed is done. We're married."

"Even if we are, you should move back to the hotel until you leave for Chicago."

"I'm not returning to Chicago."

"What do you mean? Why would you want to stay?"

"I like it here. It's an exciting place. I've been hunting and—"

"You?" said Kristin, completely confused. She felt as if she were just meeting him.

"Of course," said Jack. "I even ate the birds I shot. Very tasty."

"What a terrible thing to say."

"And I've been fishing and eating the fish. Best of all, the financial opportunities are just the type I like."

"Risky? Is that what you mean?"

"Exactly. Even riskier than spending an evening alone with an eighteen-year-old virgin."

"You're being very ungentlemanly!"

"True," Jack agreed. "That's part of my new image. Isn't that the way you're painting me in the portrait? Well, that's not me you're painting, my dear wife, but do enjoy yourself. You already have your hundred dollars, so you can do anything with my face and person you want."

He hates me, she thought, then said proudly, "I don't want to do anything with your person."

"Sooner or later you will," said Jack. "So where am I to sleep in the meantime?"

Kristin reluctantly showed him to the only extra room that had a bed in it. It was to have housed a Chicago girl or two and was accordingly utilitarian.

"Good lord," said Jack, "I can see that our first priority will be to buy furniture for this room and the drawing room. Where did you get that red-velvet stuff?"

"Hush!" said Kristin. "Ingrid thinks it's beautiful."

"What will she do if I criticize it? Throw up on me?"

Unable to help herself, Kristin began to giggle. Jack's face broke into a broad smile, and he leaned over and kissed her lightly on the mouth, causing her to jump back and trip on the ragged hall carpet. "Well, good night, my sweet wife," he said, tossed his valise into the tacky little bedroom, and closed the door in her face.

As he undressed, Jack thought about his conversation with Kristin. It had never occurred to him that the girl might think she could be impregnated by a kiss. She must have been terrified. He looked around the room and wondered where he was to hang his clothes. There was no wardrobe. Jack folded his coat neatly over the one chair, thinking that Kristin must have stayed in rooms like this since she fled the Traube mansion. No wonder she was so bitter toward him. Living like a pauper, thinking she had lost her virginity and might be with child. She didn't seem to know what virginity was.

Still, Jack was sure that he could salvage the marriage. He had always had good luck with women, and Kristin had been a soft-natured girl, not one to stand up to authority, more given to running away from trouble than facing it.

As he prepared for bed, Jack reflected that this was not the way he had imagined spending his wedding night, and he had indeed been thinking about that subject all day— to such an extent that it was difficult to concentrate on money. His associates had laughed at him. However, he had no doubt that in the very near future, perhaps tomorrow night, he would manage to seduce his wife. Innocent, virginal Kristin would be putty in his hands. Jack chuckled and hoped that she would prove to be as passionate as her conduct in her father's library promised.

He'd have her all to himself. Well, of course, there was that drunken Ingrid, but she would hardly prove to be any sort of deterrent to his romantic intentions, not when she was in the habit of drinking herself into oblivion each night. She hadn't even appeared to defend her friend in the confrontation this evening. Jack climbed into the hard, narrow bed meant for a small maid, not a tall gentleman accustomed to luxury. As he fell asleep, his thoughts were equally divided between new furniture and the anticipation of passionate seduction. *That's marriage for you,* he thought drowsily, *more practical than romantic.* But his dreams weren't practical.

Kristin plumped her pillows with a vigorous hand. She had been thoroughly bamboozled and now found herself married to a cad who expected to share her bed. Even Papa hadn't shared Mama's bed; Mama had her own room. Well, Mr. Cameron would have to stay in *his* own room. She didn't owe him any favors. Even if he hadn't taken her virginity—whatever that entailed—she had suffered almost as many consequences, and he probably would have dishonored her if her father hadn't returned when he did.

Kristin cheered herself up by picturing dapper Jack Cameron surrounded by pigs and sausage makers. That ought to drive him away. Soon. Before he realized that she still went weak in the knees every time she saw him. Before he realized how pathetic she was—still infatuated after all the awful things that had happened, while he felt nothing but duty toward her. Even if he didn't buy furniture for the house and pay Mr. Arbol-Smith or even contribute to her support, she had to get rid of him before she made a fool of herself.

For all her proud intentions, Kristin dropped into sleep and dreamed about a real marriage to Jack. The dreams were vague since she didn't know what went on in real marriages, but they were exciting. She woke up twice in the night, feeling strange sensations in unusual parts of her body.

Book III

The Disappearing Wife

Chapter Eleven

Kristin awoke because someone was pounding on her door. She stumbled out of bed and opened to Ingrid, asking, "What's wrong? Are you sick?"

"Of course not," said Ingrid. "I told you I was through with drinkin'. There's six girls at the front door, sayin' they've come to live here."

"Genevieve was more prompt than I expected." Kristin pushed a tumble of flaxen hair out of her eyes and tied the sash of her dressing gown.

"An' they say there's a herd of pigs down at the railroad station."

"The ladies' stop," wondered Kristin, "or the one in West Breckenridge?"

"I didn't think to ask," said Ingrid. "Don't reckon they'd put pigs off at the ladies' stop."

It was happening too fast. Married one day, a full-fledged entrepreneur the next. "First, we'll get Jack up. He can take care of the pigs." That ought to unnerve him.

Ingrid leaned against the door frame and stared down at Kristin. "You're not gonna keep him long," she warned, "not with me throwin' up on his waistcoat an' you sleepin' in a separate room an' handin' a bunch of pigs over to him."

"That's the idea," said Kristin. She marched down the hall and pounded on Jack's door, which opened immediately.

"Ah, my bride!" he said.

Because he was shirtless, Kristin grabbed the door and slammed it in his face.

"That's a fine body for a gentleman," said Ingrid. "Are you sure he's a banker?"

"Ingrid!" cried Kristin, scandalized. "Have you no modesty?"

Ingrid shrugged. "If you decide you don't want him, I'll take him. It's been years since I had a man."

Kristin's mouth dropped open as she watched her charge saunter down the hall with a sultry sway to her hips that Kristin had never noticed before. She knocked again at Jack's door and called out, "Don't open it. You have to get dressed and go after the pigs."

"What pigs?" Jack called back.

"At the railroad station. Kat had them sent."

"I might have known," said Jack, reopening the door. Now he was wearing an unbuttoned shirt. "Oh, for heaven sake," he said, catching sight of her expression. "Get used to me. I'm not that bad-looking. In fact, I heard your alcoholic friend pay me a compliment."

"Never mind what she said," retorted Kristin. "She has a drinking problem."

"She doesn't sound drunk this morning."

"Well, I'm sure alcohol befuddles one whether or not one's been drinking it just lately."

"You aren't befuddled," said Jack. "In fact, you're more forthcoming than you were before you took to drink."

"Oh!" Kristin gasped. "I ought to—"

"What? Kiss me?"

"Kick you," said Kristin. "Now, will you please put on more clothes and get my pigs?"

"And what am I supposed to do with them? I don't know anything about pigs. You're the daughter of sausage makers. You ought to—"

"I don't know anything about live ones," said Kristin, "so you must find somebody to bring them up here and do something sensible with them. We can't have them running all over the neighborhood."

"No," Jack agreed dryly. "The neighbors might complain. You don't by any chance know of any Breckenridge pig herders, do you?"

"Ask Mr. Chris Kaiser. He sells pork."

"Don't I get breakfast?"

"Who did you think was going to make it for you?" asked Kristin. "I'm known as a worse cook than Kat Macleod, and Ingrid's not much better."

Jack sighed. "Is every husband treated so badly the morning after his wedding night?" he asked rhetorically and closed the door again.

Kristin whirled and skimmed down the wide, curved stairway to confront her new employees. "I'm Kristin Traube—ah, Traube-Cameron," she said, trying to hide how flustered she was as a result of the conversation with her husband. "Please, introduce yourselves." The girls were clustered in the hall looking overwhelmed by their magnificent if tattered surroundings.

"Is this a sporting house?" asked one named Bea, pointing toward the drawing room with its red velvet furniture and Ingrid in a bold blue gown.

175

"No, this is a sausage factory," said Kristin. "I presume all of you know how to make sausages."

"We certainly do," said Fanny, "but I never seen a sausage factory like this one. I worked at Traube's—you related to old Heinie? Oh lord, we're in for it," she said to her companions when Kristin nodded.

"Not at all," said Kristin. "I can't stand him either. The pigs arrived this morning, I believe."

"We know that," said a third girl, whose name Kristin couldn't remember. "Makin' a terrible fuss, they were."

"Probably never been on a train before," said Pen Moriarty, giggling.

"I'm the maid," said Winifred, a tiny girl with plain brown hair.

"What is your experience?" asked Kristin.

"Don't you remember me?" asked Winifred. "I did your ironing at Genevieve's."

"Oh, goodness yes," said Kristin. "Well, at least we know you have one talent. As you see, the house is not in the best condition, so you can start right now by doing maid things. In fact, why don't all of you help her."

"Where are we supposed to put our valises?"

"Just go upstairs and find a room. I have to buy beds for you. Is there any message from Genevieve?"

"She wishes you luck and says she's sorry about telling Mrs. Maeve Macleod the story, whatever that means, and if you're successful in finding husbands for us, Chicago is full of girls who'd love to come out here."

"Good," said Kristin. "In that case, I'd better run an ad in the newspaper. Now, Winifred, if you'll direct these young women in housecleaning. There are supplies in the kitchen." Kristin waved her hand toward the back.

Ingrid had been sitting in a red velvet chair, watching

all this and trying not to laugh. Jack came down the stairs and stopped abruptly on the landing to stare at the six girls clustered around Kristin. "Who are *they?*" he asked.

"They'll clean house until we've had the pigs slaughtered. Please, ask Mr. Kaiser if he would do it for us. Then you can drop one or more of the pigs at his butcher shop if he agrees."

Jack scowled at her.

"Who's he?" asked Winifred.

"A man to beware if you value your virtue."

"What a charming wife you are," said Jack.

"Is he the one what dishonored you?" asked a girl named Frankie, who had explained during the introduction process that she was named for St. Francis.

"Well, as it turned out—"

"I most certainly did not," said Jack. "It was a misunderstanding."

"Didn't know there could be misunderstandings about things like that."

"It depends on how drunk the young lady is," said Jack, sending Kristin a retaliative grin.

The young women gasped.

"Well, you needn't worry," said Kristin. "I only took to drink once, and that was at Mr. Cameron's insistence. I certainly never intend to do it again. Now, let me introduce you to Ingrid Fitzpatrick. Ingrid, won't you come out here and meet our employees? Ingrid will be the sausage superintendent. She doesn't drink anymore either."

"I wouldn't count on that," muttered Jack.

"Just you be sure you treat Miss Kristin right," said Ingrid. "I know how to take care of gentlemen who don't treat women right."

"I'll just bet you do," said Jack. "Well, good day, ladies." He donned his hat and started for the front door.

"Where's your mustache?" Kristin called after him.

"Ah, you finally noticed. Is its removal going to give you difficulty with the portrait?"

"Not at all," said Kristin. "I remember how silly it looked."

"Many thanks, dear wife," said Jack. "You can consider my having shaved it a sign of my new status as a husband." He marched out the door and down the steps. "What are you going to give up for me?" he called over his shoulder.

"My reputation's already gone. What more does he want?" Kristin muttered. And surely, he didn't still mean to stay? She had thought the pigs would change his mind. Then she decided that Jack was just pretending that he intended to stay in order to upset her. But that wouldn't last long, not when he had to live in a sausage factory and take responsibility for incoming herds of pigs. "Well, girls, to work."

The young women took off their bonnets and headed toward the kitchen. At three in the afternoon, a herd of squealing, oinking, grunting pigs and two pig carcasses were brought up Lincoln Avenue onto Nickel Hill by a fellow who looked as if he'd been living with them for years.

"Who are you?" asked Kristin as they milled around in her front yard.

"Oakum," said the fellow. "Your husband done hired me to look after the pigs. Where you want 'em?"

"In the back yard, I guess. Will they stay in one place?"

"Not likely," said Oakum. "You got any outbuildings?"

"A few. They're not in very good condition."

"Well, I guess I could drive 'em into one for the night. Your husband hired a carpenter to build a pen."

Kristin glanced nervously from one side of the house to the other. She could see women and children on neighboring front porches, staring in horror at Oakum and the pigs.

"Where you want me to put these carcasses?" They were piled in a wheelbarrow.

"Frankie," she called desperately. "What do we do with these dead pigs?"

Frankie came running out of the dining room, where she had been scrubbing. "We can't rightly start sausage-making this late in the day, ma'am. Just hang 'em from a tree in back, fella. They'll keep overnight, cold as it gets here in the mountains. What's your name?"

"I'm Oakum."

"Oakum what?"

"Just Oakum."

"All right. On the back porch. We'll start sausage-making tomorrow morning. You got good equipment," she told Kristin.

"Goodness knows how Kat Macleod found out what one would need. Ingrid!" Ingrid appeared, still sober. "Could you choose an outbuilding in which to put these pigs? This is Oakum. Oakum, this is Mrs. Ingrid Fitzpatrick, who is the sausage superintendent."

"Ma'am," said Oakum. "You sure are a looker." His eyes were fixed on Ingrid's bosom.

"Shut your mouth before I knock you on your fanny," said Ingrid. Oakum backed up and fell off the front porch into the midst of the pigs. One little pig squealed and dashed up the steps to huddle behind Kristin.

"My goodness," said Kristin. "What a sweet piglet. She's cleaner than the others, and I think she likes me."

"Ah, there's no place like home," said Jack. He had just ridden up on a bay gelding. "I see the pigs have arrived. Furniture should follow shortly."

"Thank goodness," said Kristin.

"Five beds for your young women."

"There are six," Kristin protested.

179

"One of them can have my bed, and I'll share yours."

"You did that on purpose," said Kristin. Jack smirked. "Two of the girls will have to share," said Kristin. "You're staying in your own room until you leave Breckenridge."

"Don't count on it," said Jack. "Ah, here we are. Five beds and a dining room set. I can tell you, it's not easy to round up furniture in a town this small. Most of this stuff is secondhand."

"Secondhand!"

"You go out and see if you can do any better," said Jack. "I've more important business than rounding up furniture and pigs. Do you plan to keep them in the front yard?" he asked Oakum.

"Nope. Just waitin' to be told where to take 'em. That yard next door looks good," he announced in a loud voice.

The lady who had been on her front porch staring at them ran into her house and slammed the door.

"Well, that made a fine impression," said Kristin. "Take them around back. Ingrid will show you where."

"Only if you promise she ain't gonna do me no harm," said Oakum.

"You should be safe if you mind your manners," Kristin replied.

"Miss Kristin, I was tryin' to clean up the wallpaper in the parlor and it started to fall off," said Fanny.

"Are you sure you wouldn't rather sell this place?" Jack asked.

"It's my house. I'm not selling it."

A large wagon pulled up, and two men began to lift off furniture. "Just put the beds upstairs in whatever rooms aren't occupied," Kristin told them.

"Wonderful. We're going to sleep amongst the maids," said Jack.

"Why should that bother you? You've married one."

"If I got to sleep with her, maybe it wouldn't."

The two men who were carrying a bed past them turned around and stared. Then a bellow of rage and a great ruckus issued from the back yard.

"I think the pigs have met Mr. Arbol-Smith," said Jack. "Shall we investigate the damage?"

"I hope that paint hasn't been spilled," said Kristin. "I spent a half hour mixing a new batch right after lunch." She thought she was doing very well hiding her feelings for Jack. Being in the midst of hectic activity left one no time for the warmer emotions.

Six eligible females, ages 17 to 22, available for courtship on Sundays. No scoundrels, unemployed, or those without honorable intentions need apply. Contact Mrs. Kristin Traube-Cameron at the Fleming Mansion on Nickel Hill. A two-dollar fee will be charged to successful suitors and fifty cents for Sunday courtship attendance to cover the expenses of entertaining potential bridegrooms.

—Summit County Journal

"Miss Kristin, there's a pig in the house," cried Winifred.

"We are a sausage-making establishment," said Kristin calmly. She was in her studio, putting a few last malicious touches on her portrait of Jack. Although he had shaved off his mustache, she left it in the picture.

"It's a live pig, Miss Kristin. Walked in as bold as brass while I was sweeping the veranda. Didn't even use the back door." As if to confirm the maid's words, a small pig skirted around the girl and made for Kristin.

"It's just Gwenivere," said Kristin. "She's a sweet thing and very clean. You notice that she hasn't been wallowing with the rest of the pigs."

"Miss Kristin, you're not making a pet of that pig?"

"Of course not," said Kristin.

"Because when they slaughter her—"

"She's much too young to be slaughtered," Kristin pointed out, scratching Gwenivere gently about the ears and making the pig wiggle with delight and appear to be wagging her curly tail.

"I swan," said Winifred. "I never heard of a pet pig, especially one with such a fancy name."

"She's the queen of pigs," said Kristin, "so I named her after Queen Gwenivere in the Arthurian tales of Lord Tennyson."

"Never heard of 'em," said Winifred and bustled off to scrub down another room.

"Gwenivere," said Kristin. "I'm afraid you're not appreciated. Perhaps you'd better go to the back yard." Gwenivere was trotting around the studio, sniffing at turpentine and paint. "I shan't be doing your portrait if that's what you're hinting at, but I do wish I had a new commission. If you had enough money, I might be convinced to do one. Since Miss Weems has sold her elk picture, maybe I could sell a pig painting. I could pose you out on the mountainside. "Pig in the Wilderness." Doesn't sound like it would appeal to wealthy collectors, does it?" Kristin wondered whether Gwenivere Pig was an art enthusiast or just looking for something to eat. "You'd better watch your figure, Gwenivere," admonished Kristin. "If you eat too much, you'll end up sausage." Gwenivere trotted over and rubbed against Kristin's ankles.

"What's that pig doin' in the house?" asked Ingrid.

"She's come to call," said Kristin. "It's not as if anyone else calls on me."

"That's because I live here. No one wants to call on an ex-lady of the night an' divorced woman. I think they ought to at least let me see my children. In fact, if we ever make any money with these sausages, I think I'll hire myself a lawyer."

"That wasn't at all what Kat had in mind when she asked me to take you in," said Kristin. Ingrid's beautiful face registered her conflict of loyalties, and Kristin said hurriedly, "But you must do what you think best. Your children are so sweet. I used to tell them elk stories." She thought of painting portraits and telling .stories in Kat's house. "Ingrid," she asked impulsively, "would you let me paint your portrait?"

"Why bother?" said Ingrid. "Just look in the mirror, an' there I am. I still think we're sisters."

"Oh, I doubt it," said Kristin. "I don't think my family would have kept me for a minute if they didn't think I was a Traube, more's the pity."

"Well, better a rich Traube than a poor Leifsdatter. Maybe I'm a Traube, an' they gave me away."

"Why would they do that?"

"Who knows? They don't sound very nice. Well, I'm off to the kitchen to check on the sausages, but Kristin, you're goin' to have to get out an' start sellin' them."

"I know. I'm just trying to find out which areas would offer the best material for my debut as a landscapist."

"If you'd think less about paintin's an' more about sausages, we'd be richer. Right now this business isn't bringin' in any more than what we sell to the locals, an' Kat Macleod will expect to see us turn a profit. She's a tight woman with money. Never let me have any."

"Oh, I think you misjudge Kat," said Kristin. "She's been most generous about launching us in this business."

"An' she doesn't expect to get her money back?"

"Well yes, but not immediately."

"If you don't get on the road, I should."

Kristin thought about that. If Ingrid went, Kristin could stay in her studio painting, just peeking in on the sausage makers now and then. But if she sent Ingrid, Ingrid might disappear or get drunk, which would never do. "I'm the president. I promise I'll get out and sell sausages."

"Good," said Ingrid. "How is it that you an' Jack don't sleep together?"

"Because I don't want to."

"Well, that's no way to hold a husband. He'll be lookin' elsewhere."

Ruthlessly, Kristin suppressed a stab of alarm. She didn't care what Jack Cameron did! She wanted him to leave town, and she had no plans to commit "the act" with him. But what was it, if it wasn't kissing? she wondered. Sister Mary Joseph had said "the act" was to be committed only with an eye to procreation. Kristin liked children, especially telling them fairy tales and painting their pictures, but she didn't need the added burden of a child to raise when Jack went to Chicago. "Let's not talk about him," said Kristin.

"If he were my man, I'd have him in bed just like that." Ingrid snapped her fingers and turned away toward the kitchen. Her attitude made Kristin uneasy.

"Oh, Gwenivere," she said, patting the pig. "It's very difficult, even when you have plenty to eat and a roof over your head."

Dear Father and Mother,

    Due to the prevalence of entirely unwarranted gossip, for which we can thank Heinrich Traube, I have felt duty-bound to marry his youngest daughter, Kristin. I would appreciate your seeing Mr. Traube about turning over her dowry, Father. He is entirely responsible for this match, having forced her to leave his house for no good reason, as you know. I have no

184

doubt that if he does not hurriedly sanction our marriage and come up with the dowry, this scandal will spread through Chicago social circles as well, doing the reputations of both families harm.

I have found in Breckenridge and Colorado a fertile field for investment, and people seem intent on entrusting their money to me. Consequently, I have opened Cameron Investments and think to stay here. I would be glad of a participation by the Cameron Bank, which I can assure you would accrue to your financial advantage, Father; however, I must leave that decision to you.

You will be interested to know, Mother, that we are now living in a most interesting mansion in Breckenridge, Colorado. It was built in '87 by a New York mining financier named Medford Fleming.

In the hopes of your blessing and good wishes, I remain respectfully yours. Your son,
John Powell Cameron

Well, that took care of that, thought Jack, and precious little he'd told them about his marriage. It was not working out at all as he had anticipated. Kristin was still sleeping in her own room. He had appropriated a much larger one next to hers and furnished it for himself, but that did not give him access to his wife, who was always surrounded by sausage makers, maids, pigs, and Ingrid, who, irritatingly enough, remained sober all the time these days.

Good lord, just yesterday he had gone in search of his wife and found her in her studio keeping company with a pig named Gwenivere. What was a husband to do in the face of such bizarre behavior? And that damned portrait she had painted of him. She'd framed it and hung it over the mantel in the drawing room. Kristin had made him look like a procurer or some other decadent and immoral type.

How was he to gain ground in this battle of wills with his surprisingly adamant wife, who looked better to him every day she kept him at arm's length? Sausages, he supposed, were the key. He closed his office, untied his horse from the hitching post, and set off uphill toward his tumbledown mansion, which was now beginning to be called the Cameron mansion. Wouldn't Kristin hate that since *she* held the title.

As he rode up Washington, musing on his marital problems, he spotted his wife at the corner of French Street being harangued by Reverend Florida Passmore, the Methodist temperance crusader. Ten yards away, Jack could hear the stentorian outrage of the preacher.

"Of course it looks sinful," he bellowed. "You are sharing a house with a woman who was once—"

"—the sister-in-law of your strongest temperance supporter," Kristin interrupted.

"—who was once a woman of ill fame," Passmore finished even more loudly. "Furthermore, you are now running advertisements in both newspapers, selling off young women. It smacks of—"

"Good day, Reverend Passmore," said Jack, dismounting. "Have you some quarrel with my wife?"

"Have you seen the ads your wife is running in the *Journal*? It is your duty as a Christian, even if you are Roman Catholic, to curb her shocking activities."

Jack took Kristin's hand and tucked it in the crook of his arm. "I believe she is simply advertising for suitable men to join in holy matrimony to the young women who come out here from Chicago and put themselves in her care."

"She's selling them!" thundered Reverend Passmore.

"Indeed. I hardly think—" Jack turned and frowned at his wife. "*Are* you selling them?" he asked.

"Have any of them left?" Kristin retorted.

"But is there talk of money?"

"There's a charge if the suitors actually marry any of the girls or if they partake of refreshments at the Sunday afternoon receptions. Why not? By marrying, they are depriving me of workers, not to mention food and drink. I should be recompensed for my loss."

"Good lord!" Jack burst out laughing.

"I hardly think this is cause for blasphemy or amusement," said Reverend Passmore.

"But then, sir, you have no sense of humor," Jack replied. "That is well known all over the Western Slope. May I offer you a ride home, Kristin?" He could see that she was torn between a lofty refusal, which would leave her at the mercy of Reverend Passmore, and indebting herself to Jack for a personal service.

"Thank you," said Kristin. "I accept your offer."

Jack swung into his saddle, then held out his hand to pull her up in front of him. "I believe we've just made a step forward in our relationship," he said as he rode off after tipping his hat to the preacher. "You do at least prefer me to Reverend Passmore."

"I'd prefer the devil to Reverend Passmore."

"But then," said Jack, "you already consider me the devil, don't you?"

At the heavily carved mahogany dinner table, Jack sat at the head, Kristin at the foot, Ingrid beside her, reporting on the sausage-making events of the day, and all the young sausage makers between them. *Oh, how the sophisticated have fallen,* thought Jack wryly. He, who had once drunk champagne in the finest clubs of Chicago with beautiful women and men of his own class, now ate sausage at a secondhand table with a gaggle of female sausage makers.

"My dear," he said, addressing his wife as he watched that little pig enter the dining room and head for Kristin's chair, "have you yet planned a selling trip?"

"No," said Kristin. "I am considering which town I shall go to first, which second, which third. I'm hoping for places with saleable scenery."

"Then if I may help you make up your mind, I'm on my way to Denver and would be glad to take you along."

"I've been there. The scenery is of no interest."

"But the potential for sausage sales is, and I think you will find it much easier to do business with a husband in town in case you have any problems."

"What problems?"

"Unescorted ladies have problems, as you well know. You will be in and out of railroad stations, which can be difficult for beautiful women."

"I wish I had a husband who called me beautiful," said Winifred. She had cooked and was serving dinner—sausage. They had eaten sausage for four nights running since the supplies were piling up.

"Miss Kristin," said Fanny, "do go out and sell some. I'm so tired of eating sausage."

"Wouldn't you like to have a nice piece of beef?" asked Pen Moriarty. "A fine Irish stew. That would be so tasty."

"Anything but sausages," groaned Bea. "I never thought I'd be unhappy to see meat on my plate, but—"

"Oh, very well," said Kristin, "I'll go. I count on you to make suitable hotel arrangements." She gave Jack a sharp glance.

"You certainly may count on me," said Jack. He managed to keep from smiling, for he knew exactly what arrangements he was going to make.

"About time," Ingrid muttered under her breath.

"What's that?" asked Kristin.

"I said it's about time you stopped paintin' pictures an' started being salesman president of the company. Nobody knows about Traube's Colorado Sausages except for a few folks in Breckenridge. We'll never get rich just sellin' in this pokey town."

"How true, Ingrid," said Jack, giving her his most charming smile. "You obviously have a head for business."

Looking more sultry than ever, Ingrid smiled back at him. Kristin seemed so startled at the interchange that Jack dared to hope she was jealous.

"I myself," continued Jack, "am extending my business as far afield as I can."

"It will be like a honeymoon for you," said Fanny.

"Sean and I had a honeymoon," said Ingrid.

"You were married, Miss Ingrid?" asked Pen.

"Yes. To Sean Fitzpatrick. He's living on French Street in a bigamous union."

"Now, Ingrid," murmured Kristin, "you mustn't talk like that."

"They won't even let me see my children."

"Ooh, that's terrible," said Winifred, taking her seat and cutting up her sausage. "Why don't you sic your priest on him?"

"I wish I could," muttered Ingrid, "but I'll think of something."

Did *thinking of something* mean setting her cap for Jack? Kristin wondered.

Chapter Twelve

"Aunt Kat's gonna be really mad if she hears about this," said Bridget.

"She's not your aunt," replied Phoebe. "You're *our* aunt."

All the children giggled, while Bridget, scowling, said, "Since I'm the aunt, you should mind me."

"If you don't want to go to Kristin's, go on back home," ordered Sean Michael. "I never found out what happened to the elk prince and princess, and I want to know. We all do." Molly and Liama nodded their heads, curls bouncing vigorously as the five children scampered up the hill, having taken advantage of a rare opportunity to escape from a house full of adults. Augustina was napping, something she did often these days. Patsy, the maid, was gossiping with the lady next door. All the others were out of the house. Bridget, because the idea hadn't been hers in the first place, lagged behind sullenly, but she followed them.

"Don't you tell either, Bridget," threatened Sean Michael, "or no one will play with you anymore."

Kristin was working on "Nightscape" again, a third version. This one came closer still to her vision, for she layered her paint, letting the shadowy buildings dry, then putting in hints of their windows, doors, and ornamentation. On top of that layer she did another with a carriage and horses disappearing into darkness at the right edge of the picture, glances of light on the wheel rims, the curve of a horse's back and neck, the driver a dark huddle on the seat; in the foreground the glow of the gas lamp turned the cobblestones to swells of water like a partitioned sea. Men standing beneath the lamp were outlines with touches of white, mellow gold light glancing off top hats, faces turned to a woman, the reds of whose clothing darkened in the shadows as she hastened away. Kristin shivered at the mysterious, sinister beauty taking shape at the tip of her brush. This one she would send to Mrs. Potter Palmer in Chicago.

"We need to talk about the trip."

Kristin jumped, too wrapped up in her painting to hear Jack's footsteps in the hall. "I've decided not to go," she replied without looking toward the door where he stood.

"The devil. Why have you changed your mind?"

She didn't trust him. The idea of leaving town with Jack—just the two of them—made her uneasy. Rather than admit to her own cowardice, she began to talk about the painting, which she could not leave, not when it was going well at last. Jack walked toward the uncurtained windows where she worked and looked over her shoulder.

"Good lord," he murmured. "I didn't know you could do anything so—so—"

"Do you like it?" she asked, weak with pleasure at the admiration in his voice. For this particular painting she needed to hear praise. Kristin felt unsure of herself with "Nightscape" because she was reaching for something new, experimenting in both technique and subject matter.

"I've never seen anything like it."

"Yes, but do you—"

They were interrupted by the babble of children's voices at the front door, two of whom were shouting, "Mama!" Giggles, chatter, exclamations, weeping. Kristin hopped off her stool and ran toward the hall, Jack only steps behind. Winifred stood by the front door looking amazed; Bridget, Molly and Liama clustered around her. All were gaping at the drawing room where Ingrid knelt on the floor with her arms around Phoebe and Sean Michael.

"We thought you were dead," said Sean Michael. "You went away, and Daddy married someone else."

"But we love you, Mummy," said Phoebe. "Don't cry. We love you. I was learning to play the piano just like you. I remember all your songs, and I taught myself some 'cause the teacher doesn't know them and neither does Augustina. Then the piano went away too and—"

"Oh, Phoebe, they didn't tell me you played."

"Who's they?" demanded Sean Michael. "Why didn't you come to see us? Why didn't anyone say you were here?

"They wouldn't let me. Your grandmother—"

"Let's go into the parlor," said Kristin. "It's so nice of you to call, children."

"We came about the elk prince," said Sean Michael. "Is Mama visiting you? How long has she been here?"

"I saw her," said Bridget. "I just didn't know who she was. Is she the bad woman my mother is always—"

"Where were we in the elk story?" Kristin interrupted firmly. "Or maybe you don't want to hear it, Bridget." She gave Maeve's daughter a firm look, which caused

Bridget to close her mouth and push one toe against the other.

"Kristin, you and I were having an important discussion," Jack protested.

"Good afternoon, sir," said Sean Michael, noticing Jack in the doorway. "How are you?" He offered to shake hands, and Jack, unused to the company of children, shook the boy's hand awkwardly. "Are you making lots of money?" asked Sean Michael in the social tones he had picked up from callers at his parents' house.

"Lots," said Jack, glaring at Kristin.

"Not now, Mr. Cameron," she murmured. "So you've come about the elk prince?" She smiled at the children and invited them to sit down. Sean Michael and Phoebe pulled their mother over to the stiff red velvet settee and cuddled up to her.

"I the baby," said Liama, following and clambering into Ingrid's lap.

"She's *our* mother, Liama," said Phoebe in a lecturing tone. "*Your* mother is Augustina. Are you coming back to live at our house, Mummy? Are you bringing the piano back? That's our old piano, isn't it? Can Daddy have two wives?"

Ingrid sighed and looked to Kristin for help.

"Your mother is living here, Phoebe," said Kristin. "She's a partner in my new sausage-making business."

"I guess I could send the piano back," said Ingrid, who looked on the verge of tears again. She was holding both children clutched to her while Liama snuggled up, refusing to budge from her place on Ingrid's lap. She obviously felt that she belonged with her brother and sister, even if the blond woman wasn't her mother.

"I the baby sister," she offered at the first break in the conversation.

"If you're not coming home," said Phoebe, looking disappointed, "then we'll leave the piano here and come for lessons. Mrs. Pitts, my teacher, doesn't play at all like you used to, Mummy."

"Do you realize how much trouble this is going to cause?" Jack muttered to Kristin. "And Kat Macleod will blame me. You can bet on it."

"My mama's Kat," said Molly, who had been watching everyone, round-eyed, thumb in her mouth. "And my daddy's Connor." She removed her thumb. "But I can sit on your lap, just like I do Daddy's, while Kristin tells us about the elk princess." She was speaking to an astonished Jack.

"Prince," corrected Sean Michael from the sofa. "We never found out what happened when the Sir Bad Bear challenged the prince, who didn't have his horns any more."

"I'll bet the fairy godmother put them back," said Phoebe.

"She did not!"

"She did too."

"Actually, what happened," said Jack, remembering his first visit to Kristin, when she had pushed him out and he stood on the Macleod porch hearing part of the tale through the door, "is that the elk prince, who was very rich, paid a bunch of coyotes to chase Sir Bad Bear away, and off they went, the coyotes yiping at the bear's heels and the bear running for his life. The moral of the story is that even princes need to keep a watchful eye on their finances—"

"That's not what happened," hissed Kristin as the children all cheered.

"—and invest their money creatively. You see, children," said Jack, "the elk prince was smarter than anyone and didn't need big antlers to get the best of his enemies."

"You haven't an ounce of romance in your soul," muttered Kristin. "You're just a—just a money grubber."

"I'd be as romantic as you'd let me," murmured Jack, shifting Molly and waving a hand as if to invite Kristin to sit on his other knee.

"Horsey-back ride," crowed Molly.

"What?" Jack glanced, alarmed, at the little girl.

"Mrs. Kathleen Macleod," said Winifred, showing Kat into the drawing room. "Paying an afternoon call."

"Looking for her missing children," said Kat. "You might have sent word where they were, Kristin."

"I didn't know they hadn't asked permission," said Kristin.

Kat looked pointedly at Ingrid and her two children on the settee. "You always have your head in a paint jar, Kristin. As far as I know, you haven't even tried to sell Traube's Colorado Sausages anywhere but—"

Jack rose, handing Molly to her mother. "I'm sure you'll support me, Mrs. Macleod, in my suggestion that Kristin accompany me to Denver tomorrow. I have business and can escort her safely on her selling mission."

"I'm not—"

Kristin got no further, for Kat said, "That's a sensible idea."

"I can go on my own," said Kristin. "You do."

"So I do," Kat agreed, "but I'm older and better able to take care of myself, while you are young and extremely naive. You two can combine business with your wedding trip, which, as far as I know, you have not yet taken."

"I'm not going," said Kristin. Wedding trip sounded ominous to her, like something Sister Mary Joseph might have mentioned in her lectures about "the act." The church probably didn't approve of wedding trips.

"Kristin, I've put up a lot of money to establish Traube's Colorado Sausages, and I'm seeing no profits. I expect to hear that you have accepted Mr. Cameron's offer."

"I have painting to do. I couldn't possibly—"

"My dear, you really should stop counting on an income from art. I've showed everyone that lovely painting you did of Molly sitting on the carpet with her doll, and I'm afraid I wasn't able to talk anyone into commissioning a portrait. You'll never be self-supporting if—"

"She doesn't need to be," Jack interrupted. "I'm perfectly able to support her."

"All women should be able to support themselves," said Kat, giving him a look of haughty dislike.

"Certainly," Kristin agreed. "Considering the reason for our marriage, I'd hardly want to trust my well-being to you." She turned away from her angry husband and asked Kat why no one had been moved by the painting of Molly to want a portrait of their own.

"Oh, some think your painting is too fuzzy, and others—" Kat leaned forward and whispered, "It's Ingrid. Ladies won't come to your house because she's here. Is she, by any chance, thinking of leaving soon?"

Kristin shook her head.

"So you see," continued Kat, her voice at a normal level "you really must make a success of the sausage business."

"Why didn't you tell us Mama was back, Aunt Kat?" asked Phoebe.

"It was your father's place to do that," replied Kat "Good afternoon, Ingrid. You're looking much improved."

"Improved from what?" asked Sean Michael.

"Your mother has been ill," said Kat.

"Drunk," said Bridget. "That's what my mama says. She says—"

"That will do, Bridget," ordered Kat. "Now, children, we must all go home."

"I'm coming back for piano lessons," said Phoebe.

"So am I," said Sean Michael.

"Boys don't play the piano," said Bridget.

"Yes, they do. I peeked in a saloon door and saw—"

"Sean Michael Fitzpatrick," cried his aunt, "don't ever let me hear that you've been anywhere near a saloon."

"Aw, Aunt Kat, I just—"

"We're both coming for piano lessons," interrupted Phoebe. "Aren't we, Mummy?"

"I hope so," said Ingrid, her heart in her eyes.

Kat sighed. "Oh, Ingrid, what are we to do?" She shook her head, rounded up the children, and departed.

"We leave tomorrow," said Jack, following Kristin back to the studio, "and if you try to get out of it, I'll tell Mrs. Macleod on you."

"Sneak," Kristin hissed, and Jack grinned.

"Now maybe you'd like to tell me what she meant about Ingrid."

"Oh, nothing. Just that Ingrid used to be a—a something or other in West Breckenridge."

Jack groaned. "I can't believe I'm sharing my house with a prostitute, a gaggle of female sausage makers, and a herd of pigs."

"You're not," said Kristin, "because it's not your house. Maybe you should return to Chicago."

Even in Jack's unsettling company, Kristin was beside herself with delight. What a difference from her first train trip through the mountains! Now aspen leaves brushed her shoulder through the open windows of the train, lupine and wild roses bloomed in the meadows, and except for the high peaks, the snow was gone. On the other hand, with the train windows open, her smart blue suit and pretty hat were being showered with soot and cinders from the engine stack. Still, she refused to let Jack take the window seat. Better to arrive in Denver looking like a coal miner than to miss all the opportunities to sketch.

"Why do you keep sketching those unpainted mine buildings?" Jack asked, for he kept his eye as much on her sketches as on the passing scenery.

"Because I have a mural commission when I return. If you hadn't got Kat to persuade me to go to Denver with you, I'd be doing a mural on the walls of the Single Jack Cafe this very minute. It's owned by Hortense, who was a Chicago Girl, and Eyeless Ben Waterson, who raised Connor's older children from his first marriage. I thought since so many of the customers were miners, they'd feel at home with mining pictures."

"Or better yet, dance hall girls," muttered Jack.

"What was that?" Kristin did a quick sketch of a stamp mill backed by a hill of mine tailings. "Look! Look at that stream!" The train had curved around a base of solid rock, revealing a vista of mountain meadow, edged by pine, carpeted with swirls of wildflowers, and bisected by a meandering stream with a rocky bed. Kristin's pencil flew.

"That's good news about the mural," said Jack. "A real step forward for the town as well as for you."

She glanced at him with surprise, having expected that he'd object to any success of hers. She remembered Mrs. Hallowell doubting that a husband would support his wife's art career. Was that why Mrs. Drusilla Weems had left her husband? Mr. Cameron was surprisingly complacent over Kristin's success. She had to wonder why. Could he be proud of her talent? Her heart did a traitorous flip of happiness at the thought. Or had he finally decided to leave without contributing further to her support?

"Maybe now you can consider giving up the sausage business," said Jack.

Kristin frowned. "Without paying Kat back?"

"I could do that."

"You just don't want me to be independent."

"I just don't care much for pigs in the parlor and a house full of giggling sausage makers. What if we wanted to have a dinner party?"

"I don't want to have a dinner party," said Kristin. "And it's my duty to continue with the sausage making. For Kat's sake. And for Ingrid's. Especially Ingrid. What would she do if she had no means of supporting herself?"

"Go away and stop causing the Macleods grief? Frankly, I worry about leaving her in charge at the house."

"Yes," said Kristin thoughtfully. "I hope she does a proper job of handling the Sunday salon." For two Sundays, the drawing room had been mobbed with single men who had come in search of wives. Kristin welcomed them and oversaw their conduct, Winifred served tea and cookies, at a price, and Ingrid played the piano. Occasionally, in response to special requests, she sang a song or two. Although Ingrid's songs were very lively, Kristin had doubts about the lyrics. They seemed a bit odd to her and caused immoderate laughter among the men, even Jack, if he happened to be home.

Usually he went off to the Denver Hotel to visit with his friend, Robert Foote. Kristin suspected that they indulged in spirituous liquors on such occasions, although Reverend Passmore ran around town, especially on Sundays, preaching against saloons and drinking, demanding that people abide by the Sunday closing laws, which no one did. "We had a long discussion about her responsibilities," said Kristin, "but I must say Ingrid didn't seem to be taking much note."

"Well, she's an unusual person to serve as a chaperone," said Jack dryly.

"I think we should make every effort to be back by Sunday."

"Not possible." He smiled to himself. Although Kristin didn't know it, she was on her honeymoon.

"So how did it go?" asked Jack once the waiter had taken their orders. They were having dinner at their hotel after each had conducted an afternoon of business.

"Wonderfully," said Kristin. "It was much easier than I imagined. Everyone was so nice. I have orders from five restaurants and three butcher shops."

"That's very impressive." Jack gestured for the waiter to fill Kristin's glass from the bottle just opened.

"What is it?" she asked, glancing at the foaming, golden liquid flowing from the lip of the bottle, but Jack had hardly managed to shrug before she was off on an excited description of her sausage triumph. "You'll never guess what I did." Jack looked encouraging while he sipped his champagne. Kristin sipped too, sneezed as the bubbles tickled her nose, then giggled. "I cooked them a sample—those who had the facilities. Everyone agrees that it's very good sausage, if you like sausage. I don't, but many people do.

"And while the sausage was cooking, I drew sketches of the proprietors and presented them, free of charge. You'd be surprised at how flattered people are that an artist would want to do a picture of them." She waved to the waiter to refill her glass. Jack smiled. "And of course, I mentioned that I do portraits. No one actually gave me a commission, but I think at least three of the men are seriously considering the possibility."

"I don't doubt it," said Jack. "Are you still asking one hundred dollars a portrait?"

Kristin had the grace to blush and managed to avoid answering because the first course of their meal had arrived. "I think Kat will be very pleased, don't you?"

"I'm sure," Jack replied, watching as Kristin took a long swallow of her champagne and a spoonful of her soup. She had ordered steak as her main course, remarking, "Why anyone would eat pork when something else is available, I can't imagine."

"I wouldn't make that comment outside the family," Jack murmured.

She looked up at him in surprise, spoon suspended between her bowl and her mouth when she realized that he considered himself her family. What a strange idea! She glanced down at the beautiful ring on her finger, which Jack had insisted on buying at Sam Mayer's Diamond Palace before they went on their separate business errands. Kristin felt guilty about accepting the gift since she did not plan to honor her marriage vows, but Jack had insisted. He was generous to a fault. Perhaps to make up for his past conduct.

On their arrival in Denver, Kristin had been shown to her room in the Windsor Hotel by the desk clerk because she was covered with soot and needed to change. Jack had gone off to an appointment without checking in. So after dinner when they went upstairs, she received the shock of her life when Jack followed her into her room. His bags sat to the left of the four-poster bed. "There must be some mistake," she stammered. "This is my room."

"And mine," he replied, removing his coat and beginning to unbutton his waistcoat. "As Kat said, this is our wedding trip. Surely you expected to share a room."

"I certainly did not," Kristin declared, backing toward the door, wondering what she was to do. She had spotted her own baggage over by the wardrobe where the maid had unpacked it. Although she didn't doubt that she could go downstairs and demand a room for herself, it would be embarrassing. Still, she was quite prepared to do it— anything rather than share that bed with Jack Cameron, who had brought all this trouble down upon her with his unprincipled conduct. It was hard enough to resist his charm at a distance.

But she'd have to repack all her things—the gowns hanging in the wardrobe, her more intimate garments. What if he stood where he was now standing and watched as she removed her chemises, her corsets, her drawers and repacked them? Worse, what if he wouldn't let her take them away? She'd have to sleep in a strange hotel room with no nightdress. Kristin couldn't imagine sleeping naked. Sister Mary Joseph had said that women should always wear proper, modest clothing, including nightdresses that covered them from chin to toes, from shoulder to fingertips. She said such nightgowns were particularly important for married women so that they would not rouse the lusts of their husbands and thus promote the occasion for sin.

"I'd love to know what you are thinking, Kristin," said Jack. "Your face is a study."

"I was thinking of Sister Mary Joseph at St. Scholastica," she replied severely.

"I'm very glad to hear that," said Jack as he began to unbutton his shirt.

Good heavens, thought Kristin. Surely he wasn't going to bare any part of his body in front of her? Sister had been very clear that husbands and wives were to prepare for bed in the dark or in separate rooms and *both* were to wear modest, all-encompassing garments if they shared a bed. Sister advised against it for those who could afford separate rooms.

Not that it mattered. Kristin wasn't getting in bed with him. He probably planned to commit "the act" with her, and after that, having got her with child, he'd insist on going back to Chicago, with or without her.

She found herself staring with amazement at the interesting musculature of his now naked chest, at the pattern of hair that spread in curls around his nipples and then narrowed in a triangle toward his trousers. His shoulders and upper arms were smooth, long, and muscular, the skin over them a darker shade than her skin. She'd just like two minutes—well, maybe five—to sketch that torso, so different from her own, so intriguing.

"I'm sure Sister Mary Joseph mentioned that wives have a certain duty toward their husbands. Father Boniface Wirtner mentioned that duty in the marriage ceremony."

What had the priest said? Kristin couldn't remember. She had been so ambivalent about the marriage, torn between fascination, fear, and resentment, that she had paid little attention to the vows. Now Jack was walking toward her, stepping between her and the door, a lazy, beguiling smile on his face. Maybe he meant to leave after all, although he was only partially dressed. She tore her eyes away from his body, wishing he hadn't shaved off his mustache. She'd found him at least somewhat less attractive with it. Jack's long fingers closed around her arm well above the elbow so that the backs of his nails rested against her breasts. Kristin tried to pull away.

"You have rights over my body," he murmured in a low voice that sent shivers up her spine.

"That's all right," Kristin stammered. "I'm really not interested in—"

"And I have rights over yours, rights which I *am* interested in. And intend to exercise."

203

Elizabeth Chadwick

Kristin backed another two steps, and he followed, curving a hand over her other arm. He stroked up, then down, fingers still placed so that the nails and first knuckles brushed both breasts. Kristin felt her nipples hardening the way they did when the water went cold in her bath or she had to dress on a cold morning with no fire in the grate. Except that she was not cold. Jack's hands, Jack's body warmth, so close to hers, sent heat flooding from the lightly touched breasts outward.

"I realize that traditionally a gentleman joins his bride *after* she has had a chance to prepare herself for bed," Jack murmured.

His voice was somehow different—lower, deeper, very disturbing to her, as if by its timbre he sought to tell her something beyond words, and the words were disturbing enough—*bed . . . bride.* Kristin was trembling, moving backward, but for each step she took, his was longer, bringing him closer.

"Unfortunately, I'm afraid that if I were gentlemanly enough to leave, you'd lock the door behind me."

"You can leave," she stammered. "I won't—" She couldn't finish because he was pressing the backs of his fingers against the sides of her breasts.

"Aren't you ashamed?" he murmured.

She was. He had moved so close that the hair on his chest brushed against the crimson-and-cream silk of her bodice. Through two layers of clothing, Kristin thought she could feel that curling hair against her nipples.

"Not only have you shirked your wifely duty, but you've just lied to your husband."

"I have?" His mouth was closing in on hers, and she felt bewildered.

"You'd lock the door"—still clasping her arms, he pulled her tight against him—"if you had the chance."

Because she had taken another step backward, she found herself pressed against the bed when Jack finally kissed her, caught between the hard heat of his body and the beckoning softness of the deep mattress against her thighs, bottom, and waist.

"So I'm not going to be so gentlemanly," he murmured against her lips and deepened the kiss again. The pressure of his mouth was the most compelling, exciting thing she'd ever felt. "I'm going to play it safe for once in my life. Undress you myself."

"*What?*" The shocked response allowed him access to her parted lips, and he slid his tongue along the tender underside. Dizzy with the intimate, brandy taste of his tongue, Kristin tried to push him away. Undress her? Her heart was accelerating into a panic. Confused echoes of Sister Mary Joseph's strictures ricocheted in her befuddled mind, but Jack wouldn't be pushed. He lifted her off the floor and perched her on the edge of the mattress.

"It's too early for—" Before she could say what it was too early for, he had reached down to slide one slipper from her foot. Then he ran his hand from her foot and ankle all the way up the inner side of her limb, taking her skirt and petticoats along. "*Stop that!*" Horrified, Kristin tried to squirm away, only to find that he had stepped between her thighs and pulled her tight against him.

"Put your legs around my waist, sweetheart," he murmured.

"*No!*"

In response to her refusal, he slid his hands under her skirts, cupping her bottom and rolling her against something that bulged in his trousers. Kristin didn't know what it was and began to cry.

"Sh-sh-sh," Jack whispered and moved his hands up so that his arms encircled her waist. He began to drop kisses on her eyes, her wet cheeks, her mouth and chin, even her ears. Kristin blinked, less frightened now that he wasn't pressing against her down there anymore. The kisses were light and sweet, and he was murmuring to her in a wordless, reassuring way, stroking her neck and back, her arms and shoulders.

She sighed, eyes closed, forehead against his lips. If he'd just let her scoot off the bed, move away so that she could close her legs, but at least he wasn't—oh dear, he was rubbing the side of one breast again, making the nipple ache and tingle. She thought he'd asked if she liked that, but before she could answer, he covered her mouth, and she felt cooler air on her back as she realized that he had somehow undone the buttons on her dress while she was so bemused with new sensations and anxieties.

He moved his lips immediately to her throat. Of its own accord, Kristin's head drooped back while he kissed her throat and slid everything—her dress, her chemise—from her shoulders. She tried to stop him, but the chemise straps bound her arms, and he kissed her bare breasts.

"So pretty," he whispered, right against her nipple, and then he kissed it. Kristin went weak with shock. She had a terrible ache low in her stomach where he had pressed against her before.

"I think I'm sick," she whimpered.

Jack laughed low in his throat. "Feverish maybe," he said, mouth still fastened to her breast, fingers disposing of her corset strings.

"What are you—"

The corset came away. She heard it hit the floor and then his lips drew on her, and her whole body bucked as sensation ran like summer lightning in every direction— through her breasts all the way to her fingertips, through her aching loins and thighs and down until her toes curled.

She was helpless to resist when his hands encircled her bare waist, one thumb brushing into her navel and sending another shock through her. Somehow while she lay back, his tongue tormenting her breasts, he had undone all her buttons—dress buttons, petticoat tapes, the button that held her drawers. She felt everything being swept away, and he lifted her up, naked, to kiss her.

What she had imagined before, she now felt, the electrifying abrasion of his hair against her breasts, which were agonizingly tender. She groaned, wished he'd come closer, couldn't think. Her breasts pulsed, ached for another touch, but Jack was sitting beside her on the bed, kissing her mouth. Beside her! Kissing her ear, licking it. She shivered and tried to pull him against her breasts.

"Minute," he muttered, bending. She opened her eyes and saw that he was taking off his second sock. That he had no . . . no clothes . . . at all . . . on. What she had wished for before, she now got. He pulled her onto the bed, rolling with her, on top of her, between her legs again, his hands circling behind her thighs to—she gasped, her hips rising of their own accord. And then he *hurt* her.

"*Stop that!*" she cried, trying to squirm away. "What are you *doing?*"

Jack sighed and murmured, "Hush . . . hush," and the pressure abated. His fingers returned, touching, stroking, rubbing, sliding into her a little. She twisted beneath his touch, gasped, sighed, forgot the hurt as pleasure built and flowered, and she reached with her hips for whatever was coming, something so wonderful, so catastrophic that she let him press into her again because she had to find it, that explosion of feeling, that throbbing that burst in her and in Jack too. She felt it happen.

"Good lord!" he muttered into her tangled hair as his body went limp and heavy upon hers. Kristin lay still as the pulsing slowed, died slowly . . . slowly, leaving her as light as the kiss of sunshine on a mild spring day, light enough to float away, a spring leaf on the wind, light enough to disappear like a white bird flying into mist. Jack's weight was gone, but his warmth remained. She snuggled her head into his shoulder, smooth skin under her cheek, tickling curls against her chin.

"I must be the prince," he murmured against her hair. "Because I won the princess."

"M-m-m," she breathed, turning her face so that her lips brushed his chest. She was floating free, her mind as blank and lazy as a cloud in a blue sky.

Chapter Thirteen

Kristin awoke and wiggled deliciously under the silky sheets. She wouldn't have believed one's body could feel so happy. Turning on her side toward the empty pillow, she studied the indentation at the edge. He had slept all night beside her, perhaps holding her while she swam in exquisite dreams, in rosy, drifting hues like a perfect dawn. If any art lover would buy pictures of color without subject, she could paint such a canvas, fill it with the glowing, pearly light of satiety, cloud wisps of happiness, and brilliant explosions of dark ecstasy.

Her body stiffened as she stopped feeling and began to think. *That,* she realized, had been "the act" of which Sister Mary Joseph had had so much to say. Oh Holy, Blessed Mother of God! What had she done? Jack hadn't lied; the kiss, the touch, they hadn't been anything compared to what happened last night. The unbelievable, unimaginable *act.* How had the first people ever thought to do such a thing? How had they ever imagined that they'd *like* such a thing? If anyone had described it to Kristin, she would have run for her life.

The serpent must have put it into their heads. And she—Kristin—had fallen under the serpent's spell as easily as Eve, because, contrary to Sister Mary Joseph's warnings, Kristin had enjoyed it. She was even afraid that if Jack wanted to do it again, she'd enjoy it again, because he knew exactly how to make her do so. He was, God help her, the devil's follower; Jack too had enjoyed it, and she was willing to bet that he hadn't given a thought to procreation. Anymore than she had.

Sister Mary Joseph had absolutely said one should never, *never* commit "the act" without procreation in mind. Kristin herself hadn't had even one fleeting thought about babies. She wasn't sure she'd had any thoughts at all until just this minute. She groaned aloud and sat up in the luxurious bed. Mortal sin! That's what she had committed. A mortal sin that she couldn't mention to her priest. Good heavens! What if he asked her for details? If Sister Mary Joseph knew about "the act," no doubt Father Boniface Wirtner did. He might not even agree to absolve Kristin, no matter what the penance, no matter how sincere her act of contrition, if she ever got up the nerve to tell him what had happened.

She dropped her face into her hands, shivering. All these years she had thought herself a virtuous person, and yet lurking in her soul—no, in her body; last night had had nothing to do with souls—lurking in her body had been the seed of original sin. Seeds! How foolish she had been to think that seeds were planted by kisses. She had a very clear idea now of how seeds were planted, right where they grew, of course. But Jack would have planted no seeds. Sweet, innocent babies wouldn't grow from sin.

They would grow from proper, unenjoyable wifely submission. If anything grew in her womb, it would be a monster.

She'd stop thinking about it. But it was his fault that her immortal soul was in such danger! She could never have thought up the things he did—they did—last night. That's why he was gone, because he was ashamed of himself. And so he should be. She turned and hit his pillow with a small, clenched fist. The pillow crackled. She lifted her hand, and beneath it was a note from her husband. "Sweetheart," it said. That evil hypocrite, she thought. Calling her "sweetheart." "Sweetheart, have a lovely day shopping. See you this evening."

This evening? To do what? Well, Kristin was no dummy. She might not be able to control her sinful nature when he had his hands on her, but she didn't need to do that again. She'd—she'd leave town. That's what she'd do! What luck that Jack had given her so much money. God must have moved her to take it so she could escape.

Kristin sprang out of the bed as if the very sheets were contaminated. Unfortunately, she had forgotten how high the four-poster was and landed in a heap on the floor, discovering in the process that she wasn't wearing her nightdress. Sister Mary Joseph had been very clear about what married couples should wear to bed. Lots! That's what she'd said. And Kristin wasn't wearing anything. She was naked! Sitting on the flowered carpet in the middle of an elaborate garland, rubbing her foot, and sniffling.

What if she'd broken her foot and couldn't escape? She edged cautiously toward the bottom of the bed, pulled herself up on a hand-carved bedpost, and gingerly put weight on the injury. Oh, thank God! It didn't hurt any worse or buckle under her. She limped toward the wash basin and ewer, intent on scrubbing every vestige of Jack's touch from her body. If only she could do the same for her soul. Wishing she had time to order a tub, Kristin washed with rough haste, noting that he had injured her, remembering the pain—and the pleasure that followed.

She chose a flared navy skirt, a high-collared white blouse bedecked with tucks and ruffles, and a navy jacket to go over it, topped by a navy boater with a kelly-green ribbon and bow. Because she would be traveling, she needed something dark to hide the showers of soot from the train. Then she quickly but carefully packed her cases, memories of all those wrinkled clothes that she had brought to Genevieve's prompting her to act with care.

Kristin gathered her luggage without anyone to help her and hastened to the broad stairway. Halfway down, she peeked into the lobby. Standing on the marble floor under the great chandelier were her husband, that snake, and three other men. Kristin scrambled back up the stairs, juggling her belongings awkwardly, and hurried down a mile of Brussels carpet to her room.

Once she was safely behind the door, it occurred to her that he might return to the room, so she picked up her things, scurried out, and waited around the corner. No one arrived but maids. After fifteen minutes, she crept back down the stairway and peeked cautiously into the lobby, then hastened across to the desk.

"Was that my husband I saw?" she asked.

"Ah—" The clerk paused. "That'd be Mr.—"

"Cameron. Of Breckenridge."

"Oh yes, but I'm sorry, ma'am. He's gone."

Kristin smiled brightly. "I'm checking out. He has to stay longer on business, so he'll pay the bill."

"Yes, ma'am."

Kristin hurried out the door, looked furtively both ways, and headed for the Union Depot, which was so large and had such a distinctive mansard roof that she couldn't miss it. Once inside, she wove through the crowd to Seamus McFinn's baggage room. "Good morning, Mr. McFinn," she said.

"Why, young Miss Traube. Say, there was a fellow lookin' for you a while back. Don't recall exactly when."

"Yes," said Kristin. "If he comes around again, I hope you won't tell him where I've gone."

"Wouldn't think of it. Didn't the first time," said Seamus. He was one of several men who had proposed to her during her first stay in Denver. "Where *are* you goin'?"

"What's the first train out of here?"

"Well. Reckon that's the excursion train—to Golden, Black Hawk, Central City, Georgetown, an' Silver Plume."

"Excellent," said Kristin. "Just point me in the right direction, and I'll buy a ticket."

Mr. McFinn's eyebrows shot up. "'Tis for sightseein' an' the thrill of the Georgetown Loop, so unless you want to go to one of them towns—"

"I do. Which window?"

"Over at the Union Pacific there. They bought out the Colorado Central."

"Nice to see you again, Mr. McFinn." She picked up her belongings and scampered to the Union Pacific ticket window.

"You're in for some thrills and chills, ma'am," said the ticket seller.

Chills? "When does it leave?"

"Momentarily, ma'am. You'll have to hurry." He pointed to the gate where a crowd of gaily dressed tourists milled about. "Less you want to go this afternoon."

Kristin rushed across the depot and slipped in among the tourists. When Jack discovered her absence, he'd never

213

think of looking for her on an excursion train. Several minutes later, she climbed aboard, hauling her sketchbook, her sausage sample case, her clothing valises, and her parasol.

"What a charming hat," said her seat companion. "I'd never have thought of matching navy blue and Irish green."

"I'm delighted that you like it," said Kristin. "I changed the ribbon myself." She was about to tell the lady that she was an artist, then thought better of it. Jack would be looking for an artist, so if she were smart, she wouldn't do any drawing. It seemed a pity, for she had the window seat, and they were bound to see something of note. At the first rumble from the engine, she put up her parasol.

"That's bad *luck!*" said the woman.

"Soot and cinders are about to shower us," Kristin explained and thrust the parasol over the window opening.

"Faith, we'll all be killed with you putting up that—"

"Have you ever had a cinder in your eye? It's worse than death."

"What an unlucky thing to say," cried the woman and changed her seat. Kristin was delighted. With no one sitting beside her, she could sketch.

"Your ticket, miss." Kristin handed it to the conductor. "Finest scenery in the world coming up, ma'am," he assured her. "Just don't scream too loud when we're on the high bridge of the Georgetown Loop." Kristin swallowed hard, remembering her terror as they crossed the Gold Pan Trestle over Illinois Gulch. This trip couldn't be worse than that one. "Most ladies like to come with a gentleman," said the conductor, handing back her ticket. *Oh?* she thought. *Like Jack, the snake?*

Before she could get her sketchbook out, Kristin dozed off, having had a tiring night, and didn't awake until the train pulled into Golden. Hoping that she hadn't missed any beautiful vistas, stifling a yawn, she got out her sketch book just as a buxom lady in a plum-colored skirt and shirtwaist and a black straw hat with a twelve-inch purple feather fell into the seat beside Kristin. *If I'd stayed in Denver, I'd have had new hats,* thought Kristin. He'd urged her to buy hats, dresses, jewelry.

"Oh, my blessed Aunt Molly, you're an artist!" the woman exclaimed.

"Just a doodler," Kristin mumbled, remembering that she didn't want anyone telling Jack about a real artist.

"My name is Kelly," said the woman. "Kelly, same as the color of your hat band. That's a strange color combination, but I suppose it's because you're one of them fine ladies who likes to draw and paint because it's fashionable."

Kristin wanted to defend her, well, semi-professional status, but she couldn't really do it and maintain her anonymity. Instead she tried to look vacuous.

"I never had no opportunity for them ladylike pastimes," said the woman.

"It's very pleasant," mumbled Kristin. As if galvanized by the mountains themselves, into which they had moved while she slept, her hand began to sketch the outlines, the shadings. Oh, it was beautiful! She was glad she'd taken this particular train. "How long does the trip last?" she asked.

"You'll be back to Denver in time for dinner. It's only fifty-four miles to Silver Plume."

"What?" The train was going to carry her straight back into her husband's lascivious clutches?

"This is a tourist junket."

He'd be waiting for her in the depot, warm smile, hot eyes, tempting hands and body.

"The train goes up to Silver Plume and then comes right back, giving you two chances to have the vapors between Georgetown and the end of the line."

The thought of that body, the parts she'd seen, touched . . . "The vapors?" mumbled Kristin, trying to drive Jack's tantalizing image from her mind. Vapors? Was Mrs. Kelly a patent medicine saleswoman? Was she about to try to sell Kristin some weird—

"Most young ladies like to go with a suitor, so they can swoon into the fellow's arms on the high bridge. I'm surprised a pretty thing like you isn't with a suitor."

For the first time it occurred to Kristin to remove her wedding ring. She hated to do it; the ring was so beautiful. Still—she slipped it off under cover of the sketchpad, put it into her reticule, and resumed sketching.

"Not much of a talker, are you? Maybe you're too high-toned to chat with someone like me?"

"Not at all," Kristin protested halfheartedly. In the silence that followed Kristin did rapid sketches of everything that passed, including mines. By running away, she was passing up that commission to do a mural on the walls of the Single Jack Cafe. She had many sketches of miners from her first trip to Breckenridge and sketches of mines from the Denver trip with Jack, although mines weren't, in truth, very pretty. They were a blight on the beauty of the mountainsides.

She couldn't believe the train went back to Denver, back to her husband. Why hadn't she asked Mr. McFinn more about the route? Now she'd have to get off somewhere and stay the night in a hotel, which reminded her of the Windsor Hotel, which reminded her of Jack. Of its own volition, her hand began a new sketch. She was shading in the hair on his torso when Mrs. Kelly exclaimed, "That's a naked man!"

Kristin, caught unaware, stammered, "Only part of one."

"I ain't never been so shocked in my life!"

"He's my brother." Since she'd concealed her ring, she couldn't say that he was her husband.

"What kind of a family stares at each other unclothed?" Kristin flushed as she looked at her drawing, which showed Jack's chest, navel and some of his stomach. Fascinating musculature. She remembered it in detail, as much as she'd seen, although at the time she certainly hadn't been thinking about art, not while he was luring her into "the act." Mrs. Kelly gathered up a voluminous carpet bag that sat at her feet and stamped down the aisle, muttering to herself. Kristin flipped the page and began to sketch the approach to Blackhawk.

Having had difficulty keeping his mind on mining syndication, Jack stopped at the room to see if his sweet wife might be taking a nap or having her midday meal sent up. She was probably a bit sleepy. Jack chuckled. What a lucky man he was! And what a surprise she was! Her kisses had been very satisfactory—both in her father's house and in Breckenridge, but making love to Kristin was a real treat. A man didn't expect a virgin bride to be so ardent. He slipped his key in the lock, thinking that the new syndicate was going to make him a rich man and his new wife was going to make him happier than he was rich.

By George, if he found her in, he'd send a note to his partners postponing the finalization until tomorrow. He'd take Kristin shopping himself. Better yet, they'd stay here and enjoy . . . Jack scanned the room, puzzled. Nothing of hers in sight. He stalked over to the wardrobe. Empty!

Jack took the stairs three at a time. "Have you seen my wife?" he demanded of the desk clerk.

The man blinked. "The pretty blond lady? She checked out this morning."

"*Going where?*"

The clerk began to stammer. "S-s-she d-d-didn't say. M-maybe h-home? To B-breck . . ."

Damn girl! She'd run away again. She hadn't sniveled or cried or complained the way he'd heard some brides did. In fact, she'd had a good time. Damned if she hadn't, so why had she run off? He headed straight for Pinkerton's.

Kristin successfully concealed her terror on the three trestles and double switchbacks between Blackhawk and Central City. Surely the rest of the trip held nothing worse than that. She sketched, drawing and flipping pages as fast as she could, noting that Georgetown looked like a lovely place. Maybe she'd stop there for the night. But no, it was too close to Denver, only two and a half hours from Central City, she noted, glancing at the watch pinned to her lapel. Next time the conductor came through, she'd ask if there was a depot where she could get off and take a train to some city other than Denver.

"Georgetown Loop coming up," called the conductor. "In the next two miles, we got two horseshoe curves and a complete loop, not to mention the high bridge which is one hundred feet above Clear Creek."

And up they went, the narrow-gauge train climbing the precipitous walls of Clear Creek Canyon until they crossed the spider-web trestle in the sky. Around her, the gentlemen turned pale. The ladies shrieked. Kristin's hands shook so badly that her drawings looked like the work of a woman crippled by old age and rheumatism. But she kept trying, stopping only once when they were on the highest trestle, a thing so fragile, so high, that her dinner from last night heaved in her stomach. On that trestle she didn't shriek; she did knock off her hat getting her head out the window to throw up. Happily, the other terrorized sightseers were in no condition to notice.

When she ducked back in, the conductor, looking worried, asked, "Are you all right, ma'am?"

"Just getting a better look at the view," she mumbled, dabbing her mouth with a lace handkerchief and deciding that, escape or no escape, she would get off in Silver Plume. However, in Silver Plume her knees weren't firm enough to hold her up. She only got as far as the aisle seat. As soon as the train started back, she closed her eyes and, no matter how much shrieking went on around her, kept them closed until the conductor called Georgetown.

Then she climbed down as he followed with her baggage. "Gonna stay the night in Georgetown?" he asked.

She nodded, thinking that she might never leave Georgetown. She wasn't sure now that she could get through the Blackhawk-to-Central City section again. Georgetown looked prosperous, the scenery beautiful. Perhaps there were people in the town's fine homes who would want their portraits painted. Jack had no reason to look for her here. She'd never heard him mention Georgetown. She'd never see him again. She'd be safe. Kristin blinked back tears. "What is the best place to stay?" she asked the conductor.

"Hotel de Paris," he replied without hesitation.

"Paris?" Kristin's sad, confused heart lifted a fraction. Maybe it was an omen. In Georgetown she would make lots of money and go on to Paris. When she got to France, she might even paint naked men! She'd already drawn part of one. If she did a whole one, she'd send it to her father just for spite. Or better yet, she'd enter it in a competition in Chicago. "Nude Male by Kristin Traube." They'd never live it down.

But she'd never see another male body as beautiful as Jack's, Kristin realized wistfully. She didn't really want to. Gathering all of her paraphernalia, she trudged off toward

Sixth Street and the Hotel de Paris, to which the conductor had given her detailed directions.

It was a long, two-story building of yellow stone with dark red crowns over the windows and doors, not her idea of a Parisian building. Nonetheless, the conductor had claimed that it was the best hotel between the Missouri River and San Francisco and had superb food, cooked by the owner himself, Louis Dupuy. Kristin staggered into the lobby under her burden of luggage and requested a room.

"You by yourself, ma'am?" asked the desk clerk.

"Do you see anyone else?" Why did he care?

"One minute, ma'am." The clerk disappeared, then returned with another man. "Monsieur Louis Dupuy," said the clerk as if announcing the king of France. The Frenchman gave her a thunderous frown.

"I would like to stay the night," she said, thinking, *Perhaps the rest of my life if I have enough money.*

"Are you married?" asked the owner in a most delightful accent.

"I am an artist," said Kristin evasively and decided to try some of her St. Scholastica French on him. *"Bonjour, monsieur,"* and she stumbled haltingly through a sentence.

"Please, mademoiselle, speak English. Your French is *très* deesgusteeng."

"That's just what Sister Denis Marie used to say." Kristin sighed. "Do you think if I ever get to Paris, I will be disliked because of my terrible French?"

"You are goeeng to Paris?" asked Monsieur Dupuy.

"It is the ambition of my life, but in the meantime I need a room. I was so frightened on the Georgetown Loop that I got off as soon as my knees would hold me up."

"I suppose you shrieked all ze way up and back," said the Frenchman disdainfully.

"No monsieur, not one shriek. I didn't even faint, which three other ladies did." She didn't mention throwing up off the high bridge, the subject being indelicate.

"Are you one of zese sporteeng women?"

"Oh no," said Kristin. "We played basketball at St. Scholastica and some tennis in the warm weather, but Sister George Augustine said I would never be an athlete."

"Basketball?" Monsieur Dupuy turned to his clerk.

"It's a game where people throw balls through hoops."

"*Mon dieu,* and women do zese? Why does she tell me about ze basketball when I asked her—"

"It is a sport."

Monsieur Dupuy roared with laughter. "Zat was not ze sport I had in mind."

Kristin looked confusedly from one to the other.

"Well, mademoiselle, perhaps you can stay ze night. I don't like women—"

"Oh, that's all right," said Kristin. "I don't much like men."

The little Frenchmen raised his eyebrows and said, "Show mademoiselle to a room." Then he disappeared, and Kristin was signed in and shown to a very comfortable room, where, without even unpacking, she lay down and fell asleep.

"Well, have you found her?" Jack asked the Pinkerton manager.

"Ten people at Union Depot saw a beautiful blonde wearing a navy boater with a kelly-green ribbon—"

"That's her."

"She was getting on the Georgetown Loop excursion train."

"She went on an *excursion?*"

"Yes, sir. She got off at Georgetown with all her baggage."

"Then she must plan to stay a while." Jack shook his head. "Why Georgetown?"

"Lot of wealthy folks in Georgetown," said the Pinkerton man, "and a fine hotel. Hotel de Paris."

"That's where she'll be staying," said Jack, remembering that she had dreamed of going to France.

"You want us to pick her up for you, sir? You'll have to swear out a warrant on a runaway wife."

"I'll get her myself tomorrow morning," said Jack. "If you hear anything new, let me know."

"Yes sir," said the Pinkerton man and gave Jack the departure times for the excursion train.

It was dark outside Kristin's windows when she awoke, wondering where she was. Then she remembered. "I hope I haven't missed dinner," she mumbled to herself. She'd had nothing to eat since the sumptuous meal in Denver the night before.

Kristin was very careful with her toilette, knowing that the French were particular about fashion. She chose a pale blue satin dinner dress with pale gold lace falling in two tiers from the edge of her shoulders to her elbows, edging the low, straight neckline, plunging in a deep V over her stomach, and banding the ruffles on the hem and train. With matching ribbons at the crown of her head, long gloves and a lace fan, she was ready to impress the only Frenchman she had ever met. Evidently she impressed someone, for when she went downstairs to dinner, Monsieur Dupuy himself came out of the kitchen, wearing a white chef's hat so tall that Kristin longed to paint it. There were few parties left in the dining room. "Am I too late?" she asked anxiously.

"No, mademoiselle. Eet eez pleasing to me to meet an American who dresses so well—" Kristin blushed with happiness. "—and who wishes to dine at ze civilized hour."

Kristin replied merrily, "This American is so hungry, she could probably eat everything on your menu."

"Can you afford everytheeng on my menu?" he asked, handing it to her.

She glanced at the prices. "No." She smiled. "But a few things."

"Then I weel choose them for you, mademoiselle." He left abruptly with Kristin looking after him in surprise, then glancing wistfully down at the menu, from which she would like to have chosen herself. Still, this was very exciting. She sat back to admire the dining room and peek at the other guests. In seconds, she had her sketchbook out, drawing faces.

"I don't like oysters," said Kristin sadly when the first plate was put in front of her.

"Well, ma'am, you'd better eat 'em," said the waiter. "Mon-sewer Dupuy fixed 'em up himself, and they're the best oysters in Colorado. Probably the best anywheres."

"Are they cooked?"

"Yes, ma'am."

"Well—" Bravely, she stuck her fork into one, getting as much of the sauce as she could, and put the whole thing in her mouth with her eyes closed and her face squinched up. "Why, they're delicious!" she exclaimed a second later.

The waiter smiled. "Himself will be glad to hear you think so."

As Kristin was eating her fourth oyster, Monsieur Dupuy appeared at her table with a bottle of wine. "So, you 'ave decided you like oysters?"

"Only yours," said Kristin. "Can I have a second helping?"

"*Non, non, mademoiselle.*" He plunked down the wine bottle.

"I don't drink," she said, cowering away.

"Fine food must be accompanied by fine wine." He poured some into her glass.

"Surely, you don't expect me to drink the whole bottle?"

Monsieur Dupuy sighed. "Since you are only a woman, I suppose I can not expect zat much. Now, drink!"

Timidly, Kristin took a sip. "It's very good."

"Now, another oyster."

She popped another oyster into her mouth and chewed.

"More wine."

From then to the meal's end, Monsieur Dupuy sat at her table like a bossy mother and supervised every bite and sip.

"I have never tasted such food in my life," she said as she was eating duck.

"Of course not. Zere eez no such food anywhere else."

"I wonder," said Kristin, "if you would be interested in buying some of my sausage?"

He scowled at her.

"I have a sausage factory in Breckenridge," she explained. To which she couldn't return, unless she was sure Jack wouldn't be there as a source of mortal temptation. Still, Ingrid had to make *her* living.

"French sausage?"

"No, German sausage."

"German food eez ze worst in ze world. Except for English. Are you German?"

"I had a Swedish great-grandmother."

"Ze Swedes are not much better."

"But—"

"No mademoiselle, I weel not buy your sausage."

"But you haven't tasted it. It's very good."

"I have ze delicate palate. And now, mademoiselle. Dessert! *Crème brûlée*. Eat it."

"*Oui, monsieur.*"

"*Mon dieu.* You can't even say *oui* properly."

But Kristin was already sampling the *crème brûlée*. "Monsieur, an angel must sit on your shoulder as you cook."

Monsieur Dupuy's stern face fell into pleased lines. "And you, mademoiselle, are a woman who has obviously overcome an unfortunate heritage."

"Let me ask you, monsieur, have you ever thought of murals in your hotel? They would make a lovely addition."

"And who would paint zese murals?"

"I would, of course," said Kristin.

"But mademoiselle, you have already told me zat you have never been to Paris. If I commission murals, zey would have to be of Paris."

"Oh."

The few people in the restaurant were whispering among themselves. No one who knew Louis Dupuy and the Hotel de Paris had heard of the Frenchman spending an entire meal sitting with a young lady, much less actually smiling at her. He was a known hater of women.

"Jack Cameron?"

Jack turned at the voice. "Cal!"

Within seconds, the two men were slapping each other on the back. "Cal Bannister, what are you doing in Denver?"

"Having dinner with you, I reckon," said the young man with unruly blond hair and brown eyes. "Have you tried Pell's Fish House?"

"No, but I'm game." The two went off together toward the beckoning lighted windows of Pell's with its large marquee touting Pell's clams and Pell's oysters.

"What are you doing in Denver?" asked Cal when their first course had been served.

"What I was born to do—make money," said Jack. "What are you doing here?"

"Looking for money," said Cal. "I expect to be a millionaire by this time next year if I can come up with a little financing."

Jack's eyes sharpened. "Have you found a gold mine?"

"This place will make the whole *country* rich."

"Oh? Where is it?"

"Are you interested in financing me?"

Cal Bannister had been one of the smartest students at Yale, with a flair for science and engineering and the kind of enthusiasm that should make him a fine prospector. If he'd taken it up and said that he knew where there was gold, Jack believed him. "I can provide you exploration money, and if your prospects look good, I'll round up investors."

"By God, I knew my luck was in today."

"Now, tell me where this place is."

"Cripple Creek."

That sounded familiar. What had he heard about it? Oh, the mining hoax! "Ah—rumor has it—"

"It's a volcanic area, Jack. I'd bet my place in heaven that it's laced with veins of gold—tellurides of gold—and I'm not the only one who thinks so. The assays so far are impressive. Besides that, in the last twenty years the costs of hard-rock mining have been cut two thirds—the smelting, the shaft timbering, even the dynamite and fuses. And Jack, we could see a plunge in the price of labor costs too. If the government stops supporting silver—"

"—the silver mines will close," Jack agreed. He believed that would happen. That was why he refused to buy into Colorado silver interests.

"And the miners it puts out of work will drive the wages down. If we're going to buy in, now's the time."

"And you're sure about the gold?"

"Dead sure."

"Well, you've got your financing."

"We're going to be very rich," said Cal, grinning. The two men raised glasses of champagne to one another. "Shall we celebrate by going over to the House of Mirrors?"

"On Market Street?"

"Fanciest parlor house in town."

"With a madam who finances herself through blackmail," said Jack, thinking of his pretty wife.

"Well, if you're going to be picky, how about Mattie Silk's place?"

Jack shook his head. He really hadn't any interest in Market Street. Tomorrow he'd be in Georgetown at the Hotel de Paris with Kristin, who was both more beautiful and more exciting than any trollop. With a little experience, he imagined she'd even be more talented in bed. But why had she run away?

Chapter Fourteen

"They're in the basement," said Mrs. Hamill when Jack presented himself at the front door of William Hamill's Gothic revival house on Argentine Street in Georgetown. "The general is showing her the—"

"I'm her husband," interrupted Jack, "who would like to show her the way home."

Mrs. Hamill raised her eyebrows delicately. "Mrs. Traube-Cameron didn't mention you."

"I'm sure," said Jack. Traube-Cameron? Maybe he should be glad she hadn't dropped the Cameron. He could have been discussing gold prospects at Cripple Creek with Cal Bannister; instead he was chasing his runaway wife over high trestles and breathtaking switchbacks amid squealing tourists and pursuing her into a hotel run by a bad-tempered Frenchman who had said that "for a woman" Kristin had a "fair palate." Jack had had a bad moment there, remembering how alcohol affected Kristin, but he didn't really believe that she'd been sharing her concealed passions with the misogynistic Mr. Dupuy.

And now, in order to retrieve his errant wife, Jack was forced to embarrass himself with the family of General William A. Hamill, veteran of the Ute Wars and many a mining triumph. Mrs. Hamill led him to a narrow stairway, explaining that her husband was showing Kristin the furnace. "The general is very proud of his furnace," she said. "Almost as proud of his furnace as of his solarium and his . . ." They were making their way down a steep staircase, and Jack, hearing the light, sweet tones of his wife's voice, almost forgave her for running away.

"We've got two feet of soft brick around the furnace," boomed a man's voice, presumably the general's.

"My dear, here's Mr. Cameron, come to fetch his wife."

The general looked up, as did Kristin. How had Jack found her? Kristin wondered. And how angry was he? For her part, it was almost a relief to see him. The general didn't want his portrait painted. He had said he owned one portrait; any more would be a vanity. He also had a painting of his wife and five children; again, one was enough. Having disposed of that matter, he pointed out all the glories of his solarium, in which Kristin had found him sitting—the curved glass walls and ceiling, the exotic plants, the pewter statue of a boy.

She had inspected his office with the suspended spiral stairway that didn't reach the third floor; his stable with its dovecote for squabs; his modern, walnut-enclosed zinc bathtub; his French camel-hair wallpaper, gold-plated doorknobs, and porcelain fireplace tiles; his gas lights for which he had his own carbide gas factory—even the elaborate six-seat privy with walnut seats for family, pine for servants. They ended up here in the basement inspecting the cast-iron furnace, which she was sure would be a very nice thing in the winter, but in the meantime Kristin was tired of exclaiming politely over the general's establishment. And Jack was glowering.

"General William A. Hamill." The general shook hands with Jack. "You'll be interested in this furnace, young man." And he began all over again his description of the furnace. "It sends heat to the hall, parlor, and dining room," he told Jack. Much to Kristin's irritation, Jack *was* interested, and the two men stood discussing central heating while Mrs. Hamill beamed maternally. "Maybe you'd like to see the privy house," said the general. "It's an innovation much admired. Separate sections and entrances for family and servants. A very superior privy if I do say so myself."

"It sounds so," Jack agreed. "Unfortunately, my wife and I have a train to catch."

"Ah, well then, you won't want to miss it," said the general and led the way up the basement stairs.

"I don't have a train to catch," hissed Kristin.

"If you don't catch it," said Jack, "your baggage will go to Denver without you."

"Of all the nerve! I didn't give you permission—"

"I guess this means you won't have time to share a meal with us," said Mrs. Hamill.

"I'm afraid not, ma'am. We have business in Denver."

"Would you be the mining syndicate Cameron, newly arrived in the territory from Chicago?" asked the general.

"Yes, sir."

"Well, there are fortunes to be made in mining. No one's a better example of that than I."

Jack nodded politely, thinking that if the general didn't get out of the silver market, he might lose that fortune, or at least a good part of it.

At the mention of fortunes and the realization that she was going back to Breckenridge, Kristin was reminded of her secondary business and said to Mrs. Hamill, "I have a sausage factory in Breckenridge. Would you care to place an order for Traube's Colorado Sausage?"

"Why, I don't know, dear. We do like sausage."

"Then let me fry some up for you," Kristin offered. "I've been doing sausage tastings all over Denver and several here in Georgetown."

"We don't have time," said Jack.

"Well, Jack," said Kristin, "I don't try to interfere with your business activities. "I don't think you should—"

"I don't approve of women in business *or* missing trains," the general broke in. "To whom did you sell your sausage? Dupuy?"

"I'm afraid he doesn't like food of German origin. We got along famously—"

Jack glowered at her.

"—but he said only French sausage is edible."

"In that case, we'll take some," said the general. "Mrs. Hamill, tell the young lady how much you'll need."

Mrs. Hamill put in an order while Jack waited impatiently, never letting go of Kristin's arm. She feared he'd leave a bruise, as hard as he was holding her. As if he thought she was stupid enough to believe that he couldn't catch up with her in a foot race, she who had been such an athletic disaster at St. Scholastica.

"Why the hell did you leave?" demanded Jack once they reached the street and headed for the depot.

"*You* left." Kristin's mind was whirling. What should she say? She wasn't going to mention the sin of having enjoyed the night's activities in Denver.

"I left a note. You didn't."

"I didn't want you to find me," said Kristin.

"Why? And don't tell me any silly stories about your

shock at wedding-night doings. You had every bit as good a time as I did."

Kristin turned pink. "I did not."

"You did too."

"It's sinful."

"What do you mean? We're married."

"Well, obviously you don't know anything about sin."

"I imagine I know a good deal more than you do."

"Not about married sin."

"There's no such thing," said Jack.

"I can't believe you said that."

"Name me one. Aside from the fact that you've been shirking your wifely duty—that's a sin."

"Under the circumstances, it isn't at all."

"What circumstances? In what way do you think we've sinned?"

Two ladies passing them on the street stared, open-mouthed, from beneath their parasols.

"Sh-sh," said Kristin.

"Don't put me off, Kristin, unless you'd like to discuss our sins in front of a train full of people."

Kristin swallowed. That was a daunting thought. "Well, in the first place, you weren't thinking about procreation. That's absolutely the only reason anyone does the—*the act.*"

Jack roared with laughter. "*The act?*"

"I beg your pardon?" said a gentleman in a frock coat.

"Much you know why people perform the act," Jack added, ignoring the indignant passerby. "Actually, at this point I suppose you do know."

"I do not. I know that procreation is the only—"

"And you don't know what I was thinking. If you weren't thinking about procreation, then shame on you." Kristin turned a brighter pink. "Anything else?"

"We weren't wearing clothing."

"Clothing? It's somewhat awkward to perform *the act*, as your call it, with all your—"

"Night clothing!"

"Ah, night clothing. Well, I'll try to remember night clothing next time we're in the bedroom together."

"There won't be a next time," said Kristin angrily. "I'll not risk my immortal soul because you don't know anything about marriage proprieties. If you ever, ever approach me again in that way, I shall run away and never be found."

Jack looked at her in astonishment. "I found you this time. I found you the first time."

"Next time will be different," said Kristin.

"The hell it will."

"And you shouldn't swear."

"I'll swear if I damn-well please," he muttered. But she'd given him cause for thought. Good lord, what if she ran away and he *couldn't* find her? And Pinkerton's couldn't find her? What if she came to grief? And all over some silly ideas she had about marriage.

They barely made it aboard the afternoon excursion train to Denver, which was full of people looking pale or green or both after their experience on the Georgetown Loop. Jack wished he'd got to see it. Especially with Kristin. Since she'd hung onto his hand on the Gold Pan Trestle, she might have thrown herself into his arms on the Georgetown Loop. Well, he'd just have to find some other way to get his wife to throw herself into his arms. And in the meantime, he wouldn't be able to let her out of his sight until they got back to Breckenridge.

He glanced down to find her sketching scenery, even ugly mine buildings. "Why are you doing those?" he asked.

"Because of the Single Jack commission."

"Why, that means you *were* planning to come home."

"No, it doesn't."

"You were just leading me a merry chase. I'd never have taken you for the flirtatious, teasing type, Kristin."

"I'm not!"

"And you really don't have to go to that sort of trouble to get my attention."

"I wasn't!"

"I assure you, sweetheart, I'm as interested as a husband can be."

"You're horrible," said Kristin, pouting and flipping a page of her sketchbook. She did an unflattering caricature of Jack and then, forgetting herself, concentrated on his upper arm, the muscles of which she remembered flexing as he lay on top of her at the Windsor Hotel.

"That's a very interesting sketch," said Jack.

Kristin flushed and closed the book. How could she have been so careless? If he ever looked through it, he'd see bits and pieces of himself everywhere, all unclothed. At least there was no complete nude. But then, she hadn't seen all of him. At the thought, she had to squelch a wave of curiosity.

In Denver, Jack had time for one meeting and refused Kristin's suggestion that she go shopping while he conducted business. "I'm not letting you out of my sight."

"As long as you leave me alone, I won't run away," she promised.

"I don't believe you," he retorted and dragged her along to the meeting. The mining investors were surprised to have Jack Cameron's pretty wife sitting in on the negotiations. Kristin was appalled at the amounts of money being discussed. If he had that much, she reasoned, he could have afforded to pay her more than a hundred dollars for his portrait, even if he didn't like it.

She grinned at the thought of the picture, which was a

more accurate description of Jack the Snake than any of the sketches she'd done the last two days. And she wasn't going to do any more of those. Even if he *was* the only naked male she'd ever seen any part of.

He refused to leave the room as she dressed for dinner, although he did agree to keep his back turned. As she laced up her corset and slipped into her lavender tulle gown with its triple row of caught-up ruffles at the bottom and pink silk flowers at the waist and shoulders, she had to resist the impulse to peek at Jack. Instead, she concentrated on her gown. Although the neckline draped low, it had looked very demure six months ago when her summer wardrobe was being planned. Now it showed a surprising amount of cleavage, and Kristin had to wonder if her sinful night with Jack had increased the size of her bosom. A woman in Chicago society, who was rumored to be fast, had cleavage like Kristin's.

Then she wondered if Jack was as tempted to peek at her as she was to peek at him. He stood across the room donning evening clothes. When she finished dressing, she sat primly on the edge of the fainting couch with her head turned away.

"You're going to get a crick in your neck," he remarked, "and all for nothing. I'm decent."

Kristin relaxed, only to discover that by decent he meant he had his trousers on and was shaving in front of one of the hotel's vaunted diamond-dust mirrors. She couldn't take her eyes away. She hadn't seen his back before, and it was very interesting. The muscles curved in to his spine and formed fascinating swells on his shoulders and arms. How had he developed them? she wondered. He looked slender in his clothes, but much more substantial without them. As he turned with his razor in hand, lather covering half his lower face, she quickly dropped her eyes.

"Well, don't you look beautiful," he remarked. "Lavender's your color. Look up, will you?"

"You don't have your shirt on."

"That's all right. I'm not shy."

Indignantly she did look up, but before she could reprimand him, he said, "Just what I thought. The dress gives your eyes a lavender hue. You ought to do a self-portrait in that gown."

"How much would you pay me for it?" she demanded cheekily, much relieved that he had noticed her eyes, not her telltale bosom.

"Two hundred dollars. It's bound to be better than the one you did of me." Then, laughing, he turned back to the mirror and his razor.

"I hope you slit your throat," she muttered.

"What was that?"

But not before she got the two hundred dollars for the self-portrait. She'd never done a self-portrait. The family would have accused her of vanity. And she wouldn't have considered it except for the two hundred dollars, although Jack had given her a lot more than that to go shopping. Still, it was having *earned* money that counted, that made one feel special, talented, competent—

"Ready?"

He had his shirt and tie on and was shrugging into his coat. Kristin wished that she had taken another peek at his bare back while she had the chance, since she planned to *insist* that he get himself another room for the night. He looked disturbingly handsome in his evening clothes. She must remember not to stare.

They met Cal Bannister for dinner at Charpiot's, where the conversation turned to the Cripple Creek venture.

"Is it some sort of health resort?" Kristin asked when she heard the name of the area in which Mr. Bannister thought millions in gold were to be found. "If that's the case, I don't think you should dig gold mines there. The dust can't be good for people who are ill. Ingrid told me that Sean almost died of mine dust."

"Sean almost died of Ingrid's perfume," said Jack.

When she thought about it, Kristin realized that she herself sometimes felt she'd die of Ingrid's perfume. If it was true that Sean had become ill that way, what better reason to give Ingrid for throwing away that dreadful scent? Kristin had a moment of conscience over encouraging Ingrid to hope that she might get Sean back, but concern for her own nose overcame Kristin's qualms.

Mr. Bannister flirted outrageously with her from the first course to the last, and Kristin flirted right back as soon as she saw that it irritated Jack. When they returned to the hotel, she announced that she wasn't sleeping in the same room with him, much less the same bed. Jack replied that she could sit up all night if she wanted, but he wasn't getting out of the room because he wasn't announcing to the hotel management that his wife refused to sleep with him. As a result, Kristin spent the night on the fainting couch, Jack in the bed. Then she slept most of the way to Breckenridge, having found a fainting couch a poor substitute for a real bed.

"You're ruining my career as an artist," she muttered as they got off the train at the ladies' stop. "I didn't make one sketch on the way home."

"True," Jack agreed, "and you didn't get any new clothes either, both of which are your own fault."

"What's this I hear about your allowing suitors to call on the girls in the middle of the week?" demanded Kristin.

Ingrid shrugged. "A couple of handsome ones showed up, so I let them in. I even played the piano and sang a few songs."

Kristin felt a stab of anxiety. What kind of songs had Ingrid sung? "I heard there was dancing."

"Everyone had a fine time. Even Winifred perked up."

"And that you charged them for the dances. This is not a dance hall, Ingrid."

"Well, you charge them for refreshments."

"I don't want you to do that anymore, Ingrid. Jack and I had hardly got off the train before three different ladies approached us with the story."

"Old biddies," muttered Ingrid, but she looked crushed. "I just can't seem to do anything right."

"Now, I didn't mean that, Ingrid. I think you're doing a wonderful job with the sausage factory, and I've got orders from Denver and Georgetown."

Ingrid grinned. "I heard you ran away from him. What happened? You finally let him in your bed?"

Kristin felt her cheeks going pink.

"Good for you. But why in the world did you run away? Even if you didn't like it the first time—"

Kristin turned redder.

"—you'll change your mind. I don't think I liked it my first time. Been so long I can hardly remember."

A dew of perspiration broke out on Kristin's forehead. Even Ingrid hadn't liked it her first time, whereas Kristin had, which must make her some kind of unnatural—oh dear! She remembered Sister Mary Joseph warning against unnatural acts. Had she and Jack done anything unnatural? Probably. How was she to know?

"Well, you're a fool to run away from such a fine-looking gentleman. If he were mine, I wouldn't run away."

Kristin glanced anxiously at her partner, but Ingrid didn't

really look as if she wanted Jack. It just seemed to be the sort of remark she made. Poor Ingrid. She was so socially unacceptable, and she'd never learn how to act in respectable company if she never had any. Kristin made up her mind then and there that she'd have to teach Ingrid to be a lady and include her in social functions.

"I've some news of my own." Ingrid's face, which was so often sad, lit with a hopeful radiance, her eyes sparkling, her full mouth turning up. "Sean came to visit me. He brought the children."

"Oh, I'm so glad, Ingrid," said Kristin. "I know how you long to see them, and they are darling children."

"They were disappointed you weren't here. Phoebe wanted to hear more about the elk prince an' princess."

"I haven't thought up any more to that tale."

"You mean you make those stories up?"

"As I go along."

"I wish I could do that. I don't even read well enough to read to them. They brought along a book an' read to *me*. Pretty good story too," said Ingrid, "but the best of it was Sean stayed the whole time. An' we talked an'—oh, Kristin, I think he still loves me."

"Ingrid, you know he's married."

"He's married to me."

"He's legally married to Augustina, and they have a child."

"I have two," protested Ingrid. "It was so lovely talkin' to him. I wanted to throw my arms around him an' kiss him to death. Course, I couldn't do that in the parlor, could I? Not with the children there."

"And not on Wednesday," added Kristin.

"Wednesday? What's Wednesday got to do with it? Anyway, if I kissed Sean, Kat would hear about it an'—"

"Ingrid, Kat's not your enemy. She just never understood

239

how sad and frightened you were at that time."

Ingrid sighed. "I'm still frightened. Sean was coughin'. That's what started it all, you know. He was coughin' more, an' he sent for his sister because he didn't trust me to handle money. But I'm better about money now, don't you think?"

"I don't know how you were before," said Kristin.

"If I had it, I spent it. What else is there to do with it? That's how I felt. Now I'm investin' with Jack."

"Well, I hope it turns out well," said Kristin dubiously. "He has a reputation as a high-risk investor."

"That's how you make money out here. All the rich men gambled on the mines."

"You said Sean was coughing?"

"Yes, an' I'm so afraid he's gettin' sick again, though he promised me he wasn't goin' down in the mines."

"It's your perfume," said Kristin.

"What's that supposed to mean?"

"That's what they discovered after you'd left, Ingrid. When Sean came back from the sanatorium, he was fine until he started to take the things out of your closet. Then he started coughing and sneezing all over again."

"I was the one who made him sick?" Ingrid looked stricken.

"No, Ingrid, your perfume."

"But I love my perfume."

"Well, of course, it's up to you," said Kristin. "I suppose you could wash it off when he's coming to call. Do you know when to expect him?"

"Wednesdays. Piano lesson days."

"But maybe it's like alcohol—"

"I haven't been *drinkin'* it."

"I meant that maybe you just have to stop using it entirely so you won't be tempted. And of course, the house smells of it. It's like cigars. The odor—"

Before Kristin could say another word, Ingrid left the room, shouting to Winifred that she wanted a hot bath and all her clothes put out in the back yard to air.

Kristin smiled. She knew that she'd been manipulating Ingrid, but her partner's perfume gave her a headache. She hoped never to smell it again. "Winifred, throw open all the windows too," she called.

Chapter Fifteen

Jack sat in his office on Main Street, thinking that if he were smart he'd move his headquarters to Denver, where the money was. However, he liked Breckenridge. He liked sitting around with the Warm Stove Mine group in the back of George Watson's store listening to tall tales about gold mines and hunting adventures. He liked drinking with Robert Foote at the Denver Hotel and hunting with Connor and Sean. He considered Connor the best friend he'd ever made and the most likeable. He didn't even mind when the locals laughed at the English knickers he'd worn on his first hunting trip and the formal riding clothes for his first exploration of the area on horseback. That was just the way it was with men—good humored, rough joshing. This was a man's world

All it needed to make it complete was a pretty woman, and he had one, but he felt shortchanged there. It wasn't as if he'd debauched her in her father's library, no matter what she had thought. And she must know she'd been a virgin on their first night at the Windsor—what an experience that had been!—but she still held him at arm's length.

And why had she run away after they consummated the marriage? He'd waited longer than most men. And he'd given her pleasure. Was it some ploy to be sure she kept his attention? Well, she had it. He wanted to tumble her right back into bed, but she was locking her door at night, threatening to run again. He even suspected that she moved something in front of the door before she slept. He'd heard the scraping. A little thing like Kristin shouldn't be moving furniture around.

So how was he going to win her over? And why in the world did Fast Jack Cameron, as they used to call him in Chicago, find himself in such a position? Was it some sort of divine retribution for his success among the ladies back home? Drawing on his extensive experience with women, Jack came up with an idea. Social life! That's what women liked. Since social life here in Breckenridge hadn't been too exciting, he would treat her to a sparkling round of activities the like of which this town had never seen. Balls, performances, elaborate dinner parties. He locked his door and walked to the telegraph office to send a wire to Genevieve in Chicago asking for a French cook—Kristin had liked Louis Dupuy's cooking—and two housemaids experienced in serving fancy dinners and rich guests.

That's another thing he liked about Breckenridge—his house. Well, Kristin's house. It was going to be a real showplace when he got through with it. He'd already ordered a cast-iron furnace like the one General Hamill had in Georgetown. Couldn't have Kristin freezing this winter. She probably had no idea how bad the weather was going to be. Maybe in future years they'd winter in Denver and summer in Breckenridge.

In the meantime, he'd have to order Kristin a fur coat and some lively guests from Chicago—and do that before it got too cold. People who'd enjoy the scenery, keep his wife entertained, and invest in his mining syndicates. He'd send the telegrams off at the same time he was wiring Genevieve and a Chicago furrier. So what else? Furnace, fur coat, guests. And a lady's maid! One who was an accomplished seamstress and hairstylist. A maid who could sew the latest fashions. Women loved clothes and fancy hairdos.

Lord, but she'd looked beautiful in that lavender gown. He hoped she'd started on the self-portrait. Jack sent sixteen telegrams to Chicago and, whistling cheerfully, set off for Barney Ford's Saddle Rock Cafe to meet his friends for lunch. He'd have gone home to Kristin if he didn't have to share her with all those giggling sausage makers. And pigs. There was one damn pig that kept wandering through the house and snuggling up to his wife. Kristin had made friends with the creature and named it Gwenivere; she chatted with it while she was painting. At least the pig hadn't made any messes in the house. It had better not, since he'd ordered Brussels carpets. Maybe he should build a dormitory for the sausage girls, so he and Kristin could put their guests in the house.

No, he didn't have to move from Breckenridge just yet. Good thing too. He couldn't even consider it until he was sure his wife would agree to come with him. As it stood, she'd probably throw a party to celebrate his departure and stay here with her sausage business and her studio. He'd have to fix up that studio—chairs, maybe a fainting couch. She needed some good furniture if she was to get any portrait commissions. He'd have to invite Chicagoans interested in art as well as investments.

Investments reminded him that he'd had a busy morning. As soon word got around that he was back in town, people began to drop in and he to collect partners in the new Cripple Creek venture. Even Ingrid had put money into Cripple Creek. Good lord, she was a sultry woman, and voluptuous! He wondered how Sean Fitzpatrick felt about having divorced his first wife to marry Augustina. Not that Augustina wasn't handsome, but she didn't radiate Ingrid's brand of come-hither sex appeal. Of course, Jack supposed he favored Ingrid because she looked a bit like Kristin.

He entered the Saddle Rock and the first person he saw was Sean, looking glum. Well, what man wouldn't look glum if he had two wives in the same town, and he'd probably rather be bedding the first than the second? "You look like a man who'd be cheered at the prospect of making a lot of money, Sean," said Jack.

"So would I," said Barney Ford, and the three men, soon joined by Connor, sat down to discuss Cripple Creek and Cal Bannister's estimate of how much gold might be taken out of the unlikely-looking, bucolic, cattle-ranching valley.

Kat Macleod stopped by the Single Jack Cafe as Kristin finished her preparation of the wall for the mural, so the two women walked up the hill together. "Would you like to stop by for a cup of coffee?" Kat offered.

"I think I'd better get home and check on Ingrid."

"How's she doing?"

"She's not drinking," said Kristin.

"I'm very grateful to you for that," said Kat. "I feel so responsible for what happened to her."

"I think it was just one of those terrible misunderstandings."

"I suppose, but I never could figure out why she was always sleeping in the day and disappearing at night."

"She was sad, Kat, and frightened, and in awe of you."

"Of me? Why in the world—"

"Sean trusted you, not her. She felt deserted and useless, and of course, with her background—you do know her background?"

"I didn't then."

"Well, you can understand why she would feel uneasy around a respectable woman. She told me she was so sad that most mornings she couldn't get out of bed."

"I've never heard of such a thing," said the optimistic, energetic Kat. "If I'd known, I could have dragged her out and set her to doing something interesting. Speaking of which, how did you do selling sausage?"

"Oh, very well," said Kristin. "Even Lieukof's in Denver is going to buy our sausage, and that's a very prestigious meat firm."

"Good for you. I knew you'd make a success of the business."

"And several restaurants. I sold sausage to such places as Tortoni's and Charpiot's." At Charpiot's, Kristin had insisted on talking to the head waiter about sausage. She even visited the kitchen to talk to the chef. "A number of grocers and butchers put in orders. Not the Hotel de Paris in Georgetown, however. Mr. Dupuy—"

"Yes, Kristin, I must talk to you about that. Why did you run away from Jack? He told Connor that you didn't even leave him a note. The man was beside himself with worry and hired detectives to track you down."

"He did?"

"Yes, he did. So why did you run away?"

"Because he's an evil, sinful man," said Kristin.

"Well, I know you resent him because of what happened in Chicago, but you're never going to make a success of your marriage or anything else by running away."

"A woman could lose her place in heaven associating

246

with a man like Jack Cameron," said Kristin sternly.

Kat mouth dropped open. "Do you want to tell me about it?" she asked hesitantly.

"It's too shocking and humiliating to discuss."

"I'm so sorry, Kristin." Kat looked gratifyingly horrified. "Now I feel responsible for two failed marriages."

"Don't," said Kristin. "I'm hoping, if I stay away from him, he'll leave and go back to Chicago."

"That's a good idea," said Kat. "Maybe he'll sell us back the Chicago Girl. I could use some good news."

"Why, what's wrong?" asked Kristin. By this time, they had reached the corner of Washington and French, where Kat would turn off.

"The Sunday closing campaign is going badly. All the saloons are still open on Sunday regardless of the law. Reverend Passmore and I are going to have to do something, and that's going to make everybody angry, besides which I'm getting nowhere at all with women's suffrage."

"What you need is my Aunt Frieda," said Kristin, giggling.

"There's nothing funny about women's suffrage, Kristin."

"I was thinking of how angry she used to make my father by advocating it."

"Oh, well, that's good. And then I think Augustina blames me for the fact that Ingrid's still in town. She suspects that Sean is seeing Ingrid."

"He did bring the children to visit, but that's different, don't you think? I mean Ingrid does have a right to see her children."

"But it's not helping Sean's marriage, and the worst news of all is that Mother and James are going to stay in Breckenridge and—"

"That is bad news," murmured Kristin.

Kat frowned. "Well, I am sorry about the way Mother

247

treated you. I myself would be delighted to have her here if it weren't that she's going to open a saloon."

Kristin couldn't help herself. She fell into uncontrollable laughter.

"It may seem funny to you," said Kat indignantly, "but it's hardly going to help my credibility with the local temperance group. By the way, did you manage to see the W.C.T.U. people in Denver as I asked you?"

"No, I'm sorry. I had to run away before I got a chance."

"Damn that Jack Cameron!"

Kristin found that she resented Kat's dislike of Jack, although that made no sense when Kristin herself was so upset with him and had to shove a heavy dresser in front of her door every night to be sure that he didn't try to visit her. "I'd better get home," said Kristin.

"Me too. I'm hoping there's still time to talk my mother into something other than a saloon. Why can't she open a boarding house? Goodness, she sold the saloon in Chicago so she could do that."

"What saloon in Chicago?"

"My father was a saloon keeper," said Kat, "and my first husband too, so it's small wonder that I dislike drinking." Kat went off looking unhappy, and Kristin continued up the hill. A saloon? Wouldn't her mother and father be upset to hear that St. Scholastica had had saloon keepers' daughters as well as rich sausage makers' daughters. Giggling, Kristin decided she'd write the news to Aunt Frieda, who would undoubtedly pass it on.

Kristin had had a very satisfying letter from her aunt describing the Traube reaction, especially Minna's, to Kristin's marriage. The letter also contained lots of advice on keeping a husband in line. Aunt Frieda hadn't mentioned pushing a dresser in front of the bedroom door, but it seemed to be working.

248

* * *

Two days later, Kristin trudged up Nickel Hill toward her house. Mural painting was proving to be much more strenuous than she had anticipated. Her back hurt, her arms and shoulders ached, and she was tired. Even the bountiful meal that Hortense provided hadn't given Kristin that extra edge of energy to get her through the afternoon. Instead she gave up at two o'clock and started home, planning a nice long nap. She wasn't even sure she had the energy to shove the bureau in front of the door, although perhaps that wasn't necessary. Sister Mary Joseph had been quite clear that "the act" could only be performed at night. Kristin hoped Jack knew that.

He was trying to be nice to her. She'd get home exhausted from painting miners and mines onto the wall at the Single Jack Cafe only to find that Jack insisted on spiriting her to a Chautauqua lecture, or a ball—Breckenridge was always having balls—or a dinner party at someone's house. When she said she was tired, he said he'd order her a nice warm bath and even pick out a gown so that she wouldn't be bothered with making choices. Then he'd produce some piece of jewelry to go with the gown. Curse him! He had excellent taste and knew just what looked best on her. And he always insisted on pointing out to the people they met how beautiful she looked, putting his arm around her shoulders while the townsfolk gave them simpleton smiles and made silly remarks about newlyweds. This whole aspect of his behavior was downright alarming. She knew it to be generated by lust and a guilty conscience, but he could always send shivers up her spine with a touch or a compliment.

And then yesterday he had offered to buy a place to house the sausage girls and the factory. "We're going to need those rooms upstairs so that we can entertain."

Kristin didn't want to entertain. "Entertain who?"

"Our guests."

As far as she could see, they didn't need to move the girls out in order to entertain the folk from Breckenridge who had invited them to card parties, dances, and dinners. "I want those girls in the house where I can keep my eye on them," she'd replied. "It's my duty to the young women who come out here to see that they have a proper home environment. And I promised Kat I'd look after Ingrid."

"We could keep Ingrid in the house," said Jack, "and get another place for—"

"No," said Kristin.

"Then I'll have to think of something else."

What? she wondered. And why did he want to get the sausage girls out of the house? So he'd have her to himself? So he could do whatever he wanted? Push her protective chest of drawers aside. Invade her bedroom. These thoughts were interrupted by a great clamor coming from her house. In a surge of energized alarm, she raced up the steps and threw the door open. Pounding, clanging, hammering, men's voices. What was happening?

"We've started," said Jack, coming out of her studio, trailed by two men, who left the house.

"Started what?"

"The furnace. It's going to be even better than General Hamill's."

"But I didn't—"

"You'll love it this winter when the snow is piled six feet deep all around us."

"Six feet!"

"Breckenridge is much worse than Chicago for snow, so we'll need a furnace, unless you'd like to move to Denver."

"I would not."

"I didn't think so. There'll be warm air shot right into the drawing room, the dining room, your studio—I think that's particularly important. You'd find it hard to paint with your fingers freezing or wearing heavy gloves."

Kristin felt quite bewildered, and it took her a minute to shake off Jack's arm, which he had placed companionably about her shoulders as he offered to take her downstairs to view the beginning installation of the furnace.

"I didn't know we had a cellar."

"It's small, but we're making it bigger. I've hired an explosives expert from one of the mines."

Kristin backed away in alarm. "Won't that undermine the house? It might fall down around our ears."

"Nonsense. He's the best man on the Western Slope. Connor says he can blow a mole off a man's nose without—"

"But Jack, even if the house survives, the girls and—and the pigs will certainly be alarmed."

"We'll just send them away during the blasting."

Was he trying to destroy her house and drive away her employees because she had refused to let him into her bedroom? "What's that?" There were sounds coming from the backyard too.

"They're starting to build the girls' dormitory."

"Dormitory?"

"Since you didn't want to move the factory and the girls, I decided to build a dormitory for them in the back yard where they'll be right under your motherly eye."

"Jack Cameron, you're manipulating me. I never agreed to—"

"I'm paying for it, dear heart. Now come back to your studio. I have a surprise for you." He took her hand, which she was not subsequently able to jerk loose, and led her to her studio where, miraculously, furniture had appeared—a beautiful blue-green fainting couch with matching chairs, fine draperies at the windows, and a great scroll-framed, full-length mirror.

Kristin stood in the door, gaping with amazement. "I don't need all this."

"You can't paint portraits with the subjects sitting on the floor or standing around in a bare room."

"I don't have any portrait commissions."

"You have a commission from me to do a self-portrait. That's what the mirror is for."

Kristin shook her head. The man spent money as if he had found gold under his office on Main Street. "Are we going to become bankrupts?" she asked. Maybe that was his game. He planned to spend every penny he had and then go off and leave her to fend for herself, responsible for all the improvements he was making to her property.

"Absolutely not, my dear. We're going to be as rich as Carnegie." Jack bent down and gave her a warm, light kiss.

Before she could protest, he said, "And now I'm off to Denver. Be a good girl while I'm gone." And he left the room. Left her in a house full of clankings, hammerings, and shouting male voices. A house that might explode, then collapse. As she watched her husband's beautifully tailored morning coat disappearing down the hall and out the front door, the memory of that back, naked at the Windsor Hotel, flashed in her mind, and her fingers itched for a pencil.

Instead she tried to tell the men in the basement and the back yard to go away. They simply shook their heads and replied, "Mr. Cameron warned us you might say that and we was to pay no attention."

"Pay no attention?" she echoed, outraged. "This is my house. I hold the deed in my own name."

"Yes ma'am. He said, you being the world's sweetest wife, you never wanted him to spend his money on you, but we was to go right ahead." And they went back to their banging, clanging, and hammering.

As Kristin stalked into kitchen, Winifred said, "Ain't it exciting, ma'am? We're to have our own house."

"Oh yes, very exciting," muttered Kristin and returned to the studio. She'd never manage a nap in the midst of this chaos. She looked at herself in the ornate, full-length mirror and imagined her portrait painted looking as she did. Wouldn't that be fine hanging over the fireplace in the drawing room? Jack's portrait looking like a scoundrel and hers looking like a haggard old crone.

Kristin dropped down on the fainting couch to rest for a moment before she went to work. At least she wouldn't have to wrestle with that chest of drawers for a few days. She took her sketch pad from a pretty table beside the couch and absently sketched her husband's powerful back as she remembered it from the Denver Hotel, both the way it had felt under her fingers when he made love to her and the way it had looked while he was shaving.

Before she could recall that she had promised herself not to do any more unclothed drawings of Jack, the pad slipped from her fingers and she fell asleep. When she awoke, the workmen had gone and Winifred was saying, "I got supper on the table, ma'am, and there's a letter for you."

"A letter?" Kristin dragged herself off the couch and drifted to the dining room, still sleepy. She was greeted by all the sausage girls, atwitter over the new furnace and their new accommodations.

"A room for each of us," said Fanny. "I've never had a room to myself. And new furniture. Mr. Cameron said some lady named Augustina, who knows all about such things, was to pick it out."

Good lord, thought Kristin, *no matter what he says, we'll be bankrupt before he finishes this project.*

253

"And central heating. Mr. Cameron's putting central heating in the basement. Ain't that fine?"

"I do hear it's right cold here in the winter," said Bea, "but I expect to be married by then."

"It will be cold wherever you're living," said Kristin.

"Yes ma'am, but I'll have a warm man to cuddle up to."

All the girls giggled at that shocking remark while Kristin stared at the envelope Winifred had given her along with crusty bread and a bowl of rich bean-and-sausage soup. Winifred wasn't a fancy cook, but she fed the household heartily. Still, Kristin didn't think the dinner party Jack envisioned would turn out to be quite what he expected.

She inspected the envelope and went still. In a beautiful, flowing hand the letter was addressed to Mrs. Kristin Traube Cameron, Breckenridge, The Frontier, Colorado. And the return address. She couldn't believe her eyes. The letter was from Mrs. Bertha Honore Palmer. Fingers trembling, Kristin used her butter knife to slit the envelope. Then she took out the letter and began to read:

My dear Kristin:

I am so sorry to hear of your late troubles and that I was not in Chicago to be of assistance to you in your time of need. Your Aunt Frieda has informed me of your whereabouts and the fine marriage you have made, on which I congratulate you.

Some fine marriage, thought Kristin bitterly. If Mrs. Palmer only knew. But with any luck, she never would. Aunt Frieda wouldn't have told her about why they'd had to get married, or actually why they hadn't had to get married. Kristin skimmed over all the polite good wishes and got to the heart of the letter.

Sarah Hallowell has told me of your plan to do a nightscape of Chicago in what sounds to me like the Impressionist mode. This concept interests me greatly. If you have finished the picture and would care to send it, I should be glad to have it framed and enter it in the next exhibition of note here in Chicago.

Kristin dropped the letter, hands clasped over her thumping heart. Then she hurriedly fished the pages out of the bean soup and wiped them off with her napkin, terrified that she might have destroyed the end of Mrs. Potter Palmer's communication.

"What is it, ma'am?" cried Winifred, who had taken her seat beside Kristin. "Bad news?"

"No, but I fear that I may have ruined my letter."

"Here, give it to me." Winifred took it and patted it carefully, front and back. "Looks to me like it's all right, ma'am. The second page wasn't touched at all."

"Oh, thank you, Winifred." When she had caught her breath, she pushed the soup away and held the letter out in front of her, poring over the rest of it. How wonderful! It was just what she hoped for. She had finished "Nightscape," but had hesitated to send it to Denver, fearing that Denverites, so far from Paris and other centers of artistic innovation, might not appreciate its revolutionary style and content. "The Blessed Mother has not forsaken me, after all," Kristin murmured.

"Why would she forsake you, ma'am?" asked Winifred. "You're the kindest mistress a girl could have."

"Thank you, Winifred." Of course, Winifred didn't know about Kristin's terrible sins committed at the Windsor Hotel in Denver and still unconfessed.

"Is it good news then?"

"Yes, indeed. Mrs. Potter Palmer, of whom you've probably heard, has asked me to send a painting for exhibit in Chicago." Then she had another thought. Her parents might see the picture. And if they didn't, Aunt Frieda would tell them about it because Kristin would write Aunt Frieda immediately. She began to giggle at the thought of how distressed her parents would be. Her father didn't want her to enter exhibitions, but now he'd have nothing to say about it.

If she won a prize or even stirred interest and controversy, he'd be sorry that he'd been so mean to her. Heinrich II would worry about the family reputation with the scandal of her departure brought back to the attention of Chicago society. If they didn't know about it, her picture would bring it to the fore. And Minna, who had pinched Kristin so many times over the years, would be embarrassed because everyone would gossip about her talented sister, who had married her fiance. Kristin knew it was a sin to feel so spiteful toward Minna, but Minna deserved it.

"Ma'am, don't you think you should eat your soup before it gets cold?"

"I'm too excited to eat," said Kristin. Then she had a sudden, most astonishing desire to tell Jack about the letter, but he wasn't here. He'd gone off to Denver. Probably to associate with loose women on Market Street. She'd heard that was where gentlemen went to take their pleasure. Kristin scowled at her soup. It was shameful that men were unfaithful to their wives. Of course, she didn't care, since she didn't want him visiting her bedroom, but still she didn't like the idea of Jack on Market Street enjoying himself with some beautiful, sinful woman wearing a low-cut gown, maybe even showing her ankles.

Chapter Sixteen

Conviviality reigned at the Denver Hotel bar. Among the drinkers were Robert Foote, the owner, Jack, who was escaping the Sunday courting salon in his drawing room, and a gloomy Sean Fitzpatrick, who complained that his wife gave him nothing but accusing looks these days, which really lowered a man's natural high spirits. The gentlemen lifted their glasses to success at Cripple Creek, as all of them were investors in the claims Jack and Cal Bannister were pursuing, and to a successful 1891 deer-hunting season.

"I wanna get me a fat buck, a sixteen-pointer," said Robert, "and hang the head right over my bar." He pointed to the selected spot, then turned to Jack. "Think your lady would make me up some venison sausage?"

"Why not?" said Jack. "She might like to put in a new line, Traube's Colorado Venison Sausage. Not that she has much to do with the business. Ingrid's really running it.

She even made one of the out-of-town selling trips to all the places Kristin didn't consider scenic enough."

"Ingrid's out of town?" asked Sean.

"No." Jack poured whiskey into his glass. "She's in my parlor playing the piano, flirting, and knocking all the suitors dead. I've seen boys of twenty turn pale and stagger at the sight of Ingrid in a low-cut gown."

"Why's she wearing a low-cut gown on Sunday?" Sean demanded. "I thought she was supposed to be promoting marriage for the sausage makers."

Jack laughed. "You probably know Ingrid better than any man, Sean, so you know it's hard for any male from fifteen to sixty-five to pay much attention to some Chicago sausage maker when Ingrid's in the room."

Sean scowled.

"You did divorce her and remarry," Jack pointed out. "She's got a right to remarry too."

Sean looked even unhappier and filled a whole tumbler with whiskey, half of which he drank down at one draught. He was in the act of swallowing when the door to the bar burst open and his sister entered with Reverend Passmore.

"Sinners!" shouted the preacher.

The patrons turned and raised their glasses to the Methodist minister. "Here's to you, brother," said one and belched. Then he took a long drink.

"You're all breaking the law," said Kat.

"Now, Miz Macleod, I don't know why it is you're always wantin' to spoil a fella's fun," said the owner of a tonsorial parlor on Main Street. "Like the Lord said, Sunday's a day of rest, and we're all restin' here in the Denver bar from our week's labors."

Kat Macleod, evidently used to all sorts of comments in her campaign for Sunday closing, surveyed the room with a sharp eye as she retorted, "Shame on you, Mr. Hepburn. I ought to organize a boycott against your barber shop."

"Most of you temperance folk are female and don't shave," he pointed out. Everyone was laughing uproariously.

At that moment her eye lit on her brother. "Sean Fitzpatrick!" she cried. "What are you doing here?"

Grinning, cheering up from his gloomy contemplation of Ingrid's flirtations, Sean rose and kissed his sister on the cheek. "Can I order you a lemonade, honey?"

She picked up his glass and sniffed. "That's not what you're drinking, Sean. And to do it on the Lord's day!"

"You're starting to sound like a Methodist, Kat."

"Afternoon, Mrs. Macleod," said Jack, tipping his hat politely. He was now wearing a Stetson, having forgone his more chic Eastern headgear.

"Mr. Cameron, I'm not surprised to see *you* here."

Reverend Passmore swept the glasses off a table into the laps of various drinkers and climbed up to begin his oration. "God has his angry eye upon every one of you sinners," said the preacher.

"Then maybe you wouldn't mind askin' 'im, since he's payin' attention, to turn that eye on the feller who tried to jump my claim Wednesday last," called a prospector sitting with his friends at a large table in the corner.

"God will jump your claim himself, brother. He will spirit away the gold and silver from the lodes of sinners."

"Them's fightin' words," shouted another miner, jumping up. "An' ah'm a man who likes to fight." He danced around Passmore's improvised pulpit with his fists clenched. "Put 'em up, Reverend. Ah hear you're quite a fighter your own self. Ah'd sure like to take a poke at you."

Reverend Passmore jumped off the table and knocked the miner flat with a powerful roundhouse blow.

"Reverend Passmore!" cried Kat, "God's work is not done by violence."

"Well, if you'll excuse my contradicting you, Mrs. Macleod, you should read your Bible," said Jack. "It's got more violence in it than you can shake a parasol at."

Kat scowled. "Shouldn't you be at home overseeing that chaotic scene in your drawing room?"

"Anyone else want to take up fisticuffs against God's servant?" bellowed Reverend Passmore. Since the downed miner appeared to have lost a reasonably shapely nose in the encounter, there were no more offers.

"What are you talking about?" asked Jack.

"Give up your sinful drinking," shouted the minister.

"I went to your house to see if anyone wanted to join the temperance crusade and found Ingrid playing and singing rowdy songs in your drawing room."

"By God, that brings back memories," said Sean. "I'd like to hear Ingrid sing a rowdy song again."

His sister glared at him while Jack chuckled.

"Stop your desecration of the Lord's day." The Methodist pastor got louder with each admonition.

"And miners with muddy boots are trampling on your carpets," added Kat.

Jack stopped smiling.

"Not to mention the fact that some burly woman has frightened your wife half to death by arriving on the doorstep claiming to be her French cook."

Jack's face relaxed into a pleased smile. "Well, that's good news."

"Not if you're expecting her to be French."

"I'd appreciate it, ma'am," said Robert Foote, "if you'd take your campaign elsewhere. Connor's my friend, but—"

"You don't notice *him* in here drinking on Sunday. If fact, he rarely indulges."

"Hell awaits each person whose lips touch demon rum," declared the preacher.

"Not too much rum goin' down around here," declared the barber. "More like whiskey or beer."

"I don't appreciate your trying to scare off my customers," said Robert Foote to Kat.

"What song was Ingrid singing?" asked Sean.

"If you'll excuse me," said Jack, "I think I'll go home and see what's happening there." He rose.

"Think I'll go with you," said Sean.

"You will not," said Jack and Kat simultaneously.

Sulking, Sean settled back into his chair and poured another half tumbler of whiskey.

Kat shook her head. "You're following in our father's footsteps, Sean."

"Well, if you mean that I'm on my second wife, and the second's a lot harder-headed than the first, you're right."

"Don't you say a word against my mother *or* Augustina," snapped Kat, and that was the last Jack heard of the argument as he headed for the door with Reverend Passmore calling after him, "Look at that man. Even a papist is willing to heed the word of God and observe the Sabbath."

Jack tipped his Stetson to the minister and set off for Nickel Hill, wondering if there really had been girls on the hill in the old days who sold their favors for a nickel. He doubted they'd have been very appealing, not at that price.

"I don't know what you're talking about," said Kristin.

The woman was as tall as Ingrid and twice as heavy. "My name is Abigail Mertz, and I'm your French chef."

Ingrid was singing a song called "When the Girls Kick Up Their Heels on Saturday Night at Flossie's" with all the suitors and sausage makers joining merrily in the choruses.

"Is this a bawdy house?" asked Abigail Mertz. "I'm not cooking fine cuisine in a bawdy house."

"What's a bawdy house?" asked Kristin.

The giant woman looked at her suspiciously. "If you don't know, I don't suppose it is. How many guests do you figure on for an average dinner party?"

"None," said Kristin. "Maybe you've come to the wrong door. I'm not planning any dinner parties."

"You are Mrs. Cameron, aren't you?"

"Yes, but—"

"Well, I've been hired by your husband to do your dinner parties and the rest of the cooking for your household. I hear it's a big one, which I consider a challenge." Abigail Mertz squared her shoulders to face the challenge, and muscles rippled under her dress.

At that moment Jack bounded up the steps and said, "Where's the new cook?"

"Right here." Abigail turned, arms akimbo, a belligerent look on her face. "Are you someone else who's gonna tell me I'm not wanted for this job after I've come God knows how many thousand miles to the wild frontier?"

"Actually, ma'am, things are pretty settled here in Breckenridge. You don't look or sound French to me."

"I just cook French," said Abigail. "You wouldn't want a real French person. High-strung, high-falutin', trouble-makin' folk—that's what the French are."

"They are not," said Kristin indignantly. "Genevieve Boyer is French."

"But she's not a French *chef*. A down-to-earth French person is practical and thrifty. What you're gettin' is a down-to-earth person with a French chef's talents. Now, where's the kitchen?"

"Right down that hall, ma'am," said Jack, and he beamed at his wife. "Now we can plan our first dinner party."

"Maybe you'd better try some of her cooking before you make any big plans," muttered Kristin.

"Are you going to fire me?" asked Winifred. She had detached herself from the circle of singers and come over to listen with curiosity to what Abigail Mertz had to say.

"Of course we wouldn't fire you, Winifred."

"Well, that's just fine then, ma'am. Now I'll have time to do the housekeeping right. You won't believe the way things are gonna sparkle around here."

Kristin couldn't think of an argument to make against the presence of Abigail Mertz, not when Winifred was happy to have her. Kristin considered Winifred the center of domestic stability around which life in the house turned. When the plaster fell off the ceilings for no known reason, Winifred could always find someone to make repairs. When the necessary house began to give off offensive odors in warm weather, Winifred knew to throw in lime. When inexplicable and stubborn stains appeared on the washable clothing, Winifred knew how to get rid of them.

"My dear wife," said Jack, interrupting Kristin's thoughts. "The song Ingrid is singing is hardly proper for the ears of young, unmarried women."

Kristin glanced at him in alarm. She hadn't been paying any attention to the lyrics, being more interested to see that everyone was having a good time and the suitors weren't filching tea and cookies without paying. Actually, not many of them drank the tea. Maybe she should try to find some other non-alcoholic beverage that would please them and add to the profits.

"Excuse me, sir," said Jack to a muscular man who had just entered the house. "You're tracking mud on the carpet, which is a genuine Brussels."

"Oh yeah." The fellow looked at him belligerently. "You want to fight about it?"

"Well, we could if you insist."

"But if you do," said Kristin to the new arrival, "you'll never be allowed in again."

The miner looked crestfallen. Jack gave him a friendly slap on the back. "If you really want to fight, we can go outside where we won't offend Mrs. Cameron."

"You can not!" cried Kristin. "What are you thinking of? Your face could be ruined."

Jack leaned over and kissed her. "It's nice to know you care, sweetheart."

"Hey," said the miner, "we ain't allowed to kiss none of the girls."

"Well, that's understandable. You're not married to any of them. I am. Now about the mud on your boots."

"I don't like no one complaining about my—"

"It's hardly a complaint, my friend," said Jack. "More like a word of advice between men. Since you're obviously contemplating marriage, you should know that women become very upset when mud is tracked on their carpets or floors. You'll have no end of trouble with your new wife if you don't clean your boots off before you enter the house."

"Nobody complains up to the mine dormitory."

"They're all men. A different matter entirely."

"Suppose you're right," said the miner. "Thanks for the tip." He stamped back to the front porch to kick the drying mud off his boots.

Kristin looked on in astonishment. "How did you do that? Nobody's paid the slightest attention to me about mud. We have to clean the carpets after every salon."

"All in knowing how to be one of the boys," said Jack. "That reminds me. You're not supposed to be kissing me. Certainly not in public."

"Of course," said Jack agreeably. "Shall we retire upstairs?" He was running his thumb up and down her arm and causing tingles which she knew were preliminary to a much warmer reaction. Consequently, she backed away as fast as she could, then whirled and hastened to the piano.

"Ingrid, do you think we might have 'Old Kentucky Home'? That's one of my favorites." She didn't want to hurt Ingrid's feelings, but on the other hand, she didn't want people saying that the Sunday courting salons were a hive of improper conduct.

Ingrid obligingly broke into "Old Kentucky Home," and the courting couples again began to sing. Under cover of the music, Kristin beckoned Jack's head down, for he had followed her to the piano. She whispered into his ear, "What's a bawdy house?"

Jack grinned. "Do you know what a parlor house is or a sporting club?"

"Well, sort of," said Kristin, looking alarmed.

"Maybe you ought to make out a list of acceptable songs. Down at the Denver Hotel, they're already talking about the wild doings here."

"They are? I'll never find these girls good husbands if we become the target of unpleasant gossip."

"I wouldn't worry. There are men out here who'd marry just about anyone. You might even be able to find a suitor for Abigail Mertz, although if she can cook French, he'll have to pay a high price to buy her away from me."

"You're saying my drawing room reminds people of a bawdy house?" Kristin still worried about her reputation. "Even after you replaced Ingrid's furniture?"

"Now that," said Jack, "*was* reminiscent of a bawdy house."

She glared at him, remembering her suspicions about what he might have been doing on his trip to Denver.

*   *   *

When Kristin and Ingrid were ushering out the last of the Sunday suitors, they found two young women on the front porch, one of them weeping.

"Oh, stop it, Yvette," said the taller one, who had kinky, mud-brown hair and rosy cheeks.

"I 'ave been accosted by outlaws on ze streets of zese deesgusting town, and you tell me to stop ze weeping?" The weeper had a dark, delicate face with large brown eyes and shining dark hair pulled into a neat, but somewhat severe chignon at the base of her neck. She was primly dressed in dark clothes of a good cut, while the other young woman wore a light summer dress smudged with train soot.

Kristin could not imagine what they were doing on her porch. It was too late for the train from Denver. The men were streaming by, eyeing the two young women with interest.

"Zees must be another tavern," said the dark girl. "We 'ave once again found ze wrong place, and after being forced to walk up a mountain."

"Excuse me, ma'am," said the frizzle-haired girl, "but would this be the Cameron house?"

"Yes," said Kristin. She wasn't expecting new workers.

"Oh, thank God. We've been wandering all afternoon trying to find this place. Are you Mrs. Cameron?"

"I am," said Kristin.

"Well, I'm Maude Bottle, your new parlor maid, ma'am, and this is Yvette Molineaux, your new lady's maid."

Kristin looked astounded. This had to be Jack's doing. Was he interested in these young women for himself? Looking to them for what she refused to give him? "Are you of good character?" she asked sharply.

Before Maude Bottle could reply, Yvette wiped her eyes with a linen handkerchief and said, "Madame, 'ow could you ask such a theeng when I 'ave come all ze way to zees place of wild Indians and drunken bandits to offer ze finest fashionable care for your person and wardrobe?"

"There's nothing wrong with my person and wardrobe," muttered Kristin, but Jack had come up behind her and laid a large, warm hand on her shoulder, confusing her thought processes. She wished he wouldn't keep touching her in public when she couldn't protest.

"Well, at last. You're the new lady's maid?"

"*Oui.* Ze new French lady's maid."

"You'll be sorry for that, Miz Cameron," said Abigail Mertz. "I warned you about French folk."

"Who eez theez unfashionable woman?" demanded Yvette.

"She's the French cook," said Jack.

"Zat eez, believe me, no countrywoman of mine."

"And a good thing too," said Abigail, glaring at Yvette and then stomping back to her kitchen.

Yvette was studying Kristin closely. "Well, madame, I zeenk I can do somezing for you. You have ze exceptional figure and very good hair, if decently styled of course. Once I 'ave taken over your wardrobe, both as seamstress and dresser, you weel become *très chic*. Ze only pity is zat zere weel be no one een theez very unchic town who weel appreciate what miracles I 'ave performed."

"Including me," muttered Kristin under her breath.

"Now, sweetheart," said Jack. "You're going to love having Yvette. Everyone knows how much women like fashionable clothes and hairdos."

Kristin glared at him.

"Now, madame, eef you weel show me where my room eez and zen your wardrobe, we can begin at once. I 'ave already wasted hours trying to find you."

"I don't see how anyone could get lost in Breckenridge. Winifred, you've got a new parlor maid," she called to her housekeeper. "This is Maude, and this woman is my lady's maid." She shot Jack a dark look. "Obviously you're not satisfied with my appearance."

"My dear, your appearance is the delight of the whole population, and when Yvette gets through with you—"

"—you might even look beautiful," finished Yvette.

Kristin gritted her teeth. "Find them rooms, please, Winifred."

That night at dinner, they ate a dish called cassoulet, which Abigail said was the best she could do with what she found in the kitchen, and which everyone else, including Kristin, thought was marvelously delicious—a concoction of beans, onion, sausage and other tasty ingredients; it was the only time Kristin could remember having liked sausage.

Jack said, "Superb, my dear, Abigail," earning a superior nod from the new Amazonian cook.

"Peasant food," muttered Yvette.

To which Abigail said, "Well, being a peasant, you ought to know." Maude served the whole meal so that Winifred, for once, got to eat warm food and stay seated. Everyone congratulated Jack on having hired Abigail. The other girls took to Maude, but Yvette won no friends because she was prone to making fashion pronouncements and disparaging remarks on the clothing of her fellow employees.

"What eez zat zing you are wearing?" she asked Fanny, a look of exaggerated horror on her small, dark face.

"It's a wash dress," said Fanny. "You bein' a lady's maid, you'll probably come to appreciate 'em."

"I could never appreciate such a garment," retorted Yvette and helped herself to more cassoulet, although she had sneered at it.

"Quiet," said Ingrid after Yvette's fourth unkind remark, that one about the bold color of Ingrid's gown. "I'm one of the bosses here, so watch your tongue, or I'll tear a few handfuls out of that head of hair you've got all slicked down." Yvette looked alarmed, opened her mouth to retort, then closed it, thinking better of getting into a squabble with a woman as tall and aggressive as Ingrid.

Kristin muttered to Jack after dinner, "Look what you've done. Everyone got along perfectly until that Frenchwoman showed up."

"You'll come to appreciate the services she can offer," said Jack cheerfully.

"I didn't need any services."

"Right. And you don't need jewelry. You don't need new clothes. But I've never heard you say you don't need money, which reminds me, how's that self-portrait coming?"

"It's a good thing I haven't started," said Kristin. "No doubt Yvette would disapprove of the gown."

"If she says anything against that dress, which I happen to think makes you look like a princess, send her to me. I'll put her in her place."

As Kristin drifted back to her studio, the word *princess* reverberated in her mind. She had wanted so much to be a princess when she was a little girl, but Jack was the only one who had ever thought of her that way. Of course, why should she believe a word that came out of his mouth? It was probably just the snake offering her the apple in the Garden of Eden, the apple being another night of ecstasy. Well, she wasn't falling into sin again, not with a man who knew nothing about the proprieties of passion. He'd probably want to do the act on a feast day, or right after mass, or some equally shocking time.

By the light of the long summer evening still coming in her windows, she looked at the lavender dress, which she had hung in the studio. He was right. It *was* a pretty gown. She closed the door and put it on, then took various poses in front of the mirror. She had taken down her hair and was holding it up in back with one slender hand, her head cocked to the side in a lazy, assessing position when Yvette entered the studio without knocking.

"Madame, what time will you wish me to prepare you for bed?" Kristin whirled in surprise. "Oh madame, zat shade of lavender eez not chic zis year. You should not—"

"My husband is very fond of it," said Kristin. "He wants a self-portrait of me in this dress."

Yvette squinted from picture to picture where they leaned against the studio walls. "A strangely fuzzy style of painting," she said.

"Do you think so? I find it strange that a French woman should say that since it is all the rage in Paris."

Yvette flushed. "'Ow would you know zat, madame? Surely I 'ave been in Paris more recently zan you."

"I have never been there," said Kristin, "but I am quite familiar with what is happening in Paris art circles, which obviously you are not. You need not attend me any more this evening, Yvette. I intend to stay up painting, and you, having had a long trip, should retire early." She stared challengingly at the Frenchwoman, who curtsied and left the room, nose in the air.

Kristin giggled. Perhaps she could get the best of Yvette, after all. Even as she was talking, she had decided that she would do no standard self-portrait. Instead she would paint her own reflection in the mirror with herself standing in front of it and slightly to the side—both back and front of Kristin, her lavender gown, her hair loose and held up with one hand. It would be a challenging experiment, but if it worked, Jack wouldn't be able to say that he hadn't got his two hundred dollars worth.

She tied her hair back with a ribbon, put a prepared canvas on her easel in front of the mirror, and began to block out the picture, working steadily, her full lower lip caught between her teeth. From time to time, she posed to remind herself of the composition she wanted. From time to time, she loosened her hair and held it back. So engaged was she with her idea and its execution that she did not hear her husband when he opened the door quietly and stepped softly across the room to see what she was doing. He watched, smiling, as she posed again with her hand holding the long strands of flaxen hair away from her neck.

Jack saw immediately what she had in mind, and his face settled into lines of satisfaction. Whether or not Kristin knew it, she was displaying herself for him in a very seductive way. It would be the portrait of a woman who now saw herself as a sexual being. As such, it was extremely revealing. Jack backed quietly away and left without Kristin ever sensing his presence. He hoped she finished it quickly, for he longed to see it and how she saw herself now that she was no longer an innocent girl. He was winning the game—slowly, but winning. And she didn't even know it.

"Your breakfast, madame," called Yvette. No one answered. She turned the knob and pushed, her tray carefully balanced on one hand. Nothing happened. Yvette lowered the tray to the left of the door, turned the knob with both hands, and pushed. The door did not budge. Holding the knob open with one hand, she threw the full weight of her body against the door, which gave an inch with a scraping sound, but still she could not get in.

"'elp, 'elp!" she cried. "Somezing 'as 'appened to madame. Perhaps some villain has barred her door. 'elp!" Yvette

271

had a very piercing voice, and although everyone in the house was downstairs except Jack and Kristin, young women began to gather at the foot of the stairs.

"What's the matter? If Miss Kristin wants to sleep, why don't you leave her alone?" shouted Fanny.

Winifred came bustling in from the drawing room with Maude; they had been polishing furniture. "Miss Kristin was up late painting," called Winifred. "Let the poor woman sleep. She was so tired, she forgot to turn her lamps off."

"*Mon Dieu!*" cried Yvette. "Zere eez a large object blocking her door. Someone must 'ave dragged her upstairs from ze studio, and zat eez why ze lamps were left on." She pushed again.

The girls in the hall whispered among themselves. Abigail stormed in from the kitchen and mounted the stairs, demanding to know why the mistress's breakfast sat on the floor getting cold. Jack, who had been in his room shaving, came out wearing a blanket bathrobe with satin lapels, barefoot, wiping lather from his left cheek.

"What's the fuss?" he demanded.

"Monsieur, you must try to open ze connecting door between your room and madame's. I cannot enter madame's room. I theenk somezing terrible must 'ave 'appened, some abductor. I hear zat zees territory 'as many such persons."

Jack's mouth twitched with humor. "My poor wife!" he exclaimed. "We must force the door."

"What's going on?" called Kristin from inside the room. All the noise had awakened her.

"Madame must be 'eld at gunpoint by some bandit, who eez forcing her to zound her usual irritated morning zelf, monsieur," said Yvette.

"No doubt," said Jack dryly. "Perhaps I'd best get my rifle." He went back into his room.

The braver sausage-makers had now ascended the stairs and were standing in the hall, wringing their hands.

"Don't worry, Kristin," called Jack, coming back with his rifle. "We're rescuing you."

"What?" Inside the room Kristin had climbed out of bed, confused by all the commotion and worried that someone would discover that she kept a barrier between herself and her husband at night. She couldn't decide what to do.

Jack backed up almost to the stairs, ran forward and hurled his shoulder against the door, managing to force it open a foot, through which he squeezed, rifle first.

"What in the world is going on?" demanded Kristin, backing up hastily. She was wearing a thin white linen nightdress, ruffled at the throat and wrist, with blue ribbon and embroidery trim at the yoke. "Why do you have that gun?"

Yvette slipped in beside him as he said, "Yvette thought someone was holding you captive in here since she couldn't get in with your breakfast tray."

"Yvette, you're an idiot!"

"Well, madame, I was seemply trying to deliver your *petit déjeuner.*"

"Well, in the future don't deliver it 'till I ask for it," muttered Kristin.

Four sausage makers squeezed in beside Yvette and eyed the chiffonier which had been blocking the door. They began to giggle. Jack grinned at his scowling wife.

"Zeez eez a most peculiar 'ouse'old," said Yvette, giving the chiffonier a shove so that she could stalk out with dignity.

Chapter Seventeen

"I don't have time for all this socializing," said Kristin. "We've been to balls, lectures, dinner parties—"

"Which is exactly why we need to give a dinner party ourselves. We'll start in a simple way with a few Cripple Creek investors here in town."

"Sean would expect to bring Augustina, but she wouldn't want to be around Ingrid."

"Ingrid's going on a selling trip to Aspen. She won't be back until Sunday. Now let's see. We'll need to send invitations and alert Abigail and Yvette."

"Why Yvette?"

"For your hair and dress."

"I'm tired of having Yvette hovering over me," muttered Kristin. "I'm trying to paint, and she's fiddling with my hair. It's not conducive to artistic inspiration."

"Then give her the time to do your hair first."

Kristin was still feeling grumpy because of the embarrassing scene that Yvette had created, making it clear to everyone that Kristin and Jack did not share a bed or room. Now Yvette kept telling her that it would be much more convenient for Jack if there were a door between Kristin's room and his.

"Zat is ze proper way to handle sleeping arrangements, madame," Yvette assured her, citing such arrangements among the French aristocracy.

Kristin had to grit her teeth through all this. She couldn't tell Yvette that she and Jack did not sleep together at all, except for that once, and that Kristin had no intention of doing so again, even if she did dream of him at night and still caught herself making sketches of him—the way his hair sprang thick and lively from his forehead, his heavy brows and fine nose, the tempting definition of his lips, an elbow and biceps. She was getting compulsive about it and couldn't seem to keep either her mind or her pencil under control. Muttering to herself, she went back to her studio and her series of landscapes, the result of her trip on the Georgetown Loop. She wished now that she hadn't closed her eyes. What a sissy she was! That trestle would have made a marvelous picture.

"Come in, come in, monsieur."

Kristin, who was wearing a sheer dressing gown over her corset and petticoats, hunched her shoulders and pulled the dressing gown protectively across her breasts.

"What do you theenk, monsieur?" asked Yvette, standing back to admire her handiwork.

Jack studied his wife in the mirror. "If you shaved her head, she'd still be the most beautiful woman in Colorado, but that is a charming coiffure."

"It's too elaborate," said Kristin. A pile of curls rose at the crown of her head with wisps of fringe on her forehead.

In back a jeweled clasp held a feather decoration that rose above the curls. "None of the other women—"

"I theenk ze green dress, don't you agree, monsieur?" Three dresses were spread across the bed. "Madame wants to wear ze lavender, but eet eez a year out of style."

Jack's eyes gleamed. "I'm flattered that you chose the lavender, Kristin. Put it on for me before we go down."

Alarmed, Kristin wondered if he expected to stand there watching while Yvette helped her to dress. Obviously he did, and she couldn't say anything in front of the maid.

Pouting because her choice had been refused by Jack, Yvette swept up the lavender dress and held it out to Kristin. "Does Madame need help weeth ze dressing gown?"

Kristin scowled at them both, turned her back, and allowed Yvette to slide the sheer material off her shoulders and then button her into the dress. "Ah, madame, you must sit down at the mirror again. We have disarranged your hair and feathers." Kristin had stepped away from the mirror so that Jack could not see her reflection. Now she returned.

Jack, once she was gowned, leaned over to kiss her shoulder, whispering, "Many thanks, sweetheart."

Kristin turned pink. "I only choose it because—"

"Because you know how much I like it."

"That wasn't my reason at all," said Kristin.

"Ladies are supposed to take ze advice of zeir lady's maids," said Yvette sternly.

"What? Before the wishes of their husbands?" asked Jack as Kristin resumed her seat in front of the mirror. Jack pulled from his pocket a necklace of amethysts. "I was hoping you'd wear the lavender," he said and bent to fasten the necklace at her throat. The piece had a chain of small stones set in gold links with larger stones hanging from the chain, two to either side and one longer pendant which fell into the first rise of her cleavage. Having carefully locked the clasp at the back of her neck, Jack adjusted the pendant so that it and his fingers lay a second between her breasts. "Lovely, isn't it?"

Kristin trembled under the brush of his fingers, her eyes fastened on the mirror image of herself, of Jack, of one long, brown finger against the pale curves that rose above the low neck of her gown. He straightened slowly, both hands trailing across the sensitive skin until his fingers curved over her bare shoulders as he whispered into her ear, "Princess." His breath made her shiver again. "Hurry now," he murmured. "Our guests will be arriving."

"Wait," she called. "Do you realize that they were dynamiting under the house today?"

"It's all right," he assured her. "They know what they're doing."

"We'll be lucky if we're not all killed."

Jack laughed and walked through the door into the hall. "Five minutes," he called over his shoulder.

The table was beautifully set with a fine linen tablecloth, heavily embroidered in blue and white to match the china. When had that come? she wondered. Her husband was always ordering some new thing. There was crystal and silver, and Jack at the other end, smiling at her through the candles' glow, looking handsomer than ever in his evening clothes. She recalled too clearly the last time she'd seen him in evening clothes—just before he took them off and made love to her.

"This is some meal," said Connor, who was sitting beside her.

"Not a restaurant in town can duplicate it," said Mr. Horace Parker, who sat to her left.

Mrs. Parker and Kat flanked Jack. The Parkers' marriageable daughter, Mattie, Sean and Augustina Fitzpatrick, and Cal Bannister filled in the middle seats.

"Do you have a dog?" asked Augustina.

"I just bought two hunting hounds," said Jack.

"Their mother has the best nose this side of the Continental Divide," said Connor.

"The pigs hate them," said Kristin.

"I think one or both of your dogs are under the table, Jack," said Augustina.

Jack squinted at Kristin. Biting her lip to keep from giggling, she lifted the floor-length tablecloth and peeked under. "Gwennie," whispered Kristin. The pig, who was investigating Augustina's petticoats, ignored Kristin. Kristin sighed and rang the silver bell that summoned Maude from the kitchen. "Maude, I'm afraid that Gwennie's under the table."

"Oh, ma'am, I'm so sorry. I didn't think to look," said Maude and crawled under between Sean Fitzpatrick and Mrs. Parker, calling, "Come here, Gwennie. Come on. You can eat in the kitchen."

"What's that?" cried Mrs. Parker.

"It's Gwennie, ma'am," came Maude's voice from under the table. "She won't hurt you."

"Is Gwennie one of your hounds?" asked Augustina.

"She's Kristin's pet pig, Gwenivere," Jack replied. Mrs. Parker gasped. Kat and Connor Macleod began to laugh while Maude continued to crawl around under the table, trying to catch the elusive Gwennie, ruffling skirts, bumping into people's legs and feet, crying, "Excuse me, ma'am . . . excuse me, sir," popping out between Miss Mattie Parker and Cal Bannister. "She just won't come to me, Miss Kristin. You're the only one she ever minds."

Kristin sighed and rose, placing her napkin neatly beside her plate of venison in a superb wine-and-cream sauce. She pulled her chair away and dove under the table, saying,

"Gwennie, come here this minute." Quickly she emerged with the pig under her arm and headed for the kitchen.

"You let a pig in the house?" exclaimed Augustina.

"Well, this is a sausage factory," said Kat. "And doing very well too. If you worked as hard at interior decoration, Augustina . . ."

"I consider myself a homemaker and mother first," said Augustina, "not a business woman."

"Which is as it should be," Mrs. Parker agreed. "I've taught my daughter that when she marries"—Mrs. Parker beamed at Cal Bannister—"her husband should come first. I don't how you put up with a wife who's absent so often, Mr. Macleod," she added sympathetically.

"I'm under contract, ma'am," said Conner, referring to the pre-marriage contract he'd written to lure Kat to the alter. "Besides, Kat makes it worthwhile when she is home." Connor grinned, shocking Mrs. Parker.

Kristin reentered and said, "Gwenivere is settled for the night. Can I help anyone to more of Mr. Braddock's delicious string beans prepared in the French style?"

"I suppose Abigail's complaining about Gwennie again," said Jack.

"Yes, but it's not as if I invited Gwenivere in. Oakum says Gwenivere thinks she's one of us rather than one of them because she lost her mother at an early age. In fact, Oakum suspects her of dieting so she doesn't get fat enough to be slaughtered. She's a very intelligent pig," Kristin added to Connor. "I wouldn't allow her to be slaughtered, unless she did something really terrible."

"Like knocking over an unfinished painting," suggested Jack.

Mrs. Parker looked horrified. "Pigs are dirty. How can you allow one in your house? Especially in your dining room and your kitchen?" Mrs. Parker stared down at the food on her plate as if Gwennie had been rooting through it.

"Oh, Gwenivere's housebroken," said Kristin. "More potatoes au gratin?"

"No, thank you," said Mrs. Parker.

At that moment a loud groaning resounded under foot, and the china jiggled on the table.

"If that doesn't feel like an earthquake, I don't know what does," said Mr. Parker.

"We don't have earthquakes in Breckenridge," said Connor, who had lived in the town long enough to know.

"Well, I've been to California, and I know what an earthquake feels like."

"I told you the blasting was too strong today," said Kristin to Jack. "And I don't care how knowledgeable that dynamite man is."

"Dynamite man?" cried Mattie Parker, who was torn away from her flirtation with Cal Bannister by the fact that her venison had jumped off her plate.

"Just to be on the safe side," said Jack, "perhaps we should retire to another room." The timbers supporting the dining room floor creaked alarmingly, the table tilted slightly, and the china began to slide.

"In which direction?" asked Kristin.

Jack rose calmly, taking his wine glass and the bottle with him. "The veranda, I think," he replied. "Isn't it fortunate that we were almost through with the main course."

"I wasn't," said Kristin.

Augustina and the two Parker women fled toward the hall. Kristin followed and joined Kat, having called into the kitchen, "Out of the house, Abigail, Maude. It's collapsing because of Mr. Cameron's furnace." She had picked up her plate and silverware, for she found the venison delicious, even if Jack had shot the deer in cold blood. Kristin walked calmly through the folding doors to the hall and out onto the veranda, all the gentlemen following politely.

"Downstairs and out of the house, girls," Jack yelled up the stairs, and the sausage girls, who had been huddling upstairs, came flying down in various states of disarray to cluster in the front yard like a flock of chickens, clucking with alarm at the approach of a fox.

"Considering what I remember about the house structure, I think we're safe enough out here," said Jack and sat down on the veranda beside his wife, who was forking up another bite of venison in cream-and-wine sauce. Quite a bit still remained on her plate because she had spent so much time under the table coaxing Gwennie out.

"That ought to cure you of entertaining," she murmured under her breath. A terrible crash echoed behind them.

"What's happening?" asked Mrs. Parker, her voice trembling in a terrified quiver as she looked longingly toward the sausage girls, safe in the yard.

"What a shame you didn't bring your dinner with you," said Kristin to Mrs. Parker. "As sour a disposition as Abigail has, she cooks like an angel."

"You certainly seem to be enjoying her efforts," said Jack, grinning.

At that moment Abigail herself appeared around the side of the house, Maude trailing behind her. "Excuse me, ma'am, but the dining room furniture just fell into the basement. Not all of it, but quite a bit, taking the dishes with it. Do you want me to serve the rest of the meal out here?"

"Yes, please, Abigail."

Abigail strode back around the corner of the house, again with Maude in tow. "Elaborate dinners, *fini,*" murmured Kristin.

"Not at all," said Jack. "We can have the floor replaced, and I have a new dining room suite on the way. What man

281

wants to entertain from a secondhand table?"

"Not you obviously," said Kristin and finished her venison.

"What's the news from Cripple Creek?" asked Sean as if nothing had happened, although his wife looked pale and frightened in the fading summer light. He and Augustina were sitting as far away from each other as the arrangement of chairs on the veranda would allow.

"Good," said Cal Bannister. "All good. That's what I'm here to tell you. We just dug down to a six-inch vein on the Bull Hill Locomotive claim, and it's looking good on two more."

"Hello, Miss Ingrid," called Fanny.

"What are you girls doing out here?" asked Ingrid, who had just reached the gate with a valise in her hand.

"The dining room fell in, Miss Ingrid," said Bea. "We're waitin' to see if any more of the house falls down before we goes to bed."

"Sounds smart to me," said Ingrid and continued up the gravel walkway to the veranda.

"I can't believe this," exclaimed Augustina.

"You said she wouldn't be back," Kristin murmured to Jack.

"Sean!" cried Ingrid, a delighted smile lighting her face as she climbed the steps. "How are the children?"

"Just fine."

The gentlemen had risen. Mrs. Parker, who had been assured that Ingrid would not be in the house if she agreed to come to dinner, narrowed her eyes in ladylike indignation.

"You're back early, Ingrid," stammered Kristin.

"I got seven orders."

"Good for you," said Kat. "You're turning out to be a fine business woman."

Augustina glared at her sister-in-law.

"Well, if I do some of the selling, Kristin can spend more time in her studio, but there wasn't much use my staying in Aspen overnight, not when people kept offering me drinks. That's the idea of all this, isn't it? To keep me from drinking?" She eyed the chair beside Sean, and he eagerly rose and held it for her. The two fell into conversation about Phoebe's progress on the piano. Augustina jumped up and went into the house.

"Augustina," called Jack, "I think I'd give it a moment to settle."

"The drawing room seems safe enough," replied Augustina and turned sharply in that direction.

"I believe I'll join her," said Mrs. Parker. "Come along, Mattie. There's a chill in the air."

Mattie Parker followed reluctantly. Ingrid watched them go with a tight mouth, and Kristin felt sorry for her. They could have been less obvious in their disapproval. After all, Ingrid was sober and respectable, if a little flirtatious, all the time now. She was certainly flirting with Sean. Although they were discussing their children, the very lines of Ingrid's body trumpeted seductiveness. Kristin wondered how Ingrid did that and whether one could catch it on canvas. Painting Ingrid would be like painting herself larger than life and a hundred times more womanly. Kristin sighed and wondered why Jack continued to pursue her. Probably just for the devilment of it.

"Why the sigh, sweetheart?" Jack murmured to her. "Your dining room will be better than it ever was."

He was stroking the palm of her hand. Did he know, she wondered, how that felt to her? "Who cares about the damn dining room?" she retorted and jerked her hand away.

"I believe that's the first time I've heard you swear."

"Well, if any more rooms fall into the basement, you can

283

certainly expect to hear it again," Kristin muttered.

Maude appeared, carrying a tray with coffee and delectable cherry tarts in heavy English cream. There was after-dinner brandy for the gentlemen and a light, sweet wine for the ladies.

"You'll have to serve Mrs. Fitzpatrick and Mrs. and Miss Parker in the drawing room, Maude," said Kristin.

"Is it safe, ma'am?" asked Maude.

"There's a good support timber running down the hall that wouldn't have been touched at all," said Jack.

"You mean the kitchen will be the next to go?"

"No, there's another under the kitchen. The cross timbers that held up the dining room must have cracked."

"Sorry about that," said Connor and burst out laughing.

"Really, Connor," said Kat, "I'm sure Kristin doesn't find it funny that her dining room just disappeared."

"I suppose I should go into the drawing room," said Sean reluctantly.

Ingrid rose. "Why don't we all?"

Kat tried to catch her arm. "Ingrid, I don't think—"

"Maybe you shouldn't have let him get married again," said Ingrid. "Just because we weren't married in the church doesn't mean we weren't married. And I've looked up the law. The notice of desertion was supposed to have been published wherever you thought I might be. As I heard it, you received news that I was in Aspen."

"Yes, but we never heard of you after the first time, so we thought it must have been a rumor," said Kat.

"Well, it wasn't, and I still consider myself married."

Sean, looking stricken, said softly to his former wife, "I'm sorry, love."

"Sorry doesn't give me back my husband and children," said Ingrid. She gave him a long look, then sailed into the house, coffee in one hand, tart in the other. Everyone noticed that she had refused the wine. As the others trailed in, Ingrid sat down across the drawing room from Mrs. Parker and Augustina. When Augustina stared at her husband and patted the seat beside her on the sofa, Sean went to her, looking somewhat reluctant. Kristin saw Ingrid blink rapidly and realized that she had hoped Sean would choose to sit by her.

Kristin started toward Ingrid to offer the support of friendship and to ensure that Jack could not take her hand again, but Cal Bannister beat Kristin to the settee. "Well," said Ingrid brightly, "who might you be?"

"Calvin Bannister."

Mattie Parker's lower lip quivered in disappointment. Obviously she had hoped that Bannister would sit beside her.

"Oh, the Cripple Creek man."

"Yes. Are you one of my investors, Miss—"

"*Mrs.* Fitzpatrick." Ingrid supplied the name and glanced defiantly at Augustina and Sean. Mrs. Parker was watching disapprovingly as Ingrid set about charming Cal Bannister. Not another word was said about Cripple Creek that evening because nobody could get Cal's attention. The more Ingrid flirted, the more woebegone Sean looked.

Kristin found herself making desperate conversation, mostly with Jack, although Connor and Kat pitched in occasionally to ease the awkward silences. "Mrs. Parker," said Kristin, trying to get the woman's attention away from the drama being enacted on the settee, "you have the loveliest hairline and hair." Even the compliment couldn't distract Amelia Parker. "I'd love to do your portrait," said Kristin, her voice even louder.

That did get Mrs. Parker's attention. "I wasn't thinking of having my portrait painted," said the lady stiffly, "and certainly not in a house that has pigs wandering about,

285

sausage making going on, and—and goodness knows wha
else." She was staring resentfully at Cal, who she hac
hoped would court her daughter.

"If that's the way you feel, I'm surprised that you cam
to dinner," snapped Kristin.

"Now, ladies," Jack intervened.

"I wouldn't have if I'd known that the dining room wa
going to collapse," said Mrs. Parker.

"Now, dear," said her husband, "these things happen
Other than a few unusual events, it's been a fine evening
Just the news about Cripple Creek—"

"Come along, Horace, I think it's time we went home."
Mrs. Parker rose, took one last look at Ingrid and Cal on
the settee, bade Augustina a sympathetic farewell, which
infuriated Augustina, and headed for the door with he
disappointed daughter in tow.

"I'm still in on Cripple Creek, aren't I?" asked Horace
Parker apologetically.

"Of course," said Jack, and he saw his guests out, smil
ing as if nothing untoward had happened.

"The nerve of that woman," muttered Kristin. "I wouldn'
paint her if she were—Cleopatra. And I haven't heard tha
her housekeeping is so fine. They say that she's very sting
with the hired help."

"Does she buy Traube sausages?" asked Kat. "You can'
afford to fall out with the local customers."

"And this from the lady who causes strikes at my mine
because of her temperance crusades," said Connor dryly.

"I do not. We haven't had a strike in several years."

"We may now that Kristin controls the supply of mar
riageable women instead of you."

"I'm not toadying to a snobbish, uncivil woman with no
manners just to sell a couple of sausages, Kat. Ingrid and
have accounts all over the mountains."

"Amelia Parker could hurt you in the local market."

"I don't care," said Kristin.

Kat sighed. "Thank God, Ingrid's looking after business. I love you like a sister, Kristin, but you never have your mind on anything but art."

"You love me like a sister?" Kristin echoed, looking touched.

"Well, of course."

"My own sister couldn't stand me," said Kristin, blinking back tears. "I don't think any of my brothers liked me either, or my father and mother."

"Oh, sweetheart, you're just upset because of the dining room. Why don't you have a glass of wine?" Jack picked up the ladies' bottle and a crystal wine glass.

"Are you trying to get me drunk again?"

She gave him a furious look, and Jack began to laugh. "Not a bad idea, now that you mention it."

Kat turned on him like an avenging fury. "It's bad enough that you drink, Jack Cameron, without urging spirits on your wife. You should be ashamed of yourself."

"Come on, Kat. Can we forget the temperance lecture for one night?" said Connor.

"I never forget temperance," said Kat.

"My Aunt Frieda likes me," said Kristin sadly. "She's the only one from Chicago who ever writes to me."

"Stop looking at her," said Augustina.

"I wasn't," said Sean.

"I'd love to come to Cripple Creek sometime," Ingrid told Cal Bannister in husky tones.

Sean forgot about placating his wife and scowled at his ex-wife.

"And I'd love to entertain you," said Cal.

"Of course, it would be a trip to sell sausages." Ingrid fluttered her eyelashes at the mining engineer.

"I thought Kristin was supposed to sell sausages," said Sean. "Cripple Creek's a real pretty valley. She'll want to paint it. And Pike's Peak's right there, so—"

"I'm leaving," said Augustina. "Are you coming, Sean?"

Sean rose reluctantly; his eyes were still fixed on Ingrid and Cal.

"I guess we'll be leaving too," said Connor, "since the party seems to be breaking up." Grinning, he slapped Jack on the back. "Most interesting dinner party I've ever been to. Usually they're deadly dull."

Jack walked his guests to the door while Ingrid continued to flirt until she heard them leave. Then she rose and said, "I'm for bed. I've had a long day."

Cal grinned and said to Kristin, "I think the lady's been using me to make someone jealous, don't you?"

Kristin was still looking glum and didn't quite take in his meaning. Ingrid patted her on the shoulder and said, "Cheer up, Kristin. You have two sisters, because I love you too. Although I doubt that Kat and I will ever make it a three-way sisterhood."

"Oh, Ingrid, you should make friends with Kat. She never meant to do you any harm. One can never have enough friends, especially those of us who don't have family."

"You need a drink, my girl," said Ingrid. "A good stiff one. Ask Jack for a brandy."

Jack, who appeared through the archway at that moment, said, "Ingrid, if I offered my wife a brandy, she'd probably make me sleep in the basement, and as you probably know, our sleeping arrangements leave a lot to be desired as it is."

"Really, Jack!" snapped Kristin.

"Really what? You're the one who's insisted on this unnatural marriage."

Kristin turned pink and glanced apprehensively at

Bannister. No telling what he thought. Unnatural, her husband had said. Exactly what Sister Mary Joseph had talked about. Surely Sister Mary Joseph had never meant that abstinence was unnatural. Kristin clenched her fists and glared at her husband. How could he say such a thing? And in front of other people. She'd put *two* pieces of furniture in front of her door tonight, and she didn't care what anyone thought.

Chapter Eighteen

"Looks like the dynamitin' put two big cracks in the cross beams right under your dinin' room, an' that there heavy table caved the whole thing in. Shouldn't be no trouble to fix, though you might consider gittin' a lighter table," said the carpenter.

"Just put in extra cross beams," said Jack. "The table I've ordered is heavier than the last." Having eaten in the kitchen, Jack went to Kristin's studio. He entered quietly and stood behind her, studying the self-portrait on which she was working. The innocent sensuality she depicted so unknowingly on the canvas made him yearn to take her in his arms. Instead he murmured, "Beautiful."

She jumped.

"Sorry. I didn't mean to frighten you." Kristin immersed herself so thoroughly in her work that the house could fall down without her noticing, he thought wryly and laid a hand on her shoulder as if to steady her.

"How do you get in here without my hearing?"

"I usually do, but it's called walking like an Indian," he replied. "You can't hunt unless you learn it."

Kristin turned to stare. "You learned quickly."

"What's this Ingrid tells me about your going up to Mohawk Lake by yourself?"

"Connor was describing it to me before the dining room collapsed," said Kristin and went back to painting the pink silk roses at the shoulders of the gown. "It sounded so beautiful."

"It is."

"You've seen it?" she asked eagerly, giving him her full attention.

"I have, and you certainly can't go by yourself."

"I can too."

"How? You don't ride. You don't drive a wagon."

"I'll walk," she replied stubbornly.

"It's miles, Kristin. And the woods are full of wild animals."

Kristin looked so crestfallen that Jack was hard put to keep from grinning. "Oh, all right," he said with feigned reluctance. "I'll take you."

Her eyes narrowed suspiciously. "I'll hire someone."

"I'm not letting you traipse into the mountains with some stranger. How do we know he'd be trustworthy?"

"How do I know you would be?"

"Better the devil you know," said Jack cheerfully.

"Devil is right."

She said it so sincerely that he was taken aback. Did she truly think him evil? he wondered uneasily. She had no reason—no *good* reason. "I suppose we could go up there, camp overnight—"

"Absolutely not," said Kristin.

Jack had anticipated that reaction. "Then it will have to

be a one-day outing. Can you get what you need in, say, four or five hours? We'd have to leave early tomorrow."

Kristin wavered. She did want to paint Mohawk Lake. She needed a deep forest scene for her landscape series, and Connor's description had made the area seem perfect. Maybe they could visit the cabin where Kat had been held captive by the mad German carpenter. Life in the West was so exciting—not that Kristin herself craved excitement. But she couldn't resist Jack's offer, for she saw that if she wanted to visit Mohawk Lake, Jack was her only option.

"Very well," she said primly, "but you mustn't take advantage of the situation."

"In what way?" asked Jack, looking as innocent as he could considering his plans for a bucolic afternoon seduction.

"Well, I suppose since we'll be in the wilderness, I don't have to worry about that."

Jack nodded agreeably, thinking, *Much you know, sweetheart.*

Jack was sprawled comfortably, his back against a tree trunk, looking over papers he had just received from Cal Bannister. This was going to be one hell of an investment, he thought. By the time they'd mined out the Cripple Creek holdings, he could retire and take his wife to Europe to hobnob with the aristocracy. Somehow that prospect didn't interest him. Colorado was more to his taste. He flipped a page to read about three new claims that Cal had prospected and filed in another area of the valley.

"You'll think I'm crazy," Cal wrote, "but I had a gut feeling about this place. It may turn out to be better than any of them. Of course, you should be reassured to know that with me gut feelings are based on study of the volcanic rock, the drifts below the claim, and so forth. I won't bore you with all the geological details, but you might tell Connor." Bannister went on to describe what he had found in the new section of the valley.

Jack flipped another page to read production figures on the mine they had in operation, where they had drilled a ninety-foot tunnel. He was smiling at the latest assay reports when his wife shrieked, sending a hush of alarm through the forest. Insects, birds, small animals all went still. Kristin was frozen in front of her easel. Sweet Jesus, he thought, spotting a black bear that swayed threateningly on its hind legs in the forest shadows.

Jack picked up his rifle and called to his wife, "Move slowly to your right. Don't turn and run." The bear's shaggy head swiveled, its attention divided between Kristin and Jack. Kristin trembled so visibly that Jack could see it. Hesitantly she stepped to the right. The bear's head swung back toward her. Jack hissed, and it looked at him again. She took another step to the right, putting herself out of his line of fire. He sighted carefully and pulled the trigger in a smooth, slow motion. The bear seemed to hesitate, shudder, then it swayed and fell into the grass as Jack put a second shot into its chest. Cautiously, he walked forward.

"Don't go near him!" came Kristin's voice from his right. Jack raised one hand as if to calm her and continued his approach. When he was within three feet of the animal, he noted that he had put the first cartridge between its eyes. Wouldn't his father be surprised to know that Jack, man about Chicago, had turned into a credible woodsman? "She's dead," said Jack.

"You mean it was a mother bear?" asked Kristin.

"I don't know about mother, but it was female." He shouldered his rifle and walked toward her.

"Shouldn't you keep watching it?"

"What are you expecting?" asked Jack. "A miraculous resurrection?"

"That's blasphemous," said Kristin and burst into tears.

He glanced back at the bear, who was still dead in the grass, a shaggy mound that looked much less threatening than it had just a minute earlier. Reassured, he laid down his rifle, and took Kristin in his arms. "Now, sweetheart—"

"Stop calling me that," she sobbed.

"You weren't in danger. I'm a very good shot."

Kristin's nose was being tickled by the hair that curled at the throat of his shirt. He was turning into more than a good shot, she realized. Jack seemed like an entirely different man. Her fashionable husband was dressed in Levis, boots, a wide leather belt, a soft cotton shirt of a deep blue that matched his eyes, and a western hat. He carried a revolver in his belt and the rifle with which he'd saved her from the bear. She hardly recognized him as the sophisticated John Powell Cameron she had painted with mustache and gold-headed cane, a painting that now hung over the fireplace, embarrassing him when people came to call.

She could feel the hard muscles in his arms, the power of his body. She experienced a rush of heat and pulled away.

"Better now?" asked Jack kindly. "Why don't we take a break and have our picnic?"

"I'm not sure I could eat." Kristin was embarrassed at the way she had reacted to his body when he seemed intent only on reassuring her.

"Of course, you can. Abigail has packed us all sorts of exotic delights."

"I'm not drinking any brandy." How hard it was to be cautious and suspicious on such a lovely day when her husband had just saved her from a black bear and was being so kind and nonthreatening.

"My dear, you have a lascivious mind," he teased, embarrassing her further. He took her arm and led her toward the tree under which he'd been sitting. "Would I ask you to drink spirituous liquors at midday? Abigail has fixed lemonade and other things you'll like." He spread a blanket, helped Kristin to seat herself, and returned to the wagon to lift out the picnic hamper. The food was delicious, the air around them cool, the sky bright with sunshine, the lake a stunning sapphire blue surrounded by the deep green of the forest. Enchanted, Kristin let herself enjoy the moment.

After a pleasant half hour of desultory conversation and happy sampling of Abigail's provisions, Kristin sighed. "I *am* glad we came," she admitted, treating herself to one last spoonful of wild raspberries and cream. "Have you ever seen such colors? There's nothing like this in Chicago."

Jack nodded. He was eating cold chicken and crusty, fresh-baked bread. "The forest smells wonderful. Compare this to the Stockyard District, and it would be hard to think of moving back to a city."

Kristin bobbed her head in agreement. "The saddest thing is, I was getting used to that smell when I stayed with Genevieve. I suppose that's what happens to people. They get used to ugliness if they have to."

"I hope you've forgiven me for all the misery I caused you."

Sleepy and mellow with good food and the beauty of her surroundings, Kristin said, "My parents needn't have reacted the way they did. There's a mean streak in all of them." A frown etched her forehead. "Do you think that will come out in me as I get older?"

"Never in this world," said Jack. "You're as sweet as honey. A true changeling."

"That's what my father used to say. Not about honey, about being a changeling. When he was drunk or angry with Mother, he'd say that. I don't think he ever believed that I look like my great grandmother. He claimed—"

"Hush. They were jealous."

Kristin shook her head. "They held me in contempt."

"More fools they." Jack dropped his last chicken bone into the hamper, wiped his hands on a linen napkin, and said casually, "You've got a raspberry stain."

"Where? Yvette will be furious." Kristin inspected the sleeves and bodice of her pale green gown. "She's really irritable about paint spots. I'll never hear the end of a raspberry stain."

"It's a right—there," said Jack and leaned forward with a handkerchief to touch the corner of her mouth. Before she could object, he had leaned away again to inspect his handiwork. "Nope. That didn't do it."

Nope? He really had changed. Miners said "Nope." Henry the Burro Man said "Nope." Oakum, the pigman, said— to her astonishment Jack licked the corner of her mouth. When she gasped, he shifted and licked the *inside* of her lower lip. Then smothered her mouth with his. Sweetly. Gently. As if he had no plans to do anything but explore her lips. Minute after minute. Hour after hour. Making her feel all soft and happy. All protected and cherished.

When, still leaning back against the tree trunk, he lifted her into his lap, she nestled there. Liking the warmth of his arms. The gentle stroking of his hand on her spine. The curve of palm under her chin, the fingers cupping her cheek as she rested again him, her lips raised to his for the long, easy kiss that warmed her all over with its sweet yearning. His yearning. Hers.

After a time, they slid down to the blanket, lying on their sides, the kiss continuing. Jack nuzzled her throat where a white ruffle edged the high, boned neck of her dress. He unbuttoned the long row of buttons, one by one, continuing to kiss her mouth, eyes, ears, throat.

Kristin pulled his blue shirt from his trousers and ran her fingertips over his chest and stomach, then stripped away the shirt because she wanted to see what she was touching, what she had seen only once before. In curiosity, she touched the tip of her index finger to the nipple that peeked through whorls of soft hair on his chest. Jack stiffened and she glanced up at his face, questioning. In answer, he slid the unbuttoned dress from her shoulders, then her chemise, and touched *her* nipple.

"I felt the same thing," he whispered when she inhaled sharply at the flood of feeling he had caused. Were they really experiencing the same thing? she wondered and inched a questing finger into another whorl of hair that circled his navel. Jack sighed—a deep, almost hoarse sound that intensified the weak, warm sensation in her thighs and somewhere inside where babies grew.

Maybe that's what Sister Mary Joseph had meant about thinking of procreation—the consciousness of where babies might grow. Kristin was becoming painfully conscious of that area, low, between her hips, between her legs, because Jack had bent his head to her breast, touched the nipple with his tongue, then his lips, then both. Tremors rocked her. She wanted to squirm, to press up against him, to see more of him, as he was about to see more of her because here in the dappled sunlight, he was smoothing the clothes away from her lower body, piece by piece, even as his lips stayed at her breast, pulling ever so gently until she heard little sounds coming from her own throat.

Jack put her hands on the buckle of his heavy leather belt, and Kristin knew immediately that she could satisfy all her curiosity about men—about Jack, for she had no curiosity about other men. He stood at the center of her universe, the heart of her desire to see. She managed to unbuckle the heavy belt, to work open, one by one, the buttons on his trousers, and she felt a sort of wonder. He was so different. Not ugly or frightening. Just very different. Very exciting.

"You can touch it," he said softly.

Kristin looked up into his eyes, then down as she reached a tentative hand to him. First she ran a finger along the shaft, which was harder than the muscle in his arm, than the stones that made the mountains, as hard as the handle of the axe Oakum used to chop wood, and as smooth. Then her exploring finger touched velvet. Her husband groaned.

"That's enough," he said, his voice tight and soft. He reached for her, and Kristin was disappointed that she could no longer look or touch, for she thought of her life as being in her eyes and in her hands.

The disappointment was only momentary, for when Jack urged her gently onto her back and lifted himself above her on straining arms, she discovered that she could see for a minute the coming together of their bodies, the slow disappearance of his—what was it called?—into herself. Then they blended together in a needy, seeking, liquid blaze of excitement, the power of him, the sure stroke and heat of him inside her, plunging until the long shudders attacked her inside and out, both her and Jack. Naked in the dappled sunlight. On the soft blanket. Trembling. Stilling. Sweat on their skins like dew in the pine-scented air.

For a long time, Kristin cuddled against him, mind and body in such a state of dreamy contentment that it was hard to think of anything. She wasn't sure how long they had lain there, naked. Dozing. Happy.

"Sun's getting lower in the sky," Jack murmured lazily.

"I never finished my painting," she murmured back. She

could just see the easel over the intriguing bulge of his shoulder and biceps.

"You'll remember the scene." He had turned on his side to kiss the corner of her mouth where the raspberry stain had been, the little spot that had started it all.

"This is terrible, you know," she said sadly.

"Terrible? I thought we were superb."

"It was unnatural." Kristin could almost hear Sister Mary Joseph hissing in her ear. "Only at night." It was all coming back to Kristin now that dark urge was satisfied and the spell of pleasure spun out.

"What do you mean, unnatural?" He sounded more amused than worried.

"How can you not think so? Surely, nobody does— does what we did in broad daylight . . . in a wood where anyone could come along . . . and see . . . and know how, how sinful—"

"Who's going to come along? I'd wager there's not a soul in ten square miles, and the bear's dead." He was laughing, pleased with himself.

"I don't know how you can take this so lightly," said Kristin. She sat up and gathered her clothing, one arm shielding her breasts, really worried now. Embarrassed. "I'm sure the Holy Mother is very shocked and disappointed with us," she said.

"Nonsense. The Holy Mother expects married couples—"

"—to disgrace themselves in a public forest?"

Jack grinned. "We don't know that it's a public forest. Maybe someone owns it."

"That's even worse. About the only saving grace is that it's Tuesday." She had turned her back and hastily pulled on her drawers and chemise, her light summer petticoat, ignoring her stays, which would take too much time. She stuffed them into the picnic basket and turned to him, careful to keep her eyes on his face, nowhere else.

"Tuesday?" Jack looked confused. "You mean it's all right to make love in the forest on Tuesdays but not other days?"

He was hopeless. She couldn't believe that he'd been educated by the Jesuits and still know nothing about what was proper between married couples. "Get dressed," she whispered. Amiably Jack pulled on his trousers while she turned her back. She would *not* look any more.

"Want me to do your laces?" He had fished her stays out of the hamper while she was stepping into her dress. Since they were so hard to do herself and the dress waist didn't fit comfortably without them, Kristin agreed.

"Lord, you have a beautiful back," said Jack as he began to tug on the strings. "Such delicate shoulder blades." He leaned forward and, brushing her loose moonglow hair aside, kissed the back of her neck, then watched with satisfaction as the goose bumps rose along her shoulder. He tied the strings and then slipped his hands around to cup her breasts, to run his thumbs inside her chemise and across her nipples. She jerked under his touch, giving him even greater pleasure. She was so responsive.

"No," she said sharply.

"Just one more kiss," said Jack. He pulled her down into his lap, kissing her deeply. "And one more," he murmured. Kristin pushed him away, single tears slipping out of each eye.

"You just don't understand," she said accusingly.

"Indeed I don't, but it's been a lovely afternoon." Why did she feel that married love-making was sinful? he wondered and decided that it must be the embarrassment of a new bride. Undoubtedly, as she became accustomed to the pleasures they found together, she'd relax and stop thinking that anything unusual and overwhelming was sinful. Satisfied with his reasoning, he helped her up, reaching for his blue shirt as he rose. "All right now. Let's get you dressed." He pulled the forgotten pale green confection of a gown up and helped her into the sleeves, buttoned the row of tiny pearl buttons, then donned his shirt, laughing, saying, "If every artist looked the way you do, love, they'd never have a chance to paint anything."

"I didn't choose this dress," Kristin retorted. "It was what Yvette thought proper for a picnic."

"I didn't mean the dress, but Yvette does have good taste. You have to give her that."

"She's bossy."

"That too." Jack collected the remains of the picnic and then Kristin's art supplies, after which he helped his wife up onto the wagon seat.

She sat there, feeling glum.

"Your painting of Mohawk Lake looks like it's going to be beautiful," said Jack.

She nodded, thinking she might have come close to finishing it if she hadn't—her mind shied away from what had happened. No matter how wonderful it had *felt,* she knew she must have sinned grievously. Of course, that was the nature of sin. Its allure was the great pleasure it offered. She could almost feel Sister Mary Joseph hovering behind the two of them like a great, black, bat-winged angel of vengeance.

"Who will you send it to?" asked Jack. "Actually, someone in town might want it. Would you like me to ask among my investors?"

"That's all right," said Kristin, not wanting to be indebted to him any more than she was already. "I'll send it to Mrs. Potter Palmer."

Jack nodded. "Don't let it keep you from the self-portrait.

I have my heart set on seeing that finished."

She should be painting herself in a hair shirt, not that lavender gown, Kristin thought. *Never in the daylight,* Sister Mary Joseph whispered in her ear.

"Are you cold, sweetheart?" asked Jack.

She shook her head, thinking about pleasure, which she had certainly felt and was not supposed to, and about unnatural acts, which she had probably been guilty of, for she had touched his—what was it called? Kristin had no idea, never having known about that extra appurtenance on a man's body, not until she married Jack. This time she had seen it, since they hadn't been wearing the proper nightclothes. And because they'd participated in "the act" at an improper time, certainly in an improper place.

So what *was* it called? she wondered with intense curiosity, picturing it in her mind. His pleasure loaf? She almost giggled, then felt doubly guilty, but still the most similar shape she could think of was one of her many failed attempts at baking. A loaf that was the wrong shape to begin with because she'd got the amounts of flour wrong, and then it never rose. Although his pleasure loaf had certainly risen. Oh dear. She truly had to stop thinking about him. And it. And "the act." But how she'd love to paint him without a stitch of clothing!

Her father had been right not to send her to Europe. She was much too weak and sinful a woman for such temptations. She probably *would* have painted a naked man if she'd ever had the opportunity, although she couldn't imagine how such an opportunity would come about. Unless one were married in an unchaste union. As she was.

She had to get out of Breckenridge! That was the only way to save her soul.

"It's a pity about the bear," said Jack.

"What?" There he sat, her beautiful, tempting husband,

his soul in mortal danger, and he was thinking about a bear.

"The skin would have made a fine rug. And we could have butchered it and taken home some of the meat. I've never eaten bear."

"I don't understand how you can cut up an animal. Or shoot one, for that matter."

"If I hadn't shot it, my dear wife, you'd be the *bear's* dinner."

Kristin nodded, thinking, *I'd have been dead. Unshriven. Roasting in hell for unconfessed sins of the flesh.* She tried to picture hell and was caught up in the thought of painting it. What did hellfire look like? she wondered. What sort of flames? She hadn't seen the great Chicago fire, which occurred before she was born. And no matter how intriguing to the artistic eye a fire might be, her parents had never been willing to take her to one.

"For a woman who has a pig slaughterhouse in the back yard, you're certainly squeamish," said Jack, chuckling.

"*I'm* never there when they butcher the pigs. The smell is bad enough without having to actually watch."

"You don't have to tell *me,*" said Jack. "The neighbors are complaining."

Kristin sighed. "I'll talk to Oakum, although I don't think I can do anything about the smell."

"Move the whole operation elsewhere," suggested Jack.

"I can't," said Kristin. "That's why Kat gave me the house. She'd have a perfect right to complain—"

"All right. All right," said Jack. "Let's not quarrel after such a lovely afternoon."

Kristin looked up into his eyes. He had no idea of how much endangered his soul was. She should probably try to explain it to him, but he didn't seem to care, and she was too embarrassed to bring it up when it would remind him of her shameless conduct that afternoon.

She'd start packing as soon as she got home, she promised herself, slip out of the house tomorrow morning when he'd gone to his office. It shouldn't be too hard. Maybe he'd go out of town, rounding up more mining syndicate investors.

Where would she go? Denver? The Pinkerton detectives who had found her before were there. Somewhere else then. At least she had money that she could take out of the bank. Not to mention the fashion money Jack had given her. She'd have to pack up all her new paintings, hope that the wet ones came through the move without—

"I'm as *hungry* as a bear." Jack's voice interrupted her thoughts. "But I imagine Abigail will have something tempting for us to eat tonight."

Tempting. Sister Mary Joseph seemed to echo Jack's words in Kristin's head. *Sensualism is an abomination to God,* Sister Mary Joseph had said. The good sister had seen one of Kristin's paintings and denounced it as being *too sensual.* Kristin hadn't even know what the nun was talking about. The word *sensual* hadn't had much meaning for her in those days, when she was an innocent young convent girl who never thought about men and didn't know what a man's pleasure appurtenance looked like. She wouldn't call it a loaf anymore because that made her want to giggle, and it was probably another sin—giggling about an object of sin. Oh dear, she had to stop *thinking* about it.

Chapter Nineteen

"Dinner bell's rung," said Jack, walking into her room without knocking. "Aren't you—what the *hell* are you doing?"

The chemise she was about to pack fell from her hands.

"Now listen to me," he said. "You are not running away again. Do you understand that? You can have the room to yourself, but I'm leaving my door open. You won't be able to get out of the house without my hearing. And I'm assigning Maude to dog your every step."

Kristin stared at him.

"It's dangerous for a girl like you to be running around alone. Didn't the bear teach you anything? And you're probably accosted on trains. For heaven's sake, Kristin, show a little sense. What we did this afternoon is part of marriage. A very nice part."

"It was a sin," said Kristin.

"The devil it was."

"Exactly."

"Well, I don't care what silly ideas you have about sex. I don't want you coming to harm, and I intend to see that it doesn't happen—even if I have to hire Pinkerton's on a permanent basis." He walked out and slammed the door.

Kristin picked up the chemise. Somehow or other she'd get away. He couldn't have her watched every minute. Maude didn't have the time for it, not with Winifred wanting everything in sight waxed, polished, blackened, or lightened. Winifred was the scourge of dust and dull surfaces. Kristin went to the mirror and rearranged a few locks of hair before going down to dinner. She was ravenously hungry. Sinful activities evidently sharpened other appetites. That in itself was probably a sinful thought.

Pinkerton's? There was no branch in Breckenridge. He'd have to send to Denver. Did he really want her to stay that much? She had to squelch a thrill of pleasure. Before he could rehire Pinkerton's, she told herself severely, she'd be gone.

Kristin was at her easel, working on the painting of Mohawk Lake, every brush stroke reminding her of something that had happened between her and Jack the afternoon before. Maude sat in the corner, chatting and polishing silver. Although she seemed to have no idea why she was tagging along after Kristin, Maude did it faithfully, even to the extent of following Kristin to the necessary house, which wouldn't be there much longer. Jack had been talking at dinner last night about putting a reservoir on the roof that would catch rainwater and pipe it down into the house for bathtubs and water closets.

Kristin hadn't said so, but she figured the water tank would fall through and kill everyone beneath it or, at the least, drench the furniture and interiors. But she wouldn't be here to see it. If she had to leave her house to Jack, she was going to do it for her soul's sake.

"Mrs. Macleod to see you, ma'am," said Winifred.

Kristin put aside her brush to welcome Kat, only to find that the Mrs. Macleod entering a step behind Winifred was Maeve Macleod. Had Maeve found out about the shocking activities yesterday at Mohawk Lake? Kristin felt her cheeks turning pink in anticipation of the tirade to come.

"Well now," said Maeve, "no need to look like that. I haven't come to quarrel."

"You haven't?" said Kristin in a wary voice.

"No, I've come to employ you."

"I'm not doing maid work anymore."

"For which I'm sure all those in need of maids are grateful," replied Maeve. "But that's not my business. James and I are opening a saloon here in Breckenridge."

Kristin put her hand over her mouth to stifle a giggle. Since Kat couldn't vent her feelings in front of her temperance friends, Kristin was her chosen confidant.

"Yes, we're going to call it the Chicago Irishman in memory of my dear first husband, Liam Fitzpatrick."

The one who had died of drink?

"A fine man," said Maeve. "Always kept food on the table, unlike James, who's a dear man too but not the best provider. Nor careful with money. Nor good at making it."

"He's a wonderful photographer," said Kristin.

"Aye, but I don't want photographs on the walls of the Chicago Irishman."

Kristin's heart began to trip with excitement. Had Maeve Macleod come to offer a commission? She'd wept over the pastel of Bridget. Two tears.

"I've seen that mural you did for Hortense. An ugly thing, to be sure. Why anyone would want mining scenes I can't imagine, but still they looked just like real mines and miners, and I've a great desire to have pictures of the old country on my own walls."

Kristin's heart sank. "I've never been there."

"Of course, you haven't, but I'll tell you about it. 'Twould be a fine thing for me to look upon the beauties of Ireland while I'm serving up beer and spirits to the poor thirsty miners of the town, many of them, I've no doubt, hungering for a sight of the old country themselves."

"Well, I'd be delighted to try," said Kristin. Greens. She'd heard how green Ireland was and thought of all the luscious shades of green she could use on the walls of Mrs. Macleod's saloon. It might be disloyal to Kat, who had been such a good friend, but business was business, as men were always saying. Kristin couldn't resist the greens—chartreuse, emerald, lime, kelly, jade, forest—

"Heavens, girl. Your face is aglow. I never realized a blonde could be a beauty. I take it you're interested?"

"Oh, yes," said Kristin eagerly. "When shall we start? I'm almost through with this painting."

Maeve studied it thoughtfully. "Well, you have talent. That's a beautiful spot. Where is it?"

"Mohawk Lake."

"Mohawk Lake!"

Maeve *had* heard about yesterday's picnic sins! At the time, Kristin hadn't given a thought to the possibility of spectators. Since then, she'd been able to think of little else. Spectators and mortal sin.

"That's where that evil German carpenter took my Kathleen when he abducted her."

Brought out of her tangled thoughts, Kristin said, "I've never abducted anyone, Mrs. Macleod."

"Now, girl, don't look so distraught. I know you're not about to abduct Kathleen—or Bridget either. Why would you? Although you have no child of your own." She stared at Kristin's waistline. "You don't have one on the way, do you? A woman with child can't be climbing ladders."

She and Jack were kissing madly yesterday, among other things, but then it wasn't kissing that made babies. Unfortunately, they had been doing the other thing too. "I don't look as if I'm with child, do I?"

"You don't. But then you wouldn't. You haven't been married that long." Maeve thought a moment, tapping her forehead as if to inspire memory. "But I'd forgotten. He seduced you before—"

"Actually, he didn't," said Kristin hastily. "I just didn't know what seduction meant, so I misrepresented what happened when I talked to Genevieve."

"Are you saying you wouldn't have had to marry him if that foolish Patsy hadn't talked all over town?"

"No, I wouldn't," said Kristin and thought that she wouldn't have been so deep in sin either—or have found that astonishing pleasure, or know what a man looked like and be having sinful desires to paint him.

"Well, he seems to be getting richer by the minute. Thank your lucky stars the mistake happened with someone who has a talent for making money. Not that I consider mining a steady business. Saloon keeping is much more to be depended upon. A mine runs out of gold, but men never run out of thirst. My new saloon is on Washington Avenue. Come tomorrow morning."

"All right," said Kristin, "but we have to settle on a price," and the two women fell to haggling.

When they had at last agreed, Maeve said admiringly, "You've a lot more spirit than I gave you credit for, girl, and a head for money. I like that in a woman. A man too."

Once Maeve left, Kristin remembered that she had been planning to flee. She could hardly do that now that she had taken a new mural commission. It hurt her feelings that Maeve had thought the mining mural ugly, but the mural of Ireland wouldn't be. Kristin wondered if Maeve wanted leprechauns and fairies. Beautiful green leprechauns and dainty fairies peeking out among the greenery. Although perhaps that scene wouldn't be appreciated by men in their cups. Kristin thought she'd have liked it when she was in her cups, but then she wasn't a man.

As for running away from home—well, she'd put *two* pieces of furniture in front of her door and delay her escape until she'd finished the mural. By that time neither Jack nor Maude would be on the alert.

As Kristin was dancing with some fusty old gentleman wearing a black mask, her imagination was awash in green. While she prepared the walls at the Chicago Irishman for the mural, Maeve had described the country in endless detail between conversations with workmen, wholesalers of spirits, and grocers who would provide supplies for the free lunch. Kristin herself had a sausage order, although Maeve had balked at putting money in Ingrid's pocket and asked frequently when Ingrid would be leaving. Kristin finally thought to reply, "When she has enough money, I imagine." That was when Maeve ordered Traube's Colorado Sausages for the free lunch. Kat wouldn't sell her butter and eggs, but then Kat was a woman of principle. Kristin just wanted to be rich and avoid the more serious sins.

She was passed by the old gentleman to another dancing partner, but in imagination she was skipping through the green meadows of Ireland, hunting leprechauns and fairies in the forest, plucking wildflowers, dancing in and out of rustic cottages, circling ancient castles. Green had taken over her imagination to such an extent that she had told Yvette she wanted a green gown for the masked ball and

310

green silk flowers to put in the curls of her hair. Yvette, of course, had argued. "Blue is madame's color. To match her eyes." "Green," Kristin had insisted. "There *are* no green flowers," said Yvette. "I don't care," said Kristin. "Everything must be green. And done in time for the ball."

Grumpily, Yvette had acquiesced and performed her usual magic. Jack had purchased a Singer sewing machine. As a result, the Frenchwoman spent much of her time designing and sewing clothes. While Kristin painted in the studio, Yvette pinned things to her body, talking away about the foolishness of Kristin's modesty. One was not modest with one's lady's maid. One simply stood still and allowed oneself to be fitted, dressed, and coiffed. So Kristin had done sketches for the Irish mural as Yvette pinned and grumbled. Although the Frenchwoman was grumpy and pushy, Kristin was fast becoming the most fashionable woman in town. The new green ball gown was lovely, if a bit bare at the top. It plunged to a deep V front and back, with white tulle bows below the points and catching up the fabric on the skirt to show a green and white flocked underskirt. Jack had certainly approved of the dress, but Kristin didn't notice any other ladies so bare. Most of them had more bosom, but less of it showing.

Her second partner stepped on the toe of her evening slipper, and Kristin was brought back from thoughts of Ireland and her French maid. Who was he anyway? she wondered. Someone respectable, so she couldn't stamp on his foot in retaliation. Everyone here was respectable. The sponsors of the ball took care of that by ushering each participant into a cloakroom and having them unmask to be sure no rowdies or women of ill repute tried to attend under cover of the required mask.

Kristin's mask was green satin and edged with pearl drops which, Jack had whispered, matched perfectly the

311

translucence of her skin. Then he had leaned down, his back to the assembled sausage girls, who were there to see them off to the ball, and had flicked his tongue against her cheek, whispering, "You taste as delicious as you look." Kristin had a fair idea of the color she had turned. Red with a strong dash of cream. What a pity Maeve wouldn't let her paint any fairies into the landscape of Ireland. James had argued for leprechauns, but Maeve wouldn't have them either. Just good Irish folk and Irish cottages in the emerald hills of home. That's what she wanted.

That's what Kristin would begin to produce tomorrow. Maeve was opening on Sunday in defiance of Reverend Passmore and her own daughter. The grand opening was to feature three-penny beer, which was two pennies less than the cost in Denver, and a real live artist painting Ireland on the walls of the Chicago Irishman. Kristin sighed. She didn't much like the idea of drunken miners watching her paint, but Maeve had assured her that they wouldn't cause trouble.

Poor Kat, thought Kristin. How embarrassing to have her mother flouting the new law, opening on Sunday, when Kat was the town's foremost supporter of Sunday closing, second only to Reverend Passmore, whose fault it was that Maeve had moved her grand opening to Sunday. Saturday night had been her previous choice.

However, the previous Sunday the Methodist minister had preached a fiery sermon denouncing women in saloons, which, as he pointed out to his parishioners, was as much against the law as staying open on Sunday. He had declared that the end of the world was coming because of women like Maeve Macleod.

"I'd like to reclaim my wife, sir," said Jack. The gentleman bowed and disappeared into the throng of merrymakers. Jack put his hand at Kristin's waist and took her hand in his. He was looking so handsome in his evening clothes and mask, his hair slightly mussed above his forehead. "You've a dreaming expression on that lovely face," he said, "and I doubt that it was because of your partner. What were you thinking about? Ireland? You look delicious in that gown."

Kristin flushed. "So you said before," she replied, trying to sound prim, but knowing very well that her whole body had reacted to that lick on the cheek. "Actually, I was thinking of Reverend Passmore."

Jack groaned. "Never a more difficult person lived, although your friend, Kat, comes a close second."

"How can you say that? Kat's as fine a woman as one could hope to meet, whereas Reverend Passmore is preaching sermons against Maeve. I think that's most ungentlemanly."

"Most," Jack agreed, eyes twinkling, "although I rather imagine Maeve Macleod can take care of herself. I do believe her tongue is sharper than his, and he can't knock down a woman, even Maeve."

"I hope he doesn't preach a sermon against me while I'm painting in the saloon tomorrow."

"What?" Jack's mouth drew into a tight line. Kristin felt smug. He'd been out of town for a few days and had missed the advertisements.

"I'm the featured attraction of the grand opening."

"The three-cent beer will be the featured attraction. I'll have to talk to Maeve about this. I don't want you up on a ladder amongst a crowd of drunken miners."

"You just said Maeve could handle anything, even Reverend Passmore."

"And if she doesn't? What am I supposed to do? Offer to box with him? The man has lethal fists. I've seen him knock out a burly miner in one blow. I thought you didn't want me to be injured in a fight."

313

"I wouldn't want anyone to be injured," said Kristin, remembering her impulse to protect Jack's good looks when a Sunday afternoon suitor had challenged him to fisticuffs.

"Then don't go to the Chicago Irishman tomorrow."

"I'm contracted to Maeve."

Jack sighed. "Looks like I'll have to spend tomorrow afternoon drinking three-cent horse piss."

"*Jack?*"

"Sorry." Jack usually managed to keep from slipping into male-only language in front of his wife, who was so easily, delightfully shockable. To take her mind off his *faux pas,* he gathered her in close and whirled her around and around, her green skirts flying, a few curls coming loose from her fine French coiffure.

At first Kristin giggled at the fun of it as they circled in and out among the other couples. Then she said plaintively, "Jack, I'm becoming dizzy."

He pulled her in closer and said, "Good. Are you going to faint in my arms?"

"You're holding me too close. People will stare."

Jack extended the distance between them so that his hand rather than his arm was at her waist. Then he twirled three more times. Kristin's laughter excited him. It was so light and happy, so at odds with the chaste, glum image she was always attempting to project. His wife was a laughing, passionate, talented girl, and he loved to bring out that side of her.

"I'm going to Maeve's tomorrow," she said defiantly. "I don't care what you want."

"Maybe I should tell you what I *really* want." He pulled her back in and whispered into her ear, "Remember Denver?"

She glanced up at him, startled, giving him the opportunity to brush his lips across her cheek.

"And Mohawk Lake," he whispered. "Lying on that blanket, just the two of us. That's what I want. To make love to you until you do faint."

Kristin couldn't believe he'd said that. And in a public place.

Jack pulled her closer still. "Do you remember how it felt? When I was—"

"Hush!" Her face flamed.

"—deep inside you," he continued into her ear. "Do you remember that, my sweet, passionate wife?"

Kristin tried to break the hold of his arm at her waist, but he whirled her again, taking the full weight of her body against his when she lost her footing. He felt her trembling and was satisfied for the minute.

"You're going to get us ejected from the ball as—as the kinds of persons they were looking for in the cloakroom," she stammered, trying to recapture her poise.

"All the better," murmured Jack. "We'll go home together right now. Your room or mine?"

Kristin swallowed hard but was saved from answering when the music ended and a gentleman in a blue mask claimed her. She thought a blue mask silly on a man. Jack's looked much more dashing. Oh heaven, she mustn't let him rattle her this way! She had to think of something other than the shocking things he'd said to her, which she was sure Sister Mary Joseph would have denounced on the spot, in front of all the dancers.

"If you're feelin' overheated, Miz Cameron, we could get some air. You're lookin' sorta flushed, ma'am." She recognized the voice of Mr. Henley, one of Jack's hunting companions. He'd gone into the mountains with Jack to retrieve the bear that Jack shot the day they made love on the blanket.

"I *would* like some air, Mr. Henley. I've been whirled around once too many times." Both physically and verbally, she thought.

Mr. Henley offered his arm and gallantly escorted her to a window, which he threw open. "Is that better, ma'am?" he asked as a blast of frigid air enveloped her.

She began to shiver. Dancers in their area shouted, "Close that window. You want to start up the pneumonia?"

Jack appeared and, drawing her away from the window, murmured, "What's wrong, love? Feeling flushed, are you?"

She felt like a mouse cornered by the house cat, big black Tom, who was planning to devour her. She couldn't ask to go home because Jack would insist on accompanying her. Yet if he partnered her again and said more—

"Now, don't faint," said Jack. "I promise to be good— at least for the rest of the evening." And then he laughed, that warm, rich laugh that coated her nerves like honey or a hot biscuit.

The whole mural was blocked onto the wall in charcoals, and the Chicago Irishman had been open an hour. This wasn't too bad, thought Kristin up on her ladder, working on a forest. No one had said anything untoward or jostled her perch. Maude was no longer her shadow. Jack had taken over guard duty himself, but he sat across the room, chatting with Robert Foote, who was checking out the competition.

In fact, Jack hardly glanced her way, which was both surprising and irritating after his shockingly intimate conversation the night before. Then Connor Macleod came in and the two left together, Jack casting a glance at Kristin but not speaking to her. Well, she thought in a huff, that didn't show much concern! Some champion he was. He'd left before any real drunkenness manifested itself. Fortunately, Maeve and James were there to protect her. Kristin turned away from the swinging doors through which her husband had disappeared and began another tree.

Fifteen minutes later, when she was taking a break on top of her ladder, flexing her wrists and fingers, Reverend Passmore charged into the saloon—rugged, black-suited, breathing fire and brimstone. Kat had not accompanied him, but he was a whole army of crusaders in himself, shouting, "Abomination! Look you!" He pointed to Maeve. "Not only is God's law being broken here, so is the law of man. The Colorado legislature hath spoken long since. Women are not allowed in saloons. It hath spoken in Godly fashion, just this April. Saloons may not stay open on the Lord's Day. Get thee to thy kitchen, woman. Tend thee thy child. Be not a harlot, nor a purveyor of drunkenness, sin, and death unto thy fellow man."

"Now, see here, my friend," said James Macleod, who looked like a sprite beside the burly preacher. "That's no way to talk to a respectable woman."

Maeve walked straight up to the preacher and planted her fists on slender hips. "I've got permission from the sheriff, since it was my money that bought this place, and I've a right to look out for my own business interests."

"Sinful papist woman!" shouted Reverend Passmore, as if she were hard of hearing. "Daughter of Eve—luring men to lives of drink and debauchery."

"Off my premises!" Maeve shouted right back. "And don't be talking to me about debauchery, you Protestant hypocrite. There's no debauchery going on on any premises of mine. Just a little good, clean drinking, which every man needs at the end of a hard week's work." The patrons cheered, and Maeve, who had just hit her stride, continued. "Maybe if you ever did an honest day's work yourself,

instead of just working your mouth all over town, inter
fering in people's private and business affairs instead o
minding your own business and the Lord's—"

"Drinking is the Lord's business," Brother Passmore
shouted. "Drinking is an abomination unto the Lord."

"Poppycock. The sweet Lord Jesus himself was a drink
ing man. Why else would he change the water to wine? He
had a thirst on him, that's what!"

"Now there's a sensible woman," said Jonathan Cooper
Fincher, editor and owner of the Summit County *Journal.*

"Blasphemy!" shouted Reverend Passmore.

"Unlike her daughter, who shows signs of insanity on
the subject of tipple," continued the editor.

"Watch your tongue when you speak of my Kathleen,"
Maeve snapped, and glared at the newspaperman.

"Harken to me," shouted Florida Passmore. "If there be
any Christians among ye, follow me out of this den o
iniquity."

Kristin sat, wide-eyed, on top of her ladder, taking it al
in, covering her mouth to stifle a giggle. So far, Florida
Passmore hadn't noticed her.

"God doth abhor a scarlet woman," said Passmore to
Maeve.

She looked down at her prim gray dress. "You're color-
blind," she retorted. "Now, out of my saloon."

"The only way you'll get me out, woman, is to call the
sheriff. Do it. You're crossways of the law, so he'll have
to put you in jail."

A miner with a bottle of whiskey and two glasses in front
of him, from which he was drinking alternately, advised
Maeve to ignore the preacher. "He's entertainment, an
don't cost you nothin', ma'am. More fun listenin' to a
preacher gittin' all red-faced and hell-bent than watchin'
a girl paintin' trees on the wall. Me, I thought maybe

she'd sing a song or show her knees or sompthin' when they read yer advertisement to me." He downed another shot and squinted at Kristin. "Pretty though, but I like 'em livelier, myself. Whores, that's the ticket."

Maeve rapped him on the head, but it was too late. The miner had called the attention of Florida Passmore to Kristin, perched on her ladder, brush in hand. He strode in her direction. "Why aren't you home with your children, young woman?" he demanded, spotting the diamond wedding ring Jack had bought her in Denver.

"I don't have any children," said Kristin meekly.

"But you have a husband? Why has he let you come to this sink of sin?"

"Actually, he was here to look after me a while back, but he seems to have been called away on business."

"The only business on the Lord's Day is the Lord's business. You should not be working—unless it is in your home, looking after your family. I can see in your eyes that you are one of the innocents—"

Kristin thought it ironic that he attacked Maeve as a scarlet woman and thought of Kristin, who was a sinner in an unchaste union with the devil, as one of the innocents.

"—a simple female who has been led astray," continued Passmore in his booming voice.

"I'm just painting a mural," said Kristin. "Maybe you'd like one for your church. How about a depiction of Christ saying, 'Suffer the little children to come unto me'? I'm very good at children." Maybe if he thought he was saving her soul, she could get a commission. "I'd be glad to show you samples." She'd have to borrow from Kat and Maeve, and Reverend Passmore might not want to look at pictures of Roman Catholic children.

"My church is made beautiful by the faith of its worshippers," said the minister.

319

"Well, I could paint some of your worshippers. Maybe they'd like a portrait of you."

"Frivolities," he muttered. "I shall pray for your soul."

"Thank you," said Kristin politely, "and if you should ever want a nice mural, landscape, or portrait, do come by. I live on Nickel Hill. Kristin Traube-Cameron."

"I should have known. Another papist." Reverend Passmore backed away from her and addressed himself to a table of miners on the dangers of drink, especially drink consumed on the Lord's Day.

Jack returned a half hour later, spotted the Methodist haranguing the left side of the room, and hastened to Kristin's side.

"Did he give you any trouble?"

Kristin finished cleaning off a brush, "He thinks I'm one of the innocents. He could see it in my eyes."

"Remarkably astute of him."

"Where did you go?"

"Did you miss me?"

"No."

"Hard-hearted woman. I was just voted into Connor's volunteer firemen's group. Had to accept the appointment."

"Fires are very frightening," said Kristin. "Even false fires. I set one at Kat's house by neglecting to open the flue."

"Can't have that," said Jack. "Maybe I should give you a friendly spanking." He lifted her from the ladder and whispered, "Pat, pat, pat on your pretty little bottom. I guarantee you'll enjoy it."

Kristin turned pink and tried to squirm away from him.

"It might even remind you to close the flue. I'll make it as memorable as possible."

"I don't have to deal with flues anymore."

"But I'm still a volunteer fireman, and I'm sure it's my

duty to mete out appropriate discipline to pretty arsonists. Shall we go home and—"

Kristin, red-faced, got loose and hid behind her ladder. "I haven't finished the forest yet."

Jack snapped his fingers and said, humorously disappointed, "Foiled by a forest. We volunteer firemen hardly ever have any fun."

Chapter Twenty

Talk warmed her up, thought Jack, elated. If he whispered outrageous things into her small pink ear, out in public where she couldn't run or object, she became as flustered as a virgin in a whorehouse. He laughed aloud. By God, marriage was fun! He'd never been this intrigued with the chase before. In fact, he'd never had to do much chasing. Kristin was not only a delight in bed, but a challenge the rest of the time. He might not be Fast Jack Cameron anymore, but he was sure as hell Lucky Jack Cameron.

Now what was to be his next strategy? Another dinner party? He had Chicago investors coming this weekend. He'd mix them up with Breckenridge money and, while they were eyeing one another and distracted by Abigail's superb cuisine, he'd talk another link out of Kristin's armor. Maybe he could slip his wife a bit of wine. Alcohol did things to her—alcohol and suggestive conversation.

Of course, now that she was nearing completion of Maeve's Irish mural, he'd have to set Maude to watching Kristin again—just in case she still dreamed about running away. A man couldn't seduce a wife who wasn't in town.

Kristin trotted down Washington Avenue thinking of her mural. It was like a live thing, a community effort. The picture kept changing as patrons of the Chicago Irishman sidled up to her to share their memories of the old country, to ask if she couldn't put in a church to which they'd gone as children, a priest in black robes with a friendly red nose and a swinging stride, walking on a path by the stream, a long-dead sister picking flowers in the lee of a rock wall, a woman washing clothes as Mother used to do. Her mural was drilling memories from the hearts of men who spent their childhoods in Ireland and their adult lives underground drilling for gold and silver. The scenes grew almost of their own accord like spring weeds, stretching vines of memory to other walls.

And Maeve encouraged the spread, paid Kristin more money than originally agreed upon, delighted in each new element, remembering such people, such places as those described so nostalgically by her Irish customers. The saloon was a great success, patronized at all hours. Men took off work, climbed on trains to enjoy its green nostalgia, closed stores, and asked Kristin what she called this thing or that so they could describe it to wives and children.

Women, made daring by curiosity, peeked in on their way to town to visit the butcher, the grocer, the dry goods store. In fact, an open carriage full of boisterous, laughing women was pulling up to the Chicago Irishman even as Kristin approached it. Such costumes! Bold colors, froths of lace, satin tucks, feather boas, hats more dramatic and sweeping than any Kristin had ever seen, necklines lower than propriety allowed. Who could they be? She didn't recognize them from church or town social events. They didn't shop at Kaiser's or buy overalls at Watson's. Their children didn't attend the school.

Kristin slipped in behind them and scooted over to her ladder, which was at another wall now. James, who was tending bar, greeted the women with laughter and compliments to which they responded in kind, telling him that everyone was talking of his fine new saloon and they'd just had to see it, had slipped away when Marcie wasn't looking. They ordered drinks and took seats at the tables as if their conduct weren't shocking in the extreme. They bantered with James and the smaller afternoon crowd of male patrons.

Kristin climbed down and slipped a sketch book from her satchel, making quick drawings of the women's faces. Unusual faces. One or two were fresh and young but framed old eyes. Some looked worn under paint. All laughed and smiled even when their eyes remained unmoved, or calculating, or even frantic with merriment. There were strange hair colors under the dramatic hats, unnaturally bright hues on cheeks and lips, voluptuous bodies displayed rather than concealed, low necklines during the daylight hours. As she sketched, Kristin remembered the station manager and his words about the women of West Breckenridge.

The suspicion was confirmed when Florida Passmore burst through the door shouting, "Harlots! Repent your sins!" He bore down upon the women, preaching as he came, calling down God's wrath upon them.

Poor things, she thought. Did they really participate in "the act" all the time and with men they weren't even married to, endangering their souls, no doubt struggling under the burden of their sins and trying as hard as they could not to enjoy themselves? And she had thought *her* lot difficult one! All she had to contend with was Jack. Reverend Passmore was mean to harry them so. He reminded Kristin of her father. Always reprimanding someone. Never kind or loving. "Leave them alone!" she called impulsively. Her protest came while the minister was taking breath to launch into a new tirade. "Didn't Jesus say that people shouldn't go around casting stones if they weren't perfect themselves? Are you perfect?" Kristin asked, surprised at her own temerity.

Florida Passmore looked astounded. It occurred to Kristin that perhaps no one had ever questioned his perfection. "Spawn of the devil," muttered the preacher. "Interfering in God's holy work."

Kristin flushed and clambered up her ladder. How had he dared? When she peeked over her shoulder, Passmore had gone. The women in their bright finery were staring at her, as was James, all looking astounded. "You must be a friend of Kat Macleod's," said one of the women.

"How did you know that?"

"Ain't many respectable ladies take up for the likes of us. I'm Red Melba."

"An' I'm Genevieve," said another.

"The hell you are," said a third. "Jus' 'cause we told you about St. Genevieve like Miz Macleod told us don't mean you kin take that name. 'Tain't proper."

"Reckon we'd better be gettin' across the river before the parson goes for the sheriff," said Red Melba. She lifted her glass to Kristin, drank it down, and led her confederates from the saloon. Several of them leaned over the bar to smack kisses on James's mouth. Kristin was glad Maeve wasn't there to see it. Other patrons wanted to get in on the kissing and were told to visit Marcie's if they were feeling lonely, that loving wasn't free.

Loving wasn't free, mused Kristin when the last painted lady had departed. It was true. Men paid in money, women in guilt. She sighed, wondering how Jack would pay for the kisses he'd stolen from her.

"Afternoon, sweetheart," said Jack, coming into her studio straight from the railroad station after two days in Cripple Creek. "I brought you a present from Denver."

Kristin tried not to look eager, but Jack did bring wonderful presents. This one couldn't be jewelry because it was a large bundle. Controlling her curiosity, she unwrapped it and revealed a beautiful fabric with an intricate design woven in rich blues and greens. She ran her fingertips over it, marveling at the texture. The weaver must have mixed silk and wool, she thought. But what was it? A fabric length to make a winter dress of?

"Shake it out," Jack suggested.

Kristin tried to look nonchalant as she grasped the fabric at either edge of the bundle and lifted. As it unfolded, silken fringes rippled at the borders. It appeared to be a great gorgeous triangular shawl.

"For cold nights in summer and days in winter," Jack explained. "Thought you'd like the color and design."

Kristin sighed. She'd never seen anything more beautiful, It looked and felt luxuriously, sinfully sensuous. How could she thank him in an offhand manner, this man who was set on tying her to him body and soul? Then, in all likelihood, he'd forget all about her, treat her the way most husbands treated their wives, for she saw that danger too. She hadn't had a full night's sleep since that episode on the picnic blanket. In bed at night, dresser against the door, she thought of Jack, remembered shocking, exciting details that kept her awake. There had been nights when sleep eluded her so thoroughly that she gave up hope, pushed the dresser

326

away from the door, and went downstairs, lighting all the lamps in her studio and painting strange, dark still lifes from which fruit or flowers in luscious colors beckoned the eye. At those times the devil seemed to be her muse.

She could lose her soul for Jack's sake and then be abandoned in all but the most obvious public ways. Sometimes she wondered if she would willingly give up her principles if she were sure that Jack would continue to—but no, of course, she wouldn't. Kristin knew what was right. Sister Mary Joseph had told her.

"You don't have to say a word, love. I can see on your face how much you like it." Jack looked unbearably smug as she bundled up the trailing shawl. "And now we need to have a discussion. I heard some strange talk on the way home."

Kristin bit her lip. She knew just what he'd heard and tried to pull away from the hand he put at her elbow. She'd already been lectured by Maeve, who was furious that anyone would allow women of ill fame in the Chicago Irishman, much less stand them to a round of drinks, as James had, or defend them, as Kristin had. "Have you no sense of propriety, girl?" Maeve had demanded and given a fifteen-minute lecture on the importance of a woman's reputation.

That lecture had taken all the joy out of Kristin's depiction of an Norman-Irish castle on the second wall. Furthermore, Maeve had looked at the faces of two peasant women dancing in front of the castle and recognized them as harlots from West Breckenridge. She had insisted that Kristin paint them out and put no more strumpets on her walls. No doubt Jack had heard of Kristin's indiscretion.

He seated her in one of the chairs and took the other himself. Between them on the table sat a bowl of apples whose sheen was so delicious that no one could wonder why Eve had succumbed to the lure of their sweet, sharp flesh. Kristin tore her eyes away from the bowl and its contents, which she had painted last night and finished just before dawn; how it was hidden away behind a portrait of Phoebe and Sean Michael at the piano in the drawing room—innocence shielding temptation.

"I certainly admire the Christian charity that led you to face down Reverend Passmore," said Jack.

"You do?" Surprise jerked her from her thoughts.

"But next time you want to attack him, couldn't you do it on some more worthy subject?"

She scowled. Kat thought those women worthy of her attention. Who was Jack, of all people, to be casting stones? Kristin at least worried about the state of her soul. Jack had the moral sense of a radish.

"Sticking up for sporting ladies isn't a stand that's likely to win you many friends in a small town."

"Sporting ladies? But I thought they were harlots. That's what Maeve said."

"Same thing," said Jack.

"A sporting lady is a harlot?" Monsieur Louis Dupuy in Georgetown had asked Kristin if she was a sporting lady, and she hadn't even realized that she was being insulted. She'd thought he was talking about basketball, not "the act." Did men consider "the act" a sport? How despicable! "I suppose you've never patronized women like that," she retorted.

"Not since I met you, love. You're much more fun in that way, and prettier to boot."

Kristin flushed. Her husband had just compared her to a harlot. She felt like weeping.

"I meant it as a compliment," he protested, then burst out laughing at the look on her face.

Kristin dropped his gift on the floor in a blue-green heap, stormed out of the room, then paused in the hall because she didn't know where to go, not with Maude jumping up from her seat by the marble table, ready to follow Kristin anywhere. "Are we going out, ma'am?" she asked eagerly. Maude was enjoying the excitement of her watchdog assignment.

"Yes," said Kristin through gritted teeth. "We're going to visit Mrs. Macleod."

"You figure to tell on me?" asked Jack from the door of her studio. "It won't help." He was still laughing. "She dislikes me more than ever, but now I own *half* of the Chicago Girl instead of a fourth, and the Macleods are twice as rich, thanks to me."

"Kat is a woman of principle and Christian charity," said Kristin. "You are interested only in money."

"Wrong again, love," he replied, striding toward her so that she was caught between him and Maude. "Come upstairs and I'll tell you what else I'm interested in." He whispered the last in her ear so that Maude couldn't hear.

Kristin fled out the front door with the parlor maid in pursuit, calling, "Wait for me, Miss Kristin. You haven't even picked up your calling card case. Don't you want your hat? What if it rains? We should stop for your umbrella." Kristin had reached the street before Maude caught up, without any of the missing necessities for formal Breckenridge afternoon calls in midsummer.

"I'm interested in joining your efforts to bring—bring—" What *was* Kat doing over in West Breckenridge? "Consolation to those poor creatures on the other side of the river," Kristin finished lamely.

"I heard how you stuck up for them at Mother's, Kristin, and although I admire the kindly impulse, perhaps you should have considered that you were defending their right to drink strong spirits in a saloon."

"All right," said Kristin, feeling very ill used. Here she was offering some of her precious painting time to the pursuit of good works—and to spite her husband—and what encouragement had she got? None. Maybe Kat sensed that Kristin was in no position to be counseling women whose sins were of the flesh. "If you don't want my support—"

"Of course I do," said Kat. "We'll go this afternoon. Maybe we can talk someone into giving up the business."

"Maude goes everywhere with me," warned Kristin.

"Not to West Breckenridge, I don't," said Maude. "That's where I draw the line. Mrs. Macleod will have to protect you from yourself, ma'am, if that's where you're going."

"Protect me from myself? Is that what he told you?" Kristin could hardly contain her anger. Did Jack fear, now that he had planted the seeds of lust in her soul, that she might want to blossom elsewhere? In different soil? Of all the nerve! She didn't lust after anyone but him. And that was lust enough for any woman.

Marcie Webber, the proprietor of the Gentlemen's Sporting Club, had more curls than any three women Kristin had ever seen, even any three women in this house, where curls abounded—curls and cleavage. Kristin and Kat had been greeted like old friends, which made Kristin nervous. Although these women didn't know her, perhaps they sensed something in her. Did she communicate silently some sisterhood in sin? Or was she simply uneasy in knowing Sister Mary Joseph would have considered any association with a harlot very sinful?

Still, it was fascinating—the women with their shocking clothes, the furniture, which looked like Ingrid's red velvet suite that had sat in Kristin's drawing room until replaced by Jack's penchant for ordering anything and everything from expensive Denver and Chicago stores. Of course, Ingrid had *been* a harlot, which explained her taste in home furnishings. Poor Ingrid. Look at what harlotry had done to her—married, divorced, given to drunkenness, now a sausage factory manager. What a life!

Kat was discussing Reverend Passmore's legal action to force Sunday closing. "Finally, we've done it," she said triumphantly. "There's not a saloon left open on Sundays."

"Well, that's all very well," said Marcie, "but he'd better not come here trying to keep me from serving liquor."

More interested in Ingrid than Sunday closing, Kristin wondered whether her partner had confessed her sins to Father Boniface Wirtner. It was quite possible that Ingrid had long ago been shriven, while Kristin, coward that she was, would go straight to hell if she should meet an untimely death while she was still in a state of sin and party to an unchaste marriage. Did pushing the dresser in front of her door at night count for anything, promise her purgatory instead of hell?

"You're mighty quiet," said Marcie to Kristin when she could insert a word into Kat's discussion of the benefits of marriage, good works, and temperance. "You look enough like Ingrid to be her sister."

"We're partners, not sisters," said Kristin defensively. "And I'm an artist, so I'm naturally quiet. Artists look instead of talking." Kristin took another long look at Marcella Webber. "Would you like your portrait painted?" she asked impulsively. Kristin knew that she'd probably try to do those curls anyway, but it wouldn't hurt to be paid for the effort.

Marcie's mouth quirked in a wry smile. "Aren't you afraid for your reputation? You'll never get any commissions from respectable folk if you paint me."

"I don't get any commissions from them anyway," said Kristin. She'd love to catch that smile with its subtle mixture of experience, humor, and disillusion. Marcella Webber was a beautiful woman, and besides beauty, her face was full of character—not in the sense that most people used the word, but still—

"In that case, why not?" said Marcie. "I'll hang it in the parlor. That might snag you a few male customers."

Kristin wasn't sure she wanted that sort of male customer, but then maybe all men visited sporting houses. She wouldn't be surprised to hear it. Perhaps her father and brothers had, and Aunt Frieda's husband. She tried to imagine Aunt Frieda and Uncle Adolph engaging in "the act," but she couldn't even imagine Uncle Adolph getting up the nerve to ask. And obviously *women* didn't suggest "the act," so probably Aunt Frieda and Uncle Adolph—

"Changed your mind?" Marcie was asking.

"Oh, no," Kristin stammered and immediately drew a sketch pad from her reticule. "I'll start right now."

"We're here on a reform mission, Kristin," said Kat.

"You sound just like Genevieve," murmured Kristin, sketching, glancing up at her subject, forgetting all about sin and sex. She had a portrait commission! Finally. One that didn't come from her husband. "Genevieve took my sketch book away from me once at the railroad station when we were rescuing young women," Kristin explained. "Is this what we were rescuing them from? From becoming harl—" Kristin clapped her free hand over her mouth.

Marcella laughed heartily. "Soiled doves will do, or fallen angels, or ladies of the night. There are all sorts of semi-polite terms for women in our profession." Kristin was mesmerized by the woman's laughter. It had that full-throated enjoyment of life, that same sense of fun and good humor that Kristin loved in Jack's laughter. Jack who had compared *her* to a harlot—for which she would never forgive him. How could she even think of *love* in the same sentence with Jack. Love was solemn and holy. It had nothing to do with bodies and laughter. She had to keep that in mind.

The backyard dormitory, completed in record time, now housed the sausage makers and household servants, two of the original girls, and the rest replacements for those who had married out of the Sunday courting parlor. Kristin held the ceremonies there and let the suitors pay for the refreshments at the wedding receptions. Sometimes there were double weddings. Sausage making had been transferred to the first floor of the dormitory building.

Jack kept things changing so fast around her that Kristin didn't recognize her household from one week to the next. He had furnished all the upstairs bedrooms for out-of-town guests while she was starting Marcie's portrait, and now those rooms were filled with people from Chicago and Denver—investors. The new dining room table had three leaves in it and seemed to stretch on forever, set with the china that had replaced what fell into the cellar during their last memorable dinner party.

Kristin looked down the sparkling table, lined with well-dressed people eating and drinking, laughing and talking business. She couldn't remember all of their names. The man to her right, for instance. He had said something to her about Mrs. Potter Palmer, so he must be from Chicago. After a few dutiful remarks to his hostess, he turned his attention to Ingrid, who was wearing an outrageously low-cut gown and flirting gaily. Personally, Kristin thought the man was waiting for Ingrid to bend forward once too many times with the result that both breasts would spring out of the bodice into her soup.

"It's hard to believe, Mrs. Cameron, that you could have caused such a furor," said Mr. Wyand on her left.

"What furor?" What had she done now? Did this stranger know she had a commission from a sporting house madam? The portrait was coming along very well, a wonderful exercise in hair depiction.

"Well, no one's ever preached a sermon about me," said the man jovially.

A Chicago wife, sitting midway down the table, tricked out in diamonds and puce satin, squeaked, "Oh, do tell us, Mrs. Cameron. Who has preached a sermon about you and on what subject? Are your good works so numerous that the church has acknowledged them?"

Jack was listening and laughing, Kristin at a loss.

"Oh, Mrs. Cameron is quite the modern woman," said Mrs. Boling Wyand with discernible disapproval. Her husband owned ranches and mines on the Western Slope. Mrs. Wyand stayed in Breckenridge only during the summer and then liked to indulge her passion for gossip. "In my day," she said loftily, "women stayed home to supervise their households and to see to their husbands and children, but we did go abroad on errands of mercy and such. However, there are modern women, I believe, who devote themselves to making money and haven't time for the traditional female pursuits. Perhaps the sermon in question was on sausage-making, Mrs. Cameron's forte. Her sausages are quite famous." Mrs. Wyand fanned herself with a mother-of-pearl and lace fan. "I don't know what the world's coming to. If Mr. Cameron weren't such a talented banker"—She beamed at Jack, whose investment talents had made possible the rubies on her bony chest—"his *wife* might be outstripping him in earnings."

Kristin decided that she didn't like Mrs. Wyand, no matter how much money her husband had invested in Jack's mining ventures. "Women need to have their own sources of income," said Kristin, looking down her nose at Mrs. Wyand.

"Here! Here!" said Kat, who had been glaring at a rather tipsy investor from Chicago, who patted her hand at every opportunity. "Women in business is the coming thing."

"In case they need to support themselves," Kristin agreed. "Look what happened to me." She gave her husband a challenging look. "My parents made me leave home because of Jack, although Jack says we weren't guilty of anything. I'm sure I don't know, since he plied me with brandy."

Mr. Parker raised his glance abruptly from Ingrid's cleavage to study Kristin with astonished interest.

"We *weren't* guilty of anything," said Jack. "She just has a bad-tempered family."

"And they deprived me of my dowry. I'd probably have starved to death if friends hadn't sent me out here where Kat set me up in the sausage-making business."

Now all the Chicagoans were gaping, and Kristin had the satisfaction of knowing that they could hardly wait to get home and spread the story around. She hoped her family was horribly embarrassed. No one but Aunt Frieda had written since she'd left home. Now all the Breckenridge people would stop whispering about her. They'd heard the whole story, so what else would there be to say?

"But if nothing happened, dear, how did you and Jack happen to marry?" asked the lady draped in diamonds.

"We had to."

Everyone gasped.

"Gossip, not guilt," said Jack, leaning back in his chair as Maude removed his soup bowl. "Weren't we lucky? We might never have got together if it weren't for Connor and Kat's loose-tongued maid."

335

Kristin glared at him. Lucky? If he'd been through what she'd gone through, he wouldn't be talking about luck. "*You* didn't go hungry on the train to Denver," she said.

"No, but I'm trying to make it up to you with the best French cook in the West."

"In the country," came a stentorian voice from the pantry.

"My apologies, Abigail," Jack called. "You're absolutely right."

"If that's your cook, old boy," said the Chicagoan beside Kristin, "she doesn't sound French to me."

"I don't understand," said Mrs. Wyand, whose husband obviously hadn't told her the story about Kristin and the sermon. "If the priest wasn't speaking of sin or good works, what in the world—"

"Contaminating associations," said Jack and winked at Kristin through the candlelight. "And it was a Methodist, Florida Passmore, not a priest."

"What?" gasped Kristin. She hadn't heard that Reverend Passmore had been preaching about her. "He probably means you, Jack. You're certainly a contaminating association." She nodded to Maude to begin serving the next course—mountain trout in aspic.

"What's this stuff?" asked Ingrid. She stared at her plate suspiciously, then turned to Mr. Parker, at whom she had been casting sultry glances and who was quite surprised to find himself the object of her attentions. "I wouldn't eat that, honey," she advised. "Looks to me like the fish were sick."

"Reverend Passmore didn't mean me," said Jack. "Although he did say husbands should protect their wives from these contaminating associations. He was talking about your commission from Marcie Webber."

"He should mind his own business," snapped Kristin.

"Who is Marcie Webber?" asked Mr. Wyand. "It's hard to believe that anyone who can afford to commission a portrait would be socially unacceptable."

"As it happens, my wife is doing a portrait of one of the town's most infamous madams."

"My dear Mr. Cameron," said Mrs. Parker, who had agreed to come back to dinner at the Camerons' because her husband told her that socially prominent people from Denver and Chicago would be there, "Reverend Passmore is quite right. You should keep your wife from such associations. It is a husband's duty to dictate and a wife's to obey." She then glared at Ingrid, who was still tantalizing Mr. Parker with smiles and arm-brushing, cleavage displays, and whispered remarks that evidently shocked and titillated the poor man.

Before Kristin could explode in anger, Jack said to Mrs. Parker, "I'll do my best to live up to your standards, ma'am, but with a wife as lovely and talented as mine, I find that I can't really deny her anything she wants." He sent Kristin a besotted smile that only increased her chagrin, for she knew he was teasing her. He often played this game in public. Well, two could play. She'd show him.

"Really? Anything?" Kristin smiled back sweetly. "Do you know what I've always wanted, Jack?"

"No, sweetheart, what?"

"To paint a nude." She sent him a saucy look. "Would you like to pose?"

Mrs. Wyand choked on her trout, although Abigail later denied angrily that there had been one single bone left in that fish. Mrs. Parker fainted and had to be carried into the drawing room and stretched out on the same loveseat where Ingrid had flirted with Cal Bannister and diverted his attention from the Parker daughter. Even Ingrid looked shocked at Kristin's question. Mr. Wyand and all the gentlemen from Chicago roared with laughter, and one said to Jack, "You've got a feisty girl there, Cameron. You always did have all the luck."

Kristin tossed for several hours, then threw back the covers and slipped from bed. Cold air immediately started her shivering. And no wonder. She was clad in a nightgown that Yvette had made and then finagled her into wearing by actually shedding tears when Kristin complained that it was unseemly—pretty, but unseemly. Its sheer white cotton fabric was gathered to a wide square lace neckline which just caught her shoulders and was cut so low that the lace came halfway down her breasts before the gathered cotton began. If it slipped, her nipples would show. Other than the neckline it was chaste enough—long full sleeves gathered to a wrist band with a ruffle below, ruffles at the bottom under which just the tips of her toes peeked out.

Kristin knew that Yvette was trying to mend the Cameron marriage. She dropped hints about how Kristin could lure Jack to her bed, this gown being one of the hints. Yvette sighed each morning when she arrived with Kristin's coffee to discover only one person under the covers. Since the first disastrous attempt on the maid's part to bring a tray upstairs, Kristin had trained herself to awaken and move the furniture away from the door before Yvette arrived. Then she hopped back in bed and pretended to be asleep when Yvette came in. Obviously the lady's maid thought Jack wasn't interested. Much she knew. Jack would only lose interest when he managed to wake up in Kristin's bed, and if that happened, Kristin would have lost her immortal soul. She had to stay vigilant.

As she hunted for her dressing gown and slippers, she fretted about Yvette, Jack, and the nightgown, of which Sister Mary Joseph would have had a thing or two to say, such as the admonition that unchaste nightclothes led to unchaste thoughts as well as actions, which was certainly true in Kristin's case. Even when she managed to sleep, she had disturbing dreams when wearing this gown.

Where *was* her robe? She couldn't find it. And her slippers? Yvette kept putting things away so that she herself would be the one to produce them on demand. She didn't want Kristin to do anything for herself. Grumbling, Kristin snatched up the green-blue shawl that Jack had given her. Yvette had draped it over a boudoir chair—trust the woman not to hide anything Jack bought. Shivering, Kristin wrapped herself up in soft material. Fringe trailed almost to the floor as she edged the chest aside enough to slip through the door and tiptoe downstairs barefoot.

However, she found she couldn't paint, so she sat brooding in her studio, one lamp lit. The dinner party was over, the table cleared, guests gone to bed upstairs or to their own houses, and she sat thinking that she and her husband had acted like feuding, ill-mannered children, each trying to outdo the other in embarrassing remarks. How could he have told strangers that she was painting the portrait of a madam? How could she have asked if he'd like to pose nude? She sighed and stared at the portrait of Marcie on her easel.

"Here I am," said Jack from the doorway. "A man of my word."

"Why aren't you in bed?" she gasped, as usual taken by surprise. He'd been walking like an Indian again.

"Because you aren't there with me, love. You said you wanted a naked man, not a naked lover." As Kristin's eyes followed him uneasily, he went to the cold hearth

339

Elizabeth Chadwick

and stooped to light a fire. Flames soon danced on the stone, revealing—what was that on the floor? She stood up, staring. The bear! Its skin was spread out before the fire, looking lush, thick, and silky. Then she gasped when Jack began to undo the belt of his dressing gown.

Chapter Twenty-One

The belt loosened and slipped to the sides of the blue wool robe. Kristin could see the gleam of his eyes in the firelight. "Is this going to be one of those sensuous, sleepless paintings you've been doing the last week or so?" he asked.

"You've been in here without my permission?" She had hidden those pictures, somehow embarrassed, feeling that her restless yearnings showed through the innocuous subjects. How could he be so sensitive to her mood as it showed on her canvases? No one else would have called an apple sensuous. Or a bouquet of wildflowers picked by children in a mountain meadow and carried home in hot, grubby young fists. Ingrid had put them in water and doctored them with refined sugar because she was so touched, because she wanted to keep them fresh as long as she could to remind her that her children loved her. "I'll bet they don't bring Augustina flowers," Ingrid had said.

"What are you thinking about?" he asked.

He was holding the robe closed, just teasing her. He didn't really mean to disrobe. "About Ingrid's wildflowers. They weren't—" Kristin stopped.

"—sensuous? I'm sure the real ones weren't. But yours were. You made me inhale to catch the scent. I expected a rich, sweet fragrance."

"They had none," she protested. "Wildflowers don't—"

"Yours looked as if they did, love."

Why did he always call her *love*? He didn't love her. His interest was simply piqued because she was unwilling.

"So how are we going to do this?" He shrugged one shoulder out of the robe, so that one side of his body, quite naked, caught the firelight. Kristin could see the tiny hairs springing away from the highlighted muscles of his calf and forearm, the definition of shoulder and chest. "Back lit or front lit?" he asked.

"What?" She was embarrassed, terrified that he would drop the garment and reveal himself fully. Yet she couldn't turn away.

"Considering how alarmed you look, I guess we'd better go for back lit." He knelt, then stretched out on the rug, carelessly propped on one elbow, dressing gown tossed aside in the movement. His arm rested on his side, hand loose, one knee bent, firelight shining through hair that haloed his head—thick hair, slightly curled, reddened by the glow of the flames. She stared at the light, fascinated. She could paint just the hair, each strand aglow. Then her eyes wandered. He didn't look naked—not quite. The front of him was shadowed, a powerful promise of nakedness. Only part of his face, his hair, the line of his arm and shoulder, hip, leg, and foot showed clearly. She swallowed, telling herself she should turn away.

Even as she had the thought, she was reaching for her sketchbook, thinking that she couldn't expect him to lie

342

here all night while she painted. He'd freeze. The fire would die down and change the light. She had to catch the moment and Jack as he was now, a natural man—beautiful. Her fingers trembled as she began to sketch. Quickly. As if the devil were after her. He was.

Still, she worked, wishing her pencil could give her those colors, the red flame with its blue heart, the glowing halo of firelight on skin and hair, gold washing tendons in his feet and all the way up the muscles whose edges she could see, whose power stretched into secret shadow.

Her heart raced with her fingers. Her eyes devoured the lights and darks. She could never show this picture. *Would* never sell it. But she'd paint it. Keep it always. Not over the mantle in the drawing room. Laughter overtook her as she thought of Mrs. Parker. The woman would faint and probably never revive if she saw the portrait Kristin was going to paint of Jack. Portrait number two.

"Minx," Jack drawled. He hadn't moved an inch. "Here I've gratified your every wish, and you sit there giggling."

Kristin swallowed another giggle as she sketched the joining of his thigh and knee.

"What will the household think if they catch me this way? My reputation will be ruined." Jack managed to sound plaintive.

Was he teasing? Laughter rippled in his voice. But it would be just like him to get up and leave before she finished. At the thought, her pencil flew.

"Reverend Passmore will preach about *me* next Sunday. He'll call *you* the contaminating association instead of the contaminee."

Kristin finished the calf, the foot, shaded in the areas that were unlighted. She felt giddy with relief. Once she'd sketched a thing, it stayed in her memory. The picture was hers now.

"Finished already?" he asked when her hand rested at last.

She nodded, embarrassed at her own concentration.

"Good. Now you get to fulfill *my* every desire."

Kristin clutched the sketchbook to her chest and started to rise, but Jack had uncoiled from the fur like a snake from its place in the sun. In seconds he was in front of her, blocking the firelight before her knees unbent. He took the book and pencil and tossed them on the table. Kristin clutched his beautiful shawl around her like armor, and he let her, swinging her, still wrapped in blue and green, up into his arms. "I think you need the warmth of our fire," he murmured into her ear.

Kristin knew what he wanted. He might even have a right to expect it, given the fact that she'd just spent a fair amount of time staring at him without his clothes and drawing what she saw. Chaste wives didn't do things like that. So she had to argue or run. Talking never seemed to do her much good where Jack was concerned. Her only chance would come when he put her down, which he did before she could make any plans.

He let her slide down against his naked body. Through her nightdress and shawl she could feel the steely brush of his—pleasure appurtenance. He was ready to make love, and she herself already felt the waves of liquid heat. They started at her hip from the spot where she had brushed against *it*. From her toes where they touched the silky fur, heat spread upward. The two tides met in her loins, forming a whirlpool as Kristin's knees buckled.

Instead of holding her up, Jack lowered her onto the fur rug, and Kristin knew she wasn't going to say a word. Or jump up and run for her life. She was going to stay right here in his arms and fall into sin just the way she had on that picnic blanket and in the Windsor Hotel. Sister

344

Mary Joseph was fading from her mind like a bird flying backward, like a song dying, as Jack, on the rug beside her, carefully unwrapped the shawl.

"I like your nightdress." He slid down beside her and ran his fingers in a spreading pattern from her throat down to the lace that stretched across the upper halves of her breasts. Kristin swallowed hard, feeling her nipples tighten. He used the middle finger to pull the center down so that he could drop a soft kiss between her breasts. She sighed, transfixed already. Again he spread his fingers and hooked the corner of the low, square neckline with his thumb, first rubbing the edge of her breast, sending a tremor through her, then running the thumb up under the lace to her shoulder. She lay perfectly still, the warmth of the fire on one side, the warmth of Jack on the other, waiting to see what he would do next, eyes wide and turned to his shadowed, fire-lit face.

His smile was tender, absorbed as he slid the shoulder lace of the nightdress down inch by inch until he had bared one pink-tipped breast. "Rosebuds," he murmured and bent his head. She trembled as his lips touched, as he flicked the bud with his tongue, circled it, sucked on it. He was so gentle. She couldn't struggle against a touch so gentle, a touch that washed her in trembling pleasure.

As his lips melted her, he unbuttoned first one button, then the second at her wrists, then stroked her palms, one after the other, until her fingers curled. Then he rose and knelt over her, slipping the nightdress down her arms so that the lace band rubbed the other breast as it passed. The sleeves with their ruffled ends turned over her hands, and the lace dragged a soft abrasion down her ribs, over her stomach, catching briefly in the hair at the juncture, then scraping lightly, like fairy fingernails, over her thighs.

As the gown pulled away, the fur caressed the skin of her back and buttocks, and Jack's lips followed from her breasts down until he paused at her thighs to kiss the soft skin, to breathe heat against her soft woman's hair and secret woman's place. She squirmed, touched by shock and a little fear, breathless with excitement multiplied a hundred-fold by the silky brush of the fur beneath her and Jack above her, whispering heatedly against her thighs, then touching her so intimately with his mouth, his tongue, that wordless cries burst from her lips and heated contractions racked her body.

When the last spasm died away, he moved up over her, whispering, fastening his mouth to hers, covering her body with his. She pressed up against him, knees parting, feet sliding in the fur, rising to capture him in her body's heat. Groaning, Jack shifted to take her, setting in motion a slow, building plunge and withdrawal. Until all the slick muscles inside her clenched around him and drove him into a frenzy, out of control, filling her more deeply, more violently that he ever had any woman, and still he wanted more, and Kristin gave it. She cried out as the second run of spasms took her, lifted her, then Jack, beyond thought and sense into a world where they were one body, one melded rapture.

When he could speak again, he asked, voice hoarse and insistent, "Do you love me?" and she gasped "Yes," still holding on to him as if he were the only anchor in a stormy sea, still wrapped around him like seaweed entangled with a wharf pole driven through the sand to bedrock.

"At last," he whispered, and pulled the blue-green shawl across their nakedness. Kristin lay a long time, letting senses other than her eyes take hold—the strange contrast of heat and cold, cold air; his heat against her body, the hearth's against her back; the silken fur beneath her, the scrape and caress of the scarf against shoulder, hip, and leg; the textures of Jack's body. In her nose she trapped the hot, smoky wood smell of the fire and the smell of Jack—the wine he had drunk at dinner, the cigar he had smoked, the clean soapy smell of his skin, the man smell of his body—and threaded through was the musk of their lovemaking.

She shifted languorously so that she could rub against Jack and against the fur beneath her. "More already?" he whispered in a lazy, drowsing voice. He moved to accommodate her arm around his waist, her knee edging between his thighs, the soft pressure of her breasts as she nestled against his chest.

She was silent again, still, dozing, waking. "What time is it?" she asked.

Jack sighed. "You're right," he murmured. "We can't stay here all night." He rolled into a sitting position, then to his knees, pulling the shawl with him. The fringe tickled across her thighs, and she opened her eyes as he bent to scoop her into his arms.

Time was important, she thought hazily as he carried her up the curving stair. The great clock in the hall, which he had imported from Europe, began to sound. She counted. One, two . . . Kristin shivered. Was it before or after midnight? Three . . . four. Each echoing gong from the clock made it more likely that she had committed a grievous sin . . . five . . . six. There had been no signs of dawn in the studio. Only firelight dying on the hearth . . . seven . . . eight. She turned her head into his shoulder and wept.

"Sweetheart, what's wrong?" Jack edged through the bedroom door, then pushed it closed with his foot.

"It was before midnight."

"What was?" Jack laid her on the bed and crawled in after her.

"When we—did what we did."

"I suppose." He wrapped her in his arms after pulling up her quilt. "I wasn't looking at my pocket watch." He chuckled in her ear. "I didn't have a pocket."

"It was still Sunday!" Kristin buried her head in the pillow and wept bitterly.

Jack, still holding her, decided he knew a lot less about women than he had thought. Sunday? What did she have against Sunday?

"Want to make love again?" he asked hopefully.

"I don't suppose it makes any difference now," she sobbed.

Jack took that for a *no,* probably because he'd feel like a bounder making love to a crying woman. Even one who admitted loving him.

Kristin overslept on Monday. Jack was not in her bed when she awakened, but other things had happened in the night after Jack carried her upstairs, after she realized that they had engaged in "the act" on Sunday and he didn't understand or, more likely, didn't care about the significance. They had made love a second time in her bed, Jack lifting her sleepy, aroused body to straddle his hips. The memory started those inner shivers again, and Kristin turned over on her stomach, squeezed her thighs together and did the multiplication tables until the feeling passed.

However, multiplication would not absolve her of the many sins she had committed—engaging in "the act" on Sunday; without thoughts of procreation; enjoying it; and in unnatural ways such as on the floor, lying on a bearskin rug stark naked, and later sitting on her husband's hips while he drove her insane with his words and actions. And after he had lured her into all these sins, had she denounced him? Had she prayed or run from the house or demanded that he stop immediately? No. Instead she had told him she loved

im, let him stay in her bed, enjoyed herself with him a
third time, kissed him back when he left her room before
dawn. She was hopeless. Not an ounce of virtue in her. The
only way she could ever hope to lead a proper and chaste
life was to avoid temptation, which meant avoiding Jack,
which meant running away.

Yvette appeared with coffee. "Madame had a good night?"
he asked smugly. The nightgown, which had been left
behind in the studio, lay over her arm. Kristin grabbed her
coffee and scowled. As soon as Yvette left, Kristin leapt out
of bed, pulled the miserable, sinful garment over her head,
and packed a small bag, which she shoved under the bed.
At the first opportunity she'd be gone.

But it wasn't that day. Maude picked her up in the downstairs hall and stuck to her like flour paste all day until the
very moment that night when Kristin entered her room and
shoved the dresser in front of the door. Her only satisfaction
was that she didn't say a word to Jack. She wouldn't even
look at him. By day's end, his high spirits, manifested so
clearly at the noonday meal, had disappeared. By bedtime
he was scowling.

Jack was spending Sunday evening in the empty bar at
the Denver Hotel with Robert Foote when a great explosion
shook the town. Although Jack heard it, he didn't comment.
He was brooding on the fact that his wife, after a night of
unbelievably satisfying love, hadn't spoken to him in seven
days. It seemed to have something to do with Sunday, but
since she wouldn't speak, he couldn't ask with any expecta-
tion of getting an answer. He never saw her in the daytime
without someone else present. She never left her blockaded
room at night. Damnation! The woman had admitted that
she loved him. Her confession had come in the heat of the
moment, as it were, but love was love. It couldn't flourish

in silence and grow on scowls. Double damnation! He wa: running out of ideas.

Robert Foote, who had no marital problems to occupy his mind, took the explosion more to heart. "What wa that?" he cried, turning pale. He set his glass down. " don't know why I'm asking. It was dynamite. I guess we'd better find out what happened." He looked around the bar. A stained-glass beer sign had fallen off the wal and broken. Glasses had fallen from the shelves behind the bar. "It's bad enough that I lose my bar customers o Sunday night," said Foote. "Now I'm losing my bar."

Jack was glad to pursue any diversion that would take his mind off Kristin, so the two men went into the lob by. Various gentlemen were coming down the stairway i their nightshirts, asking questions. "We're going to fine out," shouted Foote, and they hurried to the street door Owners who lived over their businesses came downstair onto Main.

"Where was it?" asked some.

"Sounded like up Lincoln," answered others.

People emerged from their houses as Jack and Foot walked up Lincoln. "What is it? What happened?" every one asked. The largest crowd was gathered in front of th Methodist-Episcopal Church.

"Sinners have dynamited my church bell," Reverend Passmore announced. "I call down the wrath of God upo the evil, drunken rogues of this town."

Jack spotted his wife, standing among the sausage girl: and maids of his household. All the women wore long shawls, for even in August the nights were cold. Peeking beneath the shawls were white ruffled garments. Petticoats he wondered. Nightdresses?

He inspected his wife, whose golden hair spilled dow her back. She looked like an angel. Beautiful. Ethereal. An perhaps he was the devil she called him, for the sight of her didn't evoke any thoughts of God. Instead she inspired memories of their Sunday night romp. He wanted to carry her up the hill and take her to bed. Seven days was too long when a man had a wife like her. He wanted to do all the things they'd done in front of the fire—and more.

"Who do you think done it?" asked a stranger.

"Folks who wants to drink on Sunday. Who else?" replied his companion. "Hit's to git even for Brother Passmore makin' the bars close down of a Sunday."

"Think it coulda been Miz Maeve Macleod or her man? Heard she was that mad when the preacher kep' a botherin' her at the Chicago Irishman."

"Or that pretty Miz Cameron he done preached the sermon on. Confabulatin' associations or some such."

Jack stiffened. What nonsense was this?

"Women don't know nuthin' about dynamite," was the opinion of another fellow with red stubble on his chin.

Jack relaxed.

"Hell fire and damnation await all the sinners of this town," boomed Reverend Passmore.

No doubt, thought Jack dryly and noticed that Kristin had spotted him. It was time for another seduction, he decided. She looked ripe.

"Where are the police?" bellowed Reverend Passmore. "Where is the sheriff?"

Jack strolled over to his wife. "Time to go home," he murmured.

Kristin turned away, still silent. Maybe she wasn't as ripe as he'd thought. He'd have to work on it.

Tomorrow was the day, Kristin vowed as she pulled the covers up to her chin. That walk up Nickel Hill after the dynamiting of the church bell had convinced her. Just the

351

curving of Jack's fingers over her elbow as he escorted her home had set shameless sensations in motion. Accordingly she had slipped out of her room when everyone was asleep, untacked and rolled almost every dry canvas in the studio, concealed their absence by stacking the wet canvases and the failures in front of the empty frames, hauled her choice upstairs and packed them in a second valise, which she hid under the bed with the first. One case for clothes, one for paintings. This time she would travel light, make herself less easy to spot if he came after her or hired detectives again. Unfortunately, she couldn't take art supplies, but she had money under the bed. All she had to do was divert Maude, and a way to do it had occurred to her.

When Yvette brought her *café au lait* the next morning, Kristin said, "I think I'll stay in bed. You can have the day off, Yvette." The maid's smirk told Kristin that Yvette thought she knew why madame was having a day in bed. It was the result of another night with Monsieur Cameron.

"*Très bien, madame,*" said Yvette. "A day off eez always welcome." And she minced away.

One down, one to go, thought Kristin. After an hour she went to the door and spoke to Maude, who was seated in the hall knitting. Maude cooperated by asking immediately, "You're still feelin' poorly, Miz Kristin?"

"I'm afraid I am," said Kristin, trying to look sick. "I fear I caught a chill by going out into the night air for the bell dynamiting."

"I'm not surprised, ma'am," cried Maude. 'Twas right cold last night, an' us in our nightdresses. Still, I wouldn't have missed it for the world. Such excitement!"

"Yes," murmured Kristin. "You're going to have to go to the chemist's. The one just off Washington on Main."

"Yes, ma'am, but what shall I get you?"

Kristin, who was never sick, didn't know what to ask for. "See if he has Dewitt's Early Risers."

"But that's for biliousness, not the chill."

"And something for chill," said Kristin hastily. "The chemist will be able to make a suggestion. And be sure you write down the instructions."

"But ma'am, I can't write."

"Then have him write them down, and you wait for him to do it, even if he's busy. Medicine is dangerous if not taken properly. I'd rather delay than make a mistake."

"Yes, ma'am," said Maude, looking worried.

Kristin put her hand to her forehead as if dizzy and headed back to bed. "I'll just have a nice nap. You can knock softly when you return, and if I don't answer, let me sleep. My mother always said sleep is a great curative." Kristin's mother had said no such thing. Lottie had done all the home doctoring. Maude helped Kristin into bed.

"I won't wake you, ma'am. Shall I send for the doctor?"

"We'll try home remedies first." She gave Maude a wan smile.

"Or Mr. Cameron. Maybe we should send for—"

"Absolutely not! I won't have him bothered." Kristin closed her eyes and lay tensely listening for the sound of Maude on the stairs. Once she heard it, she leapt out, stripped off her nightgown, which she had been wearing over her traveling clothes, buttoned on her boots, and fished the two suitcases and her reticule out from under the bed. She could hear the front door close as she was making these preparations. After giving Maude a few minutes to turn the corner at Washington, Kristin tiptoed downstairs and out the front door. Luck was with her, luck and good planning. She knew everyone's schedule well enough to know where they'd be at this time. A valise in either hand, she walked

as fast as she could toward Lincoln, which would take her
to the railroad station. She couldn't be bothered with the
ladies' stop today. She had to make that morning train to
Denver.

"Mrs. Cameron," called Father Boniface Wirtner from
across Lincoln. Kristin tried to pretend she didn't hear.

A miner stepped into her path and said, "That there priest
in skirts is callin' you, ma'am."

The brief pause allowed the priest to cross the street and
catch up with her. "Mrs. Cameron," he puffed. "I've been
meaning to talk to you."

He's going to ask why I haven't been to confession, she
thought. Could he insist that she go right now? What time
was it? Even if she made up a few small sins and kept all
the big ones to herself, she'd miss the train.

"I saw several of your paintings at Mrs. Kathleen
Macleod's house."

Kristin stared at him helplessly. Had he found something
sinful in the portraits?

"Of the children. They were so charming. Our poor St.
Mary's lacks a good deal in the way of holy decoration,
although the ladies of the Altar Cloth Society do their
best." Father Boniface Wirtner stared at her with a mildly
accusing look.

"All right, I'll join," she offered, glancing anxiously over
her shoulder, thinking she heard the sound of the Denver
train. How great a sin was lying to a priest? Would she
have to find an Altar Cloth Society in her new home to
make good her promise? Or was she so deep in unforgiven
sin that it wouldn't matter?

"I was hoping I might talk you into doing a picture for
the church. Perhaps Christ and the children."

"All right," she said. "I'll do it." And she backed away.
"Good-bye, Father," she called over her shoulder, leaving

the priest standing in the street looking surprised. Now she'd have to send him a picture. From somewhere. *Was* that the train? Was it pulling in or leaving?

"Oh, Mr. Cameron," cried Maude as Jack entered the house for his noonday meal. "I'm so worried. Poor Mrs. Cameron was very ill this morning."

Jack felt his heart jolt with anxiety.

"She took a chill last night at the bell dynamiting. I got her the Little Early Risers and—"

"I'll go right up and see how she is," said Jack.

"But that's just it, sir. She's not there. Or anywhere in the house, and no one saw her leave. Do you think she could have been kidnapped? I've heard as how Mrs. Macleod was kidnapped. Maybe this is a bad town for it."

"You were supposed to keep your eye on her every minute," said Jack.

"But sir, she needed medicine. What could I—"

"You could have sent someone else. Yvette."

"Yvette don't run errands, sir. She's too grand."

"She can damn well do whatever she's told," snapped Jack. "Oh, what the hell! Probably doesn't make any difference now." He strode down the hall to the studio. The first thing he saw was that Kristin had finished the self-portrait. It was on the easel, beckoning him. The sight of Kristin in her lavender gown turned his heart over. She was so beautiful, so seductive in her innocence and passion. Almost as beautiful as she'd been that night on the rug in her white nightdress—and out of it. But he'd taken her too far that night, much too far. He'd let himself be carried away. Then he discovered that almost all the landscape paintings were gone. "Yvette!" he shouted.

"We're about to eat, sir," said Yvette primly. "Was there something you wanted?"

355

"Get yourself up to Mrs. Cameron's room and see if there is clothing missing."

"Missing? *Mon dieu, monsieur,* you theenk there 'as been a thief in the house, a clothing thief?"

"Just get up there and find out," snapped Jack.

Looking huffy, Yvette left. When she returned, she reported to him, lifting carefully one finger at a time, "Zee navy blue travel suit eez gone, an' zee forest green."

When Yvette got to the tenth item of clothing, Jack interrupted. "In other words, she's taken a trip."

"She said notheeng," Yvette replied. "How could she take ze treep weezout her lady's maid?"

Jack started for the door. "Damn women. You can't trust a one of them," he was muttering under his breath as Abigail appeared and said, "The meal is getting cold. Both you and Mrs. Cameron are supposed to be eating in. I expect notice if—"

Ignoring her, Jack walked out and slammed the door behind him, leaving all the sausage girls round-eyed in the hall. His first destination was the ladies' stop. Kristin had not climbed aboard there. She must have boarded in West Breckenridge. And she called *him* shameless!

He turned his horse toward the West Breckenridge Depot, where the station master was happy to give him a lecture on the proprieties of train travel on the Western Slope.

"I take it my wife boarded here," said Jack.

"She did, sir, although I told her, not for the first time—"

"What direction?"

"Ticket to Denver."

Jack nodded and left without another word, sent a telegram to Pinkerton's in Denver to be on the lookout for her, and went back to eat a cold dinner. He'd be damned if he was going after her again. Let the detectives bring her home. She was probably traveling on the wardrobe money

356

he had given her before she ran away the first time.

Well, they'd catch her. He'd given permission by telegram to detain her as a runaway wife, hoping that would be enough to get the job done. The wireless man had gaped as Jack dictated the message, so his marital troubles would be all over town by nightfall. Damn her!

Chapter Twenty-Two

Kristin kept her eyes closed as the train began the steep climb to Boreas Pass. At the Washington Spur, she started the multiplication tables, which took so much concentration that she wasn't even sure when the train crossed the Gold Pan Trestle. Once at Boreas Pass, she felt safe enough to take out her sketchbook, which fell open to the drawing of Jack, lying on the bearskin rug before the fireplace. She turned the page, but the picture stayed in her head, much more fixed than the multiplication tables.

The sketch called up that night with him, which she was even now trying to escape in mind and body. She had since discovered that as well as copulating on Sunday, which was strictly forbidden, the second *act* had been committed on Monday, which would have been acceptable except that particular Monday had been a feast day. Kristin could never keep track of all the feast days, but Sister Mary Joseph's admonitions stayed in her head. Not Wednesday through Sunday. Not during Lent, Rogation Days, Advent or Pentecost. Not on feast days. How many days did that make in all? Forty each in the case of seasons like Lent, plus all the others. It was a wonder any wedded couple ever had a baby if they were living in a chaste married union, which she and Jack certainly weren't.

Not only was there the matter of days and enjoyment, but of unnatural acts. She felt the color rise to her cheeks as she thought of the places Jack had kissed her. Certainly that was unnatural kissing. She was double-damned for permitting and enjoying it. Shocking ideas had filtered through her brain that night, ideas for things she might do to him, planted there, no doubt, by things he was doing to her.

She looked down at her sketch pad and found it covered with naked parts of Jack—biceps, abdomen, large muscles of the thigh, Jack half clad in his dressing gown, a sinewy foot, a delicious knee, a tempting ear—she had barely escaped putting her tongue in it that night. Her one consolation was that she hadn't sketched his pleasure appurtenance in either of its two states.

With determination, she put pencil and book into her reticule to keep temptation away from her naughty fingers. Because of this obsession with Jack's body, she might have to give up art. No, she had to learn control. First, she must confess her sins. She'd find some stranger priest in Denver, or wait until she reached her final destination, which wasn't going to be any tourist train making an endless loop in Colorado. Where should she go? Chicago! He'd never think of looking for her there. She'd get off in Denver and board a train to Chicago.

If she had to wait, she could make a confession in Denver. If not, there were plenty of churches in Chicago. Also in Chicago she could visit Mrs. Potter Palmer with the landscape series. Mrs. Palmer would find buyers, and with the money Kristin would go—to Paris! Even if Jack hired detectives, they wouldn't cross the ocean to look for her. In Paris, she could be the famous, mysterious American artist, whose marital status was unknown because she never spoke of it. Maybe she could meet Mary Cassatt. On that thought, she leaned her head against the seat back and fell fast asleep, dreaming of Jack all the way to Denver.

With a porter carrying her two bags, Kristin headed for the ticket window to inquire about a train to Chicago.

"Yoo hoo, Mrs. Cameron, Mrs. Cam-er-on."

Oh lord, thought Kristin. Was she caught all ready? Were there female detectives? She tried to ignore the voice, but couldn't ignore the tug at her arm.

Turning anxiously, Kristin recognized the woman but couldn't recall her name. She had been one of the guests, a silent one, at the dinner party where Kristin and Jack had made such fools of themselves.

"I'm so sorry that I didn't get to speak to you before we returned to Denver," said the lady. "To thank you for your hospitality. The dinner was—ah—" The woman blushed. So did Kristin. "—very unusual," the lady stammered. "You don't remember my name, do you? I'm Celeste Peacock."

"Oh, yes. How nice to see you again," said Kristin, glancing at the ticket window anxiously. A line was forming. What if, by the time she got away from this woman and had waited her turn, the train to Chicago had already departed? "Well, good-bye."

Mrs. Peacock grabbed her arm. "I particularly wanted to speak to you because—"

"Most kind of you," said Kristin, trying to get loose.

"—because I wanted to buy one of your paintings. If you could see your way clear—"

Kristin stopped. Her first respectable commission in Colorado from someone other than Jack. "You mean you want me to paint something for you?" she asked.

"Or sell me one of the beautiful landscapes I saw in your studio." Mrs. Peacock was a pale woman with a sweet face, mousy hair, and an expensive brown outfit. "I'm a native Coloradan, you see. I was born at Gregory Gulch during the early placer strikes, and I haven't seen any paintings that I thought captured the beauty of my state so well as yours."

A Denver socialite who wanted to buy a painting! She certainly couldn't pass this up. How much should she ask?

"I know, of course, that they'll be expensive," said Mrs. Peacock, "but my husband's very indulgent. He's already said I can have two."

"Two?"

"Yes. I don't suppose you have any with you?"

"Well, as it happens—"

"Oh, my goodness, you do. How wonderful! You must come home to tea. May I choose any I like?"

"Yes, certainly," said Kristin, casting one last glance at the ticket line. A lot more people had joined it, and the station was becoming crowded. Maybe it would be safer to get out of Union Depot, where detectives might be looking for her. They wouldn't think to look at Mrs. Peacock's.

"I have a carriage outside. Where are you staying?"

"Well, I—I haven't registered anywhere yet," said Kristin, trying to remember the name of some hotel other than the Windsor. Jack would certainly look for her there.

"Then you *must* stay with us. How exciting! To have such a talented artist as a guest!"

Kristin's heart tripped happily. She found that she really liked Mrs. Peacock. Such a nice lady. She could stay with them overnight, then slip out of town tomorrow when she had the money for the paintings. Kristin signaled to the porter and off she went with Mrs. Peacock, who invited Kristin to call her Celeste.

"Which paintings did you like best?" Kristin asked.

"Oh, I liked them all. Which have you brought?"

"Colorado landscapes."

"Those are just the ones I want."

The women climbed into the carriage chatting about art. Because Mrs. Peacock expected to pay more than Kristin would have asked, Kristin's heart was fluttering with financial joy by the time they reached Capitol Hill.

"That's H.A.W. Tabor's home," said Mrs. Peacock during the ride. "The one he built for Augusta Tabor, his first wife. He divorced her and married Baby Doe. I'm sure you've heard that story."

Kristin shook her head.

"Soon we'll pass the house he built for Baby Doe. It was quite a scandal in Colorado society, but perhaps you're not interested in gossip."

"Oh, I'm interested in everything," said Kristin exuberantly.

"Wife seen disembarking at Union Depot, Denver. Left with unidentified woman. Send instructions."

Jack stared grimly at the telegram. Who the hell had met Kristin at the station? Perhaps some female artist was hiding his wife. "Canvas Denver art colony," he telegraphed back and went about his business, feeling as bad-tempered as a man could.

In less than four hours, Kristin was on her way to becoming the toast of Denver society. They had no sooner reached the Peacock house than Mrs. Peacock whispered instructions to her servants, who scattered through town inviting people to dinner. Mrs. Peacock broke the news to her guest

362

after an hour spent exclaiming over the six canvasses and choosing the two she wished to buy.

"And now, my dear, I have a lovely surprise for you, which I hope you will enjoy as much as I intend to," she said and announced that the cream of Denver society had agreed to break whatever engagements they had in order to attend a formal dinner at which Kristin would be the guest of honor.

"I didn't bring a dinner dress," said Kristin. Even that difficulty did not deter Mrs. Peacock. She offered Kristin the use of her stepdaughter's wardrobe, which included a yellow dinner gown. Yellow was chic that year. Yvette had told Kristin so a million times, bemoaning the fact that a woman of Kristin's complexion could not wear yellow. Surprisingly, with tucking here and letting out there, the gown looked magnificent with its short train and Medici collar. She wore Jack's emerald necklace, which she had brought along to sell.

"Stunning, my dear!" exclaimed Mrs. Peacock, who was more interested in the toilette of her guest than her own. She appeared wearing brown. Again. That evening, the four remaining landscapes were snapped up at fifty dollars apiece by dinner guests, and everything Kristin said was considered witty and Bohemian. Two days later, the *Rocky Mountain News* reported that Mrs. Kristin Traube-Cameron, the beautiful, talented wife of Colorado's newest financier, John Powell Cameron of Breckenridge and Chicago, was a new star shining in the firmament of Denver society.

Appalled to see her name in the paper, Kristin stopped going out. She reasoned that Pinkerton detectives would not invade the Peacocks' house to get at her. Couples who had not had the good fortune to buy one of the six landscapes begged her to paint them one immediately, which she did. Mrs. Peacock, twittering with delight, set up a studio and sent her servants fanning out over the city buying art supplies. Kristin refused all invitations to tea, dinner, the theater, or any other out-of-house social events, claiming bondage to the artistic muse. She hoped that Denver gossip would not reach Pinkerton's or Breckenridge before she had milked every last cent she could from this unexpected good fortune.

Her greatest regret involved all the ladies who declared that they intended to spend the following summer in Breckenridge so that she could do their portraits. They asked her advice on what houses might be available to renters. Kristin hated to miss so many potential clients but couldn't warn them that she would not be in Breckenridge next summer. All these proposals kept Jack on her mind because she would not be with Jack next summer either. So she sighed and painted, getting richer and sadder as a week passed.

"Wife with Peacocks on Capitol Hill. Toast of Denver Society. Please advise."

Jack swore and crumpled the telegram. What the devil was she doing staying with his friends, the Mortimer Peacocks? Had she told them why she wasn't at home? He found himself in a foul mood, for he too was the center of attention. Four neighbors appeared at his door to demand that he control his pigs, who rooted in their yards and wandered into their houses. It did him no good to point out that the pigs weren't his. His neighbors said, "Well, where's your wife? Tell her." To take care of the problem, Jack hired a carpenter to build a pig house.

"Never built a pig house," the carpenter said. "Don't know what one looks like."

Neither did Jack. "Make it look like the main house, so it won't be too unsightly. And you'd better heat it," he added, "or the damn pigs will freeze to death this winter."

Shaking his head, the carpenter began to build a Greek revival, heated pig house in back of the old Fleming mansion. The *Summit County Journal* reported the project.

Jack wired the Pinkerton detectives, "Bring her back home discreetly, but make it fast."

Helen Henderson Shane came to call and gave Kristin the money, less commission, from the sale of Aunt Frieda's portrait, which had been acquired just the day before as a result of the many newspaper articles about Kristin's great social success in Denver.

"Newspaper articles," Kristin echoed in a weak voice. She had thought they'd stop now that she was staying in.

"Oh yes, my dear. You're the talk of Denver."

If she was the talk of Denver, her husband could have found her. Obviously, he wasn't interested anymore. And why should he be? A woman who'd sell her own aunt. Frieda should be hanging on *her* wall, not some stranger's. At least, she now no longer needed the money so badly. Feast or famine. That's what her life had turned into. But the portrait was sold. There was nothing she could do about it.

After Mrs. Shane, three more ladies came to call, one who had bought Aunt Frieda's portrait and now wanted one of herself. One wanted her children painted, one her husband, and all promised to come to the Western Slope the following summer for the sittings, although Kristin suggested that they have photographs made from which she could do the portraits wherever she might be. However, the ladies insisted on coming to Breckenridge, having heard about her deliciously Bohemian household.

Kristin was amazed to find life at the old Fleming mansion so described. What had they heard? About the dynamiting, the dining room table falling into the cellar, the pigs nuzzling the guests' ankles, sausage girls underfoot? Well, she supposed Bohemian was in the eye of the beholder.

"Mrs. Cameron never leaves house," telegraphed Pinkerton's. "Should we go in after her? Please advise."

"Lure her out," Jack telegraphed back. He returned home to find a committee of Methodists awaiting him in the drawing room, looking very grim.

"Word has it, Mr. Cameron, that your wife hired rowdies to dynamite our church bell."

"Nonsense," said Jack. "Why would she do that?"

One of the men sighed. "Because of the sermon Brother Passmore preached about contaminating associations. We're sorry about that, but she shouldn't have dynamited our bell. We think she ought to pay for a new one."

"She didn't do it," said Jack angrily. "She's terrified of dynamite. Surely you've heard that our dining room collapsed into the cellar in the middle of a dinner party as a result of dynamite."

"I had heard that," said a third member of the committee. "But we find it very suspicious that your wife left town the morning after our explosion. Rumor has it that you yourself don't know where she went."

"My wife's whereabouts are our business," said Jack, "but in her absence I am quite prepared to take you to court for slandering her."

After a heated debate, the men decided that Mrs. Cameron's involvement in the church bell explosion might be only a rumor. Nonetheless, Jack felt compelled to tell the story all over town as if it were a great joke.

"If she's not guilty, where is she?" demanded one irate Methodist, who stopped Jack several days later.

"She's in Denver socializing," he snapped, "and selling

paintings. Would a bell dynamiter be keeping such a high profile?" No one in Breckenridge yet knew that she'd run away; the wireless operator had kept his mouth shut. Jack hoped no one in Denver knew, although when the Pinkerton detectives nabbed her, there were bound to be suspicions.

Kristin was torn. She had received a note from the committee that chose paintings for an important Denver art show. The note explained that they had one of her pictures, which had been submitted by Mrs. Cherry; now they wished to speak to her about other entries. Kristin didn't want to leave the house, yet how could she pass up this opportunity? Mrs. Peacock insisted that she go. "Oh, I don't know," said Kristin, dithering.

"But why, my dear?"

"I'm always being accosted by men. On other visits to Denver, strangers on the street stopped me."

"In that case, I shall accompany you in the family carriage. You'll be perfectly safe."

Kristin considered the offer and decided that Mrs. Peacock was right. No one—not even Jack—would try to detain her against her will when she was in the safekeeping of such a prominent lady. "Very well. I suppose I must," said Kristin. She did want to. "You're so kind. No artist could have a more thoughtful patron." Mrs. Peacock beamed, all aflutter at having been named Kristin's patron. Kristin mused happily on what a coup it would be if she could take several prizes in the contest. If so, she could send paintings to Helen Henderson Shane, and they would be snapped up at marvelous prices.

On the morning of the appointment, she and Mrs. Peacock walked down the steps and climbed into the Peacock carriage, much to the distress of the two Pinkerton detectives who were hiding in the shrubbery.

Would it be discreet to take the runaway wife in front of her socialite friend? They had sent the note to lure Mrs. Cameron out but hadn't anticipated that Mrs. Peacock would be with her. By the time they had debated the issue, the carriage had gone, so they followed to the address they had given in the forged note, having decided that it was now or never.

"I'm sure I don't understand," Mrs. Peacock was saying as she and Kristin left the Tabor Building. "I shall certainly speak to the committee about their carelessness in sending the wrong address."

As they stepped onto the street, two men in bowler hats and unfashionable checked jackets said to Kristin, "We have your husband's permission, ma'am, to escort you home."

Tricked, thought Kristin. *I should have known.* "I don't wish to leave," she said.

"Who are you?" cried Mrs. Peacock.

"Pinkertons, ma'am," they replied and hustled Kristin into a waiting hack.

Mrs. Peacock, thinking her friend and protegée had been abducted, summoned the Denver police, who, accompanied by Mrs. Peacock, followed Kristin and the Pinkerton detectives to the railroad station, where there was a grand confrontation which involved a weeping Kristin, the production of Jack's telegrams by the detectives, and the confusion of the Denver police, scratching their heads and deciding that a man had a right to retrieve his runaway wife. Kristin declared that she didn't want to go back and that she had left her belongings at the Peacock house; she should at least be allowed to return for them. Mrs. Peacock twittered around the scene and decided that it was all terribly Bohemian. She promised to send Kristin's baggage and invited her to visit again if Jack ever let her leave Breckenridge.

"I consider this an abduction," Kristin told the taller of the two detectives as they assisted her aboard.

"Just doin' my job, ma'am," he replied. "You can complain to your husband before day's end."

It was a dreadful trip. She didn't have a sketchbook in her reticule, which left her with nothing to do but think about was how angry Jack must be. He hadn't even come after her himself, as he had the last time. Would he meet her at the railroad station?

He did.

"Good visit in Denver?" he asked. She sulked. "What luck you got home today," he said. "We've a house full of guests wondering where their hostess is. I hope you're not planning to give them the silent treatment too."

Kristin said nothing, and Jack guided the horses onto Main Street. "You may be interested to know that there are a number of Methodists who hold you responsible for the dynamiting of Reverend Passmore's bell."

"What?"

"Ah, so you can speak! If anyone accuses you, just laugh it off. That's what I've been doing in your absence. Actually, it was your absence that got that rumor started. They figured you committed the crime and fled."

Kristin returned to her earlier silence.

"Yvette's finished a new gown—copy of a Worth, she said. A sort of narrow dress in blue with a flowing, cream-colored coat over it. I've never seen anything like it. Blue embroidery on the cream, cream on the blue. You should look stunning in it."

"Jack, would you please stop talking," said Kristin. They had reached the house, and quite a crowd awaited them on the veranda.

Yvette said, "Welcome home, madame. In ze future, please inform me of unscheduled departures. I cannot create ze superb wardrobe when you are not here."

Maude said, looking hurt, "You tricked me, ma'am."

Ingrid said, "I hope you got some orders in Denver. The sausages are piling up again."

A strange woman, evidently one of the guests, said, "So nice to meet you at last, Mrs. Cameron. You really shouldn't wear light-colored clothes on the train. You'll never get the soot out of that gown."

"I was abducted while making a morning call," said Kristin through gritted teeth.

"Abducted?" Laughing and murmuring, the strange woman exclaimed, "Imagine! I must tell my husband. He'll love it."

"Abducted?" said Jack dryly.

Chapter Twenty-Three

While Yvette emptied the bath water and laid out clothes for the dinner party, Kristin started disconsolately out of the window of her bedroom. She was the prisoner of a man determined to engage in unnatural acts on prohibited days. Moreover, she was wildly attracted to him—but not, she tried to assure herself, in love with him. Up and down the second floor hall, she could hear the muted sounds of guests she didn't even know donning fashionable clothes, chatting with one another, completely unaware of her plight. No doubt they found Jack attractive too and failed to realize the sinful underlayer of his character.

Her gloomy musing came to a halt when she noticed the new structure rising in her backyard. It appeared to be a miniature of the house itself. "What's that building across from the dormitory?" she asked Yvette.

"Ah, madame, zat eez your new peeg house."

"Pig house?" Was this some sardonic joke on Jack's

part? His way of saying that she had turned his home into a pig house?

"Monsieur Jack has received many complaints from ze neighbors about ze peegs, zo Monsieur Jack, being ze thoughtful gentleman zat he eez, eez building ze house for ze peegs. Eet eez to be heated for zeir comfort in ze winter."

Kristin's mouth dropped open. A heated, neoclassic pig house? Her brows drew together in a puzzled frown. If he meant it as a joke, it was certainly an expensive one. Could he be building it to please her?

"Monsieur Jack, he say to ze carpenter, eet should match ze house zo eet would not be ze—how you zay?—eye illness in ze backyard."

Kristin giggled. So Jack didn't want an eyesore in the backyard. And he was worrying about the comfort of her pigs when the weather became colder. In fact, it was pretty chilly right now as the late summer evening fell. Kristin waited until Yvette had tied her corset strings before implementing her escape plan. "Yvette, I would like a few minutes to myself," she said.

"Madame, I am not allowed to leave you alone."

"What do you think I'm going to do? Jump out the window? Now go out into the hall. I wish to spend a few minutes in prayer." Kristin had estimated correctly that even the pushy Yvette would not deny her private prayer when there was no way for her to escape during her devotions.

Yvette shrugged. "Only a few minutes, madame. We haven't so much time." Kristin dropped ostentatiously to her knees by the bed as Yvette left, closing the door behind her. As soon as the door clicked shut, Kristin leapt up and hurried to the movable chiffonier for her reticule which contained, fortunately, every cent she had taken with her when she ran away from Breckenridge as well as all the money she had made selling paintings in Denver. It was a considerable amount, and her impulse to keep it with her always was a fortunate one. Although she could take no clothes this time, she would have all her money and her best jewelry.

Hands trembling, she divided the greenbacks into four equal piles and began to force them up under her corset in four different places. She was gasping for breath by the time she had finished. The corset had been very tight to begin with; now it was torturous. She blinked hard, drew a shallow breath, and scooted over to the mirror where she turned slowly to be sure that none of the money peeked out below the boning.

Safe, she thought. Now if she could just get into the new dress without any of her fortune tumbling down onto her petticoat. Drawing another shallow breath, she knelt again, folding her hands piously, bowing her head, and murmuring, "Dear Lord, do let me escape successfully tonight."

She was in the midst of that brief prayer when Yvette reentered. Kristin said, "Amen," dropped her hands, and rose cautiously from her knees.

"And now ze dress," said Yvette. "Eet eez a masterpiece."

"I'm sure," said Kristin. She'd never seen anything like it, but the flowing open coat would be welcome tonight when she was literally running away from home through the chilly evening streets. She stood still, hardly breathing while Yvette dropped the underdress over her head and pulled the waistline into place.

"Madame has put on weight?" she asked, puzzled. The dress was tight.

Kristin pointed out that she hadn't been at home to be fitted.

Yvette muttered to herself in French as she strained the buttons and snaps, tugged here and there at the fitted waist and hip line. "I deedn't notice," she muttered, "when I was pulleeng ze corset streengs. Could Madame be, perhaps, weeth child?"

"Madame could not," snapped Kristin. That's all she needed, to find herself pregnant. It was, of course, possible, but she'd better not be. She planned to stay in hiding until Jack became convinced of the unsuitability of their match.

"Madame, why do you look so sad?" asked Yvette.

"I didn't realize I did," said Kristin. Was she sad? Well, a bit. She and Jack could have had a good marriage if he'd only played by the rules. Still, there was the problem of enjoying oneself. She might never have been able to get a grip on that. Kristin sighed, then winced as four packets of money dug into her ribs and waist.

"Madame eez ill? Or faint?" asked Yvette, frowning. "Take a deep breath and—"

"Oh, stop fussing," Kristin muttered. As if she *could* take a deep breath.

"Madame eez irritable," said Yvette. "Now I shall choose zee jewelry."

"The emeralds," said Kristin. They were her most expensive pieces.

"Madame cannot wear green with ze blue dress."

"I will wear the emeralds."

"But madame—"

Kristin smiled craftily. "They were a gift from my husband. Need I say more?"

Yvette's eyebrows rose. "If madame treasures ze gifts of her husband, why did madame run off to Denver?"

"Because madame had business in Denver." Kristin walked slowly to her dressing table so as not to become noticeably short-winded. Running later in the evening was

374

going to be terrible, but she couldn't reach under her skirt on a public street and fish the money out from under her corset. Well, she'd worry about that when she had to. She sat down and allowed Yvette to clasp the necklace around her neck and thread the earrings into her ears.

"Dreadful," said Yvette. "Een terrible taste."

Kristin looked at herself in the mirror. Actually, she liked the blue and green combination. It reminded her of that lovely shawl Jack had brought her from Denver, which she would have to leave behind again. Perhaps in the separation settlement, he'd let her have it back. He couldn't use it himself. Although he could give it to some other woman. Her heart twisted at the thought of Jack with another woman. Then she remembered smugly that he couldn't remarry; the church wouldn't allow it, unless he managed to get an annulment. Could he? What were the grounds for annulment? Kristin had no idea. And he'd have to petition Rome, so it would take him a good long time.

"Eet eez nice to see ze smile on madame's face," said Yvette, "even if ze colors of her jewelry and gown are—"

"Superb," said Kristin. "You simply lack an adventurous eye for color, Yvette. Now do my hair. I thought you said we were short of time."

Grimly Yvette did her hair, using the curling iron to produce dozens of curls, which were pinned and tied into place at the crown of Kristin's head. Yvette stuck pretty much to the same style for evening, but it was a flattering one. Kristin could just imagine what it would look like by the time she reached her destination tonight. If she managed to escape.

Jack eyed the blue-and-cream gown combined with the emeralds. "I guess you like *something* I've given you," he muttered.

375

"Certainly," said Kristin. "I said thank you."

"Yes, and then ran off." He put his hand over hers where it rested on his arm and led her to another couple for another introduction. Kristin tried to remember the names this time, hoping they'd prove in the future to be art customers to whom she could make sales. Once the last introductions had been performed, Maude called the party in to dinner, still casting Kristin hurt looks. With a twinge of conscience, Kristin wondered how harsh Jack had been with poor Maude over the temporary loss of his wife.

Mr. Pembroke of Chicago escorted Kristin in to dinner and informed her with relish that the Chicago Traubes were the target of a gossip storm for their treatment of Kristin. Mr. Pembroke then sent her a jolly grin as he seated her and took his own place to her right. "You little dickens. You were probably just itching to get away. I take you for an adventurous girl."

Kristin smiled. He was certainly right about that as regarded her life these last few months, although she had never thought of herself as an adventurer. Even her daydreams hadn't been very adventurous—a handsome prince, a prize in the Interstate Industrial Exposition, that sort of thing. She wondered how the paintings she'd sent to Mrs. Potter Palmer had done. Had they sold? Won any prizes? If money came to the house, she wouldn't be here to receive it.

She sighed and again felt the breathlessness imposed by a money-stuffed corset. Being a runaway was so complicated. Doing one's duty as a chaste, Roman Catholic woman was even more so. She glanced down the candlelit table at her husband, who was flirting with a pretty, dark-haired woman.

During a lull in the conversation as soup was being

served, Kristin heard the voice of Maeve Macleod in the hall, saying, "I don't care if she's entertaining the grand emperor of China. I'll have a word with her." Then Maeve threw open the doors to the dining room. "What's this I hear about your selling those sausage makers?"

Kristin laid her napkin beside her plate and tried to rise. Mr. Pembroke knocked his chair over in his haste to pull hers back for her. Having tried to take too deep a breath, Kristin became dizzy and grasped the table for support, pulling the tablecloth an inch or two and causing a great tinkle of crystal among the place settings. Gentlemen grabbed their wine goblets, ladies their water. "I don't know what you're talking about, Maeve," said Kristin.

"The sausage girls. I heard you're charging a fee to the fellows who marry them."

"Well, of course. Those ceremonies cost me money."

"You're no better than a procurer," said Maeve.

The dinner guests gasped.

"I didn't know you were doing that," said Kat, who was seated halfway down the table.

"Don't complain," said Connor. "At least, they're not housed at our place any more. We lost money on that operation, you know."

"The idea isn't to make money," said Maeve. "The idea is to find good places in life for the girls. Marriages—"

"Or businesses," said Kat.

"I consider your actions extremely unchristian," said Maeve. "I'm going straight to Father Boniface Wirtner." She whirled and left the room.

"What was that about?" asked Mr. Pembroke as he helped Kristin into her seat again.

She had to take four shallow breaths before she could answer. "I run a courting parlor on Sundays for the girls who come out here to make sausages and find husbands," she explained. "Naturally we charge a small fee to cover refreshments, the cost of the weddings, and so forth."

"Amazing," said Mr. Pembroke. "You're—would you say—a sort of professional matchmaker?"

His wife said, "I belong to Mrs. Potter Palmer's social reform group, and we don't charge for our good works."

"I did too," said Kristin, "when I lived in Chicago, although I must say my family didn't approve. They were very snobbish about having anything to do with the lower classes, even in a charitable way."

"What a strange attitude," said another Chicago matron.

"But I persevered. I went out at least twice a week rescuing young women in railroad stations."

"Very commendable," said a lady from Denver. "We need such a service in our city."

"You certainly do," said Kristin. "I was abducted from the Union Depot." She stared meaningfully at Jack.

"The devil you were," he muttered.

"Yes, indeed," said Kristin. "I do feel the devil had much to do with it."

"But if you are in sympathy with the goals of the women's movement in Chicago, Mrs. Cameron, why are you charging these young women?"

"I'm in business now," said Kristin, "earning my own living."

Mr. Pembroke roared with laughter. "Doesn't Jack give you enough pocket money, little lady?"

Before Kristin could answer, Maude announced, "Fresh mountain trout in dill-cream sauce with a touch of white wine," and began to serve the plates.

"Wine?" Kristin stared at hers. "I don't drink."

"It's not intoxicating when it's been cooked," Jack said. He didn't want his wife getting off on the subject of brandy. She seemed bound and determined to make a scene.

"Bring me one that has the sauce scraped off," Kristin said to Maude.

"Oh ma'am, it's ever so delicious. I had some and didn't feel the least tipsy."

"Nevertheless—"

Maude sighed, picked up Kristin's plate, and plopped it down in front of Mr. Pembroke. Eyebrows rose along the table, and from the hall came the sound of a gruff voice saying, "I been waitin' to see her for two weeks. Couldn't hurt nuthin' if she just talked to me a minute. I ain't leavin' 'til you asks."

Yvette unfolded the dining room doors and stuck her head through to say, "There eez a—person—out here een ze hall, madame, who eensists on talking to you."

"By all means, show him in," said Kristin.

"There. Din' I tell you," said the gruff voice, and Yvette's slender, dark-clad form was replaced by a burly miner in heavy boots and a plaid shirt. "Ah'm Fish Eye Morgan, Miz Cameron. Maybe you remember me."

"Of course, Mr. Morgan, you're courting—ah—Lizzy."

"Right, ma'am."

"Won't you have dinner with us, Mr. Morgan? Maude, set a place between Mrs. Pembroke and Mrs. Parker."

Mrs. Parker looked horrified. She'd been angry to find herself seated by a woman, but this was really too much.

"That evens up the table," said Kristin.

"Hello there, Fish Eye," said Connor. "I didn't get out to the Chicago Girl today. How are things going?"

"Takin' out lots of gold jus' like yesterday," said Fish Eye, nervously rolling up the bill of his hat. "Say, ma'am, I din' mean to invite myself to dinner."

"Quite all right, Mr. Morgan. We were just having a discussion on how terrible I am to charge prospective bride-grooms for the wedding ceremony."

"I never give it thought," said Mr. Morgan, his fish eye rolling wildly. "It's worth it to find a wife, unmarried females bein' in short supply."

"There you are, Mr. Morgan," said Maude, glaring at him. She'd just finished squeezing a place setting in between the two ladies.

Fish Eye sat down opposite Mattie Parker, whose presence had resulted in more women than men at the table. "Scarce as women are, it's a service that's much appreciated, ma'am." He nodded his head to Kristin, then inspected Mattie. "You one a them as is on the market?"

"Certainly not," said Mrs. Parker. "Please do not address my daughter, Mr.—ah—whatever your name is. You have not been and will not be introduced to her."

"When I see Mattie's dressmaking bills, I feel like I've got a daughter on the market," said Mr. Parker jovially. He was on his fifth glass of fine wine. "Maybe I should pay your fee, Mrs. Cameron, and send Mattie over here." His wife and daughter took his remarks amiss.

"Is that gravy on that there little bitty trout?" asked Fish Eye.

"Yes," said Kristin, "and it has wine in it. If you're a teetotaler, you might want to scrape it off."

Morgan looked more distressed than ever.

"Oh, don't let it bother you, man," said Jack from the end of the table. "If you take a sip or two now and then, even on your fish, it won't disqualify you from marriage."

Fish Eye Morgan beamed at Jack and dug into his trout with elbows flying. Dill-cream sauce with a touch of white wine dripped off the edges of his mustache. Mrs. Parker and Mrs. Pembroke edged away. After he had taken a second big bite, demolishing half the trout, he said, "What I wanted to talk to you about, ma'am, was Lizzy. I done asked an' she accepted, so all we need is your approval."

"You have it," said Kristin. "Congratulations."

Fish Eye was so excited that he dropped his third hunk of trout into the sauce, causing a minor splash. Both ladies shifted farther away, almost off their chairs.

Connor was grinning widely. "Yes, sir," he said. "You do perform a service, Kristin. Particularly to me. It's a great relief to have just one maid instead of dozens underfoot as we used to."

"It's always nice to be appreciated," murmured Kristin.

While most of the guests were watching Fish Eye as if hypnotized by his table manners, Ingrid said, "I like a man with some face hair. Makes kissin' more interestin', unless the hair's got fish sauce drippin' off it. Use your napkin, for God's sake, Fish Eye."

The miner flipped up his napkin, which he had tucked under his chin, and wiped his mouth. "Sorry, honey," he said, "but even with my mouth wiped, I can't be kissin' you. I'm spoke for."

"I meant *him* for kissin'," said Ingrid, "not you."

The mustachioed Denver investor, in whom Ingrid had indicated an interest, turned pink under the furious eyes of his wife as he wiped his mustache. Kristin put a napkin to her mouth to keep from giggling, and Yvette, on door duty for the evening, reappeared and announced another caller. "I think he's a sausage buyer, madame."

"Show him in," said Kristin. Maude was clearing the fish plates in preparation for serving a lamb saddle with mint jelly, which she had announced self-consciously just after Ingrid kissed the Denver investor on the cheek.

"Would you care to join us for dinner?" Kristin asked hospitably.

The fellow, dressed in an ill-filling suit, looked quite astonished when confronted by so many people. "I've et," he said and, taking remembrance of his mission, added,

"Miz Cameron, on behalf of the Methodist Conference o
Colorado, Breckenridge branch, I'm here to inform you
that Methodists won't be eatin' your sausage no more. We
voted."

"Why?" she asked. "Have I offended the Methodists?"

"The dynamitin' of the Reverend Florida Passmore's
church bell is enough to sour any Methodist, ma'am."

"I'm sure," said Kristin. "I found it a shocking thing
myself. But I don't see what it has to do with sausages."

"Well, folks figgered either 'twas rowdies who wanted to
drink on Sunday what done it or 'twas you because of the
preacher's sermon on contaminatin' associations. Figgered
you might of took offense an' hired it done."

Jack had mentioned this ludicrous rumor. Was it one of
his jokes? Kristin wondered. Had he paid this man? "That's
a very peculiar idea," she said.

"Nothin' peculiar about it, ma'am. We done us some
detectin'."

At the word *detecting,* Kristin stiffened. The Pinkertons
were mixed up in this?

"An' we discovered that no one left town the day after
the dynamitin'—leavin' town bein' a sure sign of guilt—
'cept you, ma'am. You went off to Denver an' stayed. Ifn
you hadn't a come back, like as not we wouldn't a pursued
this no further, but soon as we heard you had, we met
an' voted on no more Traube's sausages. Respect for our
church bell's more important than any sausage, no matter
how tasty and popularly priced, like your ads say."

"What ads?"

"I've been runnin' them," said Ingrid. "Since you weren't
here to get new orders, I thought advertisin' might help."
Then she turned on the Methodist spokesman. "You're a
booby. You know that, Seth? Only a booby would think
Kristin had anything to do with that dynamitin'. Now

you come right out in the hall, an' I'll whisper in your ear who did it." Ingrid jumped up and headed in his direction.

"Now, Miz Ingrid—" cried the Methodist. "I'm a married man. I—"

Ingrid grabbed his arm and dragged him out into the hall. As the door opened to let them out, Gwenivere slipped in and made a beeline for Kristin.

Mrs. Parker shrieked, then composed herself and whispered to Mr. Pembroke, "It's no wonder she receives no portrait commissions."

"Whatever do you mean, my dear woman?" he replied. "Mrs. Cameron's artwork has been praised by Mrs. Potter Palmer herself."

"And the society ladies in Denver are falling over themselves to get sitting dates for the summer of '92," said Mr. Showalt of Denver, who sat to Kristin's left. "Half Denver society should be in Breckenridge next summer."

"Then I'll try to see that Mrs. Cameron is," Jack muttered.

"But her pictures are fuzzy," said Mattie Parker.

"My dear girl," drawled the young blade who had escorted her in. "Fuzzy is all the rage in Paris."

"Trust a Methodist to get it wrong," said Ingrid, coming in from the hall and resuming her seat. "Now, I hope it doesn't turn out that you *were* mixed up in that dynamitin', Kristin."

"Of course, I wasn't," said Kristin and gestured for Maude to begin clearing the main course. "Do we get to keep our Methodist sausage customers?"

"If we don't, I have a few stories to tell Mr. Seth Olwin's wife," said Ingrid darkly. Then she turned a bright smile on her neighbor and asked, "Miss me, sweetie?" The poor man turned red.

*   *   *

The men were safely behind closed doors indulging in cigars and brandy. The ladies were in the drawing room with their coffee and *petit fours,* that door closed as well, and Kristin, having excused herself on the grounds of an indisposition, was speeding down the hall to her studio where she stripped the unfinished portrait of Marcella Webber from its wooden slats, rolled it up with two extra lengths of canvas and all the brushes and paints she could stuff into the bag she had used when she and Jack drove to Mohawk Lake, then climbed out the window. *Free!* she thought exultantly.

It had gone just as she planned, and Kristin estimated that she had twenty minutes, perhaps a half hour, before anyone realized that she was missing again. All she needed to do was make it across the Blue without fainting from lack of air. Once in West Breckenridge, she'd have other worries, such as being taken for a lady of the night. Her only weapon was a parasol.

"Mrs. Cameron, what are you *doing* here at this hour of night?" Marcella Webber looked so shocked when the maid brought Kristin into the private parlor that Kristin would have giggled if she'd had the breath for it. She had actually run the last two blocks with a drunken miner at her heels calling out what he must have considered alluring suggestions. Kristin had been terrified.

"I'm . . . seeking . . . sanctuary," she gasped.

"In a sporting house?" Marcie eyed her unexpected guest wryly. "Isn't that something you do in a church? St. Mary's is nearer your house than mine." There was another pause while Kristin took shallow gasping breaths and wished that her hostess would invite her to sit down. "Are you going to faint?" Marcie asked.

Kristin shook her head.

"Are you with child?"

"Not . . . that I . . . know of."

Much to Kristin's amazement, Mrs. Webber lighted a cigarette. "Then what are you doing in my house during business hours? You took a terrible chance setting foot this side of the river at night and unescorted."

"Could I sit down?"

Marcie waved her to a chair, and Kristin dropped into it, closing her eyes. "I've left my husband."

"You did that last week."

"For good."

"And you've decided to take up life as a prostitute?"

"Of course not. I just want to stay with you until I can get out of town. Until he's angry enough to grant me a separation." Marcie looked uncooperative. "I can finish your portrait while I'm here," Kristin offered.

"I should hope so. I've already paid half down."

"And—and paint a mural on your walls. In return for room and board."

Marcie was starting to grin, and Kristin felt a great relief. Her plan absolutely depended upon Marcella Webber taking her in for a week or more.

"Your husband will probably swear out a warrant for my arrest if—"

"He'd never think of looking for me here."

"You're trouble I don't need." Marcie was laughing.

"Women have to stick together," said Kristin.

"That's what your friend Kat Macleod is always saying."

Kristin nodded, looking hopeful.

"Free?" Marcie asked.

"What?"

"The mural."

"Certainly."

"What would you paint?"

"Whatever you want. What about the girls? Maeve made me paint them out of the Norman Irish castle scene, but I could do them here. They looked charming as Irish peasant girls dancing around a maypole."

Marcie gave a delighted, full-throated laugh. "You painted my girls on Maeve Macleod's walls? For that alone I'd take you in."

"Oh good," said Kristin. "I'm going to need clothes and paint. I wasn't able to bring anything away but your picture and my money."

"Well, if you're running away from home, money is the best thing to bring."

"May we join you, ladies?" asked Jack, opening the drawing room doors. Then he noticed that his wife was not among them. "Where's Kristin?"

"I'm afraid she was feeling ill, Jack," said Kat, and she gave him a warm smile, which took him completely by surprise. He was used to scowls from Kat Macleod. "She's gone to her room for a bit of rest."

Jack frowned. Kristin had been in fine form at dinner—perverse as ever. He turned abruptly and, without a word to his guests, took the stairs two at a time and sprinted into his wife's room. Empty, by God! "Have you seen her?" he demanded of Yvette, who was tidying up.

"She eez downstairs in ze drawing room, monsieur."

"The hell she is!" He did a quick tour of the house, knowing all the while that Kristin had escaped once more. And right under his nose. Back in the drawing room, he faced Kat. "I suppose you helped her."

"What are you talking about?" Kat asked.

"You smiled at me. You can't stand me, so why would you smile at me unless you'd done me some ill turn?"

"Look, Jack," said Connor. "I know you and Kat don't get on that well, but there's no need—"

"She's helped my wife run away again."

"Again? Has she run away before?" asked Kat.

"You know damn well she has. Every time I turn around, she's gone."

"Well, there's no need to swear," said Kat stiffly. "I smiled at you because I thought, Kristin being under the weather, that you two might be—ah—expecting a child."

"A child! Fat chance of that! All right, gentlemen, instead of chatting with the ladies, we'll be forming a search party. There's no train out at this time of night, so she has to be somewhere in Breckenridge."

"I say," exclaimed Mr. Pembroke. "Talk about Bohemian. Your household is better than a grand opera, old boy."

Chapter Twenty-Four

The great Breckenridge wife hunt was a source of amusement to its participants, who roamed the streets of the town, knocking at doors, questioning strangers on the whereabouts of Kristin Traube-Cameron, who had disappeared from her home at the tail end of a dinner party. Now they had gone home, probably still talking about it, and Jack sprawled morosely on the fainting couch in her studio, wishing that he hadn't instituted the search. At the time, he had been worried about her safety. He still was, he supposed, but he was also irritated over the embarrassment. After all that hullabaloo, he still didn't know where his wife was, and he'd now made a jackass of himself in front of the whole town. If Breckenridge had suspected that she had run away from him before, now they knew it, unless there was someone fool enough to think she'd been abducted. No ransom note had turned up. All he'd gained was a sleepless night.

Yvette had gone through Kristin's belongings, but nothing was missing except the Worth copy gown and the emerald jewelry. He tried not to let himself think about the possibility that someone had killed her for the jewelry and hidden her body somewhere. What sensible woman ran away in a Worth dinner gown and emeralds? As for her studio, which he'd always kept a close eye on, it seemed to contain what little it had contained after she left the first time—empty canvas frames, some discarded pictures. Nor could he be sure if she'd taken paints and brushes.

She had even left her latest sketchbook behind, and it gave him an fascinating peek into the state of her mind. He paged through it slowly and found bits and pieces of himself. At least, he hoped those bits were him. By the time he reached a blank page, Jack was feeling completely confused. There was no question that his wife was enthralled with his body. She had sketched every part of him—except for a certain key area above the thighs and below the navel.

So why the devil was she running away? If he didn't have a hold on her heart, he certainly had a hold on her body and her artistic interest. How many husbands would allow a curious wife to draw them naked? He shook his head. He, who had always thought he understood women, didn't understand Kristin at all. But he still wanted her. More than ever. In fact, Jack admitted to himself, he was in love with the girl.

And he had no idea where she'd gone. His best guess was that Kat Macleod had hidden her somewhere. Kristin couldn't have left town. There'd been no trains, not even a freight, between the time she left and the time he posted a man at the railroad station and another at the ladies' stop. They'd canvassed every house and business in town. His own horses were still in the stable, and they'd checked livery stables in case she'd been fool enough to try to drive or ride out of town. No one was missing a horse or even a mule. Which left Kat Macleod.

He and Kat had certainly had words about that, Kat denying that she'd had anything to do with Kristin's disappearance. "Kristin's flight is your fault," she had said sharply and left his house without explaining her accusation.

So where was his wife? Was she dead or alive? Jack felt desperate and, for the first time in his life, grief-stricken. He didn't know what he'd done to drive her away. They should have been the most happily married of couples. Instead she insisted, on the rare occasion that she'd talk about it, that they were living in sin. It didn't make any sense. Maybe she still blamed him for that evening in her father's library and all the frightening experiences that followed.

Kristin had been given the attic at the sporting club. It had two dormer windows, makeshift furnishings, and a heavy lock on the door at the foot of the stairs. In the morning, when there were no customers in the house, Kristin worked on the mural in a room beyond the parlor. Marcie planned to knock the parlor wall out once Kristin had finished the mural and gone.

During the afternoon, when business picked up, the dormer windows in the attic let in enough light for her to paint. At sundown she went to bed and listened nervously to the noises that drifted through the closed door and up the stairs to her attic hideaway—music, laughter, screams—lord, she didn't dare think about what was going on down there. Those poor girls. Since it often took her a long time to fall asleep, she prayed for their souls and her own, still unshriven and now living in a house of ill repute. Would the Holy Mother understand that she was doing her best to be a chaste woman, even if her methods were unusual?

Kristin hated to admit it, but she was having a wonderful time painting the mural downstairs. How unfortunate that sin was so jolly! Her mural showed laughing women in bold, shocking clothing, breasts pressing up from low necklines and tight corsets. The men were faceless blurs or turned away from the artist's eye, since Kristin had never encountered any after the first night and imagined that was the way the girls saw them. Surprisingly, there had been some complaints on that score, for the girls did have favorites among their customers and wanted them included. Kristin refused. She didn't want to know who they were, the men that came here. Let them imagine themselves part of the fun, she said, and went right on doing it her way. Marcie agreed, doubting that her customers would want to be memorialized on a parlor house wall.

From her memories of Ingrid at the piano on Sunday courting afternoons, Kristin painted a woman at a piano. Another figure stood primping in front of a mirror. One smoothed stockings up above a daring knee. Marcie oversaw the whole with her enigmatic smile.

In the afternoons when Kristin was locked away in her attic with a cold supper, she worked on Marcie's portrait, but she finished that the second day, then debated how she should use the few canvasses she'd brought along, the limited supply of paint. She owed Father Boniface Wirtner a picture for the church. Would doing it here be an offense against God or a way to gain forgiveness? She blocked it out, worked on the background, and did some of the children. But she couldn't do the Christ figure, not with the goings-on downstairs, so she started another painting, hoping she could return to the picture for St. Mary's later.

After her nighttime vigils at home, Kristin was becoming used to painting in strange lights, so Marcie glowed out of the darkness—beautiful, mysterious, cynical. The finished portrait touched chords in Kristin's heart. She prepared a long piece of canvas and began to paint Jack from memory as she had seen him that night by firelight. Of course, she would have to destroy the canvas, but still she felt compelled to paint it. While she was here in this attic, she had perfect privacy. No one came up the stairs. The flames leapt out of the dark hearth on the canvas, highlighting the man on the bearskin rug. There was a satanic quality to the shadowed body, a grace that was too enticing to be pure.

As she worked, she thought of her first portrait of Jack— the shallow rake who thought of no one but himself. That painting had been an insult, deliberately so, and hadn't done him justice because, as she knew in her heart, there were many more sides to Jack than the Jack who had been a man-about-town in Chicago. The one she painted now was the man she had seen since their marriage, the sensual side that both tempted and frightened her, that had brought her to his bed and then sent her running away.

The first picture had as its background a busy Victorian room. This one had flames and darkness. It represented the danger to her soul that her attraction to Jack meant. And yet she knew in her heart that there was another level to Jack—laughing, generous, kind—a Jack she could talk to, a Jack whose company she enjoyed. That side of him drew her as well, but she could not paint Jack, the friend, lest she fall completely under his spell. Therefore, she painted Jack as the devil's tempter, and it was a brilliant picture. What a shame, she thought, that it would have to be destroyed.

"What kind of man," said Reverend Florida Passmore, "allows his wife to reside in a house of sin, in a haunt of fallen women? Or turns his head when she works in a

aloon on the Lord's Day?" The Sunday Methodists gasped
nd murmured among themselves. To whom was he refer-
ng?

"A husband has a duty," said Reverend Passmore, "to
ee to the welfare and decent conduct of his wife. A godly
usband will keep this duty in mind."

Male Methodists glanced sideways at their wives, won-
ering if any of them had visited saloons or brothels. Sure-
 not.

Kat Macleod heard about the sermon from Methodist
iends before the day was out. They wanted to know what
oman, beside her, would visit a "haunt of fallen women."
at's mission in West Breckenridge was well known and
nsidered little more than an eccentricity on her part. But
lethodist ladies knew that Kat Macleod, Breckenridge's
remost female temperance advocate, would never have
sited a saloon unless it was to demonstrate, which she
d with Reverend Passmore, and before him Father John
yer. So who was the lady in the sermon? they wanted
 know.

Ah-ha! Kat thought. That's where Kristin had gone.
ithout revealing her insight to members of the Meth-
dist Ladies' Aid Society, Kat marched across the Lincoln
venue Bridge to Marcie's house, days early for her monthly
scussion of saintliness with Marcie's girls.

"All right," said Kat to Marcie, "where is she?"

Marcie sighed, "I don't know where that damn Brother
assmore gets his information," said Marcie. "She's in the
w room doing a mural."

"I'm surprised you don't have her painting in the parlor
hile the customers are here," said Kat. "Neither you nor
ristin nor my mother has an ounce of sense."

"Give me a little credit," said Marcie. "We won't knock
wn the wall to enlarge the parlor until she's finished, and

393

I have her safely locked away in the attic during busines
hours."

"Whose idea was it that she come here?"

"Hers, of course," said Marcie. "She's running awa
from her husband."

"Well, you didn't have to take her in."

"What was I to do, let her wander the streets by herself i
the middle of the night? She claims that he makes unnatura
demands on her."

Kat frowned. "She said the same thing to me, but
thought they'd settled their differences when she cam
back from Denver."

"Evidently not," said Marcie.

"I even thought she might be with child," said Kat.

"If she is, she hasn't mentioned it. Poor thing, she's suc
an innocent. As soon as she said unnatural, I had to tak
her in. You'd think Jack Cameron, if he has strange tastes
would know enough to indulge them elsewhere."

Kat nodded. "The question is, what does she think con
stitutes unnatural? It could be quite innocuous."

"Well, she wasn't specific, if that's what you're ask
ing. Go in and talk to her. Maybe you can find out.
Marcie escorted Kat through the parlor to the door of th
new room. "As soon as the first customer knocks," sh
explained, "we send her straight up the stairs."

"So she's never seen one of them?"

"Nor they her, unless someone noticed her the first night
It's as respectable as I can make it. I don't know how tha
nosy preacher heard about her being here."

"Florida Passmore can smell out scandal," said Kat
"He's a good man for temperance, but otherwise, I'
take John Dyer any day. What do you do about feed
ing her?"

"Well, we're a two-meal house. She eats a cold suppe

in her room and takes breakfast with us." Marcie chuckled. "She's been spinning my girls some crazy tale about an elk prince and princess. I can tell you, they'll be sorry to see her go. They love that story."

"But that's the one she told my *children*."

"Well, my girls are children at heart," said Marcie. "Children in their heads, a hundred years old in their bodies, if you know what I mean."

Kat sighed. She'd rescued a few of Marcie's girls, not many.

Marcie opened the door, and Kristin called, without even turning around, "What do you think, Marcie?"

"I think a friend of yours has come to visit."

Kristin twisted, almost falling off the ladder. The two women helped her down. Kat looked first at Kristin, then at the mural. "Is that the way you see these women? Believe me, their life isn't so merry."

"No," Kristin agreed, "but it helps them to think it is."

Marcie nodded thoughtfully. "You're right. They love the painting. It makes them believe they're beautiful and happy."

"Could you leave us alone, Marcie?" asked Kat.

"It's no use your talking to me, Kat," said Kristin. "I'm not going back, if that's what you've come for."

"You can't stay here forever."

"I'll slip out of town when he least expects it."

"Is he really that terrible a husband?"

Kristin brushed back a straying lock of golden hair. "It's not only his fault. It's mine as well," said Kristin, being honest with herself and Kat for once. "Do you realize that I haven't been to confession since I arrived in Breckenridge? Jack's a sinner, and if I stay with him, he'll draw me irretrievably into his web."

"Marcie, maybe you should leave us," said Kat again.

As soon as Marcie had closed the door behind her, Kat said, "Kristin, has it ever occurred to you that the things that go on between married couples have just taken you by surprise? They may be perfectly normal, and you—"

"I hope you're not saying that you participate in unnatural acts," said Kristin, remembering all the laughter, sighs, and groans that went on in the tower room when she lived at Kat's house.

Kat flushed. "Connor and I are a normal married couple," she said with a bit of asperity in her voice. "The only unnatural thing about our relationship is that we're happy together, but we had to work at that. Maybe if you'd let yourself be happy with Jack—"

"I thought you didn't like him."

"I don't, but you're married to him. He doesn't beat you, does he?"

"No," said Kristin.

"As far as I know, he hasn't been unfaithful to you."

"I wouldn't be surprised if he had. His appetites are—" She flushed and fell silent.

"You're Roman Catholic. You can't divorce."

"We could separate. Then if he wants to, he can get an annulment—maybe. *I* certainly never want to marry again."

"Maybe you'd better tell me what's been going on."

"Absolutely not," said Kristin.

"At least go to Father Boniface Wirtner. Come on, I'll take you myself."

"No," said Kristin.

"Sweet Jesus, you're a stubborn woman! You can't stay in a whorehouse."

"Parlor house. And I've only been here a week. In another week, he'll have forgotten about me, and I can get out of town."

"You're fooling yourself," said Kat. "The man's crazy in love with you. I wouldn't be surprised to know that you're in love with him."

"I'm not," protested Kristin. "And I'm not leaving Marcie's." It would be a really terrible sin to love a sinner like Jack. She was just infatuated. As she had been when he was Minna's fiance. Wasn't she?

Jack studied Connor Macleod. He'd never seen his friend more ill at ease. Something terrible must have happened at the Chicago Girl, something for which Connor blamed himself. A flood? Explosion? Lawsuit bringing in question their ownership? Just what he needed. Another damned worry to add to those he already had about his wife. "Well, spit it out, Connor. What's happened at the mine?"

Connor looked surprised. "Well, actually, Mortimer thinks he's hit a new four-inch vein. It appears to branch off right at the edge of our claim, but he's pretty sure we hold the apex."

"So you're worried about litigation?"

Connor sighed, slumped down in his chair across from Jack's desk, and crossed his boots at the ankle. "Kat made me come," he mumbled.

"She wants me to sell out the Cameron share."

"Got nothing to do with the mine."

"Then what?" Connor was making him nervous. A man more at ease in his own skin or happy with his own lot than Connor Macleod never lived—at least, not in Jack's experience. Now Connor was acting as if he had picked Jack's pocket and come to confess.

"It's about Kristin."

"Let me guess. Kat's been hiding her. Probably got her in your house, and you never noticed."

"No, but she knows where Kristin is."

"And she didn't tell me? My lord, does she have any idea how worried I've been?"

"Surely someone's told you about Passmore's sermon."

"About contaminating associations?"

"Not that one. The one about—" Connor stopped and scratched his chin. "Look, Jack, Kat went to see your wife as soon as she heard where—well, she even advised Kristin to go home, but your wife seems to feel—ah, that you—ah—"

"For heaven's sake, man, what's she upset about this time? The Pinkertons? The heated pig house? The—"

"Unnatural demands," mumbled Connor.

"What unnatural demands?"

"How do I know? She didn't spell it out for Kat, but she thinks she's going to hell because you—ah—hell, I don't know exactly what it is, but girls—some of them come to marriage without knowing what to expect. It takes them a while—or maybe you're not used to—"

"Horse hockey," snapped Jack. "I've been with enough women to know who's having fun and who isn't. Kristin did."

"Well, hell. Maybe Kat got the wrong idea."

"Right. So where's Kristin?"

Connor thought a minute, said he guessed he'd fulfilled his part of the bargain with his wife, and admitted, "She's at Marcie Webber's."

"The whorehouse?" asked Jack, astounded.

"Yep. Mornings when there's no customers, she's painting a mural in the parlor. Rest of the time she's in the attic doing Marcie's portrait. Reckon you'll want to be getting over there right now."

"The hell I will," said Jack. "This time she's going to have to come home on her own." He opened a desk drawer, pulled out a bottle and two glasses, and poured, shoving

398

one of the glasses across the desk to Connor.

"Little early in the morning for me, and I'm not much of a drinking man anyway."

"Fine." Jack retrieved the glass and set it beside his. "A whorehouse. My wife's accusing me of unnatural demands, but she doesn't mind living in a whorehouse?"

"You still ought to go get her. If you don't, she'll sneak out and catch a train."

"No, she won't. I've got men at both stops and a deal with every livery stable in town. Now I'll hire one to watch the Sporting Club. She sets foot out of Marcie's, I'll know it." Jack downed the first glass and picked up the second. "Sure you don't want to get drunk with me?"

"There's a lady askin' for you, ma'am," said the scantily clad maid.

Marcie looked up from her weekly accounts to see a heavily veiled woman in her doorway, a woman who might have been on her way to a funeral. "Ingrid," she cried a minute later when the woman had undraped the black veiling. Marcie rose to give her a hug. "How long has it been?" she asked when they were both seated and having coffee.

"Long time," said Ingrid. "Lotta things happened since."

"I guess. I own this place free and clear, and I hear you have a half interest in a sausage business."

"That's what I've come about. My partner. I hear she's livin' in your attic."

Marcie nodded. "If you'd been a day earlier, you'd have heard her telling my girls some crazy story about an elk princess being abducted by an evil elephant who's fallen in love with the princess and stolen her from her true love. For a woman who's running from a handsome husband, she certainly has romantic ideas."

Ingrid laughed. "My children love those elk stories too,

an' I imagine your girls like them better than Kat Macleod's saint's tales."

"They're not particular. To them a story is a story. I was sorry to hear about you and Sean, Ingrid. I thought for a while there you two would make it."

"We're not through yet," said Ingrid. "I mean to get him back. Now what's this about my bein' a day earlier? Has she managed to get out of town? I thought Jack had all the escape routes covered."

Marcie sighed. "That's bad news, because believe me, I'd like to get her out of town. She's a sweet girl, and we've kind of enjoyed having her here, but we had trouble last night." The alarm on Ingrid's face caused Marcie to add hastily, "She's all right, but she had such a fright that she wouldn't come out of the attic this morning."

"What happened?"

"The maid forgot to put her chamber pot back after emptying it. I guess Kristin really had to go because she slipped down the attic stairs trying to get to the necessary house, and one of the customers spotted her. Offered ten dollars. Can you believe it? I couldn't convince her it was a real compliment if you could overlook what the ten dollars was for.

"Poor fellow won't be coming to a sporting house any time soon. She jabbed him where it hurts the worst with a parasol. Never heard such a fuss in my life—him moaning like he'd been killed, her in hysterics. I thought it would be all over town today. Or is that why you came?"

"I came to talk her into goin' home. Didn't hear about the rest." Ingrid put down her cup. "Why don't you give me the key to the attic, an' I'll see what I can do about talkin' her down."

"Take one more step and I'll unman you." Kristin stood trembling at the top of the stairs. She had heard the door opening and the footsteps, which continued even after her threat.

"That's goin' to be hard to do, honey, since I'm not a man," said Ingrid just before her head cleared the opening in the attic floor. "Good lord, how can you stand it up here? An' what's that you're wearin'? It's not your kind of dress, Kristin; take my word for it."

"I had to borrow clothes since I couldn't bring any."

Ingrid stepped out onto the attic floor and looked around, eyes narrowing as she caught sight of the picture of Jack, highlighted by the noon sun from the dormer window. Kristin followed the direction of her glance, flushed, and hastened across the room to turn the painting to the wall.

"Careful of that," said Ingrid. "Be a shame to ruin it. That's the best paintin' I've ever seen in my life. Makes me want to go out, grab me a man, an' take him straight to bed. Since I can't have Sean, I wouldn't mind havin' ole Jack there. He looks good enough to eat."

Kristin gave her a look of great alarm and chagrin.

"All I have to do is look at that paintin' to see how much you want him, honey. That bein' the case, why don't you stop this silliness an' come on home?"

"No."

"Too proud? Believe me, he wants you. Poor man's losin' weight, lookin' peaked. He's just bound an' determined that this time you'll come home on your own."

"Does he know where I am?" Kristin asked.

"Sure. Connor Macleod told him."

"Kat betrayed me?"

"Hell, Kristin, that Methodist minister preached a sermon on you an' Jack, somethin' about men who neglect their husbandly duty an' let their wives stay in sportin' houses. If Connor hadn't heard it from Kat an' told Jack, someone else would have told him. Everyone in town must know where you are by now."

"Good. If Jack's embarrassed enough, he'll give up on me and—"

"I heard what happened last night."

Kristin dropped down onto her cot. "I took care of it," she mumbled. "I can take care of myself."

"If you're so sure of that, how come you didn't show up for breakfast?"

"I'm not going back to him," said Kristin stubbornly. "The sausage business is yours, Ingrid. Enjoy it."

"You handin' over your husband too?"

Kristin glanced at her quickly, then away. "I thought you wanted Sean."

"Sometimes you take what you can get."

Kristin brushed a hand across tear-filled eyes. "Do it then. Just don't tell me I should go home. A good Catholic woman shouldn't be married to a devil like Jack Cameron."

Ingrid laughed. "I always thought the devilish ones were the most fun."

"I'm not going after her," said Jack.

"You two are as stubborn as a team of mules wantin' to pull in opposite directions. Maybe you'll change your mind when I tell you that she was tryin' to get down the backstairs to the privy last night when some fella caught her an' offered ten dollars if she'd go into one of the rooms with him."

"Who?" Jack looked enraged.

"Doesn't matter."

"Of course, it matters. Did she—"

"—get away? She did. Seems she was carryin' a parasol, which strikes me as pure good luck. Not too many women carry them after dark on the way to the privy."

"Kristin looks on a parasol as a weapon." Jack brooded on the dangers his wife faced because of her fool-headed attitude. If he rescued her, he'd have to let her leave him. Otherwise, she'd run away again and end up someplace worse. Though he couldn't think of any place worse than a whorehouse, unless it was a whorehouse where she'd be expected to take customers.

"She loves you, you know," said Ingrid.

"Not a chance," said Jack bitterly.

"She's done another portrait of you. You'd better get over there an' see it. Then you'll know what I mean."

"Why? What does it look like?"

"You'd have to see it to understand," said Ingrid, looking smug. "I'll tell you what, Jack. Bring her home. Really try to work things out. If, in a week or so, she still hasn't settled down, I'll help you convince her that you're what she wants."

"And how would you do that?"

"Jealousy," said Ingrid. "I'll go after you myself, an' you—you'll act like you're interested."

"You think that would work?"

"Sure. I already got her upset by sayin' I'd take you if she didn't want you."

"How upset?" asked Jack.

"Enough. We could put on an act. Might help you. Might help me. Couldn't hurt to try. But she's got to be here to see us gettin' cozy."

Jack grinned. "How are you going to get Sean Fitzpatrick over here to see it?"

"Leave that to me." Ingrid rose. "Now, go get her before someone beats you to it." And she left the room, hips swaying.

Jack brooded for another fifteen or twenty minutes. If there was one man who'd offer ten dollars, there'd be another who'd offer twenty as word got around town that Kristin was living at The Gentlemen's Sporting Club. Then there'd be someone who'd be willing to break down a door to get to her. Someone who didn't mind forcing a woman. Face grim, he went to his library and took a loaded pistol from the desk, shoved it into his belt, donned his coat, snatched his rifle off the rack on the wall, and called for his horse. He wondered whether Kristin was still wearing the faux Worth ball gown she'd left in. And he was curious to see the painting that, according to Ingrid, displayed Kristin's love for him.

Chapter Twenty-Five

"You don't have to shoot anyone, Mr. Cameron," said Marcella Webber, who had come out when she heard a commotion late in the morning. "She's not being held against her will." Jack Cameron stood in the hall faced off against Pascal, the mute giant who kept order for Marcie and appropriated the firearms of patrons before they were allowed in. Jack had refused to surrender his. "And please don't shoot Pascal," Marcie added. "He's just doing his job."

"I've come for my wife," said Jack, teeth gritted.

"Took you long enough. Still, if she doesn't want to go, she doesn't have to. I don't hold with men abusing women."

"I don't abuse her," said Jack.

"One woman's loving is another woman's abuse," said Marcie. "She thinks you're the devil's stepchild."

Jack got a firm grip on his temper and replied, "No matter what her opinion of me, no one can doubt, after last night, that she'll be safer at home than here. So step out of my way." He waved the rifle in the general direction of Marcie, Pascal, and the girls who were peeking out of the parlor.

"You'll not hurt her?"

"I never have," said Jack.

"She's done nothing wrong while she was here."

"I didn't think she had."

"Just finished my portrait and a mural for the new parlor addition."

What kind of mural would suit a parlor house? he wondered uneasily. Anything that he'd want his wife credited with? Morbid curiosity getting the better of him, Jack said, "Let's see them," and he forced everyone on the first floor to accompany him to the parlor where Marcie's portrait hung over the fireplace. "She's done a lot better by you than by me," he muttered. "What did she charge you?"

"Fifty dollars."

"Damn. She charged me a hundred and made me look like an ass. Now where's the mural? Here, girl." He waved the rifle at Betts. "Stick right with us. I don't want anyone warning Mrs. Cameron that I'm here." The whole crowd went through to the second room, where the finished mural glowed merrily above the wainscoting. "If she can do that with a parlor house," said Jack, "she could probably make hard-rock mining look like a weekend at the seashore."

Marcie viewed the mural with approval. "It does take the customers' fancy," she admitted. "Business is up half again since I opened this room."

"Wonderful. More lechers swarming around my wife."

"Your wife is in the attic when the lechers swarm," said Marcie dryly. "Seems to me that a charming fellow like you ought to be able to keep her home." She tossed him the key. "The door to the attic stairs is at the end of the hall on the second floor. See that you treat her well."

When hadn't he treated her well? Jack felt like retorting. He'd been a very patient and accommodating husband. Maybe too much so. Still, he'd give patience one more shot. Jack climbed the stairs to the business floor of the brothel, then unlocked the door and climbed to the attic, taking no trouble to walk softly. Kristin met him with her parasol at the ready. "You," she gasped.

"Me," he agreed. "You're coming home."

"Have you no interest in preserving your honor? I've just spent ten days in a sporting house. What man—"

"You haven't been dishonored, just inconvenienced," said Jack. "Now, gather up your things, and let's go." Patience, he reminded himself.

"No."

At that moment Jack spotted the painting. "Well, well, well," he murmured, studying it with fascination. "I can see what Ingrid was talking about. You do have some interest in me, after all."

Kristin was already racing down the stairs when Jack, whirling at the descending tap of her feet, realized what had happened and pursued her. He caught her in the first-floor hall, dropped his rifle, and swung her over his shoulder. "Package up her stuff and send it to Nickel Hill, will you, Marcie? I'd be much obliged. Stop that, Kristin."

She was pounding on his back with her fists, her feet and calves kicking below his arm, where he clasped her firmly at the knees. There was such a thing as too much patience, he decided when the toe of her boot caught him a painful blow to the thigh. He was tempted to swat her rear but didn't want to get into an argument with Marcie or Pascal. "I can carry you through the whole town kicking and yelling if you force me, Kristin, but you'll go quietly and ride if you're sensible," he muttered as he strode out the front door of the Gentlemen's Sporting Club.

"I've got some news for you," he said once they were both on his horse, Kristin held in front of him, rifle in its scabbard.

"I don't want to hear it."

"Oh, don't be sulky."

"See you found your wife," called the station manager as they passed the depot. "Comes of lettin' women git on an' off at other than the ladies' stop."

Jack ignored him. "It's about the pictures you entered in the Denver show the last time you ran away."

"What show? It was just a trick to get me into the hands of those detectives."

"Nope. There was an exhibition, and I had the paintings you left at Peacocks' entered."

"All of them?" Kristin looked horrified. "Some were failures. They shouldn't have been—"

"Thanks, Jack," he said, imitating her voice. "Not at all, sweetheart," he replied in his own. "I thought it was the least I could do after abducting you before you could score a great artistic triumph."

"I did that before you ever had me abducted."

"See you got her back," called Connor Macleod as they rode off the bridge and onto Main Street.

"Only took two guns and a lot of bluster," Jack called back.

"This is humiliating," Kristin hissed. "Couldn't you have taken some roundabout route?"

"Breckenridge is too small to *have* any roundabout routes." He swung the horse up Lincoln. "So you don't care how your paintings fared. Is that right?"

"Something's poking into my side."

"That's my pistol. If you don't treat me with wifely respect, I may just use it to shoot you."

Kristin giggled.

Jack smiled. "You took first and third places."

"I didn't!" Kristin was so excited that she forgot her quarrel with Jack. "First place? And third? Oh-h-h."

"You can kiss me if you want," he suggested.

"Abomination!" shouted Reverend Passmore. "Drinking on Sundays! Residing in brothels! Unbridled lust in the streets! Our town is turning into a Sodom and Gomorrah."

Kristin glared down at him from Jack's arms. "It would almost be worth kissing you just to spite him," she muttered to her husband.

"Spoken like the gracious, loving wife you are," Jack murmured back and spurred his horse up the hill.

"I still refuse to—to—"

"We're going to have a talk about that," he promised.

"What we need, Kristin, is to have a reasonable discussion about our problems," said Jack. They were sitting in the drawing room after dinner.

"I'm tired," said Kristin. "I've had a trying day."

"So have I," said Jack. "It's bad enough to have a sermon preached about me."

"I don't remember your being upset when he preached that sermon about *me*," said Kristin. "How do you think I felt about being called a person whose character was formed by contaminating associations?"

"How do you think I felt being called an outrage to public decency?"

Kristin giggled. "I didn't know he'd said that."

"Damn right he did." Jack grinned. "He said any man who let his wife reside in a brothel was an outrage to public decency."

"So that's why you dragged me home at gunpoint?"

"No, it's not, and I didn't point a gun at you."

"Just the fact that you had one—"

"You're trying to get me off the subject of our problems I didn't threaten you with my rifle, and I didn't bring you home because of Passmore's sermon. What the hell do care what he thinks?"

"You cared when he accused me of dynamiting his bell."

"Right. You ought to keep that in mind. You might have been arrested if I hadn't stuck up for you."

"But I didn't—"

"I know that, Kristen," he snapped, then took a dee breath. "About our problems."

"We wouldn't have any if—"

"What? If I moved out? If I didn't want to exercise m rights as a husband? If I—"

Kristin turned pink and tried to get up. Jack, quicke than she, scooted onto the middle of the sofa and held he in place with both hands. "This is all because of that nigh in your father's library, isn't it?"

"Well, we'd certainly never have married if—"

"You haven't forgiven me."

"Why should I?" Kristin wanted to go upstairs and pus the dresser in front of her door. Better yet, she wanted to b safely back at Marcie's, painting in the attic and plannin her escape from problems she couldn't solve. She certainl didn't want to be sitting in the drawing room with Jack. Sh could hardly look at him now that he'd seen that painting He probably thought she was anxious to fall into bed wit him and commit every sin on Sister Mary Joseph's lis starting with enjoying "the act" and ending with enjoyin it on some important feast day. It was probably a feast da today, and Jack was just waiting to desecrate some saint' memory.

"We need to be honest about that night, Kristin. Brand or no brandy, I'd never have kissed my fiancée's sister if weren't attracted to you."

410

"You didn't even know I was alive until that night. You couldn't have picked me out in a crowd. You probably thought I was twelve years old instead of eighteen."

Jack grinned. "Well, I certainly found out differently, didn't I?"

"I don't think that's funny." Kristin's lips quivered. It was terrible to have someone laugh at you about your sins. What if anyone else in the household saw that picture of Jack when Marcie sent it back? *If I were a good Christian, I'd have finished the suffer-the-little-children picture for Father Boniface Wirtner instead of painting that sinful, naked portrait of Jack,* she admonished herself.

"And you'd never have kissed me back if you weren't attracted to me," Jack pointed out.

Kristin's cheeks burned. He couldn't know that she'd had a long-term infatuation with him back then. Could he? "I don't know that I *did* kiss you back," she replied defensively.

"Take my word for it," said Jack dryly. "You did. That night and on several other occasions. And then you left Chicago so fast, you didn't even wait to see if your parents would relent, or if I'd help you out. I think you *wanted* to go."

Was that true? Kristin wondered. Had she wanted a career in art so badly that she'd run a thousand miles to find it? Or had the famous-spinster-artist idea been wishful thinking because she thought all her options were closed once she'd been dishonored?

"Every time you've run away from me, you've advanced your career—except for that lascivious mural at Marcie's."

"It is not lascivious," she protested. "It's just—realistic."

"The hell it is. Stylistically, it's Impressionistic, and a

411

good thing too. The fuzziness makes it a little less shock
ing. And while we're talking about your painting, I'd like
to point out that your pictures of me are a lot more flattering
than they were to begin with. Also there are a lot of them.
think you're in love with me."

"I am not."

"As for me, I followed you to Colorado, didn't I?"

"Your father sent you on business."

"And I found you."

"Only because I was at Macleod's and you owned par
of their mine."

"And I stayed here."

"That was a surprise," Kristin admitted.

"And married you."

"You didn't have any choice."

"Of course I did. I could have done business a lot more
handily in Denver and left you here ironing Connor's shirts
I married you because I wanted to."

"You did?"

"And because I wanted to start a new life. With you. So
that's what we're going to do, Kristin. Make a success of
this marriage."

Kristin bit her lip. He made it sound almost feasible.

"You've become a successful artist. I've become a suc
cessful independent banker. Why shouldn't we be a suc
cessful husband and wife?"

"Well—" Was he saying that he was willing to abide by
the rules? Kristin looked up at him hopefully. She really
did like Jack when he wasn't endangering her immorta
soul. And maybe she *did* love him. "There's the problem
of the church," she said hesitantly.

"What problem? We were married in the church."

"Yes, but—but—" She just couldn't discuss the do's and
don'ts of "the act" with him. "Maybe you could talk to

ather Boniface Wirtner about—about marriage. How it's
pposed to work and—and—"

Jack laughed. "I doubt that Father Boniface could tell me
nything about marriage that I don't know, sweetheart."

"Yes, he could," said Kristin desperately.

"All right, I'll talk to him."

She relaxed and smiled, then had another thought. "We'd
ve to get a calendar of feast days."

"Feast days?" Jack looked puzzled. "All right. I'll order
e. Maybe Marshall Fields has them."

"Jack, it's not like ordering a dining room set. You'd
ve to ask Father Boniface Wirtner where—"

"Fine. So it's all settled? We're going to make a new
art?"

Kristin nodded hesitantly.

"Wonderful." He jumped up and strode toward the door.
o from now on you'll sleep in my bed as a wife should."

Kristin froze. Every night? Was that what he meant?
ven if he left her alone during the prohibited times, which
e seemed willing to do since he'd agreed to order a cal-
dar of feast days, there was the question of enjoying it,
hich she wasn't supposed to do. How was she to maintain
proper lack of enthusiasm when he was so handsome
d charming? She'd never manage if she had to sleep
th him every night. "Jack, there's—" But it was too
te. He'd just shouted to Maude to move his belongings
to Miss Kristin's room. Everyone in the house must have
ard him, Kristin thought, mortified.

Kristin lay at the very edge of the bed, wearing her
ost all-encompassing nightdress, as Sister Mary Joseph
d advised. This was the test, she thought. If Jack slept
astely beside her because it was Wednesday, she'd know
at their marriage could work.

413

"This is the first night of our real marriage, sweetheart," he said, climbing into bed and reaching for her. Kristin stiffened as he slid his arms around her, lips closing on hers. She could feel his breath against her mouth in the dark room.

"Don't touch me," she cried, trying to wiggle loose.

"Why?"

"It's Wednesday."

"So?"

Kristin burst into tears. He'd tricked her. He had no intention of following the rules.

"Jesus Christ!" Jack let her go and rolled to his side of the bed.

And beside his penchant for marital sin, he was blasphemous. Kristin hiccupped and wiped her eyes on the embroidered hem of her pillow slip. It was uncomfortable over here on the edge of the bed with an angry husband taking up more than his share and weighing down his side of the mattress so that she had to loop her arm outside the covers and cling to the bed frame to keep from sliding downhill into his arms. She'd probably take a chill in her arm and never get any sleep for the rest of her life. She shouldn't have believed him down there in the drawing room. He didn't want a chaste marriage; he just wanted to engage in "the act" any old time. Kristin wished Sister Mary Joseph were here to give him a good talking to.

"How's it going?" asked Ingrid as she walked out of the dining room with Jack. Kristin had asked that her meal be served in the studio.

"Wonderful," said Jack sarcastically. "She tells me what day of the week it is, says good night, and sleeps falling off her side of the bed as if she'll catch smallpox if she gets closer to me than two feet."

414

Ingrid shook her head. "That girl's a puzzle. Is there anything she's asked you to do or not to do that you've ignored?"

"Hell, I even went to talk to Father Boniface Wirtner because she asked me to. Some conversation that was. I asked him if there was anything he wanted to tell me about marriage, and he looked embarrassed and said, not really. Then he asked me if there was anything I wanted to tell him, and I, being in a really foul mood, said nothing except that my wife wouldn't have marital relations with me."

Then he said, did she understand that it was her wifely duty? and I said, there wasn't a man alive who could figure out what went on in her head other than ideas for paintings and worrying about what day of the week it was. Then I asked him how to go about getting her a feast days calendar, and he gave me one and said if I wanted to, I could have her come talk to him. Of course, I could tell he was hoping she wouldn't, and that was that. I gave her the damn calendar last night, she looked at it and told me it was Monday, as if I didn't know, and we went to sleep. I'm going crazy."

Ingrid said, "I guess it's time to try jealousy."

Jack shrugged. "At this point I'll try anything."

Kristin stared moodily at the painting. She'd had to do the Christ figure three times because it kept turning out like Jack, which was completely inappropriate. Other than that problem, she thought the picture quite a success. The scene was thronged with children's faces, every child she knew in Breckenridge, including, of course, all the Fitzpatrick and Macleod children. Kristin was almost finished. She'd worked faithfully ever since returning home, considering it a sort of penance in advance in case, when Monday night rolled around and she and Jack could engage in "the act,"

415

she should lose control and enjoy herself.

Well, she needn't have worried because nothing happened on Monday night, except that she felt very disappointed after all that anticipation. Wednesday through Sunday was a lot of nights to share a bed with a man when you couldn't do anything acceptable to the church but sleep.

Jack had been very grumpy when she reminded him of the day of the week on Wednesday, Thursday, Friday, Saturday and Sunday. But then on Monday night, she'd been so pleased to hear that he'd gone to see Father Boniface Wirtner and even procured a feast days calendar that she thought everything was perfect. The calendar showed no feast day for Monday. Jack, having talked to the priest must now know what was proper in a chaste marriage. Therefore, feeling quite bold, she'd thanked him for the calendar and reminded him that it was Monday. And what had he done? Snarled good night and gone to sleep.

Kristin knew it was sinful of her to feel so disappointed. After all, why should she be looking forward to something she wasn't allowed to enjoy? Still—well, maybe he'd been tired. Or maybe Father Boniface Wirtner had said something mean to him about his previous conduct, probably assigned him a stiff penance. In fact, maybe the penance was abstinence, and Jack had been embarrassed to mention it. If that were the case, her pointing out that it was Monday had been very tactless. Kristin sighed. Being a famous spinster artist would have been a lot simpler than being a chaste wife. Although somehow, even given all her problems, spinsterhood didn't sound like much fun.

Kristin clambered up onto the bed. Jack climbed in the other side and turned out the light. "It's Tuesday," she said diffidently.

"Right," he said. She could hear him thumping his pillow. Then all was silent. Kristin sighed and settled down on her lonely side of the bed. Ingrid had been flirting with Jack tonight at dinner, and he had been flirting right back. It had really hurt Kristin's feelings, but she didn't know what she could do about it. He'd stopped paying any attention to her. It was as if once she'd agreed to a regular married relationship, within the bounds of propriety, of course, Jack had lost interest.

"Ah, Mrs. Cameron. Your husband said he might send you to see me."

"He did?" Jack hadn't said anything about seeing Father Boniface Wirtner to Kristin. In fact, he hardly ever talked to her. He was too busy talking to Ingrid.

"I understand that you've been refusing to do your wife-duty."

"Jack said that?"

"He did." The good father looked very ill at ease. "I realize that marriage and its—er—practices come as a shock to virtuous and inexperienced young women, but you do owe a duty to your husband, just as he owes one to you."

Kristin felt very confused. "Actually, Father, I came by the rectory to give you the picture you asked for."

"Picture?"

"Of Jesus and the children." She handed him the finished canvas, which Winifred had wrapped for her in butcher paper since the day was dark and threatening.

"Your husband did mention that you seem to spend a lot of your time painting. Perhaps if you paid more attention to your wifely obligations instead of trying to usurp, as it were, a man's place in the world, your marriage . . ."

Father Boniface Wirtner was going on and on about woman's place as wife and mother while Kristin fumed.

The man had asked her for a religious painting. It was▶
as if he'd offered to pay for it, he probably couldn't ev▶
afford the prices her work brought these days—and now ▶
thought she should paint less and—do what?

"Maybe you ought to talk to my husband," said Krist▶
"In fact, I'd like to know what you talked about befo▶
Ever since he visited you, he's not even interested ▶
Monday and Tuesday when it's—it's proper."

"When what's proper?"

Kristin flushed. "The act."

"What act?"

"*The* act."

"Are you talking about—ah—sexual congress?"

"I don't know. Congress? You mean like the gove▶
ment?" Kristin felt completely befuddled.

"I mean as in—ah—intimate relations between husba▶
and wife."

"Oh. Well, I guess so."

"What do Monday and Tuesday have to do with it?"

"That's when people can. I mean, if they're marrie▶
Unless it's a feast day—or Lent. Or Advent, or Penteco▶
or—"

The priest cleared his throat. "Er—Mrs. Cameron. A▶
you saying that you refuse your husband on all these oc▶
sions?"

"Well, I try. I thought it would help to have the calen▶
of feast days so I'd know. I mean, I never could *rememb▶
all the days. Of course, the nuns reminded us when we w▶
in school, but here, without a calendar—by the way, tha▶
you for sending it. Not that it matters because Jack does▶
seem interested anymore."

"To get back to the matter of ah—Wednesdays and—▶

"—through Sunday," said Kristin helpfully.

"Just where did you get that idea?"

"From Sister Mary Joseph."

"I see." The priest absently unwrapped her painting and ared at it. "My goodness, that's a very touching picture," e said.

"Thank you."

"My dear, I'm sure Sister Mary Joseph meant well, but he may have been misinformed."

"Misinformed? Sister Mary Joseph?"

"Why don't you just go home to your husband and—and orget about what day it is."

"You mean any day—"

"The Lord did tell us to increase and multiply. The church ertainly supports that view of the marriage sacrament."

"But what about enjoyment?"

"Well, child, if you can't, you can't. Just keep in mind at the end result makes everything worthwhile."

"The end result?"

"Motherhood, my dear. Sacred motherhood." Then he eld up the picture. "This is truly lovely, and if you'd care paint another for the church, you shouldn't feel that you re neglecting your wifely duties. After all, our duty to God omes first."

Completely bewildered, Kristin trudged home from the ectory. Wednesdays through Sundays didn't matter? Or east days? What about, say, Good Friday? Or Easter? urely, Father Boniface Wirtner couldn't have meant— d what about Sister Mary Joseph? How had she got all wrong? Father Boniface Wirtner had almost come t and said, "Enjoy it if you can." What an amazing onversation!

Kristin skipped several steps in sheer exuberance and eaded home. She and Jack could just do whatever they anted! And enjoy it! Then she bit her lip. She'd forgotten out unnatural acts. But then, maybe there weren't any.

That would certainly be a load off her mind—and her conscience. Why, goodness, she wasn't even in any trouble because she'd stopped going to confession. As far as she could tell, she didn't have anything serious to confess.

Humming cheerfully to herself, she opened the gate and hurried toward the house just as snow began to fall. Kristin lifted her face and stuck out her tongue to catch a flake of September snow. It must be an omen, she thought. Tonight she and Jack could snuggle under the quilts with the snow outside preparing a beautiful landscape for her to paint in the morning and Jack's furnace in the basement keeping the house cozy while they—they just did whatever they wanted and enjoyed doing it.

She opened the door and skipped into the hall where she could see, through the open doors to the drawing room, Ingrid draped all over Jack, who certainly did seem to be enjoying himself, but not with Kristin.

Book IV

Hot Pursuit

Chapter Twenty-Six

"I think it's working," said Ingrid.

"How do you figure that? She certainly hasn't thrown herself into my arms," said Jack. Ingrid had dropped by his office on Main Street to discuss the progress of the jealousy campaign.

"Well, that would be too much to expect of Kristin. She's not—flirtatious."

"Hell, she's not even friendly! How am I supposed to know when she's changed her mind?"

"Keep your eyes open," said Ingrid impatiently. "She's mopin' around. I think that's a good sign."

"Maybe she's moping because I haven't left her. Now that she can't keep me out of her room at night, she's blockading her studio so I can't get in there."

"Maybe she's painting another naked picture of you."

Jack thought that over. "You told me the picture was a good sign when she was at Marcie's, but I can't see that

423

anything's come of it. Maybe she likes my body but doesn't care for the rest of me."

"It's a start," said Ingrid. "Sean and I started that way and ended up getting married."

"Well, I'm already married. Are you saying Kristin and I will end up getting divorced? That's what happened to you and Sean."

Ingrid gave him a hurt look. "Tomorrow my children will be coming to the house. You can take us out for a sleigh ride if there's any snow left. We'll leave Kristin home."

"What good will that do?"

"It might upset Kristin. It's certain to upset Sean, and I'm supposed to get something out of this too."

Kristin wandered restlessly through the studio. She had started a second picture for St. Mary's, showing the woman caught in adultery and Jesus telling the Pharisees to cast the first stone if they were without sin. She saw it in her mind—the woman's terrified face, the malicious faces of the crowd, Jesus, eyes shining with compassion. She had even blocked it out on canvas, but she was drawn to another picture of Jack—a picture of a dashing, laughing, lovable adventurer—and she had spent more time on that, painting compulsively and secretly with a chair shoved under the doorknob. *What a pathetic creature you are,* she told herself. Now that she was entranced with her own husband, he was entranced with her partner.

"Miss Kristin!" Maude was knocking at the door. "Mr. Fitzpatrick—he's in the parlor insistin' that you come out an' talk to him. I told him you didn't like bein' interrupted but he says it's that important. Are you in there, Miss Kristin?"

Kristin threw an old sheet over the newest portrait of Jack, tugged the chair away from the door, and opened it.

"Thank goodness you answered. He come here lookin'
or Miz Ingrid an' his children, an' when he heard they was
leigh-ridin' with Mr. Jack—"

"What?"

"Well, I reckon they'd have asked you along except you
was locked up in your paintin' room, so they jus' went off.
Abigail, she's that mad, what with not a member of the
amily at the table an' her havin' to fix up a picnic besides.
Likely she'll be tearin' a piece off Mr. Jack's hide when he
omes home—him an' Miss Ingrid both."

Jack had gone off on an outing without even inviting
er? He and Ingrid? Kristin hurried into the drawing room
nd greeted Sean. "Is there something I can do for you?"
he asked.

"You can tell your husband to stay away from my wife,"
aid Sean. His face was so flushed that she wondered if
e had been drinking or perhaps had a return of his old
nalady. But no, the malady had been Ingrid's perfume,
hich she no longer used, unless she'd taken up some new
cent for Jack's sake. Kristin tried to remember how Ingrid
ad smelled the last time they'd passed in the hall.

"You mean Augustina?" Kristin asked. She hadn't known
ack was pursuing Augustina. Had the man no shame?
ristin felt like weeping.

"Of course not. He's off this minute with Ingrid."

"Ingrid's not your wife," Kristin pointed out.

Sean looked even more upset. "Well, I still feel a duty
 see to her welfare. Don't you care that he's flaunting his
fatuation for my—for Ingrid?"

Kristin did care, but she wasn't going to discuss her
eelings with Sean Fitzpatrick.

"Ingrid will get hurt," said Sean.

Kristin sighed. That was true—if Ingrid was truly in love
ith Jack. Kristin certainly understood how Ingrid could

be. After all, Jack was devilishly attractive, and Ingrid
thought Kristin didn't want him. She'd said several time
that Kristin was a fool for running away from him. Ingrid
had even said she wouldn't mind having a go at him her
self. Kristin had thought it just one of those outrageou
things Ingrid was given to saying because she didn't know
any better. Because of her background, Ingrid didn't think
engaging in "the act" was any great moral dilemma. Wheth
er or not she had fallen in love with Jack, she might commi
adultery. Lose her soul. Find herself with child. Tarnish he
already dubious reputation beyond redemption. Jack migh
break her heart, and poor Ingrid had already been hurt by
Sean. Kristin glared at him. Men were such sinners.

And Jack. What if he fell in love with Ingrid? Aske
for a divorce because he wanted to marry her and t
claim his child? He could endanger *his* soul. He coul
be excommunicated from the church. *And all those dir
consequences aside,* thought Kristin, *he's mine!* "I'll tal
to Ingrid," said Kristin.

Sean beamed at her. "I knew you wouldn't let me down.
"You don't have anything to do with it."

It was twenty-four hours before Kristin got up the nerv
to approach Ingrid about her pursuit of Jack, and the
Kristin couldn't find her. Finally she asked Winifred, wh
said, "Miss Ingrid's gone sausage selling. She left with
valise this morning."

Puzzled, Kristin drifted back to the studio. Ingrid hadn'
mentioned a trip last night at dinner. In fact, she and Jac
had talked of nothing but the sleigh ride and picnickin
in the forest. Evidently, it had been great fun. Wistfully
Kristin remembered *her* picnic with Jack. Well, at leas
he and Ingrid weren't having that kind of fun, no
with the children along, not in the snow. But really

426

Jack shouldn't be giving Ingrid false hopes. He had a wife! Kristin whipped the sheet off his new portrait and stared at it.

What a handsome devil he was! Would he take the hint that she was interested in him if she hung this portrait in place of that awful, effete, snobbish one she'd painted of him before they were married? It was hardly fair to have the pretty self-portrait of her in the drawing room and such an unflattering one of him. That's what she'd do. She'd walk downtown to the carpenter's and engage him to make a matching frame for her new painting of Jack. She might even drop in on Jack at his office. Have a friendly conversation away from Ingrid's sultry glances.

In fact, with Ingrid out of town, Kristin felt she might make some headway with Jack. He had wanted her once. And now she was sleeping right beside him in the same bed. Surely, she could think of some way to signal that she was available without actually coming right out and saying it. Which would hardly be proper, even between husband and wife.

In a more sanguine mood, Kristin redraped the portrait, cast one mildly guilty look at the picture of Jesus and the adulteress, which hadn't felt the touch of her brush in three days, stripped off her paint-smudged apron, and dashed upstairs to choose a handsome mauve plaid afternoon dress for her trip downtown—just in case she found time to drop in on Jack.

The carpenter promised to visit her house the next day to frame the new picture, but the visit to Jack's office was less successful. The office was closed; not even the clerk who slept in back with the safe and the bathtub was there. How strange, she thought uneasily, then decided that they—she and Jack—would see each other at dinner, without Ingrid sitting beside him and Kristin miles down the table. And they could talk in the drawing room, without Ingrid singing or playing the piano. Kristin loved Ingrid like a sister but not enough to hand over Jack. That thought brought her up short. She had taken Minna's husband-to-be. Was God punishing her by passing Jack on to Ingrid? No, that was silly. Jack just needed encouragement.

"Ah-ha!"

Kristin had never heard a more satisfied "Ah-ha!" in her life, even from her father. She glanced around and saw Reverend Florida Passmore. She hadn't forgiven his sermons on contaminating associations and about the insult to public decency of a man who would let his wife stay in a brothel. She supposed he had a point, but it wasn't any of his business. Jack might like her better if Reverend Passmore hadn't made a public spectacle of their problems. "Good day, sir," she said primly and increased her pace, the heliotrope parasol, which matched the heliotrope vest of her walking dress, held at an angle that blocked out the minister. Mild weather had followed the snow.

His voice followed her up the hill. "Are you not even ashamed, madam? Are you not even disturbed by this latest scandal in your household?"

What scandal?

"Now that they have run away together—"

"Who?" Kristin whirled and stared at him.

"Your husband and his paramour. They were seen leaving on the morning train to Denver. Your associations with fallen women have evidently led your husband to—"

"I don't believe you," Kristin whispered.

"They didn't even leave from the ladies' stop," said Reverend Passmore.

Ingrid had left this morning with a valise. Jack's office was closed. Sick at heart, Kristin walked away in the middle of Florida Passmore's continuing pronouncements on the many sins abounding in her household. *They've eloped,* she thought. *And it serves me right.* Kristin thought of the times she'd run away from Jack. Now he'd run away from her. Disconsolately, she trudged up the hill, opened the gate, and crossed the yard, hardly noticing that the pigs no longer roamed at will now that they had their neoclassic, heated pig house.

Would it have made a difference, she wondered, if she'd told Jack that Father Boniface Wirtner didn't hold with all Sister Mary Joseph's rules about marriage? That they didn't have to practice abstinence on Wednesdays through Sundays, Lent, Pentecost, Advent, Rogation Day, feast days, and goodness knew what other days the nun had mentioned? That perhaps some of the things he'd done hadn't been unnatural, after all? Father Boniface Wirtner had been a little ambiguous on the matter of enjoying oneself, but perhaps if one had good intentions not to and then confessed afterwards, it wasn't too great a sin. Not that it mattered now. She'd never get the opportunity to commit that particular sin again. If it was one.

"Oh, ma'am, I'm so glad you're home." Winifred opened the door before Kristin could do it for herself. "It's ever so exciting. At least, I expect it is."

"What is?" Kristin asked.

"Your letter."

Had he left her a letter? How could she bear to read it?

"From that Mrs. Potter Palmer in Chicago who's so rich and sponsors artists. She's written to you. See." Winifred waved the letter under Kristin's nose. "I remember how excited you was the last time she wrote."

Kristin took the letter. It probably said that her nightscape hadn't even been accepted for the art show.

"I thought you'd be more excited than that, ma'am," said Winifred, as she took Kristin's light mantle, parasol, and gloves.

"Well, I don't know what it says, do I?" She climbed the stairs, flopped onto her bed, and held the letter up. What difference did it make? She sighed and ripped the envelope open, tearing off pieces of two pages in her indifference. Then she saw the word *prize* on half of a line. Hastily she sat up and put the pieces together on the bed cover. "Nightscape" had taken first prize! All her paintings had sold, and a letter of credit had been sent to the Cameron Bank of Colorado in her name. She was invited to submit a painting to the Columbian Exposition in 1893. Chicago society was buzzing with the story of her family's cruelty to their talented, innocent daughter. Kristin pushed the letter aside and burst into tears.

Winifred knocked timidly and came in. "Ma'am, was it bad news? Did someone die?"

"No, it's wonderful news," Kristin sobbed. "Tell Abigail I won't be down to dinner." She wiped her eyes, blew her nose, and slid off the bed. "I'll be painting." She'd devote herself to her art. Never think of that faithless Jack again. After all, she might have run away from him, but never with another man! She'd devote herself to painting pictures for the church. Yes. She'd finish the one of the adulteress this very night. She wished the story had had an adulter*er* in it, one being pelted with stones, but she didn't suppose anyone ever got after men about their sins. Everyone would blame Ingrid.

"Miz Abigail's gonna be ever so mad," said Winifred. "What with Mr. Jack and Miz Ingrid going off unexpected, and now you—"

430

Kristin burst into tears again, all her lofty plans for a career in religious art forgotten. Evidently Jack and Ingrid had given in to impulse. If she'd been at the table for breakfast, maybe she could have stopped them. Or maybe they wouldn't have cared what she thought. How could Ingrid do that to her? Women were supposed to stick together. Kat was always saying that.

Kristin wiped her eyes a second time, blew her nose again, and announced, "I'm going to visit Mrs. Macleod."

"But what about dinner, ma'am? And look outside. I think it might storm. Rain most likely, but it did snow one day. Who ever heard of snow in September?"

"You're on the frontier now, Winifred," said Kristin. "Anything can happen, and probably will."

"He eloped with Ingrid?" Kat looked astonished as she sat on the green settee in her corridor room. "I'd have sworn he was in love with you. Why, he even wanted to fight that fellow who tried to buy you for ten dollars."

"He did?"

"Connor says the fellow offered him the same ten dollars if he'd forget the whole thing."

"And Jack took it?" asked Kristin, outraged.

"Well, not exactly. He said it wasn't worth fighting someone that cowardly, the fellow agreed, and that was the end of it."

"I don't see that as any indication that he loves me. And running away with Ingrid—"

"I'll have to admit that looks bad." Kat shook her head. "I think I'm losing my ability to judge people. I'd have sworn Ingrid was still in love with Sean. Augustina certainly thinks so, poor thing."

"Yes," said Kristin. "We're all miserable. People should never get married. I told Jack way back in March that

431

married people were always unhappy. I don't know why
I expected anything else."

"Well, I'm happy," Kat objected. "So's Connor. I'll tell
you what I think. Jack's your husband. You ought to go get
him back."

"Well, I couldn't—"

"Why not? He came after you, didn't he? He followed
you to Colorado, then to Georgetown, then to Marcie's. At
this point, I imagine his pride is hurt. Men are great ones
for pride. So you just get on the train tomorrow morning
and go after him."

"I'd be embarrassed. They're in Denver together. What
if they told me to go away, or laughed, or—"

"What if they do? At least you'll have tried. You can't
expect to get the vote if you don't show some gumption."

"The vote?" Kristin wasn't sure how that came into it.

"Right. What we need are laws that keep men from
deserting their wives and children."

"Jack and I don't have any children."

"But you're husband and wife. If women had the vote,
we could see that there were laws to protect—"

"Kat, I just want my husband back."

"Of course you do, but no sheriff's going to get him
back for you, so you'll have to do it yourself. And let this
be a lesson to you. In the future you should take a more
active interest in women's suffrage. You haven't done a
thing for the cause since you set fire to Mrs. Harby's
feathers."

All the way to Como, where she had to transfer from
the High Line to the Denver train, Kristin was bothered
by clammy palms. She didn't even try to sketch. She did
try not to think of the confrontation she faced with Jack
and Ingrid. From Como to Denver, she gave up trying

o control the direction of her thoughts. Instead she gave
herself lectures. Jack was *her* husband. Both church and
state recognized the marriage, so he'd have to give up
Ingrid. Kristin was sorry about Ingrid, and she couldn't
imagine how all this would affect their partnership in the
sausage business, not to mention their friendship, but she
still had a right to claim Jack.

Father Boniface Wirtner said they had rights over each
other's bodies. Think of that! If she wanted to, she could do
all the things to Jack that he'd done to her. Well, taking into
consideration the differences in men and women, which
were rather major when you thought about it. Kristin fell to
thinking about Jack and his differences. She wouldn't mind
painting him front-lit instead of back-lit, but first she'd like
to run her fingers over every inch of him. Trace all those
muscles. Study them. Texture was important to an artist.
Touch. And sight.

Kristin sighed. What if he didn't want to touch her anymore? Or have her touch him? What if it was too late?
What if Ingrid wouldn't even let her talk to Jack? Or
maybe she could catch Jack when Ingrid wasn't around,
if Ingrid went out to sell sausages or go shopping. Jack was
so generous. He'd probably give Ingrid a roll of money.
Then while Ingrid was spending it, Kristin could catch Jack
alone. Maybe they could go straight home and just leave
a note for Ingrid. Which wasn't very nice, but Ingrid and
Jack hadn't left a note at all. She'd had to hear about them
from Reverend Passmore. *That* wasn't very nice.

She imagined Jack coming to the door of his hotel
room—would he and Ingrid have separate rooms and visit
each other when everyone had gone to bed? Probably.
So Ingrid would be in her room, waiting for the hour of
discretion. Jack would be alone. He'd come to his door
when Kristin knocked. He'd be stunned to see her. She'd

be wearing her prettiest dress—which one? The full-length
sleeveless fitted coat of marigold faille with its bronze
silk underdress. She'd have to get a room so she could
change. Fortunately, the gown wouldn't be wrinkled, not
if Yvette packed for her. The outfit was stunning with
Kristin's blond hair. Jack would see her and fall in love
all over again.

Had he been in love with her before she'd ruined it by
trying to follow all Sister Mary Joseph's advice about "the
act"? Surely he had. He'd sweep her into his arms, and
Kristin would kiss him back instead of being a scared
ninny. Maybe she'd unbutton his shirt. Untie his tie. That
would take him by surprise! And in no time at all they'd
be on the big carved bed in the Windsor Hotel, just like
before, only better. She sighed, thinking how wonderful
was going to be when she didn't have to worry about what
day it was or anything else but being Jack's wife. If he'
take her back.

But what if they didn't care about discretion? What
Ingrid was in his room when Kristin knocked? Wearing
one of those sheer things the women had at Marcie's, with
bosoms overflowing necklines and—and Jack taking it all
in. There was a lot more of Ingrid to take in, especially
with Kristin covered from throat to toe in bronze silk. And
Ingrid would know a lot more about "the act" than Kristin
who'd only engaged in it—let's see, one, two, three—she
stopped counting because she supposed it wasn't nice to
count things like that.

Kristin wondered whether Ingrid knew how many times
she'd engaged in the act, and with how many men—besides Sean. Had she yet with Jack? Kristin decided that
maybe she shouldn't take the time to get a room and
change her clothes. But then, they had left yesterday. Maybe
be last night . . . oh, what was the use of thinking about it

She was making herself upset and nervous and scared and embarrassed and . . .

"Union Depot," called the conductor while Kristin was still wavering between hope and fear.

Chapter Twenty-Seven

He was a feast for the eyes, that muscular chest showing between the white halves of his unbuttoned shirt. If she hadn't been so tired and out of sorts from asking for him at six different hotels and from the fright of riding the vertical tram to his room, she'd probably have run a finger right down the middle to remind herself of what his chest felt like.

"I suppose Ingrid's here," she said. It had never occurred to her that he wouldn't be at the Windsor. By the time she discovered that and tried the other five hotels, she'd given up expecting anything to go right.

"In this room, you mean? No, she isn't." Jack was looking at her quizzically.

"You mean she's in a room down the hall or somewhere else in this hotel?"

"I take it you're looking for Ingrid. I was hoping you might have followed me."

"Well, I—" In a way, she was looking for Ingrid. Kristin just didn't want to find her.

"As far as I know, Ingrid's in Aspen."

"Aspen?" Kristin frowned, then rubbed her finger over the frown lines. "If Ingrid's in Aspen, what are you doing here?"

"I'm running away from home," said Jack. "You know how it is. Things aren't going your way at home. You leave."

"What wasn't going your way?" asked Kristin hopefully. "Maybe I could come in and talk about it."

Jack opened the door and waved her in. "It's my wife," he explained as he closed the door. "No matter what I do, she doesn't like me."

"I do too," said Kristin indignantly. "I lo—" She stopped and eyed him suspiciously. "You've been flirting with Ingrid. Is that supposed to make me like you?"

"She said it would. Did it?"

"No."

"There. What did I tell you?"

"I mean, I already liked you."

"But that's all?"

Kristin walked over to the bed and sat down. "No. I love you."

"Hallelujah," said Jack. "I'd have run away a lot sooner if I'd known how much good it would do."

"And you don't love Ingrid?"

"Not at all. We were trying to make you jealous. You and Sean."

"But do you love me?"

"Of course. I've been chasing you all over the country, haven't I? Rescuing you from ironing boards and furnace rooms and parlor houses. I'd say I've proved myself a very devoted, loving, and tolerant husband. Especially tolerant. I should have given you a beating."

As he talked, Kristin's smile became brighter and brighter. "Oh, do be quiet and come over here," she said when she could get a word in edgewise.

"Why?" asked Jack.

"Because I'm going to exercise my wifely rights over your body. Father Boniface Wirtner said I could."

"When did he say that?"

"A couple of weeks ago."

"Then what took you so long?" Jack sat down beside her on the bed.

"You were flirting with Ingrid." Kristin threw her arms around his neck and pulled him over on the fine silk coverlet.

"Are you sure it's the right day?" Jack asked once she'd stopped kissing him long enough to tug his shirt off.

"I don't know," said Kristin. "Father Boniface Wirtner said Sister Mary Joseph had got it all wrong about the days, so we don't have to worry about that anymore."

"That's nice," said Jack, who had no idea what she was talking about.

"I'm still not sure about unnatural acts," she said earnestly, "so if you think I'm doing something I shouldn't—"

"I'm not likely to complain," Jack interrupted.

"Does that mean you don't know either, or you just don't care?" She was rubbing the tip of her finger against his nipple but now looked up suspiciously.

"That means, love, that I find everything about you enormously seductive, so why don't we make love now and discuss these proprieties you seem to worry so much about later?"

Kristin sighed. "You find *me* seductive?"

Jack groaned. "So much so, that if I don't get to seduce you within the next two minutes, I may just die on the spot."

Kristin giggled. "Don't do that," she murmured and began to undo his belt. She had him naked in seconds.

"Well, one of us is ready for action, but you, sweetheart, are still much too well dressed."

"How much of a hurry are you in?" she asked seriously.

"Can't you tell?"

"It's really very interesting how that happens. I mean, one minute you wouldn't even notice it's there under your trousers, and the next—"

"Kris-ten!"

She reached out a finger and touched it. "It's really velvety, isn't it?"

Jack groaned and lay back on the bed. "What did you have in mind, love? A leisurely discussion of my private parts? A sketch? Maybe a pastel or an oil painting for our collection of Jack Cameron *au naturel* artwork? What are you doing now?"

Kristin had suddenly disappeared in a flurry of skirts and petticoats. "I'm taking off my drawers," came her muffled voice.

"And that's all?" Jack came up off the pillow on his elbow to watch her.

"Well, you don't seem to be interested in discussion or art, just hurrying things up, so—" Triumphantly, she tossed the lacy drawers onto the floor and scooted over him. "—we don't *both* have to be naked," she pointed out.

Jack laughed delightedly and caught her around the waist. "You sure you're ready?" he asked, even as he slid into her. Kristin gave a sigh of pleasure. "All right, now hold still," he commanded.

"But why? That's not what we did before."

"You're going to hold still because it's more fun if both of us are naked."

"That could take forever," she complained.

"Sweetheart, they didn't call me Fast Jack Cameron for nothing." He was already pulling her dress over her head and tossing it aside. "Lean down so I can get the corset laces."

"*Fast* Jack Cameron?" She allowed herself to be pulled forward and then squirmed on him because it felt so good.

"Quit that." Jack released her corset laces with one hand while he slipped a breast from the chemise with the other and guided it to his lips. Kristin gasped and squirmed again. "Don't," he whispered against her breast.

"I can't help it," she gasped.

Jack tossed her corset, her chemise, and finally her petticoats toward the floor as he began to roll his hips up against her. Her hair was sliding from its pins and falling around them as their excitement, and with it their pace increased to a frantic sprint toward fulfillment. Kristin felt the tightening excitement build inside her body until she wanted to scream, to beg him for release. Jack, feeling her clenching around him, let go, drove up, burst in her, and let the shudders overtake them both until he went limp beneath her and she sprawled on top of him in spent happiness.

"I'm so glad Sister Mary Joseph didn't know what she was talking about," Kristin gasped when she could talk again.

"Maybe you'd better tell me about Sister Mary Joseph," said Jack, settling the damp, still quivering body of his wife in the curve of his arm.

So Kristin told him about all the days when chaste couples abstained.

"Hell, we'd never have had any sex life," he remarked.

"I know. I wondered about that myself. I mean, if the

whole idea was to have babies, how did people ever manage to do it if they weren't allowed to make any babies most of the time? And then there was enjoyment. It wasn't allowed."

"Well, if I'd married Minna, that wouldn't have been a problem, but with you—not a chance."

"Why, thank you," said Kristin, looking pleased. "Since it is allowed, I'm so glad you find me enjoyable. I certainly think you are. Look at that!" She was peering down at him. "It's rising again."

"All this sexy talk," muttered Jack.

"I don't think Sister would approve. She was also worried about being properly clothed, and doing it in the dark."

"Well, you had good intentions on the clothing part."

"Not really. I just wanted to be accommodating since you said you were in a hurry."

"I appreciate the thought. What else?"

"Unnatural acts. But she never said what they were. I thought engaging in the act on a picnic blanket might be one and on a bearskin rug another."

"Couldn't be," said Jack. "Well, maybe the picnic blanket—it was sort of scratchy. But never the bearskin rug. That felt great."

"Yes, but Sister Mary Joseph didn't *want* people to feel great. Just to make babies."

"Well, we might have done that. I'll tell you what I think happened. I think Sister Mary Joseph got hold of one of those medieval books of penance and took it all to heart. When I was about twelve or thirteen, some friends and I managed to steal one from a Jesuit historian."

"You didn't!"

"Yes, we did. We had a terrible time translating the Latin, but it was pretty racy stuff. Makes you wonder why celibates are reading about stuff like that."

441

"I wondered that about Sister Mary Joseph. I mean, she never—well, you know. So why was she so interested?"

"I expect she wanted to spoil people's fun."

Jack got up and put a robe on. Then he went out into the hall to use the hotel's annunciator, calling down for a bottle of champagne and a plate of cold chicken and fruit. "We'll stay right here in bed, honeymooning," he told Kristin. "Feeding each other fruit and chicken and drinking champagne."

"I don't drink."

"Why not? You don't have to worry about my seducing you, not after you've just seduced me so effectively."

"Did I?" Kristin felt very pleased with herself.

Jack fed her a piece of chicken, then a grape, then a sip of champagne. "Now that I've prepared you with food and drink, I have a piece of news for you. Pretty shocking."

"What?" asked Kristin anxiously. She had put on the lacy nightgown she brought in her valise.

"Your parents have offered me the dowry I was promised with Minna."

"But you can't marry Minna. You're married to me."

"They've offered it for you. I gather they're getting a lot of criticism for the way they treated you. Do you want to refuse it?"

"Of course not. I want to invest it in your bank and make lots of money." She tucked a grape between her lips and leaned over to kiss him.

"Now that's a nice way of getting sustenance," Jack murmured. "You're certainly a fast learner."

"Sister Ermentrude always said so."

"Oh? Was she talking about marriage too?"

"No, art. Which reminds me. I have news too. I've been

invited to submit a painting to the Columbian Exposition. It's a great honor. Mary Cassatt will be doing a mural in the Women's Building."

"I don't even know who she is, but she can't be more talented than you. We'll have to go back to Chicago for the exposition and make our families horribly jealous."

"Oh, can we?" Kristin giggled. She and Jack were so much alike. They both liked to make love, they both liked her paintings, and they both enjoyed a good revenge fantasy.

"Absolutely. We'll be the toast of the city. Rich, talented, and beautiful. I'm rich. You're talented and beautiful."

Kristin giggled some more. She was definitely feeling the champagne and liked the feeling. Kat would be very disappointed in her. "I think you're talented and beautiful too. In fact, I've done a new portrait of you. Wearing clothes," she assured him hastily, "and looking absolutely irresistible. As for talented, you must be the most talented man alive."

"Exactly what talent are we talking about here?" asked Jack.

"The one you're going to demonstrate for me as soon as you put that champagne glass down."

"Your wish is my command, princess." He dropped the champagne bottle over the side of the bed, placed the glasses on the nightstand, swept the remains of the chicken and fruit off onto the floor, and stretched out beside Kristin. "That's a very intriguing nightgown. It appears to be held together with this one little bow."

"Yes, it is. It was a going-away present from the girls at the Sporting Club. They sent it along with my picture for St. Mary's and my naked portrait of you. Would you care to see how the bow works?"

"That sounds like a very tantalizing idea. While I untie the bow, why don't you give a thought or two to procreation. Then we can get on with the matter of enjoying ourselves in a proper fashion."

RELUCTANT LOVERS
ELIZABETH CHADWICK

"Elizabeth Chadwick writes a powerful love story...splendid!"

—*Romantic Times*

Ever since her first appearance in Breckenridge, Colorado, Kathleen Fitzgerald has been besieged by proposals from the love-starved men of the remote mining town. But determined to avoid all matrimonial traps, the lovely young widow decides instead to act as matchmaker between her new admirers and the arrivals from her old hometown. Having sworn off love, Kat finds herself surrounded by romance, while the one man she truly desires leaves her body on fire, but refuses to ask for her hand. When even the girls in the local bawdy house begin to hear wedding bells, Kat knows the marriage madness has to end—but not before she herself gets her man!

_3540-5 $4.99 US/$5.99 CAN

LEISURE BOOKS
ATTN: Order Department
276 5th Avenue, New York, NY 10001

Please add $1.50 for shipping and handling for the first book and $.35 for each book thereafter. PA., N.Y.S. and N.Y.C. residents, please add appropriate sales tax. No cash, stamps, or C.O.D.s. All orders shipped within 6 weeks via postal service book rate. Canadian orders require $2.00 extra postage and must be paid in U.S. dollars through a U.S. banking facility.

Name _____

Address _____

City _____ State _____ Zip _____

I have enclosed $_____in payment for the checked book(s).
Payment <u>must</u> accompany all orders.☐ Please send a free catalog.

Sizzling Historical Romance
by Bestselling Author Elizabeth Chadwick!

"Elizabeth Chadwick writes a powerful love story...splendid!"

—Romantic Times

Bride Fire. A renegade mustanger and a respected Comanche warrior are both determined to capture the love of seventeen-year-old Cassandra. But neither can forsee that winning the young girl's heart will be nearly as impossible as taming the wild wind.
_3294-5 $4.50 US/$5.50 CAN

Virgin Fire. As the proud owner of one of the few bathtubs in Spindletop, Jessica Parnell has everyone longing to take advantage of her precious facilities. Though Jessica is hesitant to grant her estranged husband weekly bathing rights, she changes her mind when Travis turns his Saturday-night ablution into a wet and wild seduction!
_3141-8 $4.50 US/$5.50 CAN

LEISURE BOOKS
ATTN: Order Department
276 5th Avenue, New York, NY 10001

Please add $1.50 for shipping and handling for the first book and $.35 for each book thereafter. PA., N.Y.S. and N.Y.C. residents, please add appropriate sales tax. No cash, stamps, or C.O.D.s All orders shipped within 6 weeks via postal service book rate. Canadian orders require $2.00 extra postage and must be paid in U.S. dollars through a U.S. banking facility.

Name _____
Address _____
City _____ State _____ Zip _____
I have enclosed $_____ in payment for the checked book(s).
Payment <u>must</u> accompany all orders.☐ Please send a free catalog.

WOMEN OF THE WEST

This sweeping saga of the American frontier, and the indomitable men and women who pushed ever westward in search of their dreams, follows the lives and destinies of the fiery Branigan family from 1865 to 1875.

Promised Sunrise by Robin Lee Hatcher. Together, Maggie Harris and Tucker Branigan face the hardships of the westward journey with a raw courage and passion for living that makes their unforgettable story a tribute to the human will and the power of love.
_3015-2 $4.50 US/$5.50 CAN

Promise Me Spring by Robin Lee Hatcher. From the moment he sets eyes on the beautiful and refined Rachel, Gavin Blake knows she will never make a frontier wife. But the warmth in her sky-blue eyes and the fire she sets in his blood soon convinces him that the new life he is struggling to build will be empty unless she is at his side.
_3160-4 $4.50 US/$5.50 CAN

LEISURE BOOKS
ATTN: Order Department
276 5th Avenue, New York, NY 10001

Please add $1.50 for shipping and handling for the first book and $.35 for each book thereafter. N.Y.S. and N.Y.C. residents, please add appropriate sales tax. No cash, stamps, or C.O.D.s. All orders shipped within 6 weeks via postal service book rate. Canadian orders require $2.00 extra postage. It must also be paid in U.S. dollars through a U.S. banking facility.

Name _____
Address _____
City _____- State _____ Zip _____
I have enclosed $_____in payment for the checked book(s).
Payment <u>must</u> accompany all orders.☐ Please send a free catalog.

SPEND YOUR LEISURE MOMENTS WITH US.

Hundreds of exciting titles to choose from—something for everyone's taste in fine books: breathtaking historical romance, chilling horror, spine-tingling suspense, taut medical thrillers, involving mysteries, action-packed men's adventure and wild Westerns.

SEND FOR A FREE CATALOGUE TODAY!

Leisure Books
Attn: Order Department
276 5th Avenue, New York, NY 10001